Praise f

"[*Sapphire Dream*] tak
down as Brenna and R
teenth century proves
and rewarding than Brenna could have dreamed. One of the best time-travel romances I've ever read."

—*New York Times* bestselling author Mary Jo Putney

"A terrific time-travel romance. Twists and turns abound as feisty Brenna Cameron fights her destiny, danger, and the sexy pirate who claims her as his from their first dramatic meeting. Edge of the seat suspense, heart-stopping passion, and poignant emotion make *Sapphire Dream* a fantastic, roller-coaster read. I dare you to put it down before you finish it!"

—Award-winning author Anna Campbell

"Take one feisty heroine, a to-die-for Scottish hero, a dash of magic, and an author that knows how to mix them to perfection and you have *Sapphire Dream*—an action-packed, passion-filled tale by a master storyteller. Pamela Montgomerie delivers a story that will keep you turning the pages, rooting for Brenna and Rourke, and closing the book both reluctant to leave this pair behind and anxious to see what Ms. Montgomerie will deliver next. An excellent read!" —Award-winning author Laurin Wittig

continued . . .

Praise for the novels of
Pamela Montgomerie writing as Pamela Palmer

"[A] romantic, magical, and terrifying story. A compelling debut."
—*Library Journal*

"[A] tale of supernatural danger and spine-tingling suspense . . . Pamela Palmer twists the supernatural tension, then twists it again in this story of ancient magic and newly minted love."
—*USA Today* bestselling author Rebecca York

"I loved this story! Pamela Palmer certainly delivers a riveting out-of-the-ordinary tale of paranormal suspense and romance. I couldn't put it down."
—*USA Today* bestselling author Robin T. Popp

"Scary, sexy, and with a truly disturbing villain . . . A real page-turner."
—Laura Anne Gilman

"Exciting . . . Combines sexy characters with an intense, riveting plot."
—*Romantic Times*

"The enchanting magic, passion, and danger hold the reader spellbound during every totally captivating scene . . . Takes paranormal romance to unbelievable heights."
—*CataRomance*

"The characterization, motivation, and development of Autumn and Kade are marvelous . . . Edgy, yet charming—that last due to the exceedingly likable heroine."
—*Romance Reviews Today*

"Solidifies Pamela Palmer's place as one of the top up-and-coming authors of the paranormal romance and dark fantasy genres! Without a doubt, *Dark Deceiver* ranks among the top books I've read."
—*CK²S Kwips and Kritiques*

PAMELA MONTGOMERIE

BERKLEY SENSATION, NEW YORK

THE BERKLEY PUBLISHING GROUP
Published by the Penguin Group
Penguin Group (USA) Inc.
375 Hudson Street, New York, New York 10014, USA
Penguin Group (Canada), 90 Eglinton Avenue East, Suite 700, Toronto, Ontario M4P 2Y3, Canada
(a division of Pearson Penguin Canada Inc.)
Penguin Books Ltd., 80 Strand, London WC2R 0RL, England
Penguin Group Ireland, 25 St. Stephen's Green, Dublin 2, Ireland (a division of Penguin Books Ltd.)
Penguin Group (Australia), 250 Camberwell Road, Camberwell, Victoria 3124, Australia
(a division of Pearson Australia Group Pty. Ltd.)
Penguin Books India Pvt. Ltd., 11 Community Centre, Panchsheel Park, New Delhi—110 017, India
Penguin Group (NZ), 67 Apollo Drive, Rosedale, North Shore 0632, New Zealand
(a division of Pearson New Zealand Ltd.)
Penguin Books (South Africa) (Pty.) Ltd., 24 Sturdee Avenue, Rosebank, Johannesburg 2196,
South Africa

Penguin Books Ltd., Registered Offices: 80 Strand, London WC2R 0RL, England

SAPPHIRE DREAM

A Berkley Sensation Book / published by arrangement with the author

PRINTING HISTORY
Berkley Sensation mass-market edition / July 2009

Cover art by Phil Heffernan.
Cover design by George Long.
Cover type by Ron Zinn.
Interior text design by Kristin del Rosario.

ISBN: 978-0-425-22906-4

BERKLEY® SENSATION
Berkley Sensation Books are published by The Berkley Publishing Group,
a division of Penguin Group (USA) Inc.,
375 Hudson Street, New York, New York 10014.
BERKLEY® SENSATION and the "B" design are trademarks of Penguin Group (USA) Inc.

PRINTED IN THE UNITED STATES OF AMERICA

10 9 8 7 6 5 4 3 2 1

For Laurin. Cheroo!

ACKNOWLEDGMENTS

To Allison Brandau for finding this manuscript among the slush and falling in love with it. All along, it was waiting for you.

To Helen Breitwieser, for everything.

To the many people who helped me birth this book: Laurin Wittig, Anne Shaw Moran, Denise McInerney, Kathryn Caskie, Elizabeth Fedorko, Alicia Rasley, my 99er sisters, and the wonderful men and women of the Washington Romance Writers.

And to my family for always being there.

One

THE NORTH SEA,
OFF THE COAST OF SCOTLAND,
1687

Rourke Douglas held fast to the capstan, the rain soaking his shirt as his frigate, *Lady Marie*, pitched in the gale. Lightning slashed through the storm-darkened sky, threatening to tear the masts apart. Over the roll of thunder, the eerie sound of Hegarty's chanting rose from the hold of the ship, making Rourke's flesh ripple with unease. Magic rode heavy on the air.

A high wave broke over the deck's wooden planks in a shower of seawater.

"Close the hatches!" he barked to his crew. "Secure the guns!"

"We're too close to the shore, Captain!" His bosun, Joshua Cutter, lurched into place beside him, his pitted face sharp with disbelief and a challenge Rourke was tiring of. "If the wind turns, we'll be dashed upon the rocks."

Rourke scowled. "Then we shall hope the wind doesna turn, shall we not, Mr. Cutter? Return to your post and hold our position!"

The bosun blanched, took a step back, then whirled and hurried away.

God's blood, if they survived the storm, he'd have a mutiny on his hands. As much as he hated to admit it, Cutter was right. But he'd made a vow to Hegarty to hug the shoreline until the night was through. Even if it meant damning his ship and everyone on board.

A gust of wind caused the ship to lurch hard to starboard. Rourke braced himself, holding tight.

"Order the sails furled, Mr. Baker!" he shouted to his hapless first mate. If they did not soon roll the sails up tight against the growing gale, they'd capsize. If they survived this storm, he'd happily hang Hegarty from the highest mast for manipulating him into this dire predicament.

Through the rain Rourke could just make out the rugged shoreline of his native Scotland—a sight he'd not seen since he was ten and never intended to see again. He must have been deep in his cups the night Hegarty secured his promise to go back. Naught but a sail-by, Hegarty had assured him. No need even to make port. A simple trip.

As if anything concerning Hegarty could ever be simple. Not until they arrived had the dwarf told him the ship must remain perilously close to shore for a day and a night. He'd not explained why. They both knew all too well.

The prophecy.

His gut twisted and rolled as if mimicking the churning sea. He should never have let Hegarty force him back here.

"Captain!" the pilot cried. "We're being pulled toward the rocks!"

God's blood. "Unfurl the mizzen!"

The ship leaned heavily as the wind caught the single sail. His promise be damned. But even as he braced to issue the orders to set full sail, he knew it was too late. A second sail would cause them to lean too far into the frenzied waves, capsizing the ship.

The rain slashed across his back in a pelting, stinging torrent. This was Hegarty's fault. He rued the day he'd ever laid eyes upon the little man, yet without him he'd be long dead. Hegarty was a rock in his shoe, gifted with abilities no man should possess, but Rourke owed him. Too much.

A loud crack challenged the thunder.

"Mast down!" shouted the bosun.

In grim disbelief Rourke watched the mizzenmast crash to the deck, shredding rigging and splintering deck boards.

As crewmen scurried to secure loose rigging, Hegarty appeared, cursing and stomping up the stairs from belowdecks. The dwarf wore Rourke's best waistcoat like a tunic, his wild mane of red hair dragging with the weight of the rain. He put his head down against the strengthening gale and made his way toward Rourke.

The ship pitched and Rourke grabbed the dwarf before he could be swept overboard. "Look at my ship! You'd damn well better be through."

"'Tis a poor day for magic." Hegarty glared at him as if he blamed him for calling down the storm. "We must stay until it's done."

"No more. We're through here. If we survive this storm, I'm making a new heading straight back to the West Indies." And buying that plantation on the Isle of St. Christopher he'd been eyeing. He'd bloody well had enough of the sea.

Hegarty clung to his wrist, his small fingernails digging ridges into Rourke's skin. "Today is the day, Pup. She must come to us. The prophecy will unfold at last."

The words twisted like a dull blade in Rourke's gut. "And I would be far, far away when it does. I promised to bring you back and so I have. On the morrow, I'm leaving, with or without you."

Hegarty regained his footing and smiled with that infuriating surety that always boded ill.

Rourke shook his head against the canny look in the smaller man's eyes. "You'll not pull me into this, Heg. I was not named in the prophecy. Only her."

"Named? Not precisely." Hegarty continued to smile, unnerving him.

"Dammit, man, you'll not involve me. 'Tis you who is determined to set this disaster to flight. Why can ye not leave well enough alone?"

"Well enough for whom?" The dwarf's smiled disappeared, his dark eyes flashing as he pressed the tip of his finger into Rourke's soaked chest. "Naught will be right until the prophecy unfolds. It will unfold, Pup, and it will involve ye whether ye like it or not." He flashed Rourke a smile of such certainty that the hairs rose on Rourke's sodden flesh. "Now release me so that I may return to the business at hand." He patted Rourke's chest. "Do not look so grim, lad. Ye've been waiting for this all your life, whether you know it or not. You've been waiting for me to find Brenna Cameron."

CASTLE STOUR,
NORTHEAST SCOTLAND,
PRESENT DAY

A fine tension ran the length of Brenna Cameron's spine as the tour guide's thickly brogued voice echoed off the dungeon walls. Electric lights in the shape of medieval torches lined the dank space, illuminating display cases of gleaming swords and lances. Tourists—nearly two dozen of them—milled about, studying the weapons that seemed to infuse the low, dreary room with an air of ancient menace.

Brenna shoved her hands into her jacket pockets as she wandered among the families and traveling couples, pretending an interest she didn't feel. She needed to blend in and look like one of the tourists. She couldn't afford for anyone to guess the real reason she was here. Not yet. Not until she found him.

"Imagine these kitchens as they would ha' looked in the sixteenth century, before the fire, before this space became the castle's dungeons." The guide motioned dramatically, his bald head bobbing with each word. "Imagine the tables fillin' every bit o' space. The hen wife pluckin' the fowl, the *turnbrochie* turning the roasting spit over the fireplace. Pots and cauldrons a-steamin' and a-bubblin' with stews and broths."

Brenna's fingers closed around the roll of peppermint Life Savers in her pocket. She pulled it out and popped one candy in her mouth with not-quite-steady hands. Aunt Janie had whisked her out of Scotland when she was five, then died when she was ten, leaving her with nothing but the sapphire pendant around her neck and the title of the man responsible for their flight—the Earl of Slains. He lived here somewhere, in some part of this partially restored castle. And she wasn't leaving until she found him and confronted him about what he knew.

On her deathbed Janie had made Brenna promise to return to Scotland for her twenty-fifth birthday. Unfortunately, Brenna didn't remember the name of the town or village where she'd been born. She remembered almost nothing from those early years. The earl was her only clue.

The guide motioned the group to follow, then started for the far corner, away from the stairs. Brenna sighed, her patience stretching thin. She needed to find the earl, or at least identify the way into his private living quarters. That wasn't likely to happen down here in the dungeons.

She'd tried to contact the earl from home to ask what he knew about her, but his swift, emphatic response had startled her. *Stay away*. If he'd claimed not to know her, she'd probably have let it go. The last thing she wanted to do was reopen the deeply buried wells of loneliness and hurt she'd lived with after Janie died. Yes, she'd promised Janie to return to Scotland for her twenty-fifth birthday, but really . . . who would know, or care, if she didn't?

But the earl clearly knew who she was. And she was determined to know why. Was she due an inheritance he didn't want to part with? Was her arrival likely to be an embarrassment in some way? Well, too bad. She needed to know who she was and why Janie had taken her away from everything she'd known. She needed to know what had happened to the father who'd loved her.

Once the group gathered, the guide continued his speech. "During the excavation of these kitchens, an amazin' discovery was made in this pantry." He led them to a small alcove in the far back corner, reached in, and pulled a light cord. "A hidden door that opens onto a passage out to the cliffs."

The guide ducked into the low-ceilinged pantry and motioned those closest to follow. Brenna was caught by the surge and pulled deep inside the small space.

"The door dates from the original construction over four hundred years ago," the man continued. "The first Earl of Slains conquered the castle soon after it was built, but apparently never learned of the door. During the mid-1600s, the kitchens were moved to the outer ranges and this space turned into a prison, or dungeon. In 1687, during the time of the third earl, the castle was destroyed. A fortune in weapons went up in flames—weapons hidden here during the Covenanting Wars. Had the earl and his people known of this passage, the weapons would surely have been moved to safety."

Brenna glanced toward the door, wanting out of the press of people, but for the time being she was going nowhere. While she languished in his dungeons on this never-ending tour, the earl was probably driving off in his chauffeur-driven Bentley for parts unknown.

"How did the castle burn?" a young Brit asked, his hair fanning from his head in long spikes.

"'Tis said a pirate and his lady attacked the third earl and set his castle aflame."

The young man laughed. "Did they best him?"

"Och, aye, though he was not greatly missed. A bad one, the earl was." The guide ran his hand over one of the shelves. "Can ye see the door?"

No sooner had he uttered the words than the wall behind him swung inward, causing one of the attached shelves to hit him in the shoulder. A small girl of six or seven poked her head through the opening. Short red hair framed a gamine face liberally sprinkled with freckles.

The guide clutched his chest overdramatically. "Ah, Lintie, lass. Ye stole ten years from my life, ye did."

The girl giggled. "The earl's using the observe-tory. You canna be coming in." With that, she closed the door.

Brenna's heart stopped beating for an instant before taking off like a flock of doves. She'd found him.

The guide let an expletive escape under his breath. "The one time I don't want him to be around." He shrugged. "That was the earl's granddaughter. Apparently he's chosen to use the cave this morn. I'll not be able to show you the tunnel."

A chorus of disappointed murmurs filled the small space as the guide motioned them out of the pantry. Brenna hung back, taking off her jacket in a sudden flush of nervous heat. As the tourists disappeared out the pantry door, Brenna whirled and grabbed one of the shelves, swinging the hidden door open. She slipped through and closed it behind her, holding her breath as she waited for someone to reach through and snatch her back.

The sound of small, bare feet raced away from her, down the long, primitive tunnel that wound through the rock, echoing the pounding of her heart. The musty smell of damp stone enveloped her in the dimly lit space.

She took a deep, unsteady breath, pushed away from the wall, and started into the cave, stepping lightly, silently, over the uneven rock. Her pulse raced. Her scalp grew damp with sweat at the prospect of confronting the earl. But she wanted to know, dammit. She *needed* to know why she'd been abandoned.

Her father had loved her. She was sure of it.

Her fingers reached for the comfort of the sapphire at her throat as the only memory left to her of those early years brushed over her. He'd held her in strong arms, tight against his chest, as the winds of a brewing storm whipped her straight auburn hair in a frenzy around her face. She'd laughed at the feel of it. His answering laughter had rumbled in his chest, filling her with joy. Then he'd lifted her high, twirling her once as he grinned at her with pure adoration.

She remembered the rain had started, and he'd tucked her against his chest, shielding her as he'd run for cover. Keeping her safe.

He'd loved her, dammit. He'd *loved* her. Why had he let Janie take her away? Why hadn't he come when she'd needed him?

He would have. If he'd been able. With the wisdom of an adult instead of the hurt of an abandoned child, she knew that now. The fact that he hadn't come had something to do with the Earl of Slains.

And she intended to get to the bottom of it.

Voices carried to her from deep in the tunnel, one deep, elderly, and angry. She rounded the final corner and saw him. His bent shape stood in silhouette against the upside-down Hershey's Kiss shape of the cave's mouth, the freckled girl, Lintie, standing before him.

"How many times have I told you to stay away from the tourists? If I catch you again, I will take my cane to your backside, lassie!"

Lintie darted away from him, out where raindrops

bounced on a small patch of rock that extended beyond the cave's mouth like a porch. The child climbed onto the rusted iron railing that encircled the ledge, then threw her grandfather a mulish expression and jumped, disappearing over the edge.

Brenna gasped, her heart in her throat, and ran for the rail.

"Who are you?" the elderly man demanded as she brushed past him.

"The girl . . ." She'd seen the treacherous cliffs and jagged rocks as she'd driven the coast road. The child couldn't possibly have survived such a fall. But as Brenna lunged for the rail, she heard the unmistakable sound of little girl laughter, and the tightness eased from her chest.

She peered over the rail to find the child sitting on an outcropping of rock, her face tilted up, her mouth open, catching raindrops. Behind her, the rock slid off into a crude, precarious path amongst the sharp, knifepoint turns and crevices of the cliff face.

The secret cave had a secret path.

"Who are you?"

Brenna whirled to face the distinguished-looking white-haired gentleman. *The earl.* He had to be. Anger and nervousness flared within her in equal measures as she prepared to open what she expected to be an ugly can of worms.

She strode out of the rain and back into the cave as the man moved toward her, the clip of cane on stone echoing over the rock.

"You're the Earl of Slains."

"I am. And you're trespassing."

"I have a reason. You had something to do with my being sent to America as a child. I want to know what."

He peered at her suspiciously. "And who would you be, then?"

She hesitated, watching him carefully. "I'm Brenna Cameron."

His reaction was far more than she expected. The earl's eyes widened. His cane clattered to the floor as the color drained from his face.

My God. Had she somehow inherited his castle out from under him?

The earl's expression changed abruptly, his pale face flooding red as he took a menacing step toward her. "Out!" His voice cracked with the effort of shouting. He stumbled forward and picked up his cane, then brandished it at her. "Get her out of here!"

Too late, she saw the angry-faced guide rushing toward her from the tunnel. She swung her gaze back to the earl, holding her ground against the threatening cane.

"No. You can't do this. You owe me an explanation."

But the guide grabbed her by the arm and roughly yanked her away. Brenna struggled against his hold, shouting over her shoulder, "Tell me what you know!"

The earl's hoarse voice followed her as the guide hauled her away. "You burned this castle three hundred years ago, Brenna Cameron. You'll not do it again!"

Brenna stared at him. "*What?*"

But the guide had his orders, and within minutes she found herself standing in the rain, on the wrong side of the castle's thick doors. *Dammit.*

Brenna was still debating her next move as she prepared for bed that evening, pulling on her Hard Rock Cafe T-shirt and flannel sleep pants with the curly-tailed monkeys. With a yawn, she climbed under the soft down comforter and lay in the semidarkness, tracing the cool silver that encircled the sapphire at her throat until she slowly drifted to sleep.

In her dream she was little again, held tight in her father's arms.

Brenna.

She heard his voice as if from afar. Suddenly he was gone. She was alone. *No.* Terror welled up, threatening to choke her.

Papa.

Then she glimpsed him, far off, enveloped in mist. She ran toward him. The pounding of her bare feet on the uneven ground echoed the thudding of her heart. He waited for her, tall and strong, smiling at her with boundless love. But as she reached for him, the mists swirled around him, stealing him away.

No!

"Brenna!" The voice echoed as if in her room.

Brenna opened her heavy lids and blinked sleepily. The light from a streetlamp cast shadows in the room, but there was no one there. She'd been dreaming. She closed her eyes, snuggled under the covers, and drifted back to sleep as the silver grew warm against her throat.

As the sapphire began to glow.

Two

"The captain'll kill us if'n he catches us with whiskey in the hold."

"I've only taken a nip, mate. He'll never miss it. Come on."

Brenna stirred from a deep sleep at the sound of the rough male voices. Men. *In my room.*

She bolted upright, heart pounding, then stared around her in a wash of disbelief. Gone was the quaint and quiet inn. Sounds bombarded her ears—hammering, the cry of gulls, the rhythmic splash of water. As her gaze took in the unlikely sight of a storeroom piled high with wooden barrels, crates, and sacks, the floor rolled gently beneath her as if she were on a boat of some kind.

A *boat*? She blinked at the suffocating confusion. This had to be a dream. But a host of disgusting odors assailed her nostrils—old meat, fish, outhouses—and she knew with a chilling certainty she wasn't dreaming.

Something had gone terribly wrong.

A single shaft of sunlight poured down from the stairwell into the middle of the shadowed room—or ship's hold. Against the light, two dark forms descended, then stopped suddenly. With a feeling of dread, she felt their gazes upon her.

"What 'ave we 'ere, Gordy?"

Brenna scrambled to her feet, her hand brushing the flannel of her monkey pants. With a jerk of disbelief, she fisted her hand in the soft fabric and looked down. *I'm still in my pajamas. On a boat. And not dreaming.*

What in the *hell* was going on?

Gordy released a low cackle. "Looks like we got us a stowaway."

Her mouth went dry as she stared around her. Was this the earl's doing? Had he somehow drugged and kidnapped her? Sold her to slavers or something?

Right. The real explanation was probably much more boring. Like she'd started walking in her sleep again.

Oh, crap. Her hotel was only a block from the docks. The last time she sleepwalked, she'd been thirteen and woken on the slide at a nearby playground—in the middle of the night. No one had seen her that time. This time, she hadn't been as lucky.

She pressed her palm to her forehead in rank embarrassment. How was she ever going to explain this to whoever was in charge? The captain? Especially if they'd already set sail.

What a nightmare.

But as she started toward the men to try to explain her wayward wanderings, they reached the bottom of the stairs and turned where she could see them clearly. Her steps faltered.

They were dressed in rags. There was no other word for it. Torn and stained shirts and vests. Loose-fitting pants that were filthy and threadbare. The bald man wore a patch over one eye, while his companion sported stringy hair to his shoulders, a dirty handkerchief covering the crown of his head, and a gap where one of his front teeth should have been. Knives and wicked-looking swords hung from each man's waist.

They looked like pirates. Old-fashioned pirates too perfectly horrible to be real.

Her brain scrambled for an explanation. *Actors*. Somehow she'd wandered onto a movie set in her sleep. That would certainly explain the pirates. But if the matching pair of lecherous grins blooming on the two thugs' faces were fake, these two deserved Oscars.

A burst of fear sent adrenaline surging into her bloodstream, clearing her mind and making her heart pound. If these two were actors, they had a lot more than memorizing dialogue on their minds.

The bald one, the one called Gordy, stepped toward her, his one-eyed gaze glued to her chest. "Looks like we got us a wench. Better 'n a nip any day." He reached for the ties holding up his pants, proving her instincts were dead on.

Oh God. An icy memory washed over her, turning her to stone. Another time. Another male fumbling with his pants as she lay pinned and helpless.

Her stomach clenched with raw terror. Her mind jerked into overdrive. There was a way out of this. There had to be a way.

If she could just think of it. And find the courage.

Brenna took a deep breath. Okay, she knew what she had to do. She pasted what she hoped would pass for a sultry look on her face, praying her fear wouldn't leak between the cracks of her smile, and turned her back to glance at the approaching man coyly.

"Well, well," she cooed, her voice shaking only a little. "I was hoping for a strong, handsome man." No lie there. Preferably one in a police uniform with his gun drawn on these lowlifes.

She forced herself to sidle closer just as Gordy's pants dropped around his ankles. Her stomach clenched at the sight of his aroused flesh, and she struggled to hide her revulsion.

If she failed . . .

She wouldn't fail. She *couldn't*.

Brenna edged closer and turned her shoulder. Batting her eyes at him, mentally counting one, two . . .

As he grabbed for her waist, she slammed her elbow into his nose. Gordy reared back and howled. His feet tangled in the pants around his ankles and his arms shot out and began spinning like windmills as he tried to keep his balance.

Brenna didn't wait for him to regain his equilibrium. She shot toward the stairs, praying she could dash past Stringy Hair, but he caught her from behind. As he pulled her back against him, she kicked him hard in the knee with her bare heel.

"Blimey!" He half yelled the word in her ear, his large hands squeezing her waist painfully. Throwing her head back, she slammed into his nose and he released her with a howl.

Brenna leaped onto the wooden stairs, taking them two at a time, sprinting for the ship's deck and safety. But as she raced onto the deck and into the sunlight, her steps slowed at the incredible sight before her. Shielding her eyes against the brightness, she stared at the masts criss-crossed with rigging like giant spiderwebs against the blue sky.

Somehow she'd sleepwalked onto an old-fashioned sailing ship. A *tall ship* they called them at home.

A pirate ship.

Then again, guys dressed in pirate costumes probably wouldn't be filming aboard a World War II destroyer. Her gaze slid from the masts to the men staring at her. An entire crew as realistic-looking as the two in the hold.

The hammering abruptly ceased. The dull thump of boots on the stairs behind her echoed into the unnatural silence that blanketed the deck. She tensed for the director's angry shouts, scolding her for ruining the take.

Her gaze scanned the cast, looking for the film crew. The cameramen. The makeup artist? Producer? Her gaze jerked from one side of the ship to the other. Water boy?

The warm breeze lifted her hair as a chill slid down her spine. Everywhere she looked she saw pirates. And every one was staring at her with lust in his eyes. As if in slow motion, they started toward her, climbing down from the rigging, crossing the decks. Moving deliberately, menacingly, like a pack of wolves.

Her pulse thudded in her ears. What was the matter with these guys? Her gaze skirted over the leering faces even as her heart tripped and raced. They looked for all the world like real, live, cutlass swinging . . .

Oh God. This couldn't be happening. She was *not* in the clutches of pirates.

Reenactors.

The word landed in the middle of her fears like a big, fat life ring and she grabbed hold of it with both hands. *Of course.*

They were simply a bunch of grown men playing dress up. Men did it all the time. In her part of the States, they usually reenacted the Civil War, but over here, why not pirates? They probably had boring day jobs like meter reading and auditing.

"Who's in charge? I need to speak with your . . . captain." The boat rocked, forcing her to scramble to keep her balance. A rough deck board scraped against her bare toe as gulls soared overhead, casting shadows on the deck.

"Aye now, I be thinking you'll be speaking to me first, missy."

Brenna whirled toward the voice to find a man striding

toward her, his long face badly pockmarked, his eyes cruel.

"Who are you people?" she demanded. "You need to let me go."

His grin sent fear sliding through her like cold mercury. "And why would I be doing that?"

Her gaze darted toward the others as she desperately searched for an ally. Surely *someone* would help her. But to a man they watched her without humor, without sympathy. Leering eyes, every one. Stalking the prey.

Her.

She had to get off this hell ship.

Her monkey pants flapped against her legs in the warm breeze. Out of the corner of her eye, she caught a glimpse of the coast not too far away. She could swim it. She'd swum in college, though only in pools. The ocean water would be rough and freezing, but it wasn't like she had many options. A brisk swim or gang rape. Gee, let's think about that.

As the pockmarked pirate closed the distance between them, she put up her hands, palms out. "Look, I don't know how I got here—I don't even know where here is—but I don't want any trouble." That line might actually work if she were six foot four and aiming a pair of semi-automatics.

"This'll be no trouble at all, missy." The pirate grinned and started unbuttoning his pants, filling her with pure terror.

Jesus. She wished they'd quit doing that.

Lunging sideways, she dodged his quick grasp and ran for a break in the thick wall of men. But the men saw her intent and closed in. As she tried to dash between them, one foul-smelling pirate caught her wrist and hauled her against him.

The first pirate followed, pulling a long, nasty-looking

knife. The blade flashed in the sun, momentarily blinding her.

"I claim her. She's mine until I tire of her."

The one holding her whipped out a knife of his own. "You'll not be getting 'er first, Cutter. She's mine now."

Brenna struggled against the punishing hold, taking quick breaths through her mouth against the man's stench. But as the two men circled one another, she found herself dragged along like a toddler's favorite stuffed rabbit.

Out of the corner of her eye she caught the quick flash of a blade. Her captor screamed and released her, his knife clattering to the wooden decking along with two of his fingers and a thick splash of blood.

Brenna stumbled back, fighting down the bile rising in her throat.

Reenactors gone mad.

Cutter shoved his bloody knife into the scabbard at his waist and lunged for her. Brenna twisted out of his reach, choking on her fear. These men were crazy. They were going to kill her. Rape her, then kill her.

A flash of red orange burst into the circle and lurched to a stop. A dwarf. A stocky little dwarf, his face lined and leathery, his hair springing around his head like a fireball. He looked familiar, like an actor she'd once seen on television.

He rushed in front of her, turning as if to shield her. "Leave her be, Cutter, you no-good sea swine."

She could have kissed him. A champion at last, if a little on the short side. But Cutter just sneered. With a backward sweep of his hand, he knocked the dwarf to the deck. Brenna gasped, but the small man scampered to his feet and raced away without a backward glance, taking her only hope of rescue along with him.

Cutter went back to unbuttoning his trousers as his gaze raked her from head to foot. Terror pounded through her body and she backed up, right into the arms of one of the pirates. This man didn't grab her as the other had, but shoved her back at Cutter, clearly in no hurry to lose his fingers. Brenna struggled to catch her balance and failed, falling into Cutter's waiting arms.

Fighting panic, she tried to knee him in the groin, but he was too quick. He caught her legs between his and pulled her hard against him.

Terror threatened to sweep her away. *No.* Think. She had to think. There had to be a way for her to get off this ship and into the water, or she was going to die.

Sweat pooled between her breasts and trickled down her abdomen, soaking into her T-shirt. Go limp. Make him think she was compliant.

Brenna braced herself, waiting for the right moment. As Cutter's mouth descended toward her own, she pulled a self-defense move she'd heard about, but thankfully never had a need to try before. She jerked her chin up and caught the man's nose between her teeth, biting down as hard as she could.

The pirate yelled and reared back, and Brenna pressed her assault before he could recover. She shoved her hand between his legs, reaching past the hard, distended shaft to the soft sac behind. Her hand found what she sought through the thin fabric of his trousers. Grabbing the sac, she ground his testicles together and gave a vicious twist. Cutter howled and released her, then collapsed to his knees to a chorus of hoots and laughter from his companions.

Brenna turned, sucking in air, seeking an escape, but the men had closed in tighter. The odds of one unarmed woman winning against an entire crew of pirates were nil.

Too late she saw the flash of silver coming for her leg. Cutter's blade sliced through her left pants leg, right through her calf. Her gaze snapped to where the cruel pirate knelt on the deck an arm's reach away, a vengeful sneer contorting his face.

"No one makes a laughingstock of me," he hissed. Blood dripped from the knife he gripped in his hand. *Her* blood, spotting the deck bright red.

For one surreal moment, she felt no pain. Then her leg buckled in a spasm of agony. She collapsed onto the hard sea-slimed deck of the ship.

Cutter stumbled to his feet to the cheers and taunts of his comrades, bent double from the pain she'd inflicted. He towered over her, hatred twisting his ugly face as he aimed his blade at her chest.

Her death shone brightly in his eyes.

Her heart stuttered. She wasn't ready to die. Not this way.

Frantic, she forced her arms to move, trying to propel herself, crab-style, away from the reach of his blade. But as she moved, burning pain ripped through her leg, nailing her to the deck. Dizzy with terror, she faced him, helpless to prevent her own death.

As the blade began its deadly downward arc, a shrill whistle pierced the din. The blade whipped back. To a man, the pirates jumped away from her as silence rolled over the deck like sound waves shoved into reverse.

Her body shook, sweaty and freezing, as pain spread from her leg into every cell, every nerve.

A familiar flash of red orange caught her attention, pulling her from the suffocating oblivion of pain. The dwarf broke into the circle and raced over to her, pointing. "See what yer crew's done, Rourke?" He spat on the deck behind her, glaring at the pirates. "No-good, gutter scum."

It seemed that her small champion had gone for help. But had he brought her a savior, or was he feeding her to the worst of the monsters? Her fingernails dug into the damp decking as the metallic smell of blood filled her nostrils. There would be no escape.

She was going to die without ever knowing what happened to her father. Tears burned her eyes, the pain gnawing at the edges of her sight. What other horrors would these monsters inflict upon her before they killed her?

"To your posts!"

At the booming command of the voice, she struggled to focus her vision. A man she hadn't seen before strode forward, scattering the other pirates like so much litter in a gale. Like the others, he was dressed in costume, but not the rags of his comrades. This man carried an unmistakable air of command.

The captain. But how much help could she expect from a man who surrounded himself with the dregs of humanity? The small flicker of hope that had flared to life with his appearance sputtered and died.

None. He would give her no help. The best she could hope for was that he'd let Cutter finish her off quickly. And if he didn't? If he was as bad as the others? Heaven help her.

She blinked back the useless tears and watched him approach. Ironically, he was a feast for the eyes. But then some of the worst monsters were. His light brown hair was tied back from a face that was strongly boned and sharply angled. His was a face made for movies, made for action flicks with larger-than-life heroes. But like a typecast villain, his eyes, when he peered down at her, were so pale a gray they were almost the color of ice, and just as cold.

He turned that icy gaze on the red-haired dwarf. "Ye found her." A Scottish burr colored his strange choice of words.

The little man bounced from one foot to the other. "Aye." He grabbed the tall man's forearm. "She's bleeding, Rourke. Get her to yer cabin where I can tend her."

Tend her? A tiny flicker of hope ignited even as the pain in her leg edged beyond bearing.

"Bloody hell." The tall man whipped off his shirt and knelt beside her, rolling the shirt into a makeshift tourniquet.

She stared at him. Was the cold-eyed pirate going to play hero after all? With his shirt off, his fine shape glistening in the sun, he looked every bit the part.

Her head fell back, her eyes closing. Too late. Too much blood. Unless they called for a helicopter to airlift her out of there, she was dead. She felt hands on her leg, then a searing agony that made her cry out.

"Och, lassie, he's helping ye, he is. Binding yer wound."

She tried to open her eyes and caught a flash of orange. The dwarf.

Dizzy. Too dizzy.

The captain gave a long-suffering sigh and scooped her into his arms. Her world exploded in pain. When the backs of her eyelids began to dance with little sparkly colors, she knew she was passing out. And there wasn't a damned thing she could do about it.

Except pray she woke up again.

Rourke crossed the deck toward his cabin, the woman in his arms clinging to him, her fingernails digging into his bare forearm. Her slender body was rigid, her breaths shallow, little more than tiny hisses of pain escaping her lips in a nightmarish rhythm.

He frowned at Hegarty. "Ye did it."

Hegarty bounced at his side, half running to keep up with Rourke's longer strides. His red hair waved in the breeze. "Aye, and they tried to kill her."

Aye. Rourke's scalp prickled. He had to clench his jaw against the urge to shove her into the little troll's keeping. He didn't want her here. He wanted naught to do with her.

Yet at the same time he would not have her die. Not like this. He could feel her grip loosening, though whether on consciousness or life itself, he could not tell.

As he descended the short flight of stairs to his cabin,

he felt the last of the tension drain from her body. She went slack in his arms.

Nay. Not like this.

He gazed at her as he shouldered open the door. Her head had fallen back, her sleek red brown hair swaying, leaving her slender throat exposed. A throat encircled by a thin, silver chain. A chill slithered down his spine.

"Quick, Pup." Hegarty hopped around him like an overwrought bird, mimicking the dance of the small carved birds Rourke had hung from the ceiling of his cabin. "Set her down."

Rourke laid her gingerly on his bunk. As he reached for her pulse Hegarty turned on him, teeth bared.

"Go! Now!" Hegarty pushed him toward the door. "She'll not die. I'll not allow it."

Rourke held up his hands, for heaven knew he wanted naught but to escape. He evaded Hegarty long enough to grab an extra shirt from the peg on his wall, then strode out of the cabin and up the stairs, chased by the sound of Hegarty's chanting. *Magic.*

He felt the icy fingers of the prophecy slip around his neck, and he shot into the bright sunshine, seeking to rid himself of the sensation of doom. When last he'd tangled with that foul bit of soothsaying, his life had turned to ashes. He refused to allow it to destroy him again.

THREE

Pain radiated up her leg like fire driven by a vicious wind. Discordant notes from a haunting, wordless melody swirled around her—bright, razor-sharp lashes, driving her from her body, tearing open her leaden brain. Memories escaped, flying at her like ghouls on Halloween night. Hideous faces. Cruel, leering eyes. A knife through her leg. *Pain.*

Color swirled around her, through her, spinning faster until she feared she'd be torn apart by the vile kaleidoscope and flung to the rainbows. She cried out, begging the maelstrom to cease.

"Shh, lassie. 'Tis over now. Sleep."

The dwarf. His wordless song continued, but the spinning slowed. The pain slipped away like a demon cast out of hell. The ghostlike shackles loosed their grip on her mind, if not her body, and she felt once more tethered to the living world, though she still couldn't move. She could feel herself lying on her back, a rough blanket drawn over her legs.

The bed rocked. Colors swirled. A hand brushed her throat and a thin line of pressure cut into the back of her neck. The wild-haired dwarf had hold of her necklace. The necklace had no clasp. She'd worn it since she was a little girl and the chain wasn't long enough to fit over her head. There was no taking it off without breaking it, which seemed to be what the dwarf had in mind. The song ended abruptly with a yank brutal enough to cause the metal to tear into her tender flesh. She gasped mentally, but no sound formed in her throat.

No. You can't have it. It's all I have.

But her body would not respond to her mind's demand to fight.

A string of unknown words, ripe with anger, filled her ears. The thief had not succeeded. The angry mutterings moved away, then subsided with the closing of a door, leaving her swaying in a colorful sea.

Sleep tugged at her, pulling her down into a pit of dark nightmares—dreams of pale-eyed demons, fire-breathing steel. And pirates.

"An English frigate, Captain. Heading straight toward us."

Rourke strode across his storm-damaged deck, his strides long and agitated as he reached his bosun. Joshua Cutter looked at him with an I-told-you-so expression on his pitted face. With annoyance, Rourke grabbed the spyglass out of the bosun's hand and pressed the sun-warmed metal to his eye.

Damnation. An English patrol indeed. If the winds continued, that ship would pass them in little more than an hour. He couldn't outrun them. The *Lady Marie* had been badly damaged in the night's storm and even now barely held her own against the tides coaxing her toward the rocky shore of the Scottish coast. But neither could he allow them to board. In his hold he carried illegal arms. And in his cabin . . . a dying woman.

A dull pain throbbed behind his left temple as he lowered the spyglass and tossed it back to his crewman. Hegarty had found her. The bloody little troll had found Brenna Cameron.

The pounding of the carpenters' hammers echoed across the deck, doing little to ease the ache in his head. He moved to the port rail and scanned the cliffs in the too near distance. If the wind turned against the ship, it'd be dashed on the rocks for certain. They were too close.

And anywhere within a three days' sail of his native land was too close. At the first port he would put Hegarty and the woman ashore. Then he'd sail directly for the Isle of St. Christopher and buy the Goodhope Plantation. He needed it, he realized. He needed solid ground under his feet. Some place to call his own. Some place far, far from Scotland.

'Twas a good plan, if fate would but smile upon him for once.

As if in answer, a scuffle broke out amongst the miscreants he called a crew, his bosun in the thick of it.

"She bested ye, mate!" Gordy cackled as he and Cutter circled, hands at their sides. "No sense pretendin' it didn't 'appen. We all saw the way she near ripped off yer ballocks."

Cutter's face grew more contorted by the second. The words might be true—the lass was no lady and had fought like a guttersnipe—but Cutter was not one to lose . . . at anything. He'd expected to be made first mate upon the death of the former mate three months ago, but Rourke had never fully trusted the man. In truth, he'd never sought the loyalty of any of his crew. Their respect, yes. And most especially their trepidation, for his was a crew that knew no master but greed, lust, and that most powerful of emotions—fear.

But his former mate had given him loyalty nonetheless, as had Mr. Baker. Rourke had assigned Baker the job, though he was ill-prepared to be first mate. The man was as afraid of the crew as the crew was of their captain. Still, it was better to have a loyal hand at his back.

Rourke sighed, weary of the ever-present fighting. It was like captaining a pack of ill-mannered dogs.

"I'll kill you," Cutter spat.

"Now, Mr. Cutter." Jules stood well out of the reach of the fight. "'Tis no shame in it. She bested us in the hold when we found her. Near broke my nose, she did. And Gordy won't be standin' any straighter'n you for another sennight, I vow."

Cutter whipped out his knife and slashed at Jules, missing his chest by a hair's breadth. Jules pulled his own blade.

The time had come to end this. Rourke needed every able hand to mend his ship. He could not afford to lose a man to a brawl.

The clash of steel upon steel rang over the deck as Rourke put two fingers between his lips and gave a shrill whistle. The onlookers jumped and dispersed, but the combatants were locked in battle. Jules glanced up and blanched as his gaze met his captain's cold glare.

But Cutter seemed unaware of his arrival. He fought like a rabid dog, his lip curled back, his eyes wild. His chant of "I'll kill you" slowly changed to "I'll kill her."

Rourke's blood went cold. He pulled his sword and entered the fray. With a single upward swipe, he parted the men's swords. Jules leaped back, allowing Rourke to take on Cutter unchallenged. The man lunged for Rourke, seemingly oblivious to the change in opponents. He wanted blood and cared not whose.

Rourke knocked Cutter's sword out of his hand, then

sheathed his own and rammed his fist into the man's jaw. The blow sent Cutter sprawling.

Rourke stood over him, his eyes cold. "If the lass lives, she has my protection, aye? You willna go near her again."

Cutter sneered as he rose slowly to his feet. "I know why she's here."

Rourke stared at him, dread pooling in his gut. Cutter couldn't know. Could he?

But now was not the time. He'd pursue the comment later, when his ship was no longer in danger. "Mr. Baker!"

His first mate scurried to him, looking more mouse than man. "Aye . . . my lord?"

My lord. Rourke clenched his fists against the violent urge to choke the man. "I am not a lord."

"But . . ." His voice wobbled with terror.

"Hoist the plague flag. If they query us, we've two sick with the scourge belowdecks."

"But . . ."

"'Tis a bluff, Mr. Baker. Be gone with ye." He turned his hard gaze on Cutter and the rest of his crew. "To your posts, the lot of you!"

Out of the corner of his eye he saw Hegarty emerge at last. The little man moved toward him looking weary but satisfied, his mane of wild hair bobbing in the sea breeze.

Hegarty wiped his brow with his sleeve. "She lives."

The news brought both relief and dread. "For how long?"

The dwarf's eyes shone with a mischievous glint. "Now, Pup, you know I'm a fine healer."

"I want her away, Heg." He heard a thread of desperation in his voice and cleared his throat to cover it. "Do what e'er you must, but do it off my ship. I will set you ashore at the first port."

"Ah, lad, she may not be well enough to travel that soon."

Rourke saw the gleam in the little man's eyes. "Nay. You'll not involve me in this."

"You have always been involved, Pup."

"'Twas accident, nothing more. 'Tis about her and her alone. The prophecy has naught to do with me."

Hegarty met his gaze with sharp devilment. "She'll need a champion if naught else."

Rourke's gut tightened. "You'll not foist her on me. *You* are her champion. 'Tis *you* who've been waiting for her, not I."

Hegarty looked at him with eyes that were unusually serious and far too wise. "The prophecy affects us all. Naught will be right again until its words become truth. Now I'm off for a wee bit o' sleep." He looked at Rourke sharply. "Leave her be. You can see her when she's full recovered."

Hegarty left and Rourke turned back to the work at hand, clearing the deck of storm debris alongside his men. But though he worked on deck, his thoughts remained firmly in his cabin. Hegarty's voice had made it clear he didn't want Rourke going near her. The question was, why?

His curiosity got the better of him, and he crossed to his cabin and slipped inside. He found it silent and still except for the wooden birds swaying at the ceiling. His gaze went to his bunk and the lass lying still as death. A strange blue glow emanated from the hollow at her throat. He narrowed his eyes and moved closer.

The glow came from the stone that hung from the chain about her neck. His scalp tingled, the hair rising on his arms. He took a step back, chilled to the marrow of his bones.

Hegarty's doing.

He'd avoided the prophecy for a score of years. Now it stalked him again, the evil mist washing over his ship ready to choke the life out of him.

She had to go. As soon as they reached port, he was putting her ashore.

He needed air. But as he turned toward the door, the lass began to thrash in her sleep, her head tossing one way, then the other. Rourke hesitated, then moved toward her, drawn against his will.

She appeared fragile, ethereal. How could this be the wildcat who had taken down three of his crew? Yet she was. He'd seen her attack Cutter himself. His admiration grew, thick and unwelcome, as his gaze drank of her strange beauty.

The words *Hard Rock Cafe* and *Washington, D.C.*, were emblazoned across her chest, woven into the soft fabric of her bodice—a bodice that clung to gentle curves, revealing every tip and swell of what lay beneath. He forced his eyes to move past those enticing peaks, to the outline of long legs beneath the plaid blanket Hegarty had left half covering her.

Her breeks, made of queer fabric, peeked above the blanket. Small, cheerful monkeys smiled at him, at odds with the gash that might, even now, steal her life. His gaze returned, moving upward past the glowing sapphire to the paleness of her finely boned face framed by shiny red brown hair. Her features were regular and pleasing enough, but it was her mouth that drew his attention. Ripe and full, it was a mouth made for a man's kisses.

He swore at his body's unwanted stir of interest, but found himself unable to tear his gaze away from her. It was like being mesmerized by a pistol aimed at one's face. Until he set her ashore, he would do well to stay away from her—as far as possible. She was trouble, this one. And he'd already seen enough trouble to last a lifetime.

Her lids fluttered, opening slowly to reveal green eyes clouded with confusion. She blinked, tilting her head toward him. Their gazes met and she bolted upright.

Belatedly, he realized the sapphire's glow had winked out.

She scooted to the back of the bunk, her eyes at once sharp with fear, yet hard as steel, like those of a feral animal trapped and ready to fight for its life.

He backed away. "Be calm, lass. I'll not harm ye." He'd thought her bonnie in sleep, but awake, her eyes snapping with intelligence and life, she stole his breath.

With her gaze fixed on his face, she kicked off the blanket. In one fluid move she slipped off the bunk and lunged for the door, but Rourke was quicker. He blocked her attempted escape, forcing her back toward the bunk. Her gaze darted from him to scour his cabin, then back again, and he knew she searched for a weapon.

"Easy, Wildcat. You're safe enough."

She eyed him with disbelief. "Right. You're just an eccentric cruise director." She spoke strangely, with words he didn't recognize and an accent he couldn't place but found disturbingly pleasing to his ears. "And . . . what? . . . Your friend cut off my leg to welcome me to the ship?"

She froze, her startled gaze locking with his even as realization punched him in the stomach.

"My leg," she breathed.

As one, their gazes dropped to the ragged edge of her breeks where Hegarty had completed the rending of fabric that Cutter's knife had begun.

She backed up and sat hard on the bunk, then jerked her knee to her chest to examine the appendage in question. A wicked scar now ran from her shin around to the fleshy part of her calf. Not a wound—*a fully healed scar.*

Chills rippled over his scalp.

She looked up at him, her eyes wide, her mouth open in shock. "How long was I asleep?"

He shook his head, feeling a need to clear the shock from his brain even as he quashed the need to run. "A few hours."

She paled, a shiver tearing through her. "*How?*"

Rourke swallowed hard. "'Twas Hegarty's doing." At her look of confusion he held his hand out, palm down. "The wee man." He stepped toward her.

She scooted back. "Don't come any closer."

"I've said I'll not hurt you." He heard the harsh edge in his voice and smoothed his words so as not to frighten her more. "I wish only to see your injury." He took a small step toward her and was pleased when she did not retreat farther.

Her chin went up, challenge flashing in her green eyes. "What is this? Where am I?"

He took another step and watched her visibly tense. "The *Lady Marie*." He said the name softly, willing her to calm. "My ship."

"How did I get here?"

"I dinna ken." Again that look of confusion, and he realized she was as confused by his Scots as he was by her strange words. "I do not know. You must ask Hegarty." He eased onto the edge of the bunk, careful not to lean toward her. He motioned to her, gentling his tone. "I would see your leg."

Her chest rose and fell with agitation, her gaze sharp and distrustful, but she slowly straightened her leg toward him.

With careful, deliberate movements, he took the smooth warmth of the limb into his hands and lifted it onto his lap. His mouth went dry. She was naught but flesh and blood, he reminded himself. He'd seen enough of her blood to know. He ran his thumb over the puckered length of scar, pink and white with health . . . and age.

"It doesn't hurt." Her voice was tight with disbelief. She leaned forward and touched the wound herself, her fingers brushing against his.

She looked up at him, her eyes at once terrified and bewildered. "How did he fix it?"

Rourke met her gaze, then looked away. "Hegarty's a skilled healer."

"Skilled or not," she snapped. "Wounds don't heal in hours. And this one was a doozy."

His admiration for her rose another notch. He could sense her fear, yet she met him with anger. "Aye, the wound was formidable. You bled enough for three men. My crew is still scrubbing the deck of your blood."

His thumb traced the scar, his palm brushing the strange smoothness of her skin. The feel of her warm flesh beneath his hand sent a shaft of desire bolting through his blood, causing his fingers to curl into the silken firmness of her calf as need to explore that slender expanse of leg nearly got the better of him. He swore and pushed her leg off his lap, then rose and paced away from her.

"Who are you?" she demanded. In a bare whisper she added, "*What* are you?"

He turned and met her gaze. "I am Rourke Douglas, captain of the *Lady Marie*."

She lifted a brow. "Pretending to be a pirate."

"I am not a pirate." Though he didn't doubt his crew would turn to thievery at the first provocation.

"Are you a reenactor, then? A movie actor? You're not for real."

He watched her, at once confused by her words and enchanted by the way her mouth formed them.

"I assure you, I am as real as you."

"And I'm living in the *Twilight Zone*."

He heard the sharp edge of sarcasm, but could not understand her meaning.

She stood and walked toward the small window behind his desk, her movements assured and graceful. After a moment, she turned and faced him with an intense wariness that bordered on fear. A fear she would hide.

"Why did you bring me here?"

"I didna bring you."

"The dwarf." Her eyes narrowed with confusion. "He said he did. But he couldn't have. One little man did not steal me out of my hotel room." She stepped toward him, her eyes beseeching. "You have to let me go."

"Aye." It was his most fervent wish. "I will set you ashore as soon as we make port. Two to three days unless the winds becalm us."

She watched him as if waiting for him to grow a second head. "Just like that?" Her eyes began to sparkle dangerously. "Aren't you afraid I'll call the cops, or whatever you call them in Scotland, and have you arrested?"

The wildcat was back. Her eyes speared him, her ripe mouth beckoned him. Desire hammered him hard. *God's blood.* This was the last thing he needed—his body turning traitor.

He reached for the door. "I will send Hegarty to ye when he awakens." He had to get away before he forgot he'd once been a gentleman. Before he forgot he wanted nothing to do with her. Before he got sucked, once more, into the prophecy's hell.

"Wait! Don't go!"

But he ignored her frantic plea and escaped into the sunshine, bolting the door behind him.

Brenna heard the click even as she lunged for the door. Grabbing the latch, she yanked, but the door wouldn't budge. He'd locked her in.

She whirled and faced the small room, heart pounding. Where was she? What in the hell was going on?

It should have been a nightmare, just a horrible dream. By all that was logical she should have woken up in the little room in Aberdeen. But she was still on the ship. As was the man with the pale eyes. And her scar . . .

She sucked in air as panic rattled through her. This couldn't be happening. She was *not* in the clutches of pirates.

Her frantic gaze tore over her surroundings as she searched for a phone . . . or a weapon. The cabin was rustic, museum-like in its simplicity. No electricity, no bathroom, no phone. They were taking their reenactment to the extreme.

Either they were insane . . . or she was.

She rubbed the back of her neck and winced as her hand encountered the small welt from the attempted theft of her necklace. The dwarf had tried to steal it.

Great. The dwarf was a thief, and the captain looked at her like he'd as soon drown her as save her. And they were the good guys.

She searched the room, trying the desk and the chest at the foot of the bunk, but both were locked. Panic brushed at her nerves. She needed answers, dammit. *What is going on?*

Her gaze took in the rest of the room as she searched for something. Anything. Pegs stuck out from the wall with costumes hanging from them. A vivid, sickening memory of the way the crew had looked at her had her grabbing one of the shirts and pulling it on over her T-shirt. As she rolled up the sleeves, she continued her perusal.

Movement above caught her attention. Hanging from the ceiling were at least two dozen small wooden birds, each one different. Unpainted, roughly carved, and only a few inches long, they hung on thin lines and swayed with the movement of the ship. If she hadn't been nearly sick with fear, they might have made her smile.

She walked to the small window and peered out. The glass was coated with sea spray, but not so much that she couldn't make out the rugged Scottish coastline dotted with small stone houses. She nodded, relieved. They were still close to shore.

She might yet have a chance to escape.

Sweat rolled down Rourke's shoulder blades as he paced the deck waiting for the English frigate to pass. He'd ordered his crew to maintain their posts, for he could ill afford a battle and would give the English captain no reason to think he wanted one.

Hegarty bounded out of the hold, his mane flapping like half a dozen sails in the breeze. Rourke watched him skip down the stairs into the galley. Preparing something for the woman no doubt.

Those eyes of hers flashed in his mind—eyes that were at once vulnerable yet menacing. Eyes that called him to protect her, even as they warned him to protect himself. No lady, to be sure, yet what she lacked in manners she more than made up for in courage. She would need that courage. The prophecy would demand it.

Slowly the English frigate approached them, but their heading left a safe distance between the ships, clearly not on a course to intercept. Rourke felt the relief sink into his belly like warm ale on a cold day. The plague flag had worked.

"How many dead?" the English captain called.

"Three stricken. Two dead."

"God have mercy on you."

Rourke lifted a hand in thanks, and the English ship continued on. When the ships were out of gun range, the tightly coiled tension eased out of him. The English had bought his bluff. Mayhap his fortunes were turning at last.

"Captain?" Jules called. "It's Mr. Cutter, sir. He's gone to your cabin."

Rourke jerked, Cutter's promise ringing in his ears. *I'll kill her.*

He took off at a sprint and burst through the door just as Cutter was raising his sword. The lass was trapped in the back corner of the cabin, poised for battle as if she could fight a steel blade with her bare hands. Or intended to die trying.

Even as he took in the situation, Cutter's sword began its deadly downward arc. An arc she would not escape.

In one swift move, Rourke pulled his eating knife from his belt and threw it, burying the small blade deep in the back of Cutter's sword hand.

His bosun cried out as the sword veered toward the left, landing harmlessly a hand's breadth shy of the lass. He swung toward Rourke, cradling his bleeding hand, his nose hanging at an odd angle, bleeding profusely.

The wildcat had struck first, it seemed.

Cutter stared at him, an animal's madness in his eyes. "She dies. You both die."

Rourke slammed his fist into his bosun's jaw, sending him crashing against the wall. Cutter had been with him for more than two years, a hard, mercurial man. Rourke would have set him ashore long ago had the man not been such a fine sailor.

"Captain?" Jules asked from the entry.

Rourke yanked Cutter up and shoved him at Jules. "Chain him in the hold."

"Aye, Captain."

Brenna dashed past him and out the door so fast he had to lunge to catch her before she reached the stairs. But the moment he wrenched her back against him, he knew he'd made a mistake. She twisted in his arms, turning wild.

Fortunately, he'd seen enough of the woman's fighting ways to take precautions. When she tried to slam her knee into his loins, he deflected the blow and turned her sideways, locking her shoulder against him. A growl of frustration rumbled in her chest.

"Be calm, Wildcat. I'll not harm you. You have my oath on it."

Her clean woman's scent wafted over him like a warm summer garden. He was suddenly aware of the feel of her in his arms. Too aware. The top of her head reached his mouth, her hair silky against his chin.

"Let me go." Desperation laced her voice as she struggled against him, unwittingly brushing the part of his anatomy most interested in becoming acquainted with her. Lust slammed into him.

Nay. He would not let the woman affect him in that way.

He pushed her back into his cabin, then released her as if she burned him. She spun to face him even as Hegarty pushed into the room behind him carrying a mug of foul-smelling brew.

"What happened?"

"Cutter sought his revenge on her for unmanning him. I've ordered him in chains."

"Ye should kill the blighter," Hegarty said matter-of-factly.

Rourke made a noncommittal sound.

The woman looked at him pleadingly. "I need air. I need a few minutes on deck to catch my breath."

"Nay," Hegarty said. "Ye'll not be going near that lot agin. 'Ave ye learned nothing?"

She ignored Hegarty and met Rourke's gaze, desperation growing in her eyes. "I don't like closed spaces. Just a few minutes on deck. That's all I'm asking. Surely I'm in no danger if you're there?"

Saints, but her plight tore at him.

Hegarty must have read his thoughts, for he moved between them. "Get you back on the bunk, lassie. Yer brew's await'n and ye'll drink it now."

But Brenna Cameron wasn't one to follow orders

meekly. She held Rourke's gaze as if grasping a lifeline. "Please."

Hegarty threw a hand in the air as he turned to him. "Ye let her on deck and yer crew will be all over her like dogs on a bone. Ye'll be slappin' 'em all in chains and then how will ye set this ship to sail?"

Hegarty was right. He couldn't risk it. She was dressed like a sailor and had no manners to speak of, yet even so there was something wholly feminine about her. A lushness to those slender curves that made his hands long to touch her again. She filled his senses. Stirred his blood.

And had him vowing he'd not let his crew near her again. "Ye'll remain here until we make port, lass. We'll be at sea but another day or two, if the weather holds."

He watched frustration and dismay chase themselves across her expressive features. She released her breath on an angry sigh, then turned away. Hegarty ushered him out and closed the door behind him.

Though she remained hidden in his cabin for the rest of the day and well into the night, she haunted Rourke's every thought. Her courage in the face of near-certain death, not once but twice. Her strength. Her vulnerability. The warrior's gleam that lit her gaze, and the desperation that laced her words.

Above all he saw her face. That bonnie, green-eyed siren's face.

The face of his doom.

Brenna woke to the sound of anxious shouting and the frenzied pounding of feet overhead. She sat up and shoved her hair out of her face, her sleepy gaze pulled to the little wooden birds swaying at the ceiling even as the strong, musty smell of the ship teased her nostrils.

The pirate ship.

Damn.

This nightmare just wouldn't end. And it wasn't even morning yet. The light coming through the window was soft and new. Dawn, just before sunrise.

The sounds above grew more frantic. The number of boots seemed to have multiplied.

What was going on? Her eyes widened as hope lifted her high. Maybe someone was chasing the ship.

Police.

She swung her feet over the side and ran for the window even as a voice overhead yelled, "We'll be dashed upon the rocks!"

The captain's strong voice carried clearly in reply. "Unfurl the mainsail and foresail. Tack south by southeast, Mr. Jenkins."

"Aye, Captain."

The hope that had lifted her so suddenly dropped her with a thud. Thick fog obscured her view, but she could make out the dark lump that had to be the coast.

Suddenly, she understood. They'd drifted too close to shore. This was the chance she needed. This close, she could easily swim to freedom, even with the water freezing. But she had to get out of the cabin before the ship sailed. Which meant *now*.

She needed a plan. An idea came to her and she raced for the water pitcher and tossed the contents into the corner, then ran for the door, praying the plan worked.

"Help!" she cried, pounding with both fists. "Help me!"

Her hands were nearly numb by the time she finally heard the lock click. Hegarty opened the door, the expression on his leathery face more suspicious than concerned. "What ails ye, lass?"

Brenna opened her mouth, but the words got caught in her throat, so she pointed frantically toward the corner where she'd dumped the water. "A leak!" she managed.

"Water's coming in!" Hegarty's eyes grew round and he scurried toward the corner. Without a backward glance, Brenna dashed out the door.

"The sails are catching, Captain! She's moving."

Rourke felt the pressure on his chest give way as fog rolled across his ship. They were not going to founder upon the rocks after all. He watched the two sails fill with wind, at last.

"Rourke!" Hegarty's voice carried over the hurrahs of his crew.

He turned to see the woman streak onto his deck, red brown hair glistening like silk in the patchy sunshine, his shirt a white billow around her.

Bloody hell. He was barely free of one disaster. The last thing he needed was a woman topside. Not with this crew.

As he started toward her, she glanced his way. Their gazes caught and in that instant, he understood. She meant to jump. He saw in her eyes the utter determination to escape him, even if it meant her death.

"Nay!"

But even as the word left his mouth, she leaped atop the rail. She stood there, poised for one fleeting moment like a finely carved masthead, her exquisitely sculpted face lifted to the sky. Then with a powerful, graceful arc, she dove into the frigid waters of the North Sea.

Four

"Man overboard!"

Rourke lunged for the rail, tearing off his weapons. *God's blood.* He'd not risked life and sanity to skirt the coast of Scotland only to have the woman extinguish her own life the moment Hegarty found her.

But as his sword clattered to the deck, she surfaced and started toward the fog-shrouded shore with long, clean strokes. The woman could swim. But for how long? The coast appeared much closer than it was. She would drown before she was a quarter of the distance.

"Daft wench." He should turn and walk away. Let her drown. She was naught but a tribulation he'd be well rid of.

Even as the thought went through his head, his hands tore the boots from his feet.

Aye, he should let her drown.

Instead, he hoisted himself onto the rail and dove into the sea to save her.

The cold slammed into him like a twenty-stone seaman, knocking the air from his lungs, stealing the strength from his limbs. He had to reach her before her strength gave out.

Over the rolling, cresting waves, he spotted her and set out. But as he raced toward her, the distance between them did not close as quickly as he'd expected. It didn't close at all. He knew himself to be a fine swimmer, yet the lass was keeping apace. Amazing, considering she'd nearly bled to death less than a day before.

Rourke pushed himself to his limit, ignoring the briny sea spray in his mouth and nose, the icy water numbing his limbs. Not until they neared the shore did he finally begin to gain on her. But not soon enough.

Rocks jutted menacingly from the surf between them and the shore. If a wave dashed her against one, she'd sink like a stone. She'd be dead before he could reach her.

"Wildcat!"

She turned her head, meeting his gaze for one fleeting moment. Then she pushed forward as if unaware of her looming death. Or uncaring.

Cold. So cold.

Brenna forced her arms to stroke and prayed her legs were still kicking, because she couldn't feel them. And she knew the pirate was behind her. The salt water stung her eyes. The taste of it strafed her lips and tongue with each painful breath. But she couldn't stop. She couldn't let him drag her back to that hell ship.

In front of her lay an obstacle course of jagged rocks she was going to have to maneuver between if she hoped to survive. *Just a fun day at the beach, boys and girls.*

"Wildcat!"

Her heart skipped a pounding beat at the closeness of the pirate's call. A surge of adrenaline born of pure fear set her arms to stroking at twice her previous speed until she felt herself lifted on a wave. With a burst of panic she knew the next moments would spell the difference between her death . . . and escape.

Using the bodysurfing technique she'd learned at the beach at home, she steered her frozen form around first one rock, then another, until at last she was in the surf. Her toes stubbed loose rocks along the bottom and she nearly wept with relief.

As she stumbled on stiff, numb legs through the shallow water, Brenna looked back in time to see the pirate pass between the rocks, swimming with the wave that would carry him right to her feet.

Terror lent strength to her freezing, exhausted body, and she pushed forward. She was so cold, so tired. But she had to keep moving.

Ahead, a tiny, deserted wedge of beach lay tucked into the curve of the rocky coastline. Beyond it, a steep, grassy path led to freedom, her only avenue of escape. She fought her way out of the grasping surf and lurched toward it.

At the sound of splashing behind her, her heart began to thud. *I'm not going back with him.*

Her only chance of escape now lay in outrunning him. Or reaching help in the form of a big man with a bigger gun. Anyone else would be powerless against the pirate. He was too muscular, too strong. And way too determined.

Brenna lunged for the hillside, leaping onto the grass, but that first tuft gave way to ankle-deep muddy water. She growled with frustration and scrambled up the boggy path, feeling like the devil himself was on her heels. Halfway to the top, a strong hand snared her ankle.

"No!" The word croaked through her frozen lips as she clawed at the grass, desperately scrabbling for a hold. Her attempt to kick free only made her captor yank harder, knocking her face-first onto the grassy slope. Before she could push herself up, the pirate's rough hand clamped over her mouth. His knee pressed into the small of her back, immobilizing her, bitterly stealing her brief hope of escape.

But not her fight. Never that. She slammed her elbow back, colliding with a rock-hard arm.

He snagged her wrist, holding her still. "I dinna wish to harm you." The pirate's voice, low in her ear, was as thin with cold as her own.

She tried to bite the fingers covering her mouth, but his salty hand was pressed too tightly.

"Cease! If ye draw the guards upon us, they'll kill you."

He didn't make any sense. She'd been captured by a madman. Tears clouded her vision as she struggled against his impossible hold, but he only increased the pressure on her back until she could hardly breathe.

"Wildcat, you must understand the danger we're in. You'll not make a sound, aye?"

The last thing she wanted to do was give in, but she nodded, willing to do just about anything to make him release her.

Slowly, he took his hand from her mouth.

"*Get off me.*"

"If you try to unman me as ye did Cutter, I'll let them kill you." The brittle softness of his voice told her he wasn't kidding, but the sharp pressure on her back finally disappeared.

Brenna pushed to her feet, soaked and muddy. The man's large hand clamped around her wrist and she looked up, meeting cold eyes.

"Not a sound, lass."

"Look, Pirate, if you let me go, I won't tell anyone about you or your ship. I promise. I swear I'll catch the next flight back to the States and never, *ever* come back."

The man's eyes narrowed with confusion. "Wildcat, you aren't . . ." He broke eye contact and glanced around as if surveying their surroundings. When he turned back, his gaze pinned her with keen intensity. "Where do ye think ye are?"

Brenna stared at him, a sudden uneasiness undermining her certainty. Had they sailed to Ireland overnight? Denmark?

Her gaze skimmed what she could see of the cliffs and coast until it snagged on a large edifice in the swirling mists. A castle, perched high on the cliffs above them.

The mists broke and reformed but not before she caught a clearer glimpse. She knew that place.

Castle Stour.

Thank God. She might not be welcome there, but at least she knew where she was.

But even as relief filled her, the sun broke through and the mists parted again, illuminating a whole and vibrant stronghold that couldn't be Stour at all.

She stared at it in confusion. The restored tower looked almost exactly like the one she'd toured two days ago. But that's where the resemblance ended. Stour's recently restored keep had looked strangely out of place among the crumbling ruins of its sixteenth-century ranges, like a knight in finest armor trailed by tattered servants.

There was nothing ruined about this castle. Its ranges stood as solid and impregnable as the tower itself, their crenellated ramparts rising like teeth against the misty blue sky. Teeth spotted with helmeted and armed sentries.

This was not Stour. A twin, perhaps, built by the same architect. And not destroyed by fire in the seventeenth century.

She met her captor's gaze. "Where am I, then? I thought I was in Scotland."

"You are in Scotland, lass. On the lands belonging to the third Earl of Slains."

Brenna's eyes narrowed. "How many castles does the earl own? Is he cloning them now?"

"Cloning?" That same look of confusion crossed his face. "The earl resides at Castle Stour, though I ken he's set his sights on others aplenty."

"Then which castle is this one?"

"Stour." He said the word slowly, forming it carefully as if she were an idiot.

Brenna opened her mouth, then shut it again with a roll of her eyes. Good grief, just how far was he going to take this? "Listen, Pirate, I need you to let me go. I promise, you'll never see or hear from me again."

"Ye dinna believe me." His pale eyes bore into her, sending an unwanted shiver of awareness tingling through her thawing limbs. "That *is* Castle Stour."

She huffed with frustration. "I toured Stour two days ago. Most of the castle's in ruins." Her fisted hands found her hips. "This. Is. Not. It."

He stared at her for several heated seconds, then shook his head as if to clear it. "'Tis no matter what name ye wish to call it. The earl will kill us both if he catches us. We must be away, and quickly."

Brenna stared at him. He was taking this reenactment way too far. It was almost as if he believed it. Why did all the interesting ones have to be insane . . . or married?

"Look . . . Rourke." Maybe using his name would tap a thread of sanity. If Rourke *was* his name. At least he wasn't calling himself Blackbeard or Captain Hook. "I know you *think* I'm in danger."

The quick flash of annoyance in his eyes unnerved her. Crazy people weren't supposed to be quite so quick, were they? She broke eye contact to make this easier and glanced back toward the castle.

"But . . ."

The sun, burning through the morning mist, revealed the castle in its entirety, stealing the words from her throat as her mind catalogued every eerie similarity to the one she'd visited. Even the cliffs looked the same right down to the . . .

A dull roar started in her ears as her gaze locked on the upside-down Hershey's Kiss barely visible within the folds of the rock.

No way.

Her gaze darted over the rest of the castle, frantically seeking an answer—*any* answer—as her pulse began to pound in her ears.

The earl might have duplicated his castles, but he couldn't have reproduced the cliffs and the rocks. And the cave. And if he hadn't duplicated them . . .

She tried to swallow, but her throat had gone dry. If he hadn't duplicated them . . . She swayed, but the pirate's grip held her tight.

"How can this be?" she whispered. Two days ago it had been a ruin. Today it was whole.

Foreboding rose, thudding against her chest as her mind darted about like a drunk roadrunner, crashing into the walls of her brain. Castles did not mend themselves overnight!

Neither did legs.

"Hegarty," she whispered. "He's behind this, isn't he?"

"Aye. He is the one who brought ye here."

And he'd already answered the question of where *here* was. *You are in Scotland. On the lands belonging to the third Earl of Slains.*

Her scalp tingled, the hair rising on her arms as she heard his words fully this time. The third earl.

The words suddenly took on an ominous ring. She remembered the tour guide discussing the theories behind the fire that destroyed the castle in the late seventeenth century. *In 1687, during the time of the third earl, the castle was destroyed.* The tour guide's voice rang in her head like a death knell. *During the time of the third earl. 1687.*

Her breath turned ragged, her pulse racing through her veins.

No. It couldn't be.

But she thought of the meticulously authentic pirate ship. There had been nothing anachronistic aboard that ship. No errant can of Coke. No cell phone going off in the middle of the night. No muffled sound of a soccer match over the radio. Just pirates in tattered rags as if the past had come roaring to life.

She looked up at the man who held her tight in his grip, his expression grim. If all this was somehow real, if she'd truly tumbled through time, then she was being held by an honest-to-goodness pirate.

Oh. My. God.

Her legs refused to hold her and she sank to the grass, dizzy with denial. This could *not* be happening. Chaos whirred in her ears as it hadn't since she was a child being pushed and shoved from one foster home to another.

How is this possible?

The pirate squatted in front of her and put his hand on her shoulder, his face etched with concern even as his eyes flashed with impatience. "This is no time to swoon, Wildcat. We're in great danger. We must be away before they find us."

"This is Hegarty's doing."

"Aye."

Magic. She wanted to scream, "There's no such thing!" But her leg said otherwise. *Everything* said otherwise.

She stared at the castle, glistening silver. "Why? Why did he bring me here?"

"You must ask him yourself."

Her head snapped up and she gazed out at the sea. "We have to get back to the ship." But through the breaking mist, she could see nothing on the water but a few bobbing seagulls. "Where did it go?"

"She was put to sail just before our ill-timed swim." His voice deepened with a rich vein of annoyance. "'Tis a muckle shame ye didna stay in my cabin as I bade ye, aye?"

The truth of his words slammed into her. In escaping, she'd lost her only ticket home. Hegarty.

"My crew will drop anchor and await us once they're out of sight of Stour. Shouldna take more than a day to reach them."

"A day? How fast can they sail that thing?"

"How fast do ye walk, lass?"

Walk? Brenna groaned. If this was really the seventeenth century, then of course they'd be walking. She glanced down at her bare feet, one of which was already bleeding from the rocks, and sighed. Could this day get any worse?

"Come." Rourke started up the embankment, clearly expecting her to follow. Ten minutes ago she'd been hell-bent on escaping him.

She glanced back at the empty sea, then scurried to catch up. He might be a pirate, but he was her only way back to Hegarty. And it seemed the dwarf was the only one who could send her home.

As they neared the top of the steep path, the pirate motioned her to wait. Slowly, he rose above the level of the ground, his movements as furtive as a spy's.

A shout rang out and the pirate ducked. He met her gaze, his eyes wide and disbelieving. "Bloody hell."

"They saw you?"

"Aye." His eyes turned piercingly intense. "Stay here while I engage them. I'll lead them away from you. Run and dinna stop."

"What about you?"

"I can look after myself."

"Yeah, but . . ."

He stood, hands up, and climbed to the top of the slope. "I mean no harm," the pirate shouted. "I fell from a passing vessel and was forced to swim ashore. I wish only to rejoin my crew."

"That will be for the earl to decide," a deep voice answered.

Brenna's heart thudded. How was she supposed to know when to run when she couldn't see a thing? And just where was she supposed to go? She didn't even know which way the ship was heading. Every time she'd been on board to notice, it had been at anchor.

Damn. *Damn.* The insidious helplessness she'd known as a child tightened around her like a straitjacket. She thought she'd finally shed it once and for all when she reached adulthood and was no longer at the mercy of others for her food and shelter. Yet here she was again.

Wrong. She wasn't helpless this time. She might not understand what was going on, but she knew what she had to do. Find Hegarty.

And to do that she needed the pirate.

She crept slowly up the hillside until she could see him. And, hopefully, not be seen herself. As her gaze crested the top of the hill, she sucked in her breath at the sight that met her eyes. Stour in all its prefire glory. She'd thought she understood the size of the place as she'd wandered the restored keep in her own time, but the castle in its prime was a sight to behold.

The pirate stood with his hands up, his clothes plastered to his muscled body as two men joined him. Her eyes widened at the sight of them.

The pair looked as if they'd just stepped out of a Shakespearean play, give or take a century. They wore heavy blue coats and tight black pants. One appeared to be sporting a wig, unless he genuinely had a massive head of long, curly black hair. Each wore a gun on one hip—long unwieldy-looking pistols—and a sword on the other.

Either the whole place was one giant reenactment or she was really and truly in the past.

As she watched, one of the guards moved too close to the drenched pirate. Rourke plowed his fist through the soldier's face, flattening him. But as he turned to mete out the same punishment to the second guard, the man pulled his gun and pointed it at Rourke's head.

"On your knees."

Brenna's heart went to her throat. The bluecoat was about to shoot her ticket home. She had to do something—attract the guy's attention and fast.

If they catch you, they'll kill you.

Good grief.

As Rourke knelt, hands on his head, she scrambled onto the coarse ground of the heath, her muscles tensed, every nerve in her body screeching as if she were running into the path of an oncoming car.

"Excuse me! Could you point me in the direction of the nearest Wal-Mart? I seem to have misplaced my Nikes." Did Wal-Mart carry Nikes? Like *that* mattered.

The bluecoat and Rourke glanced at her and scowled in unison, the soldier's gun never wavering from Rourke's head. The pirate looked like he was going to kill her. The bluecoat turned, ignoring her. Guess the drowned rat look didn't pose much of a threat . . . or much of a come-on. And she had too many clothes on for the wet T-shirt look to work.

The man on the ground began to stir.

She had to do something.

She knew what they'd do in the movies . . . or California. If the assets weren't showing through the shirt, then pull up the shirt.

No. No way.

The downed guard groaned.

Oh, man.

Taking a deep breath for courage, she gripped the two hems and pulled them up to her shoulders. And stood there, feeling like an idiot. The gentle breeze caressed her half-frozen nipples, but no one seemed to notice.

"Hey!" If she was going to flash, she sure as heck wanted a little reaction. A girl had her pride after all.

She started toward them. "I feel like I have seaweed stuck to me. Can you see? Do I have any seaweed stuck to me?"

The pirate saw her first. His eyes widened. His face turned to stone. The bluecoat did a classic double take as his scowl slid right off his face.

Brenna was beginning to wonder if the pirate was going to take advantage of the opportunity she'd provided him, when he finally moved. In a flash, the bluecoat's gun went flying.

She yanked the wet fabric down as Rourke and the bluecoat fought. Almost too late, she heard the sounds behind her and whirled to find the downed guard rising and pulling his sword.

The pirate didn't seem to notice. "Rourke!"

But even as she yelled, he knocked the bluecoat clean out with a right uppercut to the jaw, then grabbed the man's sword and met the charge of the second soldier.

Brenna watched them in heart-pounding fascination. A real, to-the-death sword fight, not the choreographed kind she'd seen in movies. The two men moved with amazing speed and skill, each desperate to win, for to lose meant death.

And the death had better be the bluecoat's. She still needed the pirate.

She glanced at the man lying prone and caught a

glimpse of his gun. She should get it. Walk over there and steal it. But her feet wouldn't move. It was like watching the scene, herself included, from afar.

The pirate's sword took flight. Fear propelled her forward and she ran for the gun. As her cold fingers closed around the strangely elongated pistol, she saw the pirate dive and roll, coming up with the sword in his hand.

Nice. The guy could move.

Kneeling in the grass, the gun heavy in her hands, she tried to take aim. The pounding of her pulse vibrated through her arms, making the gun shake. She didn't dare shoot. Not only couldn't she risk hitting the pirate, but she had no idea what she was doing. She'd never fired a gun in her life.

There was a first time for everything, but this probably wasn't it.

Eyeing the prone guard uneasily, she remembered how the other had popped back up. He looked dead enough, even though he'd only been clipped on the jaw. Her gaze slid to his boots and she eyed them with more than a hint of envy. His feet didn't appear to be much bigger than hers. He wasn't wearing Nikes, but leather boots would protect her feet better than nothing, even if they didn't quite fit.

Brenna eased toward him, then gathered her courage and wrenched the boots off his feet, one at a time. Grabbing up the pair, she quickly retreated and put them on as she watched the sword fight. The two men were better matched than she would have thought. The bluecoat was wiry and fast, but the pirate was bigger and clearly stronger. He fought with a ferocity and purpose that had her thanking God he was on her side.

She stood and tested the fit of the boots. They were a little big, but surprisingly not too bad. Out of the corner of her eye, she saw their owner lurch to his feet.

These guys just wouldn't stay down.

He was swaying, looking dazed, but he pulled a knife from his belt, clearly intending to join the fray.

Damn. She should have taken that knife when she had the chance. She hadn't even noticed it. Though she'd spent a lot of time learning self-defense, she wasn't in the habit of thinking in terms of life and death. Clearly, that was going to have to change. The pirate was good, but even he might not be able to handle two men at once.

As the dazed guard started toward the fray, Brenna picked up the gun, gripped it in both hands, and took aim.

I can't do it. I can't just kill a man.

But wasn't that exactly what the bluecoats meant to do to the pirate? And what about her? As soon as the pirate was gone, they'd turn on her as the pirates had done. She had no illusions about that. Especially after she'd flashed the one.

Even so, her finger refused to pull the trigger. She had to do something! Thinking fast, she grabbed the gun like a mallet and started after her target, careful to stay out of his line of sight. She'd almost caught up with him when her toe caught on a rock and she tripped, a gasp escaping her throat. Though she caught herself and kept from falling, it was too late.

The bluecoat whirled and slammed his fist into her jaw, knocking her off her feet in an explosion of pain. Brenna landed with a bone-jarring thud on a patch of hard ground.

She tasted blood. He'd hit her.

But as she tried to scramble to her feet, the hard weight of his bootless foot pinned her ankle to the ground. Above her, the bluecoat raised his knife and aimed it at her heart. The promise of her death shone in a man's eyes for the third time in less than twenty-four hours.

This wasn't happening. It wasn't real. How could she die when she wasn't even supposed to be here?

The man arched suddenly, a cry exploding from his

lips as his face contorted with pain. His knife dropped harmlessly on the ground as he began to fall toward her.

With a squeak of alarm, Brenna rolled out of the way, barely avoiding being crushed. As she sat up, she saw the dagger sticking out of the man's back.

Dead. He's dead. Oh my God. She was going to be sick.

Brenna stumbled to her feet as the pirate raced toward her. Behind him, the other bluecoat lay in a pool of blood.

Dead. He'd killed them both. He must have thrown the knife to kill her attacker. Thrown it far. With deadly accuracy.

Her forehead felt strangely hot, her hands cold, as she dabbed at her bloody lip, watching him run toward her. Her own shaking legs refused to move.

The pirate reached her and grabbed her by the shoulders, his piercing gaze on her mouth. "Are ye hurt?"

Shaken, yes. Hurt? "No, not really." What was a bloody mouth compared to a knife in the heart? She swayed as the full reality of how close she'd come to dying hit her.

"Easy, Wildcat. 'Tisna the time to swoon."

"I don't faint."

With a nod, a hint of admiration gleaming in his eyes, he released her. "Good." He grabbed the other bluecoat's gun, knife, and boots, then propelled her toward the cliffs. "Come. We must be away. It's early morn, but they'll have heard the fighting."

As if on cue, she heard a shout. Turning back, she watched half a dozen men racing from the gates of the castle.

The pirate grabbed her hand. "Run!"

Pure fear lent her strength she badly needed. Dead bluecoats meant a noose if they were caught. Or worse.

She certainly wasn't in Kansas anymore. Not that she'd ever been in Kansas, but that wasn't the point.

As Brenna ran, the boots rubbed her feet in strange ways, promising nice, plump blisters—if she lived long enough to feel them. At least the soles of her feet were cushioned against the sharp rocks.

They reached the embankment and half ran, half slid down the boggy slope, finally reaching the tiny beach where they'd swum ashore. The pirate caught her hand and pulled her along the surf's edge toward where the beach ended as the rocky cliffs met the sea.

"Where are we going?" Surely he didn't mean for them to swim again.

"These cliffs are full of caves."

They left the beach, rounding the corner to wade through the surf that lapped the base of the cliffs. The pirate kept to the outside, breaking the force of the buffeting waves. Brenna kept her free hand against the cliff face, steadying herself as they walked, until the rock opened.

The pirate peered into the cave's mouth, but didn't stop.

"You don't like that one?" she asked.

"No."

They continued on, passing three more caves before coming to a large section of rock with large, gaping holes that reminded her of Swiss cheese. Holes formed from eons of water eroding the rock.

The pirate pulled her into one of the holes, one with a roof high enough for him to stand. The cave was narrow, but deep, extending farther into the rock than the light could penetrate. If the soldiers came after them, they could well and truly hide.

As Brenna leaned against the cool, dank wall, trying to catch her breath, her companion remained by the opening, watching. If she'd known this vacation was going to entail two-thirds of a triathlon, she'd have worked harder at her training before she left home. Her breathing was finally starting to even out again when the pirate whirled on her.

"What did ye think ye were doing?" His voice was low, barely a whisper, yet as hard as his ice-colored eyes. His hair had come loose during the fight and now hung to his shoulders, brushing the shirt that clung to his muscular body—a body tensed with anger.

"I told ye to run," he growled.

Brenna swallowed hard, but met his gaze. "Yeah, but you forgot to tell me where. He had a gun to your head. I had to do something."

His arm flung sideways as he made a harsh sound deep in his throat. "I fought them apurpose to draw them from ye. I would ha' escaped them before we reached the castle."

Brenna scowled. "How was I supposed to know that?"

"Ye were supposed to follow my command!"

"Sorry, but I'm not used to following orders. I'm not one of your men, in case you haven't noticed."

"Och, I noticed." His gaze dropped to her chest, his scowl matching her own. "Ye shouldna have . . ."

"What? Lifted my shirt? I admit it wasn't the most lady-like thing I've ever done, but I had to do something. I had to get their attention."

"Aye." As he met her gaze, his eyes took on a silver cast that made heat ripple over her skin. "You got their attention, Wildcat," he said softly. "And mine."

The sudden intensity of his gaze set off tremors deep inside her that had nothing to do with fear. But when he stepped toward her, she put up her hands, warding him off.

"Don't even think about it, Pirate."

"I promise ye, I can think of little else." His voice had turned husky and raw, sending shivers of awareness rippling over her skin. He took another step and another, stopping inches in front of her, his eyes gleaming silver.

Her heart raced. He was too close. Too wild. She tried to back up, but there was no place to go.

"I'm warning you, Pirate." She fought to steady her voice as she pressed her palms against his chest and pushed. "Don't mess with me." But he didn't budge. Her heart contracted as she wondered if she'd thrown in her lot with the wrong man after all.

His hands rose to cover hers lightly. "Do you try your wee tricks on me, lass, I shall throw you into the surf to be snatched away by the earl's soldiers." His eyes were sharp with warning, but within their cool depths she saw a flash of humor, maybe even admiration.

Keeping hold of her hands, he eased back, letting her fear fall away.

Brenna watched him. "Would you really give me to them?"

"What do you think?"

Twice he'd saved her from Cutter, then dived into the frigid North Sea to rescue her, and not, as she'd originally thought, to capture her. And when the bluecoats caught sight of him, he hadn't run as he could have. He'd intentionally given himself up to give her a chance to escape.

"I think you wouldn't. You're a decent man, even though you insist on pretending you're a pirate—"

"I'm not a pirate," he said evenly.

Her gaze fell to his broad, calloused hands holding hers with surprising gentleness. "You're not like your crew." The thought of those beasts made her shudder. If one of them had come after her instead of Rourke, she'd be bleeding by now. Probably dead. "I think you're a good man."

She'd known he wouldn't admit it. Bad for the image and all. She half expected him to try to intimidate her again. What she didn't expect was the bleakness that entered his eyes.

He released her hands and turned away to peer out of the cave, his back rigid, a muscle working in his jaw. "I assure you, Wildcat. I am not a good man. Dinna make the mistake of thinking I am."

But as she watched his rigid back, she knew she was right about him. She felt it, deep down. But the bleak look in his eyes told her he'd done things he couldn't live with. She'd seen him kill with ease. He might be a decent man at heart, but he was still dangerous. Very, very dangerous. She'd be a fool to forget it.

They waited in tense silence for a long time. Brenna tried to listen for sounds of their pursuers, but she doubted she'd hear them over the crashing of the surf and the crying of the gulls outside the cave.

As the tide came in, Brenna took off her boots and set them on the rock beside her. The water soon rose until it began to lap at her ankles. Finally, the pirate turned and motioned to her.

"We must go. We'll be trapped by the tide if we stay much longer."

Brenna grabbed her boots and stepped forward as the man held out his hand to her. She reached for him, feeling a sense of rightness as his calloused hand closed warmly around hers.

She followed him out of the cave, the water now lapping at her knees with each roll of the surf. There was no sign of bluecoats.

"They have to know we were hiding."

He nodded. "They know. 'Tis unlikely they care."

Her gaze narrowed with disbelief. "But we murdered those men."

"I did only what any man would do. They'll not expend effort searching for a pair of half-drowned fisherfolk . . . if that's who they're believing us to be. Our going to ground was but a wee bit of heedfulness."

Rourke led her along the base of the cliffs, but no longer attempted to block her from the incoming waves, with the water so much higher. He kept tight hold of her hand while he braced himself against the rock face with his other. Finally, they reached another inlet, larger than the first, with a wide, grassy embankment.

Gratefully, Brenna followed him out of the water and slowly up the hill. They each donned their stolen boots, then climbed carefully to the top, watching for a sign of bluecoats, but as they crested the cliffs, there was no one waiting for them. Thank goodness.

Brenna looked back along the cliffs. Castle Stour glistened in the distance, a lone sentinel against the sea.

"Where is everyone?" she asked. "I thought real castles usually had villages nearby where the lower classes lived."

"Most of the villages are inland, away from the sea, though the coast is dotted with port towns."

Brenna frowned. "That's another thing. This is Scotland, right?"

"Aye."

"What's with the blue coats and helmets? I thought Scotsmen wore kilts."

"Kilts?"

"You know, the plaids. I thought Scotsmen wore plaid."

"'Tis a common thing in the Highlands, but few wear the plaid elsewhere. 'Tis a poor man's garb. Not quite civilized."

And it was civilized for the earl's men to be chasing them down?

They walked in silence, Brenna lost in her thoughts, the pirate's gaze glued to the sea. A movement in the water caught her eye and she turned to see a seal slide onto one of the large rocks to sun himself. The mists had burned off by now and the sun was bright against the Carolina blue sky.

The world looked so normal. So *real*. Breathing the salt air, the sun warm on her skin, she could almost forget she wasn't in her own time. She'd always imagined the past as flat. Static. Black-and-white. The way it came across in textbooks. But, of course, it wasn't. Nature had changed little, if at all. Gulls still swooped, the clouds were still white, the dirt still brown and, in some places, muddy. It was only the societies and trappings of men that would change from this time to her own. And maybe, to some extent, the men themselves.

Her gaze went to her companion, to the honest-to-God pirate walking at her side. A man capable of both violence and gentleness. A man who had risked his life to protect her.

How had a man like this wound up surrounded by the dregs of humanity? She'd love to ask, but asking questions about him would only invite his questions in return. And while Rourke seemed to accept that Hegarty had brought her here, surely he couldn't know the little man had snatched her from more than three hundred years in the future. And telling him didn't feel like a smart move. Her life depended on his sticking by her. She wasn't going to do anything that might jeopardize that.

They continued north in silence with no sign of the ship. As one hour followed the next, she could feel the pirate's frustration mount, and her own right along with it. She kept up with his long strides as best she could, but the clunky boots were rubbing blisters on top of blisters.

As gulls played in the midday sun, the pain finally became more than she could stand. Brenna stopped and pulled off the torturous footwear, staring at the oozing red welts on the top of each foot. She desperately needed a pair of socks and a box of Band-Aids. The wild grass was coarse beneath her bare feet, but better than the boots. At least for now. She grabbed the boots and ran to catch up to the pirate.

She hadn't been barefoot long when Rourke tensed and motioned her toward the cliffs. "Riders."

Brenna turned to see a tiny cloud of dust on the horizon behind them. Together, they ran for the cliff side, edging their way far enough down the rocky slope that they wouldn't be seen.

As the vibration of galloping horses' hooves drew closer, Rourke gripped her shoulder. They huddled in tense silence as the horses pounded past, swirling dust into the air. She longed to take a peek, but the pirate's firm hand held her still, his touch at once protective and restraining.

As the pounding receded, he released her and took a look. Brenna eased up beside him to peer over the ledge at the retreating backs of a band of mounted bluecoats heading north, away from Stour. Nearly two dozen of them, best she could tell.

When the riders were well past, Rourke helped her back onto the level ground and they continued in silence. Several hours later, they rounded a sharp bend in the coast to come upon a harbor encircled by a small town.

"Dunhaven," the pirate murmured, then came to a hard stop, his body going rigid. "*Bloody hell.*"

Brenna followed his gaze to the three ships sitting at anchor in the harbor. One looked disturbingly familiar.

"That's not your ship, is it?" It better not be, she thought. Because instead of ragged-clothed pirates, blue-coated soldiers scurried across the decks like ants.

"Aye." The word was little more than a sharp exhale. "It's the *Lady Marie*."

Brenna grimaced with dismay. Where was Hegarty? "I'm guessing that's not a welcoming committee."

"Nay, 'tis not," he replied stonily. "The bloody Earl of Slains has seized my ship."

FIVE

A dog barked in the distance, a discordant sound against the rhythmic lapping of the sea at the harbor's edge. A woman's laughter tinkled on the evening breeze, floating from an open window high above, in sharp counterpoint to a rough argument escaping from another window, closer by. With the sun setting on this long, long day, the people of Dunhaven were retiring to the comfort and welcome of their homes.

Would that he had such a home to go back to.

Rourke silently ground his teeth as he stood in the shadowed alley watching the last of the fishermen trudge toward supper and bed. He had come so close. So *close*. The Goodhope Plantation was all but his. Or it *had* been. It might be still, if his gold had not been confiscated along with his ship.

Anger blazed through him anew. His ship. His life. Stolen. Thanks to a green-eyed sea witch.

The rich smell of roast duck slipped through the town's

less savory scents, making his stomach rumble, reminding him he'd eaten naught since last eve's supper.

He glanced at the witch resting at his feet, her arms wrapped tight around her updrawn legs, her cheek against her knees. He felt a stab of grim satisfaction at the certainty that she, too, was miserable with hunger. It was her fault. All of it.

As she dozed, he'd watched, fists clenched at his sides, as the earl's soldiers stripped the *Lady Marie* of the last of her cargo, the last of her supplies, right down to her sails. His ship was stolen. He had no means with which to take her back. His crew was lost to the winds for all he knew.

He could buy other clothes, other weapons. He could sail another man's ship, captain another man's crew. But without his gold, the Goodhope Plantation was lost. His last hope for the future gone.

All he could do was pray they'd not found his life's savings hidden beneath the floor of his cabin. And when the harbor was asleep for the night, he would find out.

The woman murmured in her sleep, drawing his attention. Bitterness simmered deep in his gut. He'd known from the start she would be his undoing. He had sensed the danger she posed to his peace of mind the moment he'd seen her. But even he could not have guessed the havoc she would wreak in a mere two days. Worse, he knew with instinct borne of bitter experience, it was just the beginning unless he disentangled himself from her with utmost haste.

The need to escape vibrated through his very bones, a need bordering on desperation. His chest felt tight, as if he'd become tangled in the riggings and the ropes had cut off his air. Only far from this land would the tight band of pressure across his chest be released. Only then would he be free again.

Voices continued to carry on the night air from windows open to the cooling breeze, but the docks and bay were slowly becoming deserted as the earlier bustle of the harbor gave way to the night's calm. Above the night sounds, Rourke heard the achingly familiar creak and clank of his pillaged lady's bare riggings echoing across the moonlit water.

The *Lady Marie*. His home for so many years.

Desolation and frustration washed over him in equal measure. How could he leave her? Yet he must. She was his no more. And he could not stay.

On the morrow he must find Hegarty. The annoying dwarf would not have gone far, not with the lass's well-being uncertain. Nay, he was near, of that Rourke was certain. And Rourke was all too ready to shove Brenna back into the little blighter's keeping.

Once rid of her, he would sail on the first vessel leaving the harbor even if he had to earn his keep as a deck-hand.

Beside him, the lass stirred and raised her head to look up at him sleepily. Even in the faint moonlight he could see the relief etched clearly on her bruised face. Without a sound, she lowered her head back to her knees.

His jaw clenched against the quiet warmth that tried to worm its way into his chest. She'd been seeking him, reassuring herself of his presence.

The woman called forth too many conflicting emotions within him. Frustration and anger at the fates for entangling him with her in the first place. But protectiveness, too.

And admiration. Indeed, she'd thought herself in danger upon his vessel and promptly escaped. But she'd not been where she thought she was.

Chill bumps rose on his forearms.

And where did she think she was? From where on Earth had Hegarty pulled her? Part of him longed to ask her, longed to know. A very small part.

She was not his concern. The woman was trouble in ways too numerous to count.

The breeze picked up. A thick swath of clouds obscured the moon, casting the water into darkness.

Now was the time.

He shook the lass's shoulder, waking her. "I have an errand to tend to. Wait here."

He felt her tense and watched as she awkwardly rose to her feet to stand beside him. "What kind of errand?"

"I'm going to retrieve . . . something . . . from my ship."

"Don't leave me." She flinched, as if the words slipped out before she could stop them. "I'll go with you."

She was like a new sailor without sea legs, unsteady and unsure in this world of his. She clung to him as if she feared she might drown without his strength supporting her. He remembered the way she'd drawn off the soldiers rather than run as he'd bade her. Blood pooled in his groin as the memory of those small, perfect breasts flashed in his mind's eye.

She was without shame and, he'd thought, without fear.

He realized now she'd been terrified. So terrified of being alone she'd risked her life and virtue to save him when she thought him in peril. He was her anchor.

For now.

He took her arm and hustled her to where a small fishing boat lay upended upon the shore. Rolling it over, he pushed it into the water, then helped her in.

"We're rowing out to your ship?"

"Aye." He shoved off, then climbed in and grabbed the oars. His careful strokes made nary a splash as they neared the *Lady Marie*.

"Since you're here, ye can aid me. I need another distraction, if ye be willing, lass."

"What kind of distraction?" she asked warily.

He wished he could see her face. "Once I've boarded,

dive in and swim to the port side of the ship, then begin to sing. They'll think ye a mermaid."

Her laugh was low and without humor. "You've got to be kidding."

She may not have sea legs, but she was still a wildcat. "You needn't sing. Screaming will work as well."

"Pirate, there's no way I'm going back into that freezing water. It took me most of the day to warm up from my morning swim. No way."

The touch of disdain in her voice annoyed him. "Ye owe me a debt, Wildcat. If not for you, I'd still be captain of my ship."

"If not for me, you'd have been on that ship when they took it. You'd probably be in jail right now."

Perhaps. But unless he found one of his crew, he might never know what happened. He tried another tack with the lass. "There's coin on my ship. Coin that will buy us a hot meal and a warm room for the night."

"Sounds lovely, but I'm not going swimming. How many men do you think are on board?"

Stubborn wench. "Four that I've seen. One on deck, the others apt to be playing cards in my cabin."

"Okay, so what if you knock out the one on deck? I can call to the others and you can knock them out when they come up."

"Three to one, lass. They'll be armed. The only way I'll get past them is to kill them."

"Oh."

"Dinna mistake me," he continued. "I am willing enough to kill. I have no love for Slains's soldiers. But the sounds of a fight will carry over the open water. I had thought ye might offer a distraction at a safe distance. But if you cannot abide another swim, I'll have no choice. Wait for me in the boat. If one of the guards escapes my knife, untie the rope and shove off."

She exhaled loudly, part sigh, part growl. "Oh, all

right. I'll be your distraction, but I'm not getting into the water until the last minute. You are *so* going to owe me a hot meal tonight. And some dry clothes. And a warm fire."

Rourke smiled to himself.

As he reached the ship and tied the small boat, Brenna took off her boots and the shirt she'd borrowed from him and stashed them in the prow, reminding him of the last time she lifted her shirt.

He swore silently at the surge of heat to his loins and pulled himself up the rope hanging from the rail. He heard the sound of distant footsteps and knew the guard to be atop the poop deck. Moving silently to the base of the stairs, he positioned himself for attack. Pressed into the shadows, his pulse pounding a hard, steady beat, he waited, listening. Finally, he heard the guard return and descend to the main deck. Rourke slid behind him and knocked him out with the hilt of his knife, then lowered him silently.

"Did you kill him?"

With a start, he swung around. "I thought ye'd agreed to swim."

"I don't have to be in the water the whole time." She motioned toward the man at their feet. "Is he dead?"

"Nay. He sleeps. The others are in my cabin."

Brenna nodded. "I'll start my mermaid's song from up here. How will I know when you're through?"

He marveled at her grit. He'd coerced her into another frigid swim—one he'd not care to join her in—yet she acted as if the prospect disturbed her not at all. She was either a fool or possessed of more courage than he cared to admit.

He touched her arm, watching her in the lantern's light. "When I have retrieved what I came for, I'll return to the boat and make a seagull's call. Swim toward me and I'll pick ye up."

A moment went by before she replied. "If you hear me yell that I'm drowning, don't come."

He felt a smile pull at his lips. "Nay. I'll not come if you're drowning."

She laughed, the sound low and delightful. "I'm serious."

"Aye, and I know it. Now go."

While Rourke pressed himself into the darkest shadows, she sprinted for the port side and climbed upon the flat rail. But instead of diving as he'd expected, she began to sing in a clear, strong voice, moving her hands to the words.

"I'm a little teapot, short and stout. Here is my handle, here is my spout. When I get all steamed up—"

Rourke tensed at the sudden pounding of booted feet. He heard one man burst out of his cabin and clamber onto the deck.

"Get down from there!"

"I will shout. Just tip me over and pour me out!"

"Get down from there, I say!"

Rourke noted the guard kept his distance, as if not quite sure what kind of creature had landed on the ship.

More booted feet on the stairs. Two pairs. The second and third guards. "What's going on?"

Still the wildcat sang, her clear, pleasant voice ringing over the harbor. "The eensy-weensy spider climbed up the waterspout."

The moon slid from beneath the clouds, fully illuminating the nymph upon the rail. All three men advanced on her slowly.

"How did you get aboard, missy?"

Brenna acknowledged them for the first time. "The Earl of Slains sent me to entertain you."

"Did he, now?"

Rourke clenched his fist at the carnal delight in the man's voice.

"Why do ye not come down and entertain us in the cabin, eh?"

Rourke's hand went to the knife at his waist. What game was she playing?

Suddenly, she let out a scream and fell backward. Or more accurately, threw herself backward, though Rourke was certain only he realized it. Even before she hit the water, all three were running for the rail.

Rourke slammed his knife into his scabbard and slipped down the stairs into his cabin as he heard her calling from the water.

"I can't swim! Help me!"

He was glad she'd warned him. Even knowing she pretended, he had to steel himself against her piteous plea.

He looked around his cabin, glowing in the light of two lanterns. His sea chest was gone, as he'd feared it would be. As were the ship's logs and journals he'd kept in his desk. Everything he'd owned had been removed. Even the small birds he'd spent painstaking hours carving by hand.

Pulling his knife, he dove for the plank under the bunk, beneath which he'd stashed his gold. But the board was already loose.

His heart sank to the pit of his stomach as he reached into the space beneath.

Empty. Whoever had found it knew it was there, for no other board was loose. Only one man knew about his hiding place.

Hegarty.

He heard a heavy splash hit the water.

Shouted voices carried from the deck. "She can swim. Stop her!"

Rourke shoved his knife back into his belt and hurried from the cabin, sticking to the shadows. As he reached the deck, he saw only two men silhouetted against the ship's rail now. One had apparently decided to capture the mermaid.

Rourke silently crossed to where they'd left the boat and swung himself over the side. But as he slid down the rope, no rough-hewn planks met his feet. Only cold water.

A quick scan revealed no sign of the rowboat.

"*God's blood.*"

He was going to kill her. First he had to find her. With a silent curse, he let go of the rope and dropped into the freezing water, gun and all. The cold knocked the wind out of him, but he forced his arms to stroke, moving silently away from the ship.

"Rourke!"

He could hear the paddles coming nearer.

"Wheesht!" He swallowed a mouthful of salty water. As he swam toward her voice, she materialized out of the darkness. The hard wood of an oar brushed his hand and he grabbed it. Brenna pulled him to the boat, then helped him inside. He took the oars from her, icy water dripping from his nose and fingertips. "I'm going to strangle you."

"Oh, that makes me so glad I rescued you." Her voice was tight with cold and sarcasm.

He started rowing, sending the blood flowing through his frozen limbs. "Why did ye leave?"

"My leg cramped. I couldn't swim, and he was going to catch me. The rate he was going, he'd have drowned us both."

"Did it occur to you to board the rowboat, then *await* me?"

"Yeah. And it occurred to me I'd have soldiers in it with me long before you got back."

The crack of gunfire rent the air. A pair of shots exploded in the water on either side of them.

Brenna gasped and ducked. She grabbed his arm. "Get down! They'll kill you."

"They each had a single gun. By the time they reload, we'll be well out of range."

"I didn't realize it took that long to reload one of those things."

"Aye. Takes even longer to *dry one out*."

He rowed the rest of the way in silence, soaked for the second time today, thanks to the woman at his side. When they reached the shore, he pulled her out, then yanked the boat to shore and left it where he'd found it.

"Did you get your gold?" Brenna asked as they started for the alleyway. Her teeth were beginning to chatter.

He clenched his jaw. "Nay. 'Twould have drowned me if I had . . . or sunk to the bottom of the sea since there was no boat awaiting me to catch the weight of it."

"Oh." The word was small and tight. "Whoops."

Anger fueled his steps. "I've no coin, no food. No weapons except my knife and a gun that will likely never fire again. I have no ship. No crew. No cursed future. The day's been a disaster, thanks to you. The whole of my life's been a disaster, thanks to you."

He stalked into the darkened alley, his empty stomach growling his frustration. Hegarty had best have his gold. And where was the blighter?

When he stopped, the lass leaned against the wall, then sank into a huddle at his feet.

"Rourke?" The word was little more than a whisper

He glared down at her. "Aye?"

"I'm . . . r–really cold. Is there anyplace we can go to warm up?"

"Without coin? Looking like a pair of drowned kittens? Who would take us in? Nay, we'll pass the night here. 'Tis summer." But the breeze had kicked up, and he was beginning to feel chilled himself, though not unduly so. He was often wet aboard ship and was quite used to it.

He crossed the narrow alley and sat, the anger in his belly too raw to settle for her nearness. But even from this small distance he could hear her teeth clattering like shutters in a gale. For the span of a heartbeat he rejoiced in her suffering, for she'd brought all this upon herself by diving from his ship in the first place. But his sense of fairness snatched the pleasure away.

The lass was ill-suited to hardship. He'd watched her tender feet bloom with welts and blisters as the day wore on, watched as she'd alternately hobbled barefoot and then booted.

Yet she'd never complained despite the bruising pace he'd forced on her. Even without food, she'd never complained.

She was not what he'd anticipated. He'd expected a pampered lady from a golden land, a lady who would expect him to do her bidding, to be waited on, mayhap even carried. Instead, she'd turned out to be a hoyden. A wildcat with a warrior's toughness despite her tender feet, and a deep flowing river of inner strength. A woman who intrigued him far more than he wished.

With his anger abated, he moved to where she sat huddled and shaking. He lowered himself beside her and pulled her against him to share what warmth he had. She was more than shaking, he realized. The tremors racked her body with alarming force. He grabbed her icy hand, then felt her face, the back of her neck. As cold as her hand.

His heart gave a sick thud.

"Wait here," he whispered, as if she were in any condition to wander off. He found Dunhaven's stables, broke the lock off one of the doors, and slipped inside. Feeling his way through the dark, he found what he'd been hoping for—an empty stall halffilled with soft hay.

Returning to the alley, he scooped her into his arms. She would not die this night. He'd not allow it.

He carried her to the stall and laid her on the hay, then searched through the dark until he found a horse blanket.

"I know ye're cold, Wildcat, but I must remove these wet garments or you'll not get warm. I found a blanket."

She made a sound that seemed to be acceptance, though she was shaking so hard he could not tell. He'd never felt a body so cold. He peeled off the shirt of his she wore again and reached for her strange shirt with the words on the front.

"How do I remove this?"

She moved, but could barely help him. "P–pull it over my head. Careful. I . . . I don't want it to rip."

"There isna room for your head, lass."

"It stretches."

With a frown, Rourke did as she directed. He grabbed the hem of the shirt and gently pulled it upward. Amazingly, it slipped off with little effort.

He eased off her boots. "Now yer breeks." He grasped her slender waist, feeling for a button or tie, but found neither. "Will these be stretching, too?" The garments fascinated him, but now was not the time to marvel at them.

"Uh-huh," she murmured. "H–hurry. I'm so c–cold."

He slipped his finger into the waistband of her breeks and pulled. Sure enough, they yielded. Amazing. He pulled them down over her hips, encountering a wee scrap of silk with his knuckles. Silk covering her most precious gifts.

The thought tantalized him as he pulled the breeks off her, and then retraced his path, running his hands up smooth, frozen legs to the silken scrap. He gently pulled it over her hips, leaving her bare and damp and vulnerable.

His eyes longed for a glimpse of the womanly curves his fingers had skimmed, wishing for even a single candle's light to break the dark. Instead, he pulled the horse blanket snug around her. "Lie ye down. I'll pile the hay about you to help hold in a little of your heat."

"I . . . have . . . n-no . . . heat."

He stared into the darkness toward her voice. He had no broth to warm her from the inside, no fire for the outside.

All he had was himself. *Bloody hell.* But he had to get her warm. With grim determination, he yanked off his sodden clothes, opened the blanket, and lay down beside her. He gathered her frozen body into his arms and wrapped the musty wool around them both.

Her quakes tore through him as he rubbed her cold skin, seeking to build some warmth within her, regretting his insistence she swim this eve. He prayed her warrior's strength would see her through this night, for he feared, if he didn't get her warmed, she'd soon be fighting for her life. She was too soft for such mischief.

His hands rubbed her back, her buttocks.

She was too soft. His hand ran down one long leg. Too . . . smooth.

His breath caught as his mind caught up with what his body had already realized. He held a naked woman in his arms, her small distended nipples pressing against his chest. A shaft of hot desire surged between his legs.

Ah, Christ.

He was no saint. He was all for having a lass in his bed, but not *this* lass. *Never* this lass.

His body shuddered with a need that would likely tear him asunder before daybreak. He must hold her . . . simply hold her . . . until she warmed.

Even if it took every bit of strength he possessed.

Six

The night was cool, the stable dark as a blackguard's soul and rich with the smells of horse and hay. Smells Rourke had had little contact with since he'd left Scotland as a lad. Smells that brought back a wealth of memories he wished to forget.

The lass shifted against him, burrowing closer as if she would crawl inside him. Heaven knew, his body strained to do the same to her. The feel of her soft flesh pressed against him was nearly beyond bearing.

She shivered violently and he wrapped his bare leg around her frozen hips, blanketing her in every way he could. He knew she could feel the hardness of his arousal, but was either too dazed to notice, or too cold to care. She merely squeezed closer to him, her soft breasts tight against his chest.

Breathe.

It was torture to be but inches from the source of her

womanhood and not slake his desire, but he'd never taken advantage of a woman and he'd not start now. Never would he tie himself to her in that way—in any way. Desperately, he sought to think of something other than the soft flesh pressed against him.

Hegarty. Now there was a thought to cool his ardor. Where was the little bugger tonight? Holed up in a warm room with a fire and hot stew? Or under lock in the village gaol? On the morrow he would find him and hand Brenna Cameron over to him once and for all.

The woman moved her head, her hair brushing against his chin. Slowly, after what felt like an eternity, he felt her shivers begin to subside, felt her warming beneath his hands. She'd be all right now. He could slip away from her, leave her wrapped in the horse blanket until morn.

She sighed and rubbed her cheek against his chest.

He should move away.

But she felt too good. Even with his need unabated, the feel of her in his arms was heaven.

She made a faint snuffling sound and he knew she slept.

When was the last time he'd held a woman as she slept? Never. He'd never wanted such closeness. He didn't want it now.

But despite the command from his brain, his arms refused to release her. So he lay, uncomfortable with need, but warm. And surprisingly content.

He yawned deeply. Exhaustion was beginning to take its toll on him despite his arousal. He might not sleep, but he would at least rest his eyes.

But sleep he did.

He half woke to the feel of soft lips against his bare shoulder. His wildcat. Kissing, nuzzling, her warm, damp tongue darting out to mark him. He half remembered where he was. Half didn't care. All that mattered was that he was on fire for the woman in his arms. And by the sounds coming from her throat as she ran her small hand through the hair on his chest, she returned his ardor.

That same hand slid over his shoulder and into his hair as she tipped her face to his, seeking his kiss. He needed to taste her. He needed to feel her hard nipple in the palm of his hand. As his mouth covered hers, she opened to him and their tongues met and slid together, igniting a need inside him that raged.

He was ablaze, unable to get enough. His hand found her breast, cupping and kneading the gentle swell that had obsessed him, while his lips moved from her mouth to taste her cheek and jaw. She tasted salty and womanly, like a sea nymph should.

His lips moved to her neck and she shivered, but not with cold this time. The moan that escaped her throat was pure desire. Raw, feminine desire that sent his hunger for her spiraling out of control.

She wrapped one bare leg around his hips, opening herself to him. He was helpless to deny her, knowing he'd die if he didn't bury himself inside her soon.

He pushed her gently onto her back, sliding his finger into her woman's sheath to test her readiness for him. She was open and wet. Ready. *Wanting*. Shaking with desire, Rourke moved over her as she opened her silken thighs for him. He guided himself to her slick opening, then slid inside her, feeling a rightness he could barely fathom, let alone understand. She fit him like a glove. Filled him with a glimpse of peace. Of brilliant perfection.

She thrust her hips hard against him, letting him know without words that his gentleness was neither needed nor particularly welcome. With a groan of pure pleasure, he pulled back and buried himself deeply within her again. Never had anything felt so right, so good.

She bucked against him, driving him with her need.

"Harder," she begged, her voice rough with disuse. The sound of her voice seemed to startle her.

He thrust into her as she demanded, harder and harder, his body's excitement rising with every thrust.

It was several moments before he realized the wanton in his arms had turned to stone.

The confusion had barely registered in his passion-clouded brain when she turned wild beneath him.

"Get off me!" Her voice echoed in the small stable.

One of the horses whinnied in alarm.

"Wheesht, lass!" Rourke slammed his hand over her mouth even as his body continued to drive into her, desperate for completion.

She bit him as she bucked. His every instinct cried for release, but she pushed and pummeled until her desperation forced its way through the madness. With herculean effort, he pulled out of her and rolled, shaking, onto his back. He tore deep, ragged breaths into his lungs as unabated need roared like a fire in his loins.

Covering his face with his hands, he willed the throbbing pain of his arousal to abate, willed some semblance of sanity to return as he listened to her scramble away, out of his reach.

What just happened? She'd been open and ready for him. Crazy for him. *Harder.*

He'd not dreamed the word.

But perhaps she had. She'd kissed him, initiated the joining in her sleep. And he knew precisely when she'd woken. At the sound of her own voice. *Harder.*

The soft sound of her crying carried from the far edge of the stall.

Bloody hell.

"I didna take your maidenhead, Wildcat. I didna mean for that to happen, but 'twas not my doing alone. I awoke to the feel of your tongue upon my shoulder."

"Don't touch me." Her voice was low, shattered. "I don't want you to touch me."

He stared into the night as something withered in his

chest. All he wanted to do was get away from here. Away from Scotland. Away from this woman.

As he ran a shaking hand through his damp hair, the full import of what he'd almost done hit him. He'd nearly spilled his seed inside her. What kind of madness . . . ? He'd been half asleep. Unthinking.

If not for her awakening, he could have gotten her with child, binding himself to her for all eternity. The thought made him go cold. He had to find Hegarty, for he wanted nothing more to do with her. *Nothing.*

Except to bury himself deep inside her and finish what they'd started. *God*, he wanted to do that. Instead, he sat up and pulled his wet breeks up his now dry legs. The discomfort was almost enough to temper his raging need. Almost.

He sat on the bare stable floor as far from her as he could, and leaned his head against the wall, a sense of doom enveloping him like a fine, malevolent mist.

Brenna woke with a start.

Rourke was standing over her looking grim as he dropped her clothes onto her blanket-wrapped body. "Get dressed. 'Tis morning. We must leave before someone finds us." He turned his back to her and left the stall.

His voice was cold this morning, unlike last night when they'd . . .

Squeezing her eyes closed, she buried her face in her hands as memory and humiliation washed over her. *Last night.* She'd dreamed she was having the most incredible sex of her life, then woke to discover it was no dream. She'd panicked. The feel of him on top of her, his weight pressing her into the hay, had triggered her terror and she'd lost it.

How was she ever going to face him again?

Her whole body hot with humiliation, she sat and

pulled the coarse blanket tight around her. She'd been wild with need for him. Out of control until . . .

Brenna shuddered. The terror lingered like a bad aftertaste, making her feel shaky and disjointed even as the unreleased tension still throbbed between her legs.

God, she needed to get out of here. She wanted to go home, to her own world, her own time, where she didn't have soldiers in blue coats ready to plunge knives in her heart and where she wasn't tempted to make disastrous love to handsome pirates. But to get home she had to find Hegarty.

With unsteady hands, she eased out of the blanket's warmth and reached for her T-shirt, then scrambled into the rest of her damp clothing. Running her fingers through her hair, she grimaced at the sticky, salty feel. The first thing she was going to do when she got back to civilization was take a shower. Her stomach growled. Or maybe the shower would come second. First she'd find food.

She pushed open the stall's low door to find Rourke waiting for her, his hard good looks diminished not at all by the wrinkled clothes and his weather-beaten appearance. If anything, he looked more appealing. Definitely less civilized.

Their gazes met only for a second, but the look in his eyes shot straight to her core. Accusation, certainly, but heat, too, as if he were remembering what it had felt like to be inside her. Embarrassment flooded her cheeks. Damp heat gathered low in her belly as she remembered the exciting fullness of him as he'd driven into her.

He turned and started off without a word, expecting her to follow. Or not.

Brenna pressed her fingers to her eyes and tried to banish her X-rated thoughts. Oh man, she did *not* want him. She didn't.

They walked in silence through the small town, tension and unresolved passion thick between them. The sun was up, though not high in the sky. The mist lay heavy on the water, its ghostly fingers sliding through the alleys and streets. Brenna shivered from the damp clothes and prayed for an unseasonably warm day.

She glanced around her as they walked beneath the overhanging upper stories of the buildings lining the street. Dunhaven was cute, though it would have been more pleasant without the ripe smell of decaying fish. The buildings ringed the small harbor, attached like some kind of medieval strip mall. The line was broken only by alleys in a couple of places. She could see other buildings, or maybe homes, on the hillside rising beyond.

Her stomach rumbled and she pressed her hand to it. Humiliated, hungry, and sexually frustrated, with painfully blistered feet. Great way to start the day. She prayed Rourke was searching for food, but wasn't sure how they were going to eat when they didn't have any money. Then again, he *was* a pirate.

"How are we going to find Hegarty?"

Rourke threw her a disgusted look and kept walking. He didn't have to say the words for her to hear them loud and clear. It was her fault they'd lost Hegarty in the first place.

The aroma of food suddenly broke through the dead fish smell as they approached a door. Above swung a classic tavern sign: The Ram and Lamb. Rourke pushed the door open and went inside.

Brenna followed him through the low-ceilinged, smoky room. The smoke emanated from the hearth rather than the patrons, of which there were few. A pair of fishermen in the center of the room laughed and chatted with the waitress in their thick Scottish brogues. In the back corner sat a lone, familiar-looking man. One of Rourke's pirates, though she'd had no dealings with this one.

Thank God.

He waved toward them, then nervously looked away.

"How did you know he was going to be here?" Brenna asked.

"I didn't." Rourke pulled out a chair and sat across from the man. "Mr. Baker."

Brenna slipped into one of the empty chairs, her mouth watering as she took in the bounty laid out in front of the silent pirate. The plate in front of Baker was laden with eggs and ham, a bowl of what looked like watery oatmeal, and a small loaf of bread. Rourke grabbed the plate of eggs and shoved it in front of her, then stole the bread for himself.

"Eat." He lowered his voice to a bare whisper. "What happened to my ship, Mr. Baker?"

Brenna dug into the food without protest. He hadn't forgotten her after all. No wonder the timid pirate had looked at him nervously. He must have sensed the imminent demise of his breakfast.

"When you dove . . . well"—he colored and looked away—"the lads . . . they did not think me capable of leading the ship, sir. They let Mr. Cutter out of the hold and ordered me to stand down or they'd throw me off the ship." His pink cheeks turned red. "I cannot swim."

Rourke said nothing, just nodded and kept eating.

"Mr. Cutter directed us into port here," the man continued. "Then he left the ship to have a word with a pair of soldiers on the docks. Several hours later, Slains's soldiers were swarming the decks."

Brenna grabbed the man's mug and took a long sip of ale. Funny how manners disappeared when one was starved.

"And my crew?"

"They let us go. The lads are in town awaiting another ship to sign aboard."

"Hegarty?"

Mr. Baker set a small leather pouch in front of Rourke that rattled with coins when it hit the table. A letter quickly joined the purse.

Brenna glanced at the latter with dismay. She needed to find Hegarty. A letter was not a good sign.

"He made me vow to wait for you here or he'd turn me into a toad. He said to give you these."

"Where's the rest of it?" Rourke growled, his eyes suddenly narrowed, his expression fierce.

The poor man paled and visibly shrank back in his seat. "'Twas all he gave me, your—Captain. I vow it." He leaned over and picked up something from the floor. "I brought your boots and weapons. You left them on the deck when you dove into the water."

Rourke traded the borrowed boots for his own, then shoved his own gun into his belt beside the waterlogged one he'd taken from the bluecoat when they first got to shore. As a serving maid set mugs of ale in front of them, Rourke grabbed his sailor's oatmeal and began shoveling it into his mouth. When he was through, he picked up the letter and turned it over.

"The seal is broken."

"'Twasn't me, Captain."

Rourke frowned as he pulled out the letter and read it. The frown turned into a scowl. "I'm going to kill him."

"Hegarty?" Brenna asked, drawing his cold gaze.

"Aye. He's left. We are to meet him"—he visibly clenched his jaw—"several days' ride from here."

Brenna made a croak of dismay. *Days?* She couldn't possibly stay here for *days*.

"Captain?" Mr. Baker nodded pointedly at her. "The Earl of Slains's soldiers were asking about your lady. They're turning the town inside out looking for her."

Brenna's mug stilled halfway to her mouth. "Why would they be looking for *me*?" Unless they'd somehow figured out she and Rourke were the ones who'd killed the bluecoats.

Rourke drained his mug in a single gulp, then rose and grabbed her wrist. "Come. We must be away."

Brenna glanced longingly at the few remaining bites of ham. "Do we have to—?"

They'd barely taken two steps when the door burst open behind them.

"'Tis she!" Cutter shouted, two bluecoats close behind him. "Brenna Cameron!"

Brenna's jaw went slack as Rourke drew his sword, an icy numbness spreading through her. *Brenna Cameron?* How in the world did he know her name? She'd told no one. *No one.*

Mr. Baker drew his own sword and moved between them and Cutter. "Run, Captain. I'll hold them off."

Rourke hesitated only a second before pulling her through the kitchen and out the back door into the fog-shrouded sunshine.

"Run, Wildcat."

Brenna tore through the narrow alley in her clunky boots, dodging a woman shaking out bed linens. A dog barked. Children shrieked and scattered.

How did they know who she was? This had to be a joke. One huge, elaborate joke. It wasn't real.

And yet it was. She'd watched men die.

Rourke drew up beside her and grabbed her arm. "This way." He drew her right, toward the stables.

"Hold!" a deep voice shouted from far behind them as they turned the corner.

Ahead, a teenager led a sturdy-looking horse out of the stables. Rourke dug into his bag of coins, then grabbed the reins from the lad and pressed a coin into the startled boy's hand.

"I'll return her when I'm through." He leaped onto the animal's back, then pulled Brenna up behind him as two soldiers rounded the corner of the stable yard. "Hang on."

Brenna locked her arms around his waist as the animal shot forward, the soldiers shouting behind.

A shot rang out. Brenna flinched and grabbed the pirate tighter around the waist.

"Now I know why you brought me," she shouted over the sound of the wind. "I'm your shield, aren't I?"

Another shot exploded into the ground several yards to their right and she swallowed a shriek.

Cutter knew her name. How did he know her name? Hegarty was the one who'd brought her here. Did they *all* know who she was? No, they couldn't. They thought they did, but they couldn't possibly.

A final shot rang out as they rounded a corner and followed the road up a shallow hill.

"Pirate!" she yelled. "If we make it out of here alive, you're going to tell me what the hell is going on."

Seven

Fate was playing him for a fool.

Rourke *knew* he should never have returned to Scotland. The moment he'd stepped foot on his native soil, he'd been ensnared like a hare in a trap. His ship and possessions seized, his gold . . . God knew where. His bosun had mutinied. And the bane of his existence had shown him heaven, then cast him straight to hell.

A pox on the woman. A pox on them all.

Rourke urged the horse faster, sending the villagers in the narrow street scattering. Another shot rang out behind them, causing Brenna to flinch and tighten her grip.

"Faster," she urged against his shoulder.

Harder. Memory sliced through him, sending the blood surging between his legs. She'd been like fire in his arms, aflame with a need that had burned them both until she'd woken and realized it was he deep inside her and not some soft-spoken swain.

He gripped the leather reins until his shorn nails dug into his palms. It was as if she could see the darkness within him and wanted no part of it—or him. And he couldn't blame her.

The sun broke through the morning mist, setting the dew-laced roofs to glistening as if thatched with a million wee daggers. He forced his thoughts away from her silken thighs and back to the problem at hand.

They would never outrun their pursuers. The earl's soldiers would be mounted and after them soon enough. The poor animal beneath him would tire quickly with two riders. He had to throw the soldiers off their trail before they hit the open moor. He urged the horse down a narrow lane. Out of sight of the guards, he searched for a likely pair to help him carry out the ruse and spotted two youths mending a wagon. He pulled up beside them and dismounted, then reached for Brenna.

As his hands gripped her slender waist, their gazes collided. Her eyes widened, memory flaring in their green depths. Not memory of the anger and revulsion she'd thrown at him as she'd struggled to free herself from his intimate embrace last eve. No, not that.

In her eyes he saw only heat, echoes of the passion he'd tasted in the moments before she'd awakened, passion that had threatened to drive him higher than he'd ever flown. Aye, she'd eventually rejected him, but at first he'd been certain she'd wanted him. Now he knew she wanted him still.

Though his pride demanded he steel himself against the pull of her, his body had a will of its own. As he swung her down, he drew her close, drinking in the feel of her soft body pressed to his as she slid to her feet, daring her to deny the attraction between them.

She turned her face, her body stiff, her cheeks reddened. Her discomfort at once pleased and shamed him. He released her, and she took a hasty step back.

"What are we doing here?" she asked, not quite meeting his gaze.

His gaze fell heavily to her chest. "Remove your shirt."

Green eyes flashed wide, then narrowed. "Excuse me?"

"The shirt of mine ye wear, not your own. I've a wee plan."

He watched the expressions flit across her face. A flash of stubborn refusal quickly conquered by reason and, finally, resignation.

She sighed and bent her head to untie the linen shirt. Her gaze flicked up, spearing him from beneath her lashes. "Tell me how Cutter knew my name."

"We've no time. When we are safely away, we'll talk."

She let out a soft snort. "The twelfth of never."

His gaze snagged on those fingers, on the soft garment and softer mounds they revealed. When she reached for the hem, he helped pull the garment from her shoulders and called to the lads. When they approached, he tossed the elder of the two a few coins. Interest lit their faces.

"I've a task for ye." He handed them the reins. "Ride north and west until you lather her. Then rest her and return her to the stables."

He tossed the shirt to the smaller of the two. "Wear this and ride behind. Now be off with ye."

The lads glanced at one another, a grin flashing between them. The smaller of the two donned the shirt, then leaped onto the animal behind his companion, who whirled the horse and took off.

Brenna made a worried sound deep in her throat. "The guards will shoot at them, thinking they're us."

"Nay. They'll realize their mistake long before they're close enough to shoot. This ruse will buy us a little time."

A slender young woman about Brenna's size, a babe on her hip, stood before one of the structures watching them curiously.

Rourke called to her. "Mistress, have ye an extra gown for my lady?"

Laughter filled the woman's eyes as she looked from him to Brenna and back. Clearly, she thought he was jesting by his use of the term *lady*.

"I'll pay ye good coin for a gown, mistress. A poor one, at that."

The woman lifted an eyebrow as she eyed Brenna. "I've a skirt. And a bodice that belonged to my sister." She motioned them to follow. "Come in, my lord, while I fetch them."

My lord. The words felt like a kick in the gut. He hated the title, yet he had led her to believe him such by calling Brenna his lady. This time he'd done it to himself. Then again, it was better she thought him a lord than a pirate. They followed her into the narrow dwelling, poorly lit and smelling of warm bread and stale urine.

As she disappeared into a second room, Brenna turned on him, her hair swinging free around her shoulders, eyes flashing. "We're hidden, now. Not in imminent danger. How did he know my name?"

He had no intention of involving himself in this. It was Hegarty's place to explain, not his.

He reached for her hair, twining a thick lock around one finger, seeking the evidence of her attraction once more. His pride demanded it.

"Tell me," she said.

"I have naught to tell." As his finger brushed her cheek, he heard the quick intake of her breath and watched her eyes darken, fanning the flames of a desire he would never quench. He should back away, stop torturing himself with her nearness. But pride demanded this. He would not be satisfied until he was convinced she, too, felt this maddening need.

With his knuckle, he traced the graceful line of her jaw, watching the pulse beat in her throat. Aye, she felt it. His gaze dropped to her mouth, and her lips parted as if he'd commanded they do so. Nay, she was not unaffected by him.

He tugged gently on her hair, closing the distance between them until their mouths were but a hand's breadth apart.

"Here," the young mother said, dousing the insanity that had stolen over him. "I've no shift to spare."

Rourke released Brenna's hair and stepped back.

"Will ye be changing, then?" the woman asked.

Brenna looked at her, then him. "I'll just put them on over my pajam . . . clothes."

The woman nodded and handed Brenna a worn black skirt that had been mended many times. Brenna pulled it on, then laced up the front of the gray bodice, hiding the yellow sun. The young mother handed Brenna a servant's cap and stepped back.

Rourke stared, nonplused, at the transformation. By all rights, the peasant's garb should have dampened her allure, yet its effect was the opposite. Eliminating the distraction of her strange dress, the clothes became a perfect foil for her vibrant coloring, the red brown of her hair and the green of her eyes. Against the poorness of the garments, her beauty shone like a rare gem.

A gem his body longed to possess.

Brenna stared at the cap as if she knew not what to do with it. He took it from her hands and put it atop her hair as she stood, still as stone, her gaze focused on his heart. His own gaze fell to her mouth.

She ducked her head as if suddenly shy, and grabbed fistfuls of the skirt. "My aunt would have loved this. She could never get me into dresses."

His fingers stumbled as they adjusted the cap. "Your aunt?"

"She raised me for a while. Until she died."

He stepped back, frowning. "When was that?"

Shadows entered her eyes. "When I was ten."

"There, now," the young mother exclaimed. "She's presentable, at least. She'll be needing a few more things, but this is all I have to spare ye."

Brenna looked at him uncertainly, with a hint of feminine vulnerability he'd not seen before. She held out the skirts still gripped in her hands and turned from side to side. "Will it do?"

Something softened inside him. She'd most likely not had an easy life. He knew what it was like to be ten and alone in the world. He'd not wish it on anyone. Aye, she might be the bane of his existence, but she needed him. For now. Until they found Hegarty. Neither the Earl of Slains, nor his men, would touch her. Which meant he had best get her away before the lads led the earl's soldiers right back to them.

The ruse seemed to have worked. At least it had worked well enough to give them a fighting chance of escape. They'd been riding across open fields so long she'd lost all feeling in her rear and in the fingers clasped tightly around Rourke's hard waist, yet still they'd seen no sign of Cutter or the bluecoats.

After getting her the clothes, Rourke had borrowed yet another horse. Unfortunately, this one had the same lousy shock absorbers as the last. She really preferred to ride *inside* her transportation, not on its back.

As she eyed the thick clouds rolling across the sky, she wondered what would happen to her little rental car. And the rest of her stuff. Would time in her world stand still until she returned, or had it moved on without her, leaving her a missing person?

The wind whipped against her face and she turned to press her cheek against Rourke's linen-clad back, dodging the breeze. The sad part was, she might be a missing person, yet there were few who would actually miss her. No family, certainly. No boyfriend. A few casual friends and a handful of staff at the restaurant where she worked and that was about it.

Her fingers laced tighter around Rourke's waist. At least she had the pirate. What would she have done if he hadn't followed her over the side of the ship? The thought made her shudder. There was no denying he wasn't an easy man, yet she felt totally safe with him. If she'd had any doubts before, last night proved it. Not many men could have found the strength to break off sex halfway through. Far fewer men *would* have. Yet he had, confirming her earlier belief that within that hard exterior beat the heart of a good man.

If only she weren't so ungodly attracted to him. She'd never met anyone who affected her like this. A simple touch of her hair, a glance from those pale eyes, and she was out of her head with wanting him.

She didn't want this attraction. Her forays into intimacy had always been a disaster, and she couldn't afford any more of those with the pirate. She'd never find Hegarty without him.

Fear pressed in on her and she clung to the pirate harder. She'd thought life was through tossing her about like a tin can in a thunderstorm. For eight years, from the time Aunt Janie died until she turned eighteen, Brenna had been shuffled from one foster home to the next. No control. Never knowing what tomorrow would bring.

When she turned eighteen, she swore she'd never live like that again. She'd make a home for herself, a life where no one was in charge but her.

Now, here she was, the tin can all over again, with no more idea how to live alone in this world than she had in her own. *So* not fair.

With a sigh, she lifted her head from the pirate's back

and caught sight of another village in the distance. He seemed to be heading straight for it.

"Are we going to stop there?"

"Aye. We need supplies and a fresh mount."

They were going through horses faster than a Hollywood starlet through fiancés. They pulled up behind a stone building on the outskirts of town where laundry hung from lines, drying in the warm breeze.

Rourke took her hand, and she slid awkwardly to the ground, then groaned when her legs threatened to buckle beneath her. She hobbled back far enough for him to dismount, feeling the sticky sea grime chafe her skin with every move. What she wouldn't give for a long soak in a warm tub. Soap. Shampoo. Heaven.

"Wait here, Wildcat. I'll no' be long."

She caught her breath. "I'm coming with you."

He scanned every building, every bush, his expression grim. "I want ye to hide amongst the laundry until I return."

"No way, Rourke." A flush of dread turned her hands damp. "I want to go with you."

He turned his full attention on her, gripping her shoulders and meeting her gaze. "I'll be back for ye forthwith. I'll not have you marked."

She tilted her head. "Marked?"

"Remembered."

Her gaze slid to his mouth, watching his lips form the word. She could almost recall the feel of his lips against her neck. Her pulse leaped with a mix of desire and real fear. What if he didn't come back?

"I'm wearing a dress. I'll fit in perfectly." She hated the panicked edge to her voice, but was helpless to control it.

His gaze softened and warmed as it traveled slowly to her feet and back up again. "Even in servant's rags, ye are bonnie enough to make a man lose all reason."

The heat in his eyes shimmered through her, making her catch her breath. He pulled her toward him and slowly lowered his head, giving her every opportunity to pull away. But she didn't. She couldn't. She longed for the taste of him.

His mouth covered hers, opening as his tongue swept inside. His hands slid over her back with a pressure that spoke of unbearable need, turning her limbs weak, sending heat arcing to her womb. She grabbed hold of his shirt, feeling as if she'd be swept away if she let go.

He pulled back, his eyes gleaming silver, his damp mouth turned up in a sliver of a smile—pure male satisfaction.

The look nearly sent her up in flames.

Before she could recover, he swung back into the saddle. "I willna be long."

As the horse trotted off, she swore softly, feeling like the victim of a hit-and-run. Every time she thought she was gaining even an ounce of balance, he knocked her feet out from under her again. And this time it had been intentional, straight out of Pirate Deportment 101: Charm the lass, then desert her before she comes to her senses.

Brenna wiped her mouth with the back of her hand, then ducked into the waving laundry. That might be *his* game, but she wasn't playing. Instead, she followed him, staying behind the laundry as far as she could. She figured she had two choices: either wait where he'd told her to, which she'd already decided against, or keep him in sight. Anything else and she might lose him for good.

She hated this feeling of utter dependence.

When the laundry line came to an end, she kept to the shadows, head down so as not to attract undo attention, and followed him into town. As he rode into what appeared to be a stable, she ducked into a narrow alley across the street to wait for him. The sun had broken through the clouds again, but the alley was shaded and cool even if it smelled like an outhouse.

From the relative safety of the shadows, she watched the people pass by. A woman in an outfit similar to the one Brenna wore, her feet bare, walked side by side with a little girl dressed much as her mother. Around the two of them scampered a boy of maybe three or four, circling them, squeezing between them, then darting off to explore a weed growing between the cobbles at the side of the road.

"Duncan!" The woman's scolding was tinged with laughter. "Get back here, ye wee scamp."

The little boy grinned and ran back, his chubby hand clinging to a small wildflower. He thrust it at his mother and was gifted with a smile filled with such love it made Brenna's heart ache.

She'd been loved like that once. She knew she had. Sometimes she thought she remembered a woman singing her to sleep at night. A woman who wasn't Aunt Janie. Could she have been her mother? If only she could remember. If only she could get back to her time to find out.

The pirate emerged from the stable with a different horse, shielding his eyes as he looked around. With a smooth, practiced move, he mounted and turned the horse down the cobbled street, away from her.

Brenna remained where she was until he turned the corner, afraid he'd look back and spot her, then hurried after him. She heard the loud clank of a hammer striking metal as she neared the corner. A flash of sparks caught her eye. The village blacksmith.

She picked up her skirts and leaped over a puddle just as a figure stepped into her path on the other side. She collided solidly with the young man.

"Whoa, lass!" He grabbed her upper arms and steadied her when she would have fallen. He was tall and lanky, his skin freckled, his eyes friendly. "Are ye hurt?"

Brenna shook her head and stepped out of his reach with an apologetic smile. "No. Sorry. I'm in a bit of a hurry." She turned and dashed the short way to the corner.

She peered around it, praying the pirate was still in sight. To her vast relief, she spotted him immediately, tying up the horse. He climbed the stairs of one of the buildings with an air of total confidence, as if he owned this town. Powerful, strong, arrogant as hell. Why did she find that so darned sexy?

As she watched, he entered a door with a sign swinging over it: Alex. McDonald, Merchant.

"Are ye lost?"

Brenna jumped and swung around.

The young man she'd run into grinned apologetically. "Och, I didna mean to scare ye."

Brenna returned his smile ruefully. "Sorry. I'm a little jumpy. And no, I'm not lost. I'm waiting for my . . . brother. He had to meet someone and told me to wait by the creek . . . the burn."

"Och, aye. And ye fancied ye'd see what he was up to, eh?"

Brenna raised a rueful brow. "Something like that."

"Yer not from around here. Yer not Scottish."

"You know, the funny thing is, I am. Or at least I used to be. I've been living . . . away." Way away. Other side of the world and about three centuries to the right.

"If ye be needin' anythin', I work at the smithy's, there." He motioned to the building behind her where all the clanking and hammering was coming from. "Come find me, eh? I'm Rabbie."

Brenna smiled warmly, then froze as she heard a low rumble—a rumble she was starting to recognize. Horses. A moment later, she saw them. Bluecoats entering town, riding a wave of dust.

Her mouth went dry, her heart pounding in her chest. *Rourke.* She had to get to him, warn him. She ducked her head, wishing she had a wide-brimmed cowboy hat to hide beneath.

Rabbie made a growling sound deep in his throat and stepped in front of her, his lanky height shielding her as the riders approached.

Seconds felt like hours as the pounding hooves tore up the road, pelting her with bits of mud and pebbles. Chills danced over her skin. With every dust-filled breath she feared discovery.

But the pounding continued past her. No shots rang out. No shouts of her name.

Rabbie turned to look down at her. "They're by."

She stared at him, head whirling. "You protected me."

Rabbie's lip curled as his gaze followed the bluecoats. "Aye. The Earl of Slains sends his soldiers to one village or another near every month to fetch lasses to entertain his guests. Some little more than bairns." He held his hand out, hip-high.

Brenna blanched. "That's terrible."

"Och, aye. Beltane last, one of the villagers was killed trying to stop them from taking his wee daughters. The earl returns the ones who survive the bed sport, but they're ne'er the same."

"Someone needs to kill that man," she said heatedly, even as she shivered. These were the same men looking for her.

"Some have tried. But the earl's too powerful. Two years past, the village of Dunlochy rose against him. He burned it to the ground."

"The whole village?"

"Aye. He claimed they were harboring witches, but all kent the truth. 'Twas retribution, plain and simple."

She had to get out of here. Find Hegarty and get out of this nightmare world. But Rourke . . .

She swung around to see the bluecoats pulling up in the center of town. They dismounted and split into three groups, each drawing their swords and guns and heading toward a different building.

Her heart stuttered. They'd kill Rourke before he had a chance to defend himself.

What chance did she have without her pirate? She couldn't let him die if she could save him.

Brenna grabbed her companion's arm. "Those men are after us. I've got to distract them before they find . . . my brother. Can you help me?"

She slipped around the corner and pulled the cap off her head, then began pulling at the laces of her bodice. She turned her back to him. "Untie this skirt, will you?"

When he didn't reply, she glanced over her shoulder to find the young man's eyes had swallowed his face.

"I have clothes on underneath, Rabbie. Help me, please?"

He blinked, then nodded, and had her out of the skirt in seconds. Clearly, the guy had had some experience disrobing females. When she turned around, he stared at her Hard Rock tee and torn monkey pants with a mixture of disbelief and dismay.

Okay, maybe not the greatest clothes.

"Thanks. I'll be right back. I'll need your help again."

"Ye play with fire, lass."

"I know. If he'd just carry a cell phone . . ." She raked her fingers through her hair, digging deep for courage, and met his somber gaze. "They'll kill him if they catch him."

He pursed his lips and nodded.

Her legs felt stiff as she rounded the corner. The soldiers and Cutter had all disappeared inside the various shops and buildings. The breath caught in her throat. Was she already too late?

Then Cutter and a bluecoat strode out of one shop and started toward the next. Alex. McDonald, Merchant. Cutter had his back to her. She had only one option and scant seconds to execute it.

Forcing her legs to move, she ran into the street. "Rourke! Watch out!" She couldn't have drawn any more attention if she'd run into the street stark naked. Passersby—the few who hadn't hightailed it out of there at the first sign of the soldiers—stopped and gawked at her.

"Get her!"

Cutter. Mission engaged. Now for the hard part—surviving it.

She turned and ran, her clunky boots tearing at the blisters they'd rubbed yesterday. As she rounded the corner by the smithy's, she almost plowed into Rabbie again.

He was waiting for her. Without a word, he threw the skirt over her head, then followed with the top. While he tied the skirt, she tried to pull her front laces closed, but they were stuck.

Rabbie brushed her fingers aside and tried to make the laces cooperate, but he had no better luck. "They're tangled," he hissed.

She was starting to shake. The bright yellow of her Hard Rock tee showed clearly through the knotted laces. She needed to hide, but where?

The vibration of booted feet grew stronger. Any second Cutter would turn the corner and find her. *Dear God.*

Brenna grabbed the cap out of the dirt, twisted her hair and shoved it inside as she looked up at her companion. He seemed so much older than the men his age she'd known in her time. There was a wisdom and a solidness in his eyes that she'd always thought took years to acquire. But perhaps not so long in this place. Either way, he'd proven himself to her.

"You shielded me once," she said. "Will you do it again?"

Without waiting for his reply, she pressed herself against him, hiding her gaping bodice. "Kiss me and act like you mean it."

The young man's eyes widened, but she saw a grin

bloom in their depths as he did as she commanded. His warm mouth covered hers. Sweet, tentative. She reached up and grabbed him about the neck, moaning for good measure. Rabbie followed her lead, turning the chaste kiss real even as he kept a small measure of distance between their bodies.

This kind of ploy always worked in the movies. *Please let it work for real.*

"You there!"

Cutter. She'd know that voice anywhere. Her heart leaped, then began to pound until she thought she'd have a heart attack. *Oh God, oh God, oh God.* She kissed Rabbie harder, praying he'd take the hint and ignore the command.

Rabbie didn't seem to have heard the command at all.

"Never mind them," snapped a second voice. "They didn't see anything. You two go left. Mr. Cutter, come with me. She couldn't have gone far. Find her!"

As the sound of pounding feet retreated, Brenna opened one eye and peaked over Rabbie's shoulder, afraid one of the men had remained behind. Amazingly, they'd been left alone.

She pulled back, ending the kiss. "It worked. They're gone."

The young man rubbed his mouth with the back of his hand and stared at her with a mixture of dismay and thorough arousal.

Brenna winced. "I'm sorry. I shouldn't have used you like that. I think you just saved my life."

A grin bloomed on his face, his eyes crinkling at the corners as his capable hands untangled the strings of her bodice and put her back together. "Ye may use me any time ye wish, lass."

Brenna smiled, then froze as she heard the sound of a horse racing toward them from around the corner.

Rabbie wasted no time in pulling her back into his arms.

"Unhand her," a voice growled as the horse came to a sudden halt beside them.

Relief turned her legs to Silly Putty. Brenna pulled out of the embrace, then turned and stared at the sight before her. The pirate in a coat and long black curly wig.

She grinned, then turned and kissed the young man's cheek. "Thanks."

Rabbie eyed the cold-eyed pirate warily. "Ye'll not hurt her."

"I aim to throttle her." He extended a hand to Brenna, his eyes glittering like ice, filling her with a strange joy.

She flashed a quick grin at Rabbie. "Isn't he sweet?" But as she reached for the pirate's proffered hand, she heard shouts and the sound of horses cutting off their escape.

Bluecoats.

Rourke leaped from the horse. "We'll not outrun them. We'll have to hide."

"Come!" Rabbie yelled, running beneath the smith's canopy and motioning them to follow him into the brick building behind.

Rourke tied the horse to a nearby post, grabbed her hand, and pulled her with him after Rabbie. They dove into the sweltering building a second before the soldiers' horses thundered past.

For a moment she thought they'd taken the short route to Hades, for the room was hotter than a sauna and glowing red from banked coals in a huge oven standing in the middle of the room. The forge. A broad, muscular man stood before it, heating what appeared to be iron on a long pair of tongs, staring at them.

"Da," Rabbie said. "We must hide them. The earl's soldiers seek them."

The older man, whose bald head glistened with sweat in the stifling heat, frowned. "I want no trouble."

"Nay, Da. They've done no wrong. I'll not have them killed."

"The soldiers . . ." He shook his head. "Ha' ye no sense?"

Rourke stepped forward. "Ye needn't shield me. Just the lass. I shall pay you well."

Brenna leaped after him. "Rourke, no. You're not facing them alone."

He turned to her, his expression grim. "Hide, Wildcat, and heed my command this time, aye?"

"They'll kill you."

"Mayhap. If they do, make your way to the village of Monymusk. Hegarty will find ye. Soon or late, he will find ye."

Outside, the sound of booted feet pounded at a small distance.

"Come." Rabbie grabbed her arm. "You can hide in the coal bin."

The blacksmith grunted. "You'll be needing to move his mount to the rear," he told his son.

Rabbie grinned. "Aye, Da."

"Have you a second mount?" he asked Rourke.

"Nay."

The older man turned to Rabbie. "Then ye'll saddle mine and tether him there as well. They'll not make it far on one."

Rourke gave a nod that was almost a bow. "My thanks."

Brenna swallowed hard. That meant she'd be riding alone. Assuming they made it.

The blacksmith finally looked at Rourke. "Get yourself hid. I want no trouble, but . . ." He shrugged. "As trouble is here, I'll be helping you."

As Rabbie ran to get the horses ready, the blacksmith took the hot ingot out of the coals and went outside under the canopy to hammer.

Rourke turned and closed the distance between them.

He grabbed her waist and lifted her into the filthy coal bin. Oh, she was going to be dirty.

"Get down," Rourke commanded. He took off his black jacket and put it over her head. "'Twill cover the brightness of your hair and cap."

Then he pulled off his wig and thrust it at her. "Hold that for me."

"Aren't you getting in, too?"

"Nay. I must be able to fight." The coldness in his eyes evaporated in a wash of heat. "I could flay you," he growled. "I commanded ye to remain hidden, yet you disobeyed."

"Oh sure, don't thank me for saving you."

He threw her an incredulous look. "We are not *saved*."

"No, but at least you're still alive. I was afraid they were going to surprise you. I couldn't let that happen."

"You did not think I could take them?"

"There are six of them!"

"So you yelled for me, then found yourself a laddie?"

He was jealous. "Rabbie helped me get in and out of the dress, then—"

"He *undressed* you?"

Brenna jerked the jacket off her head. "Oh, for heaven's sake, Rourke. I thought they'd kill you if I didn't do something."

He grabbed her shoulders and shook her. "What if they'd caught *you*?"

The raw emotion in his eyes took her by surprise. She'd been nothing but a thorn in his side.

"Why do you care? Why do they want me, Pirate?"

His hands stilled. Then he released her and turned away. "Christ, I need to get back to sea. Get ye hidden."

"Not until you tell me." It was a bold threat. If one of the bluecoats walked in now, she was as good as caught. But she had to know what was going on.

He turned, glaring at her with those cold, cold eyes.

Brenna stared right back. "I'm waiting." She lifted the hair that had tumbled down her neck, desperate for some respite . . . *any* respite . . . from the suffocating heat. Sweat rolled through her hair, making her scalp itch.

He broke eye contact and turned away.

"Why are you afraid to tell me?"

He scowled, the accusation pricking his pride as she'd intended. "I am not *afraid*."

"Then tell me what's going on, Rourke. They're trying to kill me, and I have a right to know why."

"This is not the time," he growled.

"It's never the time, is it? It's never going to be the time." She stared at his strong profile, the stubborn jut of his chin, the line of his straight, arrogant nose. She saw the moment his rigid stance softened ever so slightly, the moment his shoulders seemed almost to droop.

Turning, eyes bleak, he met her gaze. "He wants you because of the prophecy." He turned back and started for the door, leaving her staring after him.

Brenna dropped his wig in the coal and climbed out of the bin.

Rourke swung toward her, blocking her movement. "*Wildcat*."

"You can't just drop a bomb like that and walk away."

He glared at her, but with that glint of confusion she was becoming used to when she said something strange. *Not too many bombs around here, eh?*

"Hegarty should be the one to explain, not I."

"Hegarty's not here, in case you hadn't noticed."

"Aye. I am aware of that." His words contained a wealth of frustration. "It has naught to do with me. I only know that Hegarty brought you here to fulfill your part, and the Earl of Slains is disinclined to allow it."

"Because?"

He lifted her and deposited her once more into the

coal bin, his eyes grave. "Because . . . according to the prophecy . . . ye will destroy him."

Brenna stared at him, brows creased in disbelief even as she forgot to breathe. *I'm hearing, but definitely not comprehending.*

She grabbed his forearms as he released her. "What do you mean, *destroy*? Financially?"

"No."

"You can't mean I'm supposed to kill him."

"Aye. You are."

Brenna gaped at him. "Me?" The idea was absurd. There was no denying the man deserved to die, but she was the last person anyone should expect to be his assassin. Not unless a man could die from a knee to the groin. But she suddenly remembered the earl in her time railing at her. *You burned this castle three hundred years ago, Brenna Cameron. You'll not do it again!*

Whoa.

There had to be a mistake. That was the only explanation. She wasn't the right Brenna Cameron. Hegarty must have flipped through some kind of cosmic phonebook and picked the wrong woman.

Rourke was already making his way back toward the door.

"I'm not the one you want, Pirate. I can't be."

He stared out at the street, then turned and eyed her meaningfully. "You wear the sapphire."

She squinted in confusion as her fingers went to the small pendant at her throat. "I've had this forever. What could it possibly have to do with . . ."

Rourke's body tensed, and he levered himself back into the shadows and motioned her down. Someone was coming. She squatted low in the coal bin and pulled Rourke's jacket over her head as the sound of heavily booted feet drew near.

Eight

Brenna's pulse set up a reggae rhythm in her ears, nearly blotting out all other sound as she huddled in the coal bin. The worst of it was not knowing what was going on. She couldn't see a thing but black. Black coal, black skirt, black jacket over her head. Her heart was beating too fast, too hard.

She heard the muted thud of footsteps enter the smithy. Her breath caught and held, the heat and musty wool smell of Rourke's jacket filling her lungs. Even if it weren't like a sauna in here, she'd be sweating from the sheer fear that discovery was only seconds away.

Footsteps moved closer.

Don't move. Don't breathe.

Through the thudding in her ears, she heard movement, then the crash of metal on metal. Swords.

Don't you die on me, Pirate.

At least now she knew where to find Hegarty. Monymusk, wherever that was. But how would she get there without Rourke? How would she survive without him? In the interminable hours since she'd arrived in this place he'd become more than her guide. He'd become an ally and a champion—something she'd sorely lacked in her life. Even now, if he died here, it would be protecting her.

The blacksmith's hammer joined the noise of the swords, the clanging outside synchronized almost perfectly with the ringing of the metal . . . almost as if the hammering were designed to mask the sound of battle.

Brenna eased up and lifted the jacket until she could peek over the top of the bin. Not six feet away, the pirate and a bluecoat were going at it in earnest, thrusting and parrying with deadly skill. The pirate would win. She had to believe that.

A shadow darkened the doorway. The flash of steel and the blue of the man's coat made Brenna's heart sink. Two against one. Rourke had told her to stay hidden, but once they killed him, they'd almost certainly find her. Hiding wasn't going to save either of them.

She surreptitiously peered around, her gaze snagging on the poker sticking out of the forge. For a second, she hesitated, heart thudding violently. But she couldn't let the pirate die. She threw off the jacket, slipped out of the coal bin, and ran for the poker. At the last minute, Brenna snatched up a rag before grabbing the scalding handle, as she'd seen the blacksmith do. As her hand closed around it, one of the bluecoats shouted and started for her.

Staring at the brute, who was twice her size and armed, she wondered what in the world she'd been thinking. She couldn't possibly beat this man. An idea came to her. Lifting her skirt with one hand, she turned and ran the other way, around the forge until she was behind Rourke's opponent. Swinging with all her might, she slammed the hot poker across the back of the bluecoat's head.

He yelped with pain and whirled on her. As his swinging sword stopped at the top of its arc, Rourke's blade erupted from the bluecoat's throat in a shower of blood.

"Wildcat!" Rourke yelled. "Behind you!"

She heard the heavy footsteps of the brute and turned, swinging her poker, but he caught it easily with an upward thrust of his sword and sent it flying from her hands into a pile of rags by the door.

The bluecoat's sword came at her again, aiming for her neck. Brenna tried to jump back, but her foot caught in her skirt, and she went down, catching the tip of the sword on the jaw. As she hit the ground, the pirate leaped over her and took on the soldier, sword to sword.

Brenna scrambled to her feet, her jaw burning, damp warmth sliding down her neck. A flash of light caught her attention and she turned to find the poker had set the rags on fire.

As she watched, Rourke lunged toward his opponent, backing the bluecoat into the quickly growing blaze. Too late, the earl's man realized his mistake. With a scream, he turned and ran from the smithy's, tearing the smoldering coat from his back.

Rourke leaped for her and grabbed her hand, pulling her toward the back door. "Are ye hurt?"

"Just a nick." She touched the stinging wound and felt the damp stickiness of blood. "I think."

Rourke eased out the door, sword drawn and ready, then opened the door wider for her to follow.

Rabbie and half a dozen townsmen were running toward them, carrying buckets. Water for the fire, no doubt.

Rabbie saw them and ran over, his face drawn. "One of the soldiers is searching for you in the church. The others and your scalawag are watching the south and west roads out of town. No one is watching the east."

"My thanks," Rourke said. "When I am able, I will send money, for what little good it will do. You helped us and we brought ruin upon you. I am sorry."

Rabbie's expression lightened a little. "Dinna fash yourself. 'Tis no more than what happens every time the earl's soldiers come."

"You'll have one less to worry ye, then," Rourke added with a rare bit of rueful humor.

"Bye, Rabbie," Brenna said.

"God be with ye both. May he deliver ye to safety." The young man turned and rushed into the back door of the smithy's.

Rourke helped her mount, then leaped atop his own horse and they hastily left town. Brenna held on to the reins for dear life, terrified she was going to crash the beast, or at least fall off. But she did neither. Riding seemed to come more naturally to her than she'd expected. She glanced back at the curl of smoke rising into the sky. No sirens rent the air, no fire trucks roared to the rescue. If the townspeople didn't get the fire under control soon, they could lose their whole town.

She was beginning to feel like one of those cartoon characters with the black cloud hanging over his head, bad luck following him everywhere he went. Her black cloud was beginning to resemble a hurricane.

He'd almost had them.

Rourke gripped the reins of the agile gelding with frustrated fingers as the animal raced across the open moors. Beside him, Brenna rode with determination, if little skill.

The wind blew through his hair, doing little to cool his battle lust. God's blood, he'd been ready to take them all. He'd been ready to take *Cutter*. He'd heard the horses from inside the merchant's and knew the earl's soldiers had arrived. If Brenna hadn't interfered, he'd have taken them down, one by one.

Instead, her shout had turned his blood to ice. Never

had he felt anger and fear in such measure at the same time. *They could have killed her.*

If she'd stayed where he'd left her—where he'd *ordered* her to remain—he'd have cast down Cutter and the earl's soldiers once and for all. But she'd refused his direct command.

She'd sought to save him.

A strange heaviness shifted within his chest, pinching his heart. She'd risked her life for him. And then she'd done it again, breaching her hiding place in the coal bin to attack one of his opponents when he'd been outnumbered. Indeed, she had fought beside him, protecting his back as best she could. His pride tried to protest the affront to his ability, but he could muster no real resentment.

An unwelcome wash of soft emotions flowed over his skin, slipping into his pores, making him *feel*. Warmth. Gratitude.

He fought the unwanted feelings like he would any foe, refusing to let them weaken his defenses against the darker emotions he kept at bay—the soul-crushing guilt that he had carried with him all these years.

The familiar need to escape swept over him. He wanted only to return to the sea where the turmoil of his past would no longer swirl around him, threatening to suck him into oblivion.

But intertwined with that need was a new one, equally strong and growing stronger with every hoof beat. A driving need to smite his traitorous bosun and the rest of the soldiers who would drag Brenna to her death.

He'd find Hegarty and turn her over to him in a thrice, but not until they were safely free of their pursuers. Then he would live the rest of his bleak life without her.

Turning, he caught one last glimpse of the town, now crowned by a wreath of black smoke. Either the fire in the smithy had not been controlled, or the soldiers had set flame to additional buildings in their quest to find Brenna.

The prophecy's claws had torn asunder yet more lives, adding to his guilt that he'd inadvertently been an instrument in that destruction.

They backtracked east until they came to a shallow burn, then followed it for nearly half a mile, riding through the water, hiding their tracks. As they crossed the open moor, turning slowly toward Monymusk, he soundly cursed Hegarty, knowing precisely why the little troll had chosen the place.

Above the village of Monymusk stood Picktillum Castle, Rourke's childhood home. A place to which he would never return, no matter how hard his uncle begged. His life there was through, destroyed on a dark day twenty years before.

If Hegarty thought to lure him to Picktillum, he'd be sorely disappointed. Not even for his gold and the Goodhope Plantation would he ever again set foot in his home.

When he'd pushed them as long as he could without rest, he led the horses into a copse of pines growing beside a small, sparkling loch.

"Are we stopping?" The raw hope in Brenna's voice made him smile.

"Aye."

"Hallelujah." She dismounted. "I had no idea it was so hard to drive one of these things!"

"Drive?" He led both horses to the water's edge.

Brenna sank to her knees beside him. Her straight fall of russet hair had fallen loose beneath her cap, framing a face and neck liberally streaked with both coal dust and blood. And still she was the bonniest woman he'd ever seen.

She dipped the hem of her skirt in the water and began to wipe the soot from her face. "I like it so much better when you're driving the horse and I'm just a passenger."

As did he. He missed the feel of her pressed close behind him, her breath soft in his ear, her hands locked at his waist. He wanted her that close again, but this time facing him as she had in the stable, their clothes discarded . . .

A flare of heat roared through him, and he dunked his head, needing to extinguish the fire. The cool water closed over his scalp and face, doing little to cool his ardor. Never had a woman had such a raw effect on him. Lifting his head, he shook his wet hair, spraying them both.

Brenna gave a small shriek and backed away, laughing. "You're worse than a dog."

He was unsure why he felt this lightness of heart when their situation was so dire. When so much had gone amiss this day. It was her. How had the bane of his existence become the one woman who could make him smile?

Brenna made a sound of dismay. "I forgot your wig. And your coat. They're still in the coal bin."

"'Tis no account. I dinna like the wig."

He reached for her, pulling her back down beside him, then tilted her chin up to take a look at the cut the soldier's blade had inflicted. The wound was shallow, little more than a nick, as she'd said. He brushed the soft skin beside the cut with his thumb.

"Does it hurt?"

"A little. No big deal."

The movement of her lush mouth intrigued him, enchanted him. His thumb moved, tracing the fullness of her bottom lip as his gaze moved to her eyes—eyes alight with a fire that set his blood aflame. Slowly, he cupped her face and drew her closer, allowing her to flee, yet coaxing her forward. Her green eyes flicked up to his, uncertainty rimmed in desire. To his surprised delight, she reached for him, pressing her soft palm to his cheek, and met him halfway.

He'd meant to take it gently—nay, he'd meant to not touch her again at all—but the moment he tasted her, he was lost. And so, it seemed, was she.

The kiss turned frantic. He drank of her, his mouth

open, devouring, needing her with a violence that set his limbs to quaking. Brenna melted against him, strength and softness, her mouth opening to his seeking tongue. His hands swept up her back as she filled his senses, her taste at once sweet and infinitely arousing, her scent a strangely heady combination of coal dust, sea nymph, and pure, captivating woman.

As her hands slid around his neck, her breasts pressed against him, nearly sending him over the edge. Memories raged through him—her perfect breasts gleaming in the morning sun, the feel of her tight sheath as he'd driven into her in the dark of the stable.

His palm found her breast, pulling a moan of pure bliss from his throat. So soft. He *needed* . . .

Brenna wrenched out of his embrace and pushed him away, lips swollen with passion, her eyes shadowed.

"I can't do this," she whispered, stumbling to her feet.

Rourke stared at her retreating back, aching as if his lungs had been ripped from his chest, as if she'd kicked him in the ballocks. He clenched his fists at his side. He was a fool to touch her, to want her like this.

He dunked his head into the cold water a second time, holding it there until the fire that raged in his loins cooled to a low burn and his lungs begged for air. Finally, he pulled himself out and squeezed the water from his hair. The woman was destroying him in more ways than he'd believed possible.

She stood gripping her elbows, staring into the distance, looking lost. As if he were the one who'd pushed her away and not the other way around.

After he saw to the horses, he untied the rolled plaid that held the items he'd bought in town and laid it on the grass. Brenna came to stand beside him as he opened it.

"What does my necklace have to do with the prophecy?"

He sighed wearily and met her gaze. The woman had no mercy. "Lift your skirts."

She blinked. "Excuse me?"

He made impatient lifting motions with his hands, then reached for the small weapon tucked in the plaid. "'Tis a lady's knife for your thigh. Sharp enough to cut a man's throat."

Emotions flitted across her expressive face. "The way to every woman's heart," she said dryly.

"Have ye ever wielded a knife?"

She shook her head. "At the dinner table or the cutting board. Never as a weapon."

"Then ye need to learn. This knife is not meant for fighting, but for defending yourself. The reach is not enough to take on a full-size blade, but 'twill slice a man's throat. Or slide with ease through his heart."

"Lovely." She lifted fistfuls of faded black skirt.

Rourke pressed the scabbard against the soft fabric of her breeks, high on her thigh, and fastened the small belt around her leg. Even through the breeks he could feel the tightness of her thigh . . . and the softness. Memory of the way those thighs had cradled him as he thrust into her crashed through him anew, and he fastened the buckle with suddenly unsteady hands and pushed back, silently swearing.

Taking a deep breath, he pulled two apples and a pair of oatcakes from his small stash, and handed her one of each.

"Dinner, as it were," he said, then rolled up the plaid again.

"Thank you." She stared at him a moment as if waiting for him to answer her question, then finally gave up and went to sit on a nearby rock to eat.

Rourke rose, a tight knot of frustration making his movements quick and jerky as he retied the bundle to his saddle. As much as he'd like never to speak of the prophecy again, there were things she needed to know.

He picked up his food and went to sit beside her. "The sapphire is how Hegarty found you."

She met his gaze, her eyes confused, her fingers going to her necklace. "I don't get it. I've always had this. How could Hegarty have anything to do with it?"

"The stone is magic when in the proper hands."

"Hegarty's hands."

"Aye. I believe he used the sapphire to heal your leg."

They ate in silence, then Rourke rose and went looking for a chunk of wood suitable for carving. He pulled out his own knife and sat once more beside her.

She glanced at him. "Who *is* Hegarty? *What* is he to have magic like that?"

"I dinna ken," he said, peeling the bark from the wood in long strips. "He is what he is. Most times a pain in my arse."

"He reminds me of Rumpelstiltskin."

His hand paused. "Of who?"

"A character from a story. A mischievous little man who makes magic."

"Aye, that sounds like him well enough. In truth, he's not a bad sort as long as you dinna mind his thievery. He has a liking for clothes . . . other people's clothes." The knife caught his finger as it was wont to do, drawing a prick of blood. "Whene'er I've had a need for him, he's come."

"There's a lot to be said for having someone like that." There was an emptiness in her voice that tugged at him and he felt a pang of sorrow for the small lass she'd once been. "Who made the prophecy?"

"The Cruden Seer." As he worked, a tiny creature emerged from the wood, one cut at a time. With regret he remembered his other creations that had hung in his cabin were gone now. "Some called her the Cruden Witch. The Earl of Slains wished to ken his death so he could avoid it, aye? She told him."

"And she named me as the one who would kill him?"

"I dinna ken the particulars. I've heard it said ye would be the one to destroy him."

Brenna's expression was troubled as she fingered the stone at her neck. "I'm not a killer. I shouldn't even be here. There has to be a mistake."

Her shoulders sagged as her gaze dropped to the half-eaten oatcake in her hand. "I just want to go home."

He gazed at her bent head, the fragile curve of her neck and shoulder. Strength, yet so much vulnerability.

"Do you have a family awaiting ye?" He'd never thought to ask. Never truly wondered despite finding her no virgin. He was a fool.

"No. No one like that. Just friends and a job."

"But you're happy there?"

She looked up at him, her eyes clear and sure. "It's where I belong."

Aye, and he knew it well. "Wildcat . . ." His knife stilled and he met her gaze. "Hegarty will want that stone you wear."

"Yeah, I know. He tried to take it from me when I was half drugged after he healed my leg."

"'Tis your only way home. Ye must not let him take it until he sends ye back."

Her gaze sharpened and bore into his. "Do you know where I came from?"

"No. And I dinna wish to. All I ken is Hegarty can send ye back. Or take ye there himself."

Green eyes, dark with shadows, turned toward the landscape. "He's not going to send me back until I kill the earl, is he?"

"Mayhap we can convince him to. The prophecy is old. The earl older. He canna live forever, aye? And once he dies the prophecy dies with him. What matter would it make if you are here, or . . . your home?"

She turned to him, her eyes troubled even as they filled with a warmth that spread through his chest like brandy. A small smile spread across her features.

"Thanks for helping me, Rourke."

Something clenched deep in his chest. He was going to miss her, he realized.

A raindrop splattered on his arm, then a second. Rourke rose and offered his hand to her. "Come. We must be away."

"We're going to ride in the rain?"

"Aye. 'Twill hide our tracks."

She took his hand, the feel of her soft palm against his somehow right. As if she'd always been by his side. As if she belonged there.

He shook off the untoward thought and helped her mount. But as he swung into his own saddle, he felt the loss of her at his back and dreaded how much more alone he would feel when she was gone.

Brenna lay restlessly on the huge length of plaid and stared up at the stars. She was exhausted, every muscle of her body aching from the ride, yet sleep eluded her.

It had to be past midnight, but without a clock, she had no way of knowing how much of the night had passed. They'd ridden until well into the evening before stopping, but she felt like she'd lain here for hours.

She swatted at a night bug that was trying to settle on her face and rolled onto her side. Rourke lay beside her, barely an arm's reach away. His deep, even breathing calmed her. His presence, even in sleep, was comforting.

With a sigh, she marveled at how dependent upon him she'd become in a mere two days. It was disturbing, really. She knew better than to depend on anyone other than herself, yet she didn't have a choice here. How could she possibly get along without him? He protected her, fed her, and, hopefully, led her to Hegarty so she could get home. She needed him, but her feelings for the man were becoming a lot more complicated than simple gratitude.

"Canna sleep?" Rourke's voice rumbled low, startling her.

"No."

"Is aught amiss?"

The warm concern in his words wrapped around her. "I'm fine. I'm not used to sleeping on the ground. Do you know, I've never slept under the stars like this?"

"Never?"

"No. Then again, I've never seen them like this. So bright. So many of them."

"The stars are the lifeline of a seaman. They're as familiar to me as the back of my own hand."

Brenna smiled. "It's hard to believe some of them no longer exist."

"If we see them, how can they not exist?"

"Time delay. The stars are actually faraway suns with life cycles of their own. Their light takes so long to travel to Earth that they can die and we won't know about it for thousands, sometimes millions, of years."

Silence met her words. The warm feeling of camaraderie slipped away, to be replaced by a cool dread. Why did she tell him something like that? Something that people in this time, without powerful telescopes, couldn't possibly know?

"Where did Hegarty find you, Wildcat?" His words were softly spoken, but there was an edge to them that told her clearly that she was spooking him.

"You told me before that you don't want to know. You were right. You don't."

He didn't answer. The silence dragged on, deep and dark as the night as she lay there, her breathing shallow and as silent as his. She wished she could see his face. Read his expression. Finally, she couldn't stand it anymore.

"Where do you *think* he pulled me from?"

His silence stretched for nearly another minute before

she heard him sigh. "I dinna ken. Knowing the little troll, he could have gotten ye from anywhere." The tightness was gone from his voice, leaving him sounding weary. "I know only that women there dress unlike here, wear their hair differently, speak differently. And ye know things, like the stars."

She heard him move, as if rolling toward her. "How do ye know these things?"

Part of her desperately wanted to tell him the truth. But a larger part was terrified.

She rolled onto her stomach and lifted up on her elbows, feeling as if she stood on the edge of a precipice. "I'm afraid to tell you."

She heard him move closer, felt his hand touch her shoulder, then slide down her arm until it rested upon hers. "What frightens ye?"

"It's too strange. I don't want you to think I'm crazy, or . . . or a witch or something. I'm just a woman, Rourke. Maybe the one named in the prophecy, maybe not. I'm just who I am."

He squeezed her hand. "I ken that. 'Twas Hegarty's doing that brought you here. I know I said earlier that I dinna wish to know from whence ye came. But I do. Where have you been, Wildcat?"

Brenna lowered her head until her forehead rested on the back of his hand. His scent filled her nostrils and she closed her eyes against the powerful longing that swept through her. A longing to be closer to him in every way. She lifted her head and turned toward him in the dark.

"The future. He brought me from the future."

Again that long pause. "What future?"

"Yours. The Earth's. Over three hundred years, I think."

Slowly, he pulled away. Physically, as his hand slipped from hers, and emotionally. She could almost hear the hair rising on his arms.

"I shouldn't have told you." She sat up, cold congealing in the pit of her stomach. "I knew you weren't ready to hear it."

Still, his silence stretched.

"Rourke . . ."

"I . . . must think." She heard him move. "*Three hundred years?*"

Good grief, why had she told him? "More, I think. I came from the year 2009. Isn't it the late 1600s now? I've wanted to ask, but been afraid to."

"The year is 1687," he said stiffly.

A chill went through her like a knife. She'd known. And yet . . . "How is this possible?"

"Hegarty." From the sound of his voice, she knew he'd sat up. "I ken your oddity now. Things have changed in three hundred years, aye?"

"More than you can imagine. More than I could ever explain."

"Try."

She stared into the dark, toward the sound of his voice. *How?* How could she possibly put her world into terms he could understand.

"I'm never cold. Never wet unless I want to be, never hungry. If I get sick, there's usually a cure. I make good money, have a nice place to live, and have no one chasing me or shooting at me. Ever."

Even to her own ears, twenty-first-century Baltimore sounded like paradise. What she hadn't mentioned was the loneliness—a loneliness she hadn't fully understood until the past few days when it had been strangely absent.

She heard him rise. "Where are you going?"

"No' far. I need to think. Go to sleep, Wildcat."

She felt his departure more than heard it, and felt isolation rush back to envelope her. She shouldn't have told him. He couldn't handle it—of course, he couldn't.

Brenna lay on her back and stared up at the stars,

unshed tears burning her eyes. He was a moody man, grumpy and silent, or demanding and dictatorial. But he was also kind. And honorable.

Over the past couple of days, they'd developed a bond of some kind. A friendship, maybe even something more, something steeped in an attraction like nothing she'd ever felt.

With a spurt of painful anger at herself, she flung one arm across her eyes. *Stupid, stupid, stupid.* If her erratic childhood had taught her anything, it was that developing bonds with anyone was only going to get her hurt. Sooner or later, they always left.

The worst part was, this time she'd done it to herself. With a single, ill-placed truth, she'd turned herself into a freak in his eyes. And lost her only chance of having a real friend in this world. *Of having a true friend at all.*

Nine

The sun was low in the evening sky the next day when Rourke spotted a familiar sight ahead, sending dread snaking through his belly. High atop a steep rise, a fairy ring overlooked the burn he and Brenna had been following most of the day. Two stones stood upright amongst their fallen companions, silhouetted against the orange sunset.

A chill ran down his spine. He knew this place. He'd been here once before, as a lad. The night his parents died. Memories rushed over him, bitter and painful. It was only the beginning. For the sight meant they were not far from Monymusk . . . and Picktillum Castle. A half-morning's ride at most.

The thought wound around his chest until he thought he would suffocate. It was all he could do not to turn his horse and ride back to the sea as fast as the animal would take him. He would sign aboard another ship. With his reputation, he'd soon be captaining *someone's* ship even if not his own.

But even as dread and thoughts of flight filled his mind, his gaze turned to Brenna. How could he leave her to them?

Nay, he could not. He'd take her with him. They'd sail the seas together, her fighting off the crews with her clever hands while he struck down the rest with his sword.

He grimaced. *Mayhap not the best of plans.*

His gaze returned to the fairy stones as a hard shudder went through him. Until he found Hegarty, he could go nowhere but forward. Hegarty must send her back . . . to her time. She would never be safe here. And he wanted that for her. To be safe. Happy.

"A stone circle," Brenna breathed. She turned to him, pleasure lighting her eyes. "I've always wanted to see one."

"Ye've heard of them?"

"I've seen photos."

"Photos?" The word sounded strange on his tongue.

She gave a small grimace. "Paintings . . . sort of."

But he knew she was speaking of something from the future he wouldn't understand. *The future.* Three hundred years. He looked at her as if seeing her for the first time, as he had on and off all day. She was the same woman he'd dived into the sea after. But though his mind reminded him, his skin rose with chill bumps.

He shouldn't be surprised, not when Hegarty was involved. Nothing the wee scamp did should have the power to startle him anymore.

Even so. *Three hundred years in the future.*

"Can we go up there and walk through it?"

At Brenna's question, his gaze caught sight of the smile that danced at the edges of her mouth. Warmth spread through his chest, chasing away the chill, reminding him she was still his bonnie companion.

A companion who would not be with him much longer if he had his way. *If* Hegarty agreed to send her back to her own time.

The thought caused a hollowness in his heart that surprised him. He gazed at her as she awaited his reply, taking in the smudge of coal dust on her cheek that she'd missed when she rinsed her face, and the small, angry red welt that cupped her jaw. Her eyes glowed with strength and life, her ripe mouth tilted in that smallest of smiles. A smile he suddenly longed to see bloom.

"Would ye like to make camp by the stones for the night? We'll ride into Monymusk on the morrow."

The smile that broke over Brenna's face exceeded his fiercest wishes, stealing the breath from his body. Her green eyes sparkled, her lush mouth curving to reveal white, perfect teeth.

The need to pull her into his arms and cover that mouth with his own knocked him back even as her smile drew him in, pulling him like the strongest of whirlpools. A whirlpool he would gladly sacrifice himself to.

With a start, he realized he was smiling himself.

"I swear, I am *so* ready to get off this horse," Brenna said. "I'm never going to walk straight again."

A chuckle escaped his throat, sounding odd to his ears.

"Are we going to try to ride up there?" She eyed the steep incline.

"The horses need watering, as do we. We'll dismount below."

They rode the short distance to the hill, then dismounted and walked the horses to the water's edge. Brenna's first steps were indeed stiff and ungainly, but as he watched, her graceful movements slowly returned.

The need to touch her again, to taste the beauty of her smile, was becoming a physical ache. He thirsted for her like a man too long without water, but she wasn't open to his advances. She'd made that painfully clear.

Running his hand over his mouth, he scanned the horizon in every direction. A distant croft. Open moors and rolling heath. There had been no sign of Cutter or the earl's men since they'd left the burning town. He might have taken heart that they'd truly lost them, except for one thing. Hegarty's missive had been opened when Rourke received it, the seal broken. Someone had read it before he did, and he didn't think it was Mr. Baker. He feared it was Cutter. Which meant Cutter likely knew they were on their way to Monymusk and might well be waiting for them there.

As he pulled some soft grass with which to rub down the horses, his gaze returned to Brenna. He watched as she dipped her hands in the water, lifting them to cool her face. Suddenly he remembered the gift he'd purchased for her earlier. They'd stopped midday at a small croft and bought a round of cheese, some salt beef, and a pair of hard-cooked eggs for their meals. Then he'd taken the crofter aside and made a small additional purchase he'd not shown Brenna.

With sweet anticipation, he fetched it from the plaid.

"Wildcat. You might be wanting this, lass." When she glanced at him, he tossed the small ball to her.

She caught it with ease, her expression curious. Suddenly her eyes widened and she gasped with delight. "Soap!" She gifted him with a smile of such pleasure he felt his heart contract under the pressure.

"Did you find this?" she asked.

"I purchased it. I thought it might please you."

"You thought right." She grinned. "I think I love you, Pirate." Then she whirled toward the water and dipped her hands in.

He watched her, unable to move. *I think I love you, Pirate.* The words meant naught and were merely an expression of deep gratitude. He didn't *want* them to mean anything.

Yet the simple words warmed him as little ever had.

With an oath, he turned back to the horses, damning himself for a fool for letting a woman disturb his mind so.

With every smile, every word, every courageous act, he felt as if he were being spun around until he could no longer tell up from down.

He had to find Hegarty, and soon, or he'd find his determination to be rid of her wavering. He'd wake one morning to find himself embroiled in the prophecy, leading an ill-fated charge against the earl's entire army.

Nay, he would not be so foolish.

Not even for a green-eyed sea nymph.

The man was an enigma.

Brenna sat on one of the fallen rocks in the stone circle, chewing the last bites of her dinner while Rourke whittled his piece of wood a few yards away. The stones were huge and ancient, though she had to use her imagination to call it a circle. Time and weather had knocked all but two to the ground, reducing what had once been a circle to little more than a pile of pick up sticks.

Rourke's knife strokes were smooth and even. The resulting sound calmed the tension that had ridden her ever since she'd told him where she was really from. She'd fallen asleep before he returned last night and had not woken again until morning.

He'd said no more about her origins and was acting as if nothing had happened. As if he was determined to ignore the truth. But he was brooding. He'd spoken little the entire day, and that only when necessary.

And yet, he'd bought her soap. Just when she thought she was figuring him out, she realized she didn't really understand him at all. All she knew was she wanted him to accept her. To not be spooked by her. His gift of the soap seemed to indicate he wasn't. Not too spooked, anyway.

She rose and walked over to the rock where he carved and sat down beside him to watch. All day, she'd kept her distance, wanting to give him time to come to terms with her. Now that she thought maybe he had, she longed to breech the gap, if only a little.

As his strong, capable hands formed a small crude head a vague memory teased her mind. "I used to know someone who whittled. I vaguely remember watching him make little animals, kind of like your birds." She watched his clever movements form wings and a tail. "Will it fly?"

He met her gaze, his expression sardonic. "'Tis no' real, Wildcat."

Brenna gave him a wry smile. "So I noticed. But it doesn't have to be alive to fly. If it's made to catch the air, it'll soar when you throw it."

He gave her a look that was a mixture of disbelief and keen interest. "Things fly in your time."

It was a statement, not a question. She searched his expression for signs that he was disconcerted by her comment—or by her—but saw nothing to warn her to keep silent and move away. So she did neither.

"Yes, things fly. But they have engines. Power to make them soar. Sometimes, though, small objects will sail on the air if they're made right. I used to make paper airplanes when I was in school. I have no idea if a small wooden bird could be made to soar."

His pale eyes sparkled with intellect and excitement. "Shall we find out?"

Brenna laughed, as much with relief that he really seemed to be accepting her as by the pleasure in his eyes. "Why not?"

A huge weight lifted from her shoulders. Finally, she could talk with him freely about the things she knew and had done. Though maybe she'd wait awhile before she told him about space travel. Or MTV.

She looked at the small bird nestled in the palm of his hand.

"Flatten the bottoms of the wings, but keep the tops

rounded." She met his gaze. "I don't know a lot about flight, but I do know that much." She'd taken so much for granted. Airplanes flew because . . . they just did. Who cared about the details so long as your flight arrived on time, *with* your luggage?

He scraped the underside of the wings flat, then handed the carving to her. "Show me what to do."

The little bird was small and light, but solid. Would it fly without a propeller or rubber band? Or a turboprop jet engine? She knew paper airplanes, how to make them, how to launch them. Wooden birds were virgin territory.

One way to find out. She held the bird as if she were launching a paper airplane, intensely aware of Rourke's eyes upon her.

"Here goes nothing." She gave the crude little bird a good throw and watched as it arced up, rolled, and dove toward the earth in an unfortunate imitation of a rock landing on the hard ground with a snap.

"Oh no." She hurried over to find the little bird lying at an angle, its wing broken, held together by only a weaving of wood splinters.

Rourke came up beside her.

"I guess it was too heavy to fly after all." She reached for the broken little bird.

"Leave it."

"But—"

"*Leave it.*"

Brenna cringed at the coldness of his tone. She glanced at him in disbelief, but he was already turning away.

"Pirate . . . *Rourke*. I'm sorry."

He ignored her and started down the hill toward the stream, his back stiff with anger.

Brenna stared after him, totally confused. It wasn't like she'd *meant* to break his toy. Surely he knew that.

She watched from the stone circle as he came to a stop by the water's edge, his arms across his chest. A conqueror surveying his land. But this conqueror's shoulders were a little too tense, his head a little too low.

As if he'd lost his prized possession and not simply one of a hundred birds he'd carved.

Except he'd lost those birds. *All* of them. Along with his entire ship. His gold. All his possessions.

He'd lost *everything* when he dove off his ship thinking to save her. The bird was merely the last straw. In three short days she'd all but destroyed his life.

When Rourke finally returned to the campsite, he found Brenna asleep. She lay on her side, curled into a ball as if she were cold. Or miserable.

Self-loathing washed over him.

She hadn't deserved that outburst. He wasn't even sure where the anger had come from. He'd put little enough effort into the carving. The bird had only begun to take shape. He'd wanted to see if it would fly as much as she had; it wasn't her fault it had broken.

The anger had come from elsewhere.

From the dislike he felt for being in this place of memories, for being so close to the place he'd once called home. And also for a place buried deep inside him, carried on a memory of another time. Another broken bird. A long-necked swan he'd spent painstaking hours carving as a birthday gift for his mother. He'd been but a lad when he'd watched selfish little hands break it the morning of his mother's birthday, unleashing an anger and a need for vengeance that had ultimately called hell itself down upon his head, destroying everything and everyone he'd loved.

He couldn't fight the memories much longer. With every mile closer to Picktillum, he felt the hellhounds gaining on him. His own personal demons snapping at his heels.

He had to end this and soon. Find Hegarty and get out of here before he went mad.

As he sat down on the plaid, the lass rolled toward him in sleep. Her expression was not peaceful. Her dreams were not sweet this eve, of that he was certain. Likely she was dreaming of pig headed pirates.

His hand reached out and lifted a strand of her hair. It was no longer as silky as when she'd first arrived, but still soft, the rich reddish brown was bonnie in the fading light.

Brenna Cameron. The bane of his existence.

For so long he'd blamed her. Yet when he thought about the few things she'd told him of her life in the future, he knew she'd lost as much as he. And more. Far more.

She'd lost not only everything she had, but everything she'd known, when Hegarty called her through time. At least he understood the world in which he lived. And he stood a fighting chance of regaining what had been taken from him. She'd lost *all*.

And he wasn't certain Hegarty would give it back.

She'd tried to share some of her world with him, teach him something he'd longed to know, and he'd thanked her with anger when the trial went awry.

He tucked the errant strand behind her ear as he gazed down at the bonnie, yet troubled face that was becoming more familiar to him than his own, and far more dear.

She hadn't deserved his anger. It was the whirlpool swirling around them that made him crazed. But for the first time he realized she'd not cast him into the maelstrom—they'd fallen in together. She was not the cause of his troubles. She was as much a victim as he.

More so.

If the prophecy had ensnared him, so, too, had it ensnared her. They were in this together. Had always been.

As he ran a finger over the line of her jaw, her hand reached up and took hold of his own, tucking it close to her heart. He closed his eyes against the flood of soft emotion that wove through him. His plan to send her home sank like a rock to the pit of his stomach.

Brenna woke to the rising sun, squinting at the yellow orange orb with dismay. She never could sleep past sunrise, which presented something of a problem when the sun rose at 4:30 A.M. She didn't need a watch to know what time it was. She'd arrived on the summer solstice . . . in both centuries.

And it was too early to get up.

She tried to get comfortable, but the stickiness was driving her nuts. Nothing like a saltwater bath to make a person feel gross. And she'd taken two of them.

Rolling over, she was relieved to find Rourke sleeping soundly a few feet away. He'd stayed by the stream so long she wasn't sure he meant to return. Two nights in a row, she'd driven him away. She'd tried to stay awake, to apologize to him for all the trouble she'd caused him, but sleep had overtaken her.

He slept now on his back, one arm flung over his eyes, his other hand resting on the hilt of his long knife. If possible, he looked even more dangerous in sleep, his jaw clenched, his expression hard and uncompromising. She wondered if he was taking out an opponent in his dreams. He wouldn't kill in his sleep, would he? A real concern since she was the only one within striking distance.

With that not-so-calming thought she knew she'd never go back to sleep. She shifted again, feeling like she had sand in her clothes. She probably did.

On a silent groan, she sat up. He'd bought her soap—if she only had a hot bath to go with it. What she did have was the stream. Definitely not hot, but it was water, and at four in the morning, probably safe from onlookers. A combination she couldn't resist.

She grabbed the soap from where she'd laid it on her skirt and made her way down the slope to the shallow river. A cool breeze blew her hair into her face and she tucked the strands behind her ear, wondering at her sanity. That water was like ice—she'd tasted it last night.

But the night had remained warm and the sun was already rising in a clear blue sky. She'd warm up soon enough. She'd go mad if she didn't get rid of this stickiness.

Scanning every direction for sign of an audience, she found only a couple of cows watching from the other bank, so she stripped off her T-shirt and monkey pants. As she slipped her fingers into the waistband of her hot pink bikini panties, she hesitated. They were nylon. They'd dry quickly enough. Leaving them on, she waded knee-deep into the gently flowing ice water.

Freezing, freezing, freezing.

Why couldn't she have gone back in time to Jamaica?

The soap didn't lather like the ones at home, but it smelled wonderful and did the trick. Once she'd washed her body, she took a deep breath, more for courage than air, and sank all the way under the surface of the frigid stream.

Sputtering with the cold, she worked the soap into her hair one hand at a time, careful to keep a good grip on her precious treasure. Finally satisfied she'd done all she could to exorcize the salt water and grime, she leaned forward and rinsed her hair thoroughly. As she squeezed the excess water from her hair, a movement at the top of the rise caught her attention.

Rourke, his expression hard and angry.

Instinctively, she crossed her arms over her breasts and started to sink into the water to find some cover, but the water was just too cold. Embarrassment crawled over her skin. If only she could call her clothes out to her, but unfortunately, she'd never taught them that trick. Unless she wanted to risk freezing to death, she was going to have to tough it out and go fetch them herself.

Dark memories of another time nipped at her courage.

She could do this. He might be mad, but he wouldn't hurt her. Even if he *was* stalking down the hill, his expression thunderous.

As she started toward the shore, her stomach tied itself in knots and her breath began to come in quick, shallow pants. She'd barely stepped out of the water's icy grasp when he reached her, looming over her, barely an arm's reach away.

With his long hair and his beard stubble, he looked thoroughly disreputable and more than a little dangerous. *He won't hurt me*, she told herself over and over, but her pulse began to thud as he stared at her with those cold, pale eyes. "What do ye think you're doing?" His gaze raked her near nakedness, sending a shiver of fear down her spine.

Memories crowded her. *Naked. Helpless.*

She forced back the rising fear and struggled to keep her shoulders back even as her arms remained locked across her chest. "I needed a bath. Why did you think I wanted soap?" The breeze wafted over her cold, wet skin, bringing back miserable memories of two nights ago when she'd been so cold she thought she'd die.

Lifting her chin, Brenna tried to step around him, but he blocked her path. She managed a look of annoyance. "Can I get dressed before you rip me to pieces?"

His expression remained hard. "Ye should have told me you were leaving."

"So you could watch me? Maybe join me?"

His eyes narrowed, darkened, as his gaze slid over her, heat following the chill. He scowled. "Have ye learned nothing of the dangers of this world?"

"Can we have this discussion *after* I get dressed? I'm cold, Pirate."

His gaze turned hot. Liquid. "Aye. I noticed." He half choked the words as he reached for her, running his warm finger down the wet skin of her breast to the very tip where her hard nipple touched her arm. Her breath caught. Fire swirled low in her stomach, a heat that seemed forever ready to flame when he came close.

Why was he so different? Why couldn't she control her body's response to him? A moment ago, she'd been half afraid of him, and now she was melting.

"Ye need to be dry before you dress." As she watched, bemused, he took off his shirt and began to pat the moisture from her cheeks. She stood rooted as the musky-smelling linen touched her neck, then her shoulders, slowly following the path down her arms she'd taken with her soap. As her skin flushed, she watched him, transfixed by the play of muscles across his broad chest. There wasn't an ounce of fat on the man. He was nothing but tight, hard muscle from the waist up. Below the waist . . .

The thought made her legs go weak. She was sinking fast into a sea of sensation and heat. When he turned his attention to her breasts, she knew she was lost. He took an inordinate amount of time lifting one, then the other as he dried every inch.

She longed to feel his hands grip her, craved the touch of his lips. But he was all business in his determination to get her dry. As he abandoned her throbbing, needy breasts, a small groan escaped her lips, drawing a very male smile from him.

He made quick work of drying her back and abdomen, then knelt before her, encircling first one leg, then the other, lifting away the cold stream water with his shirt.

Her gaze remained riveted on his bare chest, entranced by the hair that hung loose about his shoulders, mesmerized by his arms rippling with muscle as they worked to dry her legs. His handsome face tight with concentration, he could have stepped out of a fantasy. A very erotic fantasy.

He ran the shirt up the inside of her thighs again and again, and she suspected the water dripping from her panties was thwarting him. With a growl, he dipped his head and ran his rough, warm tongue up the path the water drops had followed, nearly buckling her knees. Shards of excitement tore across her sensitive skin as his tongue reached the very edge of her panties.

She gasped and grabbed his head, digging her fingers into his thick hair. A moment ago she'd been freezing. Now she felt only heat. And need. And wondrous anticipation.

He didn't disappoint her. His finger slipped beneath the elastic of her panties and pulled the slip of fabric aside. Then he pressed his lips against her, tasting her.

"Rourke."

His tongue ran along the slit of her womanhood, then thrust inside her.

Pleasure shot down her legs and up into her womb as his clever tongue moved, teasing her, driving her up. His whiskers scratched and tickled her sensitive skin as his warm fingers dug into her thighs, holding her tight. Her own fingers clung to his hair, her hips writhing against his mouth with unbearable need.

As his tongue retreated, his mouth closed over the place where his tongue had been and began to suckle, driving her quickly over the top. She moaned and held on to him as wave upon wave of intense contractions tore through her, leaving her gasping with pleasure and disbelief.

Without warning, the pirate stood and swept her into his arms. She looped her arm around his neck and buried her face in his neck as he strode purposefully back to their small camp at the top of the rise. He laid her down on the plaid, then knelt beside her and unbuckled his belt.

He was going to try to make love to her.

"Rourke, no." Brenna scrambled to her feet, searching for her clothes. With dismay, she realized they were still by the water along with her soap. As she turned to fetch them, Rourke rose and gently took hold of her wrist, pulling her around to face him. If he'd been rough, she'd have fought him, but he exerted no force she couldn't easily escape.

He gazed down at her with a look of such longing, such sadness, she couldn't pull away. "I know ye want me."

She shook her head. "It's not that I don't. It's just—"

He stole her words as his lips covered hers in the sweetest of kisses, carrying her right back into the turbulence of passion. His fingers slid down her bare back and inside the waistband of her panties, cupping her cold cheeks. Pulling her hips against him, he let her feel his hard arousal, making her want him as much as he wanted her.

The kiss lost its sweetness, turning hungry. As her arms encircled his neck, his hands moved to cup her breasts. Her mind no longer functioned. She wanted. And the wanting was everything.

He held her tight and lowered her to the plaid, following her down. Then he was on top of her, his hard arousal pressing against her abdomen through the fabric of his pants.

Flashes of memory clawed at her. Fear leaped in her chest and she began to push at his muscled chest. She pounded on him with her fists, tried to kick him, to knee him in the balls.

Rourke leaped off her, his lips full and reddened from her kisses, his expression one of total disbelief.

Brenna scrambled to her feet, shaking.

Clothes. She needed clothes. Some defense. *Anything.*

She turned and grabbed the blanket off the ground,

pulling it around her in a flurry of dust and dirt, then started for the hill. *She needed clothes.*

Tears stung her eyes, blinding her. She didn't even see the pirate until he blocked her path.

"Wildcat?"

She tried to dodge around him, but he stopped her, gripping her shoulders with a gentle firmness. As he touched her, she began to sob.

Rourke stared at the woman before him in utter confusion. He knew women were hard to understand at times, but this one was beyond fathoming.

He pulled her cautiously into his arms, afraid she would pull away at any moment, but she leaned into him, accepting his comfort.

She'd been so ready for him, thrusting herself against his tongue, falling apart beneath his mouth. She'd wanted him. Until he'd been ready to make love to her. Once more she'd rejected him.

Memory of her expression flashed in his mind. Not rejection. *Fear.* She'd been wild with it.

God's blood. Suddenly he understood. Someone, somewhere, had hurt her. He closed his eyes and ran his hand over her hair, almost afraid to touch her.

Slowly her sobs turned to sniffles and hiccoughs. She pulled away, not meeting his gaze.

"I need to get my clothes."

"I'll fetch them, Wildcat."

She looked up at him with red-rimmed eyes glossy with tears, then wiped her damp face on the plaid. "And my soap?"

His heart clenched and a small smile found its way to his mouth. "And your soap." A wildcat could only be brought so low.

He gathered her things, then returned to the fairy ring

where she now awaited him. He turned away as she quickly dressed herself. He would not take advantage of her again.

"I'm done."

When he turned back, he found she'd donned the skirt and bodice as well as her underclothes. She was seated on one of the fallen stones, her hands clasped tightly in her lap.

Slowly, he sat beside her, keeping some distance between them, not wanting to crowd her. "I would never hurt you, Brenna."

She stared at the dirt at her feet and sighed. "I know."

"But someone did, didn't he?"

She tormented her bottom lip with her teeth, finally looking up to meet his gaze. "They. There were three of them."

His hands turned to fists. "I'll kill them."

She shook her head. "They didn't . . . they tried but they didn't. But they would have."

"When?"

"I was fifteen."

"I'll kill them."

"They were boys. Teenagers. They didn't . . ." She looked away, then met his gaze with painful defiance. "They didn't actually rape me."

The air left his lungs on a harsh relief, but her fragile strength told him there was much she wasn't saying. "They still hurt you. They still frightened you."

Her lower lip started to wobble, and she clamped down on it, closing her eyes. "Yeah."

He felt a great weight lift from his heart. She'd never truly rejected him. He'd frightened her, which didn't please him, but he'd not been the cause of the fear. Not directly.

"Tell me, Wildcat, if ye can. What happened?"

She was silent for a long time as tears leaked out from under her closed eyelids, and he regretted asking her to speak. Finally, she swiped at the tears and looked into the distance, as if seeing into the past. Her past.

"I was living with the Prestons—a family who'd taken me in. I was alone in the house, doing laundry in the basement, when Brandon, the Preston's fifteen-year-old son, came home with a couple of friends and started heckling me and saying . . . nasty things. They were all fifteen. Little creeps, though they were taller than I was. And stronger. I told them to go away, but . . . one of them grabbed me. Then the other two joined him. They . . ."

She buried her face in her hands and started trembling.

It tore at Rourke to watch her. He longed to pull her back into his arms, but feared he would scare her again. Instead, he moved closer and touched her hair, letting his palm slide down onto her back.

"They pulled off my clothes and dragged me to the floor. I tried to fight but they were too strong. They groped at me, squeezing my breasts and . . . and . . . touching between my legs. And laughing. Then Brandon laid on top of me, crushing me. I couldn't move. I couldn't breathe."

Her voice broke, stabbing at Rourke's heart. "He rubbed himself against me, his jeans tearing at my skin. He was so heavy. I was furious. And terrified. Finally, one of his friends pushed him off me. He knew how to do it for real. He was going to rape me. I fought them, but Brandon and the third boy held me down while their friend unfastened his pants and started to pull them down. I saw his . . . penis. How big it was."

Rage seared through Rourke, and with it a burning need to hurt the creatures who had terrified her.

Brenna straightened and turned to him. "Then Mrs. Preston came home and the three of them ran off."

"But ye've ne'er forgotten."

She sighed deeply and shook her head. "It's not the sex that scares me. It's being pinned."

He reached for her and cupped her jaw, running his thumb over her small chin. "If ye want me, there are other ways."

"I know. I'm not a virgin, Pirate. I just . . ." She closed her eyes.

"'Tis all right, Wildcat." He cupped her far shoulder and gave a gentle tug, wanting to hold her. To his relief, she leaned against him, laying her head against his chest, and he wrapped his arm around her with gentle care.

"You don't scare me, Pirate. Not really. I can't help my reactions when you get too close."

The unfamiliar sensation of warmth curled in his chest, a tenderness he'd not felt in many, many years. He ran his free hand over her head, following the line of her wet hair. Slowly her trembling stopped, but he continued to stroke her head and her shoulder, comforting her and, amazingly, himself. Peace seeped into him, quieting his demons.

He hadn't realized how much he'd missed this, the closeness. The tenderness. As a small lad, he'd spent nearly every evening curled up on the lap of one of his parents, listening to the *seannachie*, a visiting bard, or a musician, or simply listening to the adult conversation around him. In the years since their deaths he'd had no one to share such kindnesses. He'd had women by the score, but there had been no caring. Lust, sex. But he'd never stayed afterward for he'd known he would never find what he sought with any of them. Why Brenna? Why did simply holding her feel so right?

Her head slipped, then righted itself with a jerk, and he knew she'd fallen asleep.

He roused her. "Come, lass. We've time for a wee bit more sleep." He rose and pulled her up with him, then spread out his plaid and waited for her to lie down. As he started to cover her with the blanket, she stopped him and gazed at him sleepily, her eyes unsure.

"You make a good pillow, Pirate."

He smiled. "Ye wish me to stay?"

She nodded sleepily.

He lay down beside her and gathered her against him, utterly content to hold her for as long as she'd allow.

Her slender hand moved over his chest and she snuggled closer to him. "I don't know why or how, but you drive out the cold."

"I thought you'd warmed."

"That's not the cold I mean."

He understood. She drove out the cold of his own soul.

What would he do when she left?

TEN

With every mile closer to his childhood home, Rourke's dread grew. It was a good thing they rode horseback, for he doubted he'd be able to convince his feet to take the steps. Twenty years since he'd been back. Twenty years since he watched his home burn, his parents die.

Picktillum Castle sat high on a hill overlooking the village of Monymusk. If there were any other way to reach Hegarty, he'd not be going near either. But Hegarty had told him to meet him here.

Tension grew in his chest, wound through his innards like adders, a brutal reminder of why he'd been so anxious to avoid Scotland, why he'd wanted naught to do with the prophecy again. Why Brenna had to go home. For herself. For her safety.

For his sanity.

This was Hegarty's doing, this attempt to draw him home. Hegarty could try to manipulate him all he wanted, but he would never go near Picktillum again. Not for any reason. If Hegarty did not appear within a day or two, he and Brenna would leave Scotland. Hegarty would have to find *them* if he ever wanted to see her or the sapphire again.

Brenna rode at his back, her slender arms circling his waist. They'd turned over her mount to a pair of travelers soon after they started out. She'd have ridden alone without complaint, but he knew it took a toll on her. And their ride would be short this morning.

As much as he hated to admit it, he had selfish reasons as well. He wanted her close. These might be the last few hours he would have her near if Hegarty was indeed awaiting their arrival.

But the closer they got to Monymusk, the more certain Rourke became that Hegarty wasn't the only one waiting for them. They rode into a trap, he was certain. Cutter and the earl's soldiers would be there.

Brenna could not be with him. He knew what he had to do, though she would be most displeased with him.

Displeased, aye.

But safe.

"That's Monymusk," Rourke said.

Brenna peered around him to get a good look. The small village sat nestled between river and hills. The sun glistened off white stone buildings, most roofed in thatch. In many ways this village resembled the others she'd seen, bustling with activity as people went about their daily business.

Instead of riding into town, Rourke made a wide circle, finally climbing into the low, rocky hills behind.

"What are we doing?" Brenna asked as they dismounted.

"I need to change."

She eyed him with surprised amusement. Last time she looked, he didn't have any luggage.

He saw her expression. "I'll don the plaid." He tied the horse to one of the pines, removed his plaid bundle, then led her up a path in the rocks to the mouth of a small, well-hidden cave. He ducked inside.

"Do you want me to wait out here?"

"Nay. Come in."

Brenna followed him. The cave was small, about the size of her tiny bedroom at home, and well lit since the light found its way into the corners easily enough. The ceiling was high enough for Rourke to stand straight with room to spare.

She stretched her legs as she watched Rourke lay his belt on the ground and the long plaid blanket on top of it, gathered so that it more or less fit the belt.

He pulled off his boots, then unbuttoned his pants, turned his back to her, and dropped them without a single seductive glance or comment. Since she was certain he didn't have a shy bone in his body, she suspected the show of modesty was strictly for her. Of course, his shirt fell halfway to his knees, so it wasn't like he was flashing her in any way. But the shirt was thin and she could tell he wore nothing beneath. A frontal view would have been interesting.

It seemed she was the only one having lecherous thoughts, though. Ever since she'd woken the second time, he'd treated her like a fragile china doll. She'd shaken him up this morning. She'd shaken them both.

Is this how it would end, then? They'd find Hegarty, convince him to send her home, and this would be it? Part of her wanted that desperately. An end to the confusion and chaos. A return to her world, her well-ordered life.

But part of her dreaded the thought of never seeing Rourke again. He'd become important to her so quickly—for obvious reasons. He knew where they were going, how to get food, how to fight with actual weapons. But his importance somehow transcended the obvious.

As she'd told him this morning, he drove out the cold. In a matter of days, they'd formed a bond she couldn't explain. A bond that, at least for her, went far beyond their mutual attraction.

She liked him. A lot. Maybe too much.

And in a matter of hours she might never see him again.

He lay on the plaid, fastening the blanket and belt around him. He then stood and tossed the extra length over his shoulder, tucking it into his belt.

"What think you?"

Oh, man. Braveheart come to life. "Amazing. Instant Highlander. It may be a poor man's garb, but it looks good on you, Pirate." The understatement of the year.

He cocked his head with a small grin. "Do ye think?"

She laughed at the pleasure in his eyes. Her gaze slowly slid down his strong, muscular legs. "Oh yeah."

He reached for her and pulled her lightly against him, then quickly stepped back to keep distance between them even as his hands clasped at her back.

"I wish to kiss ye, lass," he said, his eyes warm silver.

Sweet heat washed through her and she lifted her hands around his neck and pulled his face down to meet hers, but he resisted, taking it slow. He kissed her, lips closed, for long moments, a mere press of one mouth to another.

He was being excruciatingly gentle with her, but the tremors in his hands telegraphed his desire loud and clear. Rather than tell him she wasn't quite so breakable, she showed him, opening her mouth over his and sliding her tongue between his lips.

With a groan, he took her invitation, his mouth slanting over hers, his tongue sweeping inside on a thrust of hot possession.

The heat intensified until her breath was ragged, and her pulse raced. They tasted, devoured one another, her hands deep in his hair, his own becoming more and more frantic as they moved over her back and lower, pressing her against him, against the hard evidence of his arousal.

She pushed her hips against him, wanting the feel of him. *Needing* him.

Rourke wrenched back. He cradled her face and rested his forehead on hers as he took a deep, unsteady breath.

"Forgive me." His tone was worried, regretful. "I lose all reason when I touch you." He lifted his head, his hands sliding over her shoulders and upper arms. "You're shaking."

She met his silver gaze and smiled. "Not from fear." She couldn't hold the smile. "From wanting you."

And she did want him. *Her* way. Slowly, carefully. Her in control. And she had no doubt that he would do that for her—when the time was right.

His eyes drifted closed as he visibly struggled for control. "Ah, Wildcat. Ye slay me." He opened his eyes and gazed at her with such thinly controlled passion, she thought she would melt in his hands.

"I want you more than breath. If you'll have me. If ye can. But now is not the time."

"I know. We have to find Hegarty."

He released her slowly, then grabbed his boots and sat on one of the rocks in the cave to pull them on.

"How fare your feet, Wildcat?"

"My feet?" Not the part of her anatomy that was currently drawing her attention. "They're surviving."

"I wish to see them." He stood and pushed her gently down onto the rock.

Why did she get the feeling he was up to something?

He knelt before her and took first one boot off, then the other, and examined each of her feet.

"You've blisters."

"It's not a problem since we're riding now. I haven't had to walk much."

"Close your eyes."

Brenna narrowed her brows with confusion. "Why?"

He reached up and cupped her jaw with his warm hand. "Trust me."

A smile tugged at her lips. Had he somehow hidden another gift like he had the soap? Comfortable shoes, maybe?

As she closed her eyes, she felt his hands on her ankles, pushing her feet together. Then the brush of rope against the backs of her heels. With a gasp, she realized what he was up to.

"Rourke!" Her eyes flew open and she tried to kick free of the rope, but he was too quick. And too strong. She stared in disbelief as he tightened the knot binding her ankles together.

"What are you doing?"

Rourke stood, his eyes filled with regret as he backed away from her. "Forgive me, Wildcat. I canna take you with me. 'Tis too dangerous. The knot is firm, but you'll cut yourself free quickly enough."

She tried to tear at the rope, but like he said, it was too tight.

"You couldn't simply ask me to stay here?" Her chest hurt, a physical pain.

"Would you have said aye?" His tone told her he already knew the answer. So he would force her. Betray her unquestioning trust.

He backed out of the cave slowly, carefully, shoulders hunched like a man who knew he was destined to live the rest of his life in the doghouse.

Her heart began to pound with unreasoning fear. "Rourke, don't do this! Please don't leave me here like this."

Frantically, she dug at the uncooperative knot, breaking a fingernail down to the quick.

"Cutter and the others are awaiting me in Monymusk. I'll not endanger you again."

"What if he kills you? You'd leave me here to die?"

He turned, the sun sparking golden highlights in his brown hair. "You have a knife, Wildcat. Use it to cut through your bonds, but I'll be away before ye do."

His face filled with regret. "Trust me, lass. I'll return for you. Be here so that I can find you, eh?"

Then he turned and left.

"Rourke! Don't you dare leave me here. I'll kill you, Pirate!"

But he didn't reply. Moments later, the sound of retreating hoofbeats met her ears.

"Damn you!" She cursed him with every word she knew as she lowered herself back onto the rock and dug the knife out from the scabbard strapped to her thigh. As soon as he returned, she'd kick him in the balls so hard he'd never stand straight again. *Then* she'd kill him.

As she worked to cut the heavy rope, fear overwhelmed her anger. What if he didn't come back? What if he'd simply decided she was too much trouble and wanted to be rid of her?

What if they killed him?

The rope came loose in her hands and she ripped it off her ankles and ran out of the cave, but he was already little more than a speck in the distance. She stood there, shaking with the magnitude of her powerlessness, with the utter devastation of his betrayal, until the speck disappeared.

"*Damn* him."

Unshed tears burned her eyes. She'd sworn she would never be helpless again. Now here she was, without a horse, without money. Without Rourke.

What if he never came back?

This was all Hegarty's fault. What right did he have to rip her away from everything she'd worked for? If it weren't for him, she'd be worrying about tomorrow's menu selections, not men trying to kill her. She'd be at the restaurant, or the gym, not trapped in a cave in the hills of seventeenth-century Scotland with no horse. With no pirate.

Alone.

Again.

Anger and apprehension tore at her nerves, shredding her courage and her heart.

She'd trusted him, dammit, and he'd betrayed her. He'd been so gentle this morning. So sweet. Then he'd turned around and stripped the last ounce of control from her fingers. Without asking. Without discussion. He'd made the decision she wasn't coming.

The sun beat warm on her shoulders. Too warm, so she turned with leaden feet and returned to the coolness of the cave. As she sank down onto the rock, her gaze caught the contents of his bundle, wrapped loosely in his discarded pants. He'd left her the food. And her soap.

She pressed her fingers to her closed eyelids.

He hadn't betrayed her. She hated the way he'd handled it, but she knew deep down he'd done it to protect her. He was captain of his ship, used to giving orders. *She* wasn't used to following them, which he knew all too well by now, so he'd avoided the confrontation altogether.

He'd come back for her.

If he could.

She wasn't sure how much time had passed when she first heard it. Faint thunder, but continuous . . . and moving closer.

Horses. More than a couple. Three? Maybe four?

Brenna jumped up and moved toward the mouth of the cave, then stopped. She needed to stay hidden. The pirate knew where to find her. If he wasn't one of the riders, she didn't want to be found.

The pounding of the horse's hooves grew stronger, echoing the beating of her heart. They sounded as if they were coming straight for her.

She dug out her knife.

Please let them go by and not see the cave.

She heard the horses slow, stop. But there were no voices, no sound of men at all.

Moments later shadows darkened the mouth of the cave and three men stepped into the opening, swords drawn. Two wore blue coats. The third man faced her, an evil, leering grin slicing across a heavily pock marked face.

Cutter.

Rourke rode toward Monymusk, his heart heavy as iron. Brenna's green eyes, clouded with confusion, brittle with the knowledge of betrayal, haunted him.

He'd had to do it. There had been no other way.

But the knowing brought no relief to the hollow ache in the pit of his stomach.

As guilt rode his shoulders, he vowed to make it up to her by finding Hegarty and convincing the wee troll to send her back where she belonged. He knew he could do it. He'd want his sapphire, of course, but Hegarty could take her there himself, then return with his gem. And Rourke would insist he did. Brenna needed to be away from here. He wanted her safe.

Ahead rose the familiar sight of the town where he'd spent so many hours as a lad. Here he'd gotten into his first fistfight at the age of seven and stolen his first kiss from pretty Isobel McPherson at the age of nine. Here his mother had taken him for sweet treats and his father had bought him his first knife.

Here, burning with vengeance over a minor injustice, he'd brought the evil of the Earl of Slains down upon them all. The lad within him who was to inherit Picktillum had died that day, twenty years ago. Rourke had spent two-thirds of his life keeping him buried. He was not resurrecting him now.

A pox on Hegarty for his meddling. For all his strange and sly ways, Hegarty poked and prodded him like the worst of fishwives. Indeed, there were times when he'd likely not have survived if Hegarty hadn't appeared, weaving in and out of his life at critical moments.

His knuckles turned white on the reins as he urged the horse forward. He would not find Hegarty by standing out here. And he would not be rid of the ghosts of his past until he accomplished what he'd come for.

As he rode toward the village, he stopped a tall youth leading a cow.

"Slains's soldiers. Are they here?"

The lad's eyes widened. "Nay. Are they comin'?"

"Aye. I fear so." Had he gotten here ahead of them? As ready as he was to fight Cutter to the death, it was far better to snatch Hegarty and be away before the soldiers' arrival.

"Och, 'tis a dark day, then." The lad tugged harder on the cow's lead, hurrying away.

As Rourke continued toward the village, he wondered if he'd truly beaten them here or if the trap they'd laid for him was farther out. They were likely watching the roads into town. The main road from the east, in particular. But Rourke and Brenna had circled around and Rourke had entered town from the west. They'd not have been expecting that. Mayhap his fortunes were beginning to turn.

The village bustled with activity, people scurrying about their business before the dark clouds on the horizon dumped their rain. Monymusk was much as he remembered, though smaller somehow. He'd grown since then.

Without giving conscious thought to his destination, Rourke found himself before the door of Jamie McBean's, his favorite shop as a lad. Memory crashed over him. He wanted nothing to do with the place, but even as the thought pounded through his brain, his hands and knees urged his mount forward, directly toward the shop. As if pulled by an invisible force, he dismounted and tied up his horse, then climbed the stairs to the merchant's.

A small bell tinkled as he pushed through the door. Memories assailed him with the familiar scents of new linen, tangy cinnamon, and spun wool. His gaze took in the shelves stocked high with fabrics in every weight and hue. Everything from ribbons and buttons to caps and spectacles lined the shelves. A glass case in the back was filled with sweet candies as it always had been.

He had a sudden vivid memory of walking into this shop, his father beside him—the viscount and his whelp. The shopkeep had treated them like royalty, offering Rourke a piece of candy—a cinnamon drop, his favorite.

The memory was painful, but strangely pleasing, for he'd long ago banished such thoughts from his mind. The good years. The happy years. Long, long gone.

The shopkeep of his memory stepped out of the back, wiping his hands on his apron. He'd aged much over the intervening years. His once dark hair was now white and thinning. But as he adjusted his spectacles and peered at Rourke, he somehow seemed the same as he'd always been.

"Can I help ye?"

"Mr. McBean."

"Aye." The man squinted, eyeing him with faint recognition. "Do I know ye?"

Rourke suddenly regretted speaking the name aloud. "Nay. I'm looking for a man. He's—"

"Rourke," the man said suddenly, a grin blooming on his weathered face, revealing large gaps in the rows of his teeth. "It's ye, isn't it? All growed up. We heard ye was alive."

Before he could answer, he heard the sound of footfalls on the steps outside. Grabbing his sword, he turned as a matronly woman entered the shop behind him.

"Maggie!" McBean exclaimed. "Ye'll ne'er guess—"

Rourke shoved his sword back in its scabbard and hooked his arm around the old proprietor's shoulders. "I have need of a word with ye." He led the man into the back of the shop.

When they were out of earshot of the store, he turned the man to face him. "No one must know I'm here."

"Are ye in trouble, lad?"

"Aye, in a manner of speaking. I'm looking for a man. A dwarf, about this high." He held his hand even with the bottom of his rib cage. "Red hair. You'd know if you'd seen him, aye?"

The proprietor scratched his chin. "I havena seen such a creature, but I'll ask around for ye, if ye'd like."

"I havena much time."

"Yer sure he's here?"

Rourke sighed. "He told me to meet him here, but nay. I'm sure of nothing."

The shopkeep started toward the front, motioning Rourke. "Maggie will know. Maggie McCloud knows everything that goes on in this town, oft before it happens."

With reluctance, Rourke followed him back to the front where the wide-girthed woman admired a collection of ribbon. She looked at Rourke with great interest as McBean approached her.

"Have ye seen any strange little men in town in the past days, Maggie? This lord is searching for a redheaded dwarf, if ye can be believing such a creature exists."

The woman eyed Rourke with interest. "A lord, are ye? Och, and ye have the Douglas eyes." She peered at him suspiciously. "Are ye of the castle then?"

"Nay," Rourke said curtly. If he was not careful, the entire village would soon know of his arrival. "The dwarf, mistress. I would know if you've seen him."

"Well, now, I've seen no such creature." Her eyes narrowed thoughtfully. "Though 'tis said there's something strange going on at the Wellerby cottage. For two nights now, passersby have heard laughter and cackling, and strange, eerie singing, but when they've knocked, Old Inghinn refuses them in. Says she's entertaining none but herself."

Rourke turned to the merchant. He remembered the cottage. "Is hers still on the north road?"

"Aye. Ye'll know it by the red door."

Rourke thanked him and leaned close. "Say naught, I beg of you."

Mr. McBean nodded unhappily. "'Tis time you came home, laddie."

Rourke shook his head. "I cannot." He turned, and with a polite nod to the matron, left the shop, the bell tinkling after him. Keenly alert for signs of Cutter or the soldiers, he mounted and kept to the side streets as he made his way through the town.

The Wellerby cottage stood much as he remembered. As a lad, he'd heard it said a witch lived there. A fitting place to find Hegarty, to be sure.

The red door stood open. A toothless old crone perched on a stool out front, beneath a large elm, plucking a hen. Two cats played at her feet.

"Excuse me," Rourke said when he reached the low, gated wall. "Are ye Inghinn, perchance?"

The woman eyed him balefully. "And who would be askin'?"

"I'm looking for a friend. A man by the name of Hegarty. About this high, red hair."

"I havena seen anyone." She went back to her plucking.

"Old mistress, if ye do meet such a man, will ye tell him Rourke got his missive and awaits him? 'Tis most urgent I find him."

To his surprise, she met his gaze. "What stone does yer lass wear?"

"My lass?"

"Aye."

Stone? *Of course.* Hegarty *had* been here. "A sapphire, mistress."

The woman nodded. "'Tis time that one returned, though I'll have Hegarty's hide if'n he doesna get me my amethyst. You'll be coming inside, then, to await his return."

Rourke went through the gate. "He's not here?"

"Nay. He'll return this eve." She eyed him sharply. "Where is the lass?"

"Safe."

Before the red door she stopped and looked at him with shrewd eyes, a touch of pity in their depths. "Nay, lad. She's not."

"I assure you . . ." But even as he said the words, cold seeped into his veins. The woman before him was a friend of Hegarty's with all his unnatural ways. A witch.

"You know she's not safe."

"Aye."

His blood turned to ice.

Without a word he turned and ran for his mount. Cutter and the soldiers weren't awaiting him as he'd expected. They must have been trailing them.

Brenna.

He vaulted into the saddle and urged the horse into a run. Dirt flew out behind as they shot down the lane. Brenna was well hidden. Cutter wouldn't find her. *Please don't let them find her.*

Villagers ran for safety as he rode at a full gallop back through the center of town. Never had the miles passed so slowly as they did as he raced back toward the hills. Finally, he reached the track leading to the cave and noted the recent marks of multiple horses. His heart plummeted.

Rourke drew his sword, rode up the path, and dismounted, approaching silently. No sound met his ears. He swung into the cave. Empty.

"Wildcat!"

But even as the word echoed off the walls, he saw it. The large pool of fresh blood lying on the floor.

"*Nay.*" They had not killed her. He would not let it be so.

She had a knife. Maybe she had sorely injured one of her attackers before being dragged away. It was her attacker's blood he saw. Not hers.

It cannot be hers.

But as he scanned the cave, he caught sight of her knife lying discarded, clean and unused. He could not even hope she'd gone after him, for not far from the knife lay the food he'd left with her. And her soap.

His throat ached with despair. His fingers closed around the soap and he lifted it to his nose to drink in the clean scent of heather that had enveloped her that day. The joy in her eyes at the simple gift swam in his memory, mocking him.

Fury, raw and primitive, rose up to choke him. He'd been a fool to leave her alone. Unprotected. In a fit of self-loathing, he threw the soap against the wall, shattering it, then strode from the cave.

Cutter would die this day. They all would, every last man.

He leaped onto his mount and took off in a spray of dust, vowing to find her. He'd not give up until she was back in his arms.

Even if there was naught left to be done but bury her.

ELEVEN

The wind slashed at Rourke's face, whipping his hair into his eyes, driving stinging rain across his cheeks as he rode his mount hard over the moors. The tracks that led from the cave had skirted the main road and cut toward the northeast. He continued in the direction the tracks had begun, though now the rain obscured any sign of the horses. All he could do was pray he followed correctly, for the alternative was not worth thinking about.

His hands clenched the reins tighter, his palms sore from the bite of the leather. His jaw ached. His heart thudded, pounding a desperate beat in rhythm with the racing horse.

Brenna. Brenna. Brenna.

He had to find her before the soldiers reached the Earl of Slains. Before they killed her.

If she wasn't dead already.

Guilt devoured him. He deserved to hang, to be drawn and quartered, his entrails shoved down his throat. Brenna's cry would haunt him for the rest of his days. *Rourke, don't do this! Please don't leave me here like this.* He'd seen the fear in her eyes just before it dissolved into a warrior's promise of vengeance. But he'd ignored her demand as he had her plea, arrogantly sure of the rightness of his actions. He'd left her tied and helpless.

No, not helpless. The wildcat had taken down half his crew with her bare hands. She was never helpless.

He clung to that thought like a drowning sailor to a useless splinter of driftwood. He'd seen the blood. Blood her knife had not drawn.

As the landscape before him rose in a gradual slope, he rode on. Cresting the hill, he saw movement far below.

Blue-coated riders. *Soldiers.*

The rain grew stronger, slashing sideways as if even the wind sought to punish him. Drops obscured his vision.

He swiped the water from his eyes as he urged his mount faster. Three horses. Only two riders, and neither of them Brenna. Or Cutter.

It was not them. He'd not found them after all.

Despair crashed over him like a storm wave.

Where is she?

He was soaked to the skin and chilled from the inside out. These were not the soldiers he sought. But even as the thought went through his head, he noticed something curious. The third horse was not riderless. Across the saddle hung a third, blue-coated figure.

Lifeless.

Hope flickered within him. Could the blood in the cave belong to the dead soldier? The hope was doused moments later as he caught sight of a flash of white bobbing near the knee of one of the riders. A lady's cap still upon the head of the lady.

Brenna. He was sure of it. But she was as limp and lifeless as the dead soldier draping the third horse.

Blood pounded in his head. Denial flashed quick and hot through his brain. She was not dead.

But even as the denial sliced through him, so did the rage, white-hot, liquid fire.

He urged his mount into a full gallop and raced down the hillside, the wind lifting the edges of his sodden plaid, sending the last remnants of the stinging rain over his thighs. He pulled his sword and lifted it high as bloodlust raced savagely through him, making him feel as wild and barbarous as his Highland ancestors.

One of the soldiers must have heard him for he turned, spotted him, then called to his companion. As the soldier holding Brenna urged his mount into a run, to escape, the other turned to fight.

Rourke gave free rein to the war cry that had been building in his chest since he saw them. His enemy pulled his gun and fired, but the shot went wide. The soldier drew his sword instead.

Rourke could ill afford to fight the man. Not with Brenna's captor disappearing with her over the next rise. He shoved his sword into his scabbard and pulled his gun.

He had one chance, one shot.

He aimed at the soldier who'd tried to kill him, and fired. Rourke did not miss. The man flew from the saddle and plummeted to the ground. His now riderless horse danced skittishly into the mount carrying the dead soldier.

Without slowing, Rourke shoved the spent gun into his belt and took off after Brenna and her assailant. He bent low, urging his mount on, cresting the rise to see them below. The distance slowly closed between them.

The wind blew wet strands of hair across his face as anguish tore another cry from his lungs. "Brenna!"

If she were conscious she would have heard him. He prayed for some sign that she had, for some movement, but saw nothing to give him hope.

He started to draw his sword, then hesitated. How was he to swing with Brenna's prone form within his striking arc? Every thrust, every strike, would endanger her.

But even as he slammed his sword back into its scabbard, deciding he could not risk it, the soldier circled his mount to face Rourke's oncoming charge and he had no choice but to defend himself.

The soldier raced toward him, his face alight with battle, his sword held high, Brenna's lifeless form across his lap. The clash of metal against metal rang over the heath as Rourke parried blow for blow. He was stronger than his opponent, but never had he fought with such fear that his blade stroke would be too long, would pierce that which he did not intend. The sooner he ended the clash, the better.

With a quick, hard swipe, he knocked the sword out of the soldier's hand. But the man was quick. Before Rourke could finish what he'd begun, the soldier pulled his dagger and raised it, point down, over Brenna's back.

"Drop your weapon or I'll kill her." The hard look in the man's eyes gave Rourke no doubt he would indeed.

But the man's words sang through him: *kill her.* He could not kill a woman who was already dead.

Hope flared.

He tossed his sword to the ground, but in the same move, whipped out his small eating knife and flung it. The knife buried itself cleanly in the soldier's arm, whipping it back, sending the dagger that threatened Brenna's life flying.

As the soldier cried out, Rourke pulled his own dagger and hurled it, end over end, burying it deep in the soldier's chest.

He leaped off his mount and grabbed Brenna before the dying soldier knocked her off and crushed her beneath him. Narrowly missing the man's arcing boot, he pulled her safely into his arms and backed away. The scent of bile filled his nostrils and he knew why when he saw her stomach's meager contents streaked down the forelegs of the soldier's mount.

Cradled against his chest, she groaned, the sound melting the fear that had encased his heart since he'd found the blood.

"Wildcat." He pulled her tight against him, burying his face in the curve of her neck, inhaling her warm scent.

As he laid her on a patch of soft, rain-pearled clover, he caught sight of the dark bruise on her cheek and the swell of her bloody lip. Rage sliced through him all over again and he was suddenly sorry he'd killed the two soldiers. He would happily kill them all over again, slowly this time. Painfully.

Sliding his hand out from beneath her head, he saw the blood. His hand came away streaked with thin stripes of red.

Her eyes fluttered open. "Rourke?"

"Aye, lass. 'Tis me. You are safe now."

"I think I'm going to throw up again." She tried to roll over and he helped her onto her side as she heaved what little was left in her innards onto the ground.

He wiped her mouth on his wet sleeve and helped her sit up.

Brenna sneezed, then sneezed again. She was as soaked as he from the rain, but she was injured and far more fragile. Her wounds needed tending. What she needed above all else was a dry gown and a warm bed. Food. And safety.

He closed his eyes against the knowledge of what he must do, then took a deep breath and lifted her carefully into his arms. Setting her on his mount, he swung up behind her and cradled her in his lap, then turned the horse toward Monymusk. He would take her where he should have this morning. The one place she would have been safe. The last place he wanted to go.

Picktillum Castle.
Home.

"Did you find Hegarty?"

Rourke glanced at the woman tucked against his chest, half hidden by the plaid he'd thrown around her. She'd slept fitfully during most of their long ride back to Monymusk, but now her green eyes peered out at him from the wool.

"Nay. I will go back another time," he told her. "How do you feel?"

"Like I've been used as the puck in a hockey game, but I think I'm through throwing up."

He didn't know what a hockey game was, but from her strained tone understood that she hurt. "Forgive me, Wildcat. I shouldna have left you behind."

She shuddered and leaned against him, as if seeking protection from what she'd endured. "Remind me to kick you in the balls when I feel better."

He smiled and pulled her closer. "I shall. 'Tis the least of what I deserve." He stroked her arm, offering the comfort he'd stolen from her when he'd deserted her.

Slowly they made their way up the steep track to Picktillum. The rain was through, but the sky remained as gray as death and the wind tore at his hair. Though he'd kept a keen eye out, he'd seen no sign of Cutter.

"Wildcat . . . was Cutter with the soldiers who took ye?"

Her head moved against him, but he could not tell which direction. "He tried to kill me."

"He was the one who clouted you?"

She stiffened, but instead of pressing closer, she straightened, pulling away. "No. Soon after you left, Cutter and the three bluecoats showed up. They rode right up to the cave as if they knew I was there. I think the bluecoats wanted to capture me for the earl. Cutter just wanted to kill me."

Rourke ran his hand down her back, needing to touch her, to reassure himself his Judas of a bosun had not succeeded.

She glanced up at him, meeting his gaze. "He pulled his knife and started toward me, but one of the bluecoats stopped him. He said the earl wanted me delivered unharmed." Her expression turned wry. "What fun is killing me if I'm already dead?"

She sighed and leaned back against him. "Cutter has a real ego problem. When the bluecoat pushed him away from me, Cutter killed him. Shoved his dagger right into his chest. The other two bluecoats turned on him, and he took off running."

"He escaped?"

Brenna shrugged. "I was more concerned with getting away than worrying about what happened to him. I almost made it. Unfortunately, they saw me before I could get the horse in gear."

"The soldiers stopped you."

"One of them yanked me out of the saddle and backhanded me." She touched her injured cheek. "Then he hit me in the mouth and sent me flying. I remember falling on the rocks, but nothing after that."

"Ye hit your head."

"Yeah, I guess. It feels more like they took a jackhammer to it."

"I killed them, Wildcat. I killed both the soldiers."

"But not Cutter."

"Nay. I never saw him."

He felt her stiffen again. "He might be waiting for us back at the cave."

"We are not going to the cave."

She pulled away and looked up at him. "But your pants are there. And my soap."

He'd shattered her soap in his self-anger. "We'll get them later."

She slowly leaned back against him and lapsed into silence as he pushed the mount forward along the muddy, puddled track. As they climbed, his gaze was drawn to the painfully familiar stronghold at the summit. Picktillum Castle stood over the glen, looking the same as it always had despite the fire he'd fled twenty years ago.

He'd imagined the castle destroyed. Had it been rebuilt so perfectly? Its pink harled stone glistened with rain, more welcoming than he could have imagined. It beckoned him, promising sanctuary and peace.

Sudden, intense longing blindsided him, along with a wave of excruciating homesickness. He hadn't known—hadn't realized—how much he'd missed the place. How had he not known?

Maybe he had. It was why he'd stayed away. He'd known all along he wanted to go home. But he could never undo the past.

He ran an unsteady hand over his eyes, wanting only to escape as he had for so many years. "I need to get back to sea," he said fervently.

"You miss the ocean," Brenna murmured.

"'Tis where I belong. If I had my gold . . . 'Tis no matter. I dinna need money to go back to sea."

As his gaze drank in the sight of the castle, he wondered at the reception he would receive after all these years. For nineteen winters they'd thought him dead. 'Twas not until a year ago they'd learned the truth when his father's youngest brother recognized him in London and sent the glad tidings of Rourke's survival back to Scotland.

A letter from his eldest uncle, James, had quickly found its way into Rourke's hands. In it, his uncle had expressed joy at his nephew's survival and begged Rourke to return home. Though he'd stated his heartfelt wish to welcome Rourke back into the clan, a man's words and a man's deeds were oft different things.

And Rourke knew he deserved no homecoming.

The horse ambled beneath him, splashing through the mud. His kin would take him in this day with or without welcome. Brenna needed refuge and protection and he would walk through the very fires of hell to see that she got them. He owed her that much.

The rain began to fall once more as they approached the familiar gates of his childhood home. Like the village, the castle seemed smaller than he remembered. Thick stone walls joined the four towers that made up the corners of the fortress. Three rectangular towers and the single round one with the conical roof that had housed the laird and his family in the old days.

"Who goes there?" the sentry called from high atop the wall. The long-faced man looked familiar, yet not quite, like a reflection of a friend shimmering on a not-quite-still loch.

"Angus?" Rourke replied. "Is that you?"

"Aye, and who be asking?"

Rourke stared up at his childhood playmate, now a man. A strange stillness dropped over him, a sudden, deep reluctance. He could turn and ride away and none would ever know he'd been here.

Brenna sneezed.

"'Tis I. Rourke."

"Rourke? *Rourke?*" The man let out a whoop of joy. "Open the gates! Lord Kinross has returned!"

Brenna stiffened in his arms. "*Lord?*" She glanced up at him, her eyes round.

A shudder tore through him. "Aye."

"You own this place?"

If things had been different. If *he* had been different. "'Twas my father's."

She shifted in his arms, meeting his gaze. "Why are you a pirate if you own a castle?"

Leave it to Brenna to cut to the heart of the matter. He kissed her hair. "I'm not a pirate."

The gates opened on loud, squeaky hinges and people began slipping through. Men, women, and children alike ran to greet him, heedless of the rain and mud, their faces full of welcome, their eyes filled with tears. He tensed as if for battle as the people swarmed around him, their faces familiar, yet not.

One stooped old man peered up at him suspiciously. "Rourke, is it ye, lad?" Finlay, the blacksmith. He'd always had patience with Rourke when he'd slip inside the warmth of the smithy to watch, loving the way the man could make things out of what seemed like nothing. Horseshoes, kettles, even keys, out of molten iron. 'Twas the blacksmith who'd taught him to whittle, sensing in him a need to make creations of his own.

Rourke met the old man's gaze. "'Tis I, Finlay."

"Of course 'tis him," an older women said. The old henwife, if he was not mistaken. "'Tis the spitting image of his father, he is. Just look at those eyes."

"All these years we thought ye lost. They told us last summer ye'd been found, but I didna believe." Tears began to run down Finlay's weathered cheeks. "I didna believe."

He'd not be shedding tears if he knew the truth. If he knew what had really happened twenty years ago, he'd be spitting on his lord's feet instead.

Brenna's head felt like someone had taken a hatchet to it.

She nestled tight against Rourke's warm chest as the crowd of people swept the pair through the gates and into the castle's courtyard. The people were laughing and crying, treating the pirate like a returning hero. If streamers and colorful confetti had been invented, Brenna was sure they'd be cascading down from the high towers.

Rourke swung off the horse and pulled her into his arms.

"I can walk," Brenna protested. She wasn't a complete invalid, despite the rock band jamming on her head.

But Rourke ignored her. She levered herself into a better position to watch, looping her arm around his neck, feeling his soft hair brush her knuckles. The movement caused a small groan to vibrate through her nose as pain shot up the back of her skull. *Bad, bad headache.*

Rourke gripped her tighter as people gathered around them like paparazzi on a movie star. She half expected them to start whipping out cameras . . . or shoving pens and paper at him for his autograph. The tension running through him told her he expected even worse.

This wasn't the fairy-tale homecoming it might look like from a distance. She didn't understand what was going on, but she did know the man who held her—the pirate who could set his crew to cowering with a single look—was edgy as a new waiter the first night on the job.

The lord of the castle was not happy to be home.

A man pushed his way through the crowd toward them, the same one who'd first shouted from the wall. Tall and thin as a needle, he moved with the tightly controlled movements of a well-trained athlete.

He slapped Rourke on the back. "Welcome, old friend. Your uncle will be most pleased ye've returned, as we all are."

"I would speak with him," Rourke said tightly. "But first I must see to my lady's well-being. She's injured and in need of a dry gown."

"Then come."

"Rourke!" A very pregnant woman in an expensive-looking red gown pushed through the crowd and grabbed his arm. "It *is* you." She slugged him on the upper arm.

"How could ye not have told us where ye were? All those years ye let us think the soldiers had kilt ye."

"Kerrie, ye've still an arm on ye, lass."

Brenna watched tears fill the woman's eyes—eyes the same pale shade as Rourke's. She was pretty, with delicate features and blond curls to die for.

"Where were you, laddie?"

"'Tis a long story." Rourke's tone was weary, yet filled with affection.

"One you'll be telling us right enough." Kerrie dashed at the tears on her cheeks and peered at Brenna with both curiosity and welcome. "Is this your wife?"

"Nay." The word came out like a shot. "She is . . . the Lady Marie."

Brenna caught her breath on a laugh. He'd named her for his ship. Now *that* was a switch.

Kerrie peered at her bruised cheek and clucked her tongue. "Thrown from a horse, were you?"

"Aye," Rourke said.

Clearly, he wasn't ready to enlighten his family about either her or their situation, just as he'd failed to enlighten her about *their* existence. Was he intentionally keeping secrets, or just being a man?

"I thought the castle burned." Rourke carried her across the courtyard, accompanied by what seemed to be half the population of Scotland. She felt the brush of his rough stubble against her hair as he looked around.

"The south range went up," Angus said. "But the storm kept the fire from spreading to the towers."

Brenna could see no sign of a fire at all. High stone walls surrounded a courtyard far smaller than Stour's. Or, at least, far more crowded. Then again, the Stour she'd seen in the twenty-first century had been a ruin. Other than the single restored tower, nothing had been left of it but the stone.

Picktillum was still in its heyday, a fully functioning castle. Against the inner walls stood more than a dozen small buildings, almost like a small village tucked within the castle's walls. But these structures, made of wood, wouldn't survive the centuries. By her time, nothing would be left but the stone shell. If that.

They entered the nearest tower by way of a long outdoor stairway. Rourke swept her into a dimly lit entryway, then followed Kerrie up a narrow, curved stairwell off to the right. As the stair turned and turned, Brenna was suddenly very glad she didn't have to walk. She was getting vertigo just being carried.

Finally, they moved into a hallway to the open door of a pretty blue and yellow bedroom. An old-fashioned four-poster bed sat in the middle of the room, hung with floral bed curtains. The walls were covered in cheerfully elegant yellow and white wallpaper.

The room had a slightly old and musty smell as if it hadn't been used in a while. Then again, without central air and heat, maybe it smelled this way all the time.

Kerrie turned to them. "This will be Marie's room, Cousin. I will fetch clothing for the both of you. Will your own things be following you?"

"Nay. We have naught but what we wear." He looked down at her. "Would ye like a hot bath, Wildcat?"

At her gasp of delight, a smile lit his eyes, crinkling the corners for the space of a couple of seconds.

Kerrie put her hand on Rourke's arm. "I'll have baths sent up to both your chambers. Since you've admitted she's not your lady wife, you'll not be sharing her chambers, my cousin." She laughed and turned away. "Put her down and come along, Rourke. Though I should call you Kinross now. I'll show you to your chamber."

"I'll be there forthwith. I would speak with my lady alone."

Kerrie turned back, her mouth opened as if to argue. Then her gaze moved between the two of them, and she rolled her eyes with a wry smile.

"Aye, have your time alone. I'll send for the baths."

Brenna smiled at the woman. "Thank you, Kerrie."

Kerrie grinned at her, tears suddenly sparkling in her gray eyes. "'Tis a great day, this. A muckle great day." Then she turned her pregnant bulk and made her way from the room, closing the door behind her.

As the latch clicked, Rourke buried his face in Brenna's hair. She felt an earthquake of a shudder rip through him.

"That bad, huh?" She reached up and stroked his hair.

"Aye."

"You never intended to come home, did you?"

He didn't answer. He didn't have to. Instead, he carried her to an upholstered chair before the cold fireplace and lowered her carefully, then went to tend the hearth.

She watched him, admiring his strong profile, the jut of his chin, the line of his straight nose. He was a good-looking man. An amazing man, really. A sea captain. A warrior. Yet there was something in the bend of his shoulders as he lit the already-laid fire that made him seem lost somehow.

"Why haven't you ever come home, Rourke?"

"I dinna wish to speak of it, Wildcat." Despite a heavy dose of weariness, his voice brooked no argument. He turned to look at her. "Dinna tell them who you are or where you're from. I dinna think any of my kin would hurt you, but I've not been here for a long time and there may be those loyal to Slains. In the morn, I'll seek Hegarty."

Brenna nodded, waiting for the familiar rush of relief at the thought of finally going home, but all that came was a trickle. Gumming the flow was a pervasive melancholy at the thought of leaving the pirate. She couldn't stay here. She didn't want to stay here. But the thought of never seeing him again lodged like a rock beneath her breastbone. As badly as she wanted to go home, she had a feeling she'd be leaving a piece of herself behind.

Once he had the fire going, Rourke came to squat in front of her, his gaze doing a serious inspection of her face.

"How do ye fare?"

The concern in his voice was mirrored in his eyes. His worry warmed her. It had been a long time since anyone had worried about her.

"I'm okay. My head hurts, but not too bad."

Rourke nodded, his eyes shadowed. He rose and scooped her up, then settled on the chair with her on his lap. He pulled her head against his shoulder, silently willing her to settle against him as he stroked her hair.

Tears pricked her eyes at his gentleness, at the sweet caring of his touch, and she melted against him in absolute trust. If only she could stay here, just like this, forever.

"After your bath I wish ye to rest until I fetch you for supper. We'll go down together." Something in his tone told her that facing all those people over the dinner table was going to be an ordeal of the first order for him.

She lifted her hand and stroked his cheek, needing to return some small measure of the comfort he offered her. "They love you, you know."

She felt a faint tremor go through him as he looked down at her. "Aye. 'Tis the worst of it." His gaze searched hers as if he sought answers to questions he wouldn't ask.

Lifting her head, she reached up and framed his lightly stubbled face, a face she was coming to adore. As she leaned toward him, he met her halfway. The kiss was chaste and exquisitely gentle. A mere press of lips, yet so much more. It was as if they were joined beyond the physical. As if in this simplest of touches they'd opened a small conduit between their innermost selves.

She felt him shudder and gather her tight against him, his body shaking with emotion she didn't understand, an emotion all the more powerful for its desperate silence. He needed her, as she needed him. But it was a need that went beyond the flesh. He clung to her as if she alone could save him from his demons.

Tears stung her eyes. Her chest filled with emotion until she could hardly breathe for the pressure. And she knew.

She'd fallen in love with a pirate. A man from the wrong century. A man who could never be hers.

God help her.

TWELVE

Brenna watched in the mirror as Kerrie's clever hands slowly transformed a twenty-first-century assistant restaurant manager into a woman who belonged in a painting in an art museum. Less the bruised cheek and fat lip, of course.

Kerrie had found a beautiful gown for her to wear—a green silk that was a bit low-cut, but which set off her complexion to a T. Forget the painting. She felt like a princess.

Kerrie had shooed the servant away and now rolled fat locks of hair on an old-fashioned curling iron, one she'd heated beside the hearth instead of plugging into an electrical outlet. The woman was warm and funny, regaling Brenna with tales of Rourke as a small boy. He'd always been too serious, she said, as if weighed down by his looming responsibilities from a tender age.

"How long have you known my cousin?" Kerrie asked as she set the iron beside the now roaring fire and began to pin Brenna's hair in place.

Long enough to fall in love with him.

Denial raced behind. No, she didn't love him. She was just . . . dependent upon him. That was all. This kind of thing happened to kidnap victims all the time. It was documented. Plus, he was a nice guy who just happened to be incredibly attractive. No wonder she thought she was in love with him.

Even if she were, it wouldn't matter. They had no future. She was going back to her own time, and he had eyes only for the sea.

Brenna realized Kerrie was still waiting for an answer. "I haven't known Rourke long. I became separated from my . . . guardian . . . and he's helping me track him down."

The woman was too curious by far. She'd kept Brenna company while she bathed, firing off questions worthy of a FOX News reporter. Where was Brenna from? Who were her kin? Were she and Rourke . . . involved? So far, Brenna had either managed to come up with false answers—she was Lady Marie Osmond from Castle Utah—or dodge the questions with vagueness, but she couldn't keep this up forever.

"I've not heard of Castle U-tah," Kerrie murmured as she worked Brenna's hair. "Is it far from here?"

"Very." She had to get the woman onto a different track. "So, when was Picktillum Castle built? I'd love to know its history."

Kerrie complied and rambled away as she finished dressing Brenna's hair, giving Brenna a welcome respite from the interview.

Brenna closed her eyes, letting Kerrie work. She was feeling better, having slept most of the afternoon after the most wonderful bath of her life. The tub had been small and the water cooler than she preferred, but after her dip in the freezing cold stream, it had felt like heaven.

Kerrie had woken her when she brought a gown and

accessories to dress her for supper. More clothes than Brenna had ever worn at one time, with all the under whatchamacallits and outer thingamajigs. Surprisingly, the thing she'd been most worried about—the corset—wasn't bad. Really nothing more than a long, stiff bra. It was snug, but not uncomfortably tight.

Kerrie was still talking when a rap sounded at the door.

Brenna turned and gaped as Rourke ducked into the room. He was breathtaking. Dressed in what she supposed was the height of current fashion—pants that ended just below his knees, thin socks that molded to his muscular calves, a royal blue coat that fell to midthigh—he looked the part of the gentleman pirate. More handsome than any movie star. He'd shaved and bathed and his thick hair now hung loose and clean around his shoulders.

"Och, Cousin," Kerrie exclaimed. "You're a fine-looking man." She turned to Brenna with a grin. "Is he not?"

All Brenna could do was nod as her gaze met Rourke's and held.

Kerrie laughed. "I'll return forthwith." She patted Rourke's sleeve and disappeared out the door.

Brenna drank in the sight of him. "You do look wonderful, Pirate."

"And you." His silver gaze slid slowly over her gown, then up to her face and hair. Raw male appreciation sparkled in his eyes. "As bonnie as ever a woman born."

Brenna stood and ran her hands over the slick softness of her silk skirt. "It's a pretty gown."

Rourke crossed the room and took her hands. "Aye. The dress is bonnie." He lifted one hand and kissed her knuckles. "But 'tis the woman who steals my breath." No laughter tugged at his mouth. No teasing. The heat in his eyes told her he meant every word.

Hot awareness shimmered through her. A blush warmed her cheeks. "Thank you. That's quite a compliment for someone with a fat lip."

His mouth quirked into a small half smile and he cupped her jaw, running his thumb, featherlight, across the cut. "Your lips are perfect, lass. *You* are perfect."

Her heart jolted even as she shivered at the sweet intimacy of his touch. His warm, male scent wrapped around her.

"You smell good, Pirate."

His smile deepened as he dipped his head to kiss her.

"Enough of that," Kerrie scolded. "I havena finished her hair and your uncle James awaits you both in the Laird's Hall."

Rourke pulled away, his hand lingering on her cheek, his eyes liquid silver, filled with promise. Kerrie pushed between them and he stepped back, but didn't go far. He crossed his arms over his chest and stood beside the hearth to watch.

"Sit ye down, lassie." Kerrie ushered Brenna back to her stool. "'Twill take but a moment."

Kerrie chattered about the fuss being made over the evening's supper as Brenna met Rourke's gaze in the mirror. The heat in his eyes melted her insides until she thought she'd slide off the stool into a single puddle.

"There, now," Kerrie declared. "Ready at last." She turned to Rourke. "And a fitting companion to you, Cousin."

As Brenna stood and turned around, Rourke crossed to her and held out his arm.

She smiled at him cheekily. "I never thought I'd see you playing the part of the gentleman." She'd meant to tease him, but the shadow that stole across his face told her she'd said the wrong thing.

Rourke escorted her in silence down one turnstile stair and up another to a large, sumptuously appointed room. The walls were covered in rich red, trimmed in gilt, and adorned with all manner of crests and shields and weapons. In the center of the room stood a massive dining table, beautifully set with silver utensils, china plates, and crystal goblets.

People milled about, talking and laughing until they noticed the two of them standing in the doorway. The room quieted. One by one, all heads turned their way. Rourke's hand tightened its hold on hers, which was tucked into the crook of his arm.

A stately looking older gentleman, dressed similarly to Rourke, with a wig of long black curls, came toward them. His bearing contained an aura of power and aged masculinity, but in his eyes, she saw only kindness. And joy.

When he reached them, he broke into a grin and slapped Rourke on the back. "Good saints, it's good to have you back, lad. I feel years younger just looking at you." The shadows of melancholy dulled the edges of his smile. "The image of your father, you know."

He turned to her, his grin turning bright again as he took her hand and bent low over it.

"Your taste in women is as fine as my brother's was, Kinross."

"The Lady Marie, Uncle."

"Charmed, my lady. I am most pleased to welcome you to Picktillum." His gaze swiveled back to Rourke. "As pleased as I am to have the viscount back where he belongs."

Brenna's gaze flew to Rourke. "*Viscount?*"

She felt him stiffen.

Rourke's uncle chuckled. "He didna tell you?"

"Uh . . . no. He must have forgotten to mention it."

"'Twould seem he has forgotten much of his heritage." He slapped Rourke on the back once more. "'Tis time we ate, aye? We will talk over dinner." He led the way to the table and motioned for Rourke to take the large chair at the head.

Rourke stilled. "Nay, Uncle. That seat is yours."

"Only while you were away, lad. I've merely been keeping it warm."

Brenna could feel Rourke's tension as if it were her own. He didn't want to be the laird of Picktillum, let alone the viscount. He hadn't even wanted to come home. She wished she knew why.

Rourke gave in and seated her on his right, then slowly took the large chair at the head of the table. The rest of the assemblage sat, then burst into conversation as if nothing had happened.

Moments later, the far doors opened to the wonderful smells of roasted meat. Servants carried platter upon platter into the room, circling the table as they served the diners with silent precision.

Impressive, Brenna thought. She eyed the variety of dishes with delight, though her eyebrow rose over a platter of small birds, fully cooked with heads and feathers attached. A special treat to celebrate the homecoming of the lord, or the usual dinner fare? She wondered if she'd have time to explore the kitchens before she left. She was dying to see how they prepared the birds.

This was her first real taste of seventeenth-century cooking. What had passed for meals these past few days hardly counted—beef jerky, cheese, and oatcakes.

She served herself from a platter of fragrant roast lamb. "Now *this* is food."

Rourke nodded, but there was no anticipation in his expression, no pleasure in his eyes. He remained tense and rigid.

Beneath the table, she patted his knee, then dug into the sumptuous meal. Brenna marveled at the strangeness of some dishes and the utter familiarity of others, intrigued by the food almost as much as the people. The women were beautifully gowned, their dresses all on a par with the one Kerrie had loaned her. The men were dressed in the same style as Rourke, about half sporting wigs like his uncle's.

She felt strangely detached as she watched them, as if she weren't part of the scene at all, but only viewing from the audience. She still found it hard to fathom she was in the past. Everything was so strange, yet so real.

Beside her, Angus reached for something and knocked his goblet over, sending red wine halfway across the table. In the opposite direction from her, fortunately. He cursed roundly, then glanced at her, abashed.

"Beg pardon, my lady."

Brenna swallowed a laugh at the normalcy of the accident. Yes, their clothes were different, and the castle lacked many of the amenities she was used to—running water, electricity, cable TV. But people were still just people.

Some were so much more.

Her gaze turned back to Rourke, who was attacking his meal as if it would be his last. At least nerves hadn't affected his appetite.

"Well, Kinross," Angus said, mopping up the wine with his linen napkin, "where have you been? Have you truly been at sea all this time?"

Every head at the table swiveled toward Rourke expectantly.

Brenna turned her attention back to her meal, not wanting to add further pressure. Out of the corner of her eye, she saw him put down his fork and knife with hands that appeared surprisingly steady.

"I will say this but once." His deep voice resonated down the table, accompanied by the clink of two dozen knives and forks being set on the china.

Brenna set down her own utensils and put her hands in her lap, not about to be the only one eating. She jerked, startled, at the feel of Rourke's hand covering hers under the table. She turned her palm to his and their fingers laced. Their gazes met in unspoken accord.

He needed her. The knowledge squeezed her heart.

"I fled the fire, all those years ago, but Slains's soldiers spotted me and gave pursuit."

Brenna looked at him, surprised. She'd thought the earl was only after her.

"Somehow I made it to Aberdeen, but I'd not been there three days when I was set upon by a pair of scalawags and carried aboard one of the ships docked in the harbor. I was one of a score of young lads kidnapped to be sold as servants in the Colonies."

Brenna hadn't even realized her grip on his hand had spasmed until she felt him squeeze her back in return.

"'Twas my fortune that a week into the voyage smallpox struck the ship. I didna succumb to the disease, but many aboard the ship died. Those of us in the hold were released to help sail the vessel, and the captain took a liking to me and kept me on board after we docked in the Colonies."

"And you remained at sea, then?" Angus asked.

"Aye. A sennight past is the first I've walked on Scottish soil since."

"You should have sent word," Rourke's uncle said, a hint of reproach in his tone.

Rourke squeezed her hand briefly, then released it. "I was but a lad when I left Picktillum. Ten years old. By the time I was grown, and free to set my own course, I had responsibilities too numerous to name and too important to walk away from. My parents were dead. I believed my home and all those I loved were gone. I put the past behind me."

There was something about the shift of his eyes and the slightly defensive tone of his voice that made Brenna think he wasn't telling them everything.

"I regret that you thought me perished all these years."

And that was the crux of it, she realized. He didn't. He hadn't wanted to be found. He'd *wanted* them to think he was dead. But why?

The silence of the room suddenly erupted, everyone talking at once.

"Some say you're a pirate, my lord."

"You could have sent word, Kinross."

"Where is this ship of yours?"

Rourke narrowed his eyes in that way she'd seen him do when he wanted to scare his crew. "I am not a pirate. Nor am I Viscount Kinross, Laird of Picktillum. The lad who was to inherit that title died twenty years ago. The man who grew up in his stead is a sailor. Nothing more. Nothing less."

But his cool glare was having no effect on his family. They continued to watch him with warmth and curiosity.

Brenna laughed to herself. Why would that cold stare work on these people? Half of them had eyes the same pale color as his.

She could feel his tension, feel the slight shift in his body that told her he was getting ready to leave the table, to flee his relations if they didn't back off.

As much as she sympathized with him, she couldn't let him do it. He had *family*. Precious, precious family. And all he wanted to do was run from them. He needed to work out whatever was bothering him, but leaving wasn't the way to do it.

"My lord," several people said at once.

The sudden tension in his body told her he was getting ready to rise, so she grabbed his knee, holding him down and turned to his uncle across the table from her.

"This meal is the best I've had in ages," she said loudly, drowning out most of the questions. "Did the ingredients come from this estate?" She flicked her gaze to Rourke and back to his uncle.

A flash of impatience darkened the older man's eyes,

then disappeared as his own gaze swung to Rourke. When he turned back to her, he gave her a quick wink before launching into detailed accounts of the estate's workings. He was a good man, Rourke's uncle.

She felt Rourke's tension ease, but when she would have pulled her hand back, he caught it and held fast. His eyes held a hint of laughter over the capture, but also gratitude. And her heart swelled until she thought it would burst.

Oh, she wasn't ready to be in love. Not with this man. Not here.

Because there was nothing in it for her but heartache.

Rourke checked the passage outside Brenna's bedchamber for the third time since he saw her to her door. The sun was now long set, the castle asleep. Except for him. He could not sleep for worrying about her. He'd spoken with Angus and his uncle, warning them of Cutter, begging them to be on guard for such a visitor.

The castle was closed tight and well guarded. None would get in uninvited. Still, he worried.

He would go to his death with the image of Brenna draped across the soldier's horse engraved upon his mind. The icy terror lingered still and probably would for days to come.

He would sleep in the chamber with her, and most happily, if not for the damage it would do to her reputation. He would not have his uncle and his kin believing her of ill repute even if she would be leaving this world for her own in a very short time.

A pain twisted his heart.

If only things had been different. His life was to have followed a different path—he should have been laird. At supper this evening, he'd felt awash with a feeling of longing and regret. What if he *were* laird of Picktillum and all her lands? What if he could keep Brenna as his bride? What if he were to live the life he was born to?

But events had long ago destroyed any possibility of that. *He* had long ago destroyed any possibility of that.

As he made his way back to his own bedchamber, he passed a short staircase that led to the small chamber that had been his as a young lad.

He eyed the closed door deep in the shadows for long moments. An unknown force made him grab a lantern from the wall and climb the stairs. He didn't want to face this. He wasn't ready. Yet his feet continued to climb.

With each step, the years peeled away. The simple act of approaching the door was so familiar. So strangely familiar. As he reached for the door latch, a frisson of apprehension tore through him. He knew not what he would find on the other side. A sleeping servant? The chamber unrecognizable as his own? Or the memories he both sought and dreaded?

He rapped on the door. When no one responded, he pushed it open . . . and stood rooted in the doorway. He lifted his lamp high. The room, awash with lamplight, remained unchanged. Indeed, by the looks of the thick dust and cobwebs, he was unsure anyone had been here since he left.

Twenty years.

He felt as if he himself traveled back in time. His small bed sat next to the wall, the bright blue bed curtains now faded to a dull purple. His desk stood as it always had, littered with a child's assortment of treasures.

With feet suddenly turned to lead, he crossed to the desk and peered down at his past. Two oddly shaped rocks that had caught his fancy sat on either side of a feather from a falcon's tail. Beside them, his first crude attempts at carving.

His heart snagged and tore as his gaze fell upon the broken swan. He set the lamp on the desk with a clatter and reached for the broken bird with shaking fingers. In one hand he picked up the body, in the other the head.

Grief, raw and painful, ripped through him. He sank onto the stool by the desk and stared at the two pieces that should have been one. His mother had loved swans. He'd spent long, painstaking hours trying to make this one perfect for her birthday. For her.

His eyes burned as his hands pushed the pieces together, fitting them as they'd originally been. He squeezed his eyes closed and wished with everything inside him he could make them one again. That he could undo the past.

But the pieces fell apart in his hands just as his life had so many years before. The body slipped out of his fingers and bounced onto the desk. Guilt crawled over his skin as he stared at the beheaded creature, the catalyst of the destruction that had followed.

If only he'd accepted the small disappointment of the broken gift instead of seeking retribution. But he hadn't. In his childish, righteous rage, he'd betrayed them all. And his mother's birthday had become the day she died.

Brenna froze at the faint squeak of the door's hinges. She wasn't sure if she'd been asleep or dozing, but suddenly she was wide awake.

Footsteps. Someone was in her room. *A man.* The nearly silent footsteps still had the heavy sound that could only be a man.

Her heart set up a hard percussion. What if Cutter had found her? The bed curtains were drawn, but of course the bed would be the first place he'd look in the middle of the night. She needed to get under the bed.

Swinging her legs over the side, she slipped out as silently as she could.

"Wildcat?"

Clearly, not silently enough. "Rourke?"

"Aye."

She moved around the bed to where she could see his dark form in the shadows. "What's wrong?"

"Naught." But the misery in that single word was palpable. He continued across the room into one of the alcoves and stopped, silhouetted against the faint moonlight.

Brenna remained at the corner of the bed, watching him. Waiting. But he said nothing, as if the moonlight had turned him to stone.

She took a step toward him. "Are you looking for something?"

"Nay."

Just standing in her room in the middle of the night. Alone.

She was reminded of the night shortly after Janie died, when she'd woken from a nightmare. She'd only been with her foster family, the Changs, a few days and was too proud to cry out to strangers for comfort, so she'd crept down the hallway to her foster parents' room. Reassured they were still there, but unable to face her empty bed again, she'd curled up in the hallway outside their door and fallen asleep.

What nightmares had driven Rourke into her room in the middle of the night?

Sympathy and warmth bound her heart as she crossed the wooden floor to the alcove and the dark figure standing before the window. She slipped her arms around his waist and pressed her cheek against his back as she had so many times on horseback. He shuddered and covered her hands with his own, then turned in her embrace and wrapped his arms around her.

"Ah, Wildcat." He pressed his cheek against her hair and held her as if she were his last hope. He turned his face, brushing her cheek as he sought her mouth. His kiss was infinitely tender, careful of her cut lip, and she felt herself falling, spinning head over heels, until she was lost in the taste of him, lost in the feel.

Completely, totally, in love. She reached up and slid her arms around his neck, her fingers burrowing into the soft fullness of his hair. He smelled warm and heavenly.

His hands slid over her back, gentle yet tense, as if he held their great strength in careful check. He wanted her. She could feel it in the tightness of his muscles and in the hard ridge of his arousal against her stomach.

The spinning intensified until she was dizzy with wanting him, too. He pulled away from her mouth only to trail kisses down her sensitive neck to the top of her nightgown. He dipped his head and took one of her breasts into his mouth, fabric and all.

Sensation shot through her. "*Rourke.*" She dug her hands into his hair, shaking with love and desire.

Rourke released her breast and stood before her, close, but apart. She couldn't see his expression in the dark, but could feel his seriousness. Gently he cupped her face with his calloused hands.

"Wildcat. *Brenna.* I want ye, lass." His words trembled with yearning and hunger. "But I dinna wish to frighten ye."

Turning her face into his hand, she kissed his palm. "Make love with me." She felt the shudder that went through him. "Just don't . . ." She took a deep breath. "Don't lie on top of me."

"Och, aye." He lifted her and swung her around so that his face was in moonlight. Fierce joy transformed his features, making him look rakish and charming. He wasted no time in removing their clothing, then he pulled her against him, holding her as if he would never let her go. Slowly he pulled back, his hands sliding over her back . . . and lower.

Brenna groaned. The soft furring of his chest tickled her breasts. His arousal pressed damply against her abdomen. In the darkness of the room, she had to use her hands to see. And she wanted to see . . . everything.

Her palms roamed the hard planes of his chest and the solid rock of his shoulders, then slowly moved down. She stepped back, wanting to reach his taut stomach . . . and the most fascinating part of his anatomy. That part followed her, springing toward her, still pressed against her stomach.

Reaching for it, she cupped the hard length in her hand and felt a tremor go through him. She'd never touched a man like this before. Then again, she'd never trusted a man like she trusted her pirate. There was irony there. But all she felt was an overwhelming desire to be closer to him . . . as close as a man and a woman could be.

She touched the tip of his penis with her thumb and felt the drop of moisture.

"Wildcat."

"You're ready for me." The knowledge pleased her tremendously.

"I have been ready for you since I first watched ye lying in my bunk." He swept her into his arms and strode across the room to place her, sitting, in the middle of the bed, then followed and knelt before her.

Brenna scrambled onto her knees and they came together, chest to chest, mouth to mouth. He held her face in his hands and kissed her with a passion bordering on desperation that set her pulse to racing and sent hot syrup flowing through her veins.

His hands left her face, sliding over her bare shoulders, down her rib cage. She felt his hand between her knees and caught her breath as he coaxed her legs apart. Shifting, she gave him the access he demanded. His hand slid against the perfect center of her sensitivity, his finger finding her warm, moist core.

Brenna gasped and clung to him, her fingers digging into his hard shoulders. Rourke cradled the back of her head and kissed her hard. Her fingers slid into his hair as they kissed, mouth to mouth, tongue to tongue.

But it wasn't enough. She wanted more. *Needed* more.

She pulled back from his kiss. "*Rourke.* I want you."

He released her to slide his hands over her breasts. "Aye, lass. And I you. But I want ye to be sure."

"I'm sure." *I love you, Pirate.* But she didn't say the words out loud. She couldn't. Because they couldn't matter. All she wanted tonight, this moment, was this man and the joy they could bring one another.

Rourke lay on the bed and pulled her down beside him, then leaned over her to take her breast in his warm mouth, his soft hair sliding against her shoulder. Desire spiraled hot inside her as she clung to him.

"I thought . . . I thought we were going to . . ."

His devilish chuckle sounded low in her ear as he released her damp breast to the air. "Soon, Wildcat. I'll have my way with ye first." He took her other breast into his mouth, warming the first with the caress of his hand.

The need inside her tightened until she thought she couldn't stand it anymore. Her hips rocked, wanting.

"*Rourke.*"

"You taste of honey," he murmured, his voice shimmering with raw desire. "And smell like wildflowers."

"Rourke, I want you. *Please.*" He'd reduced her to begging, but she didn't care.

"Do ye now?"

"Yes."

He rolled onto his back and pulled her on top of him. "You lead, Wildcat. I'll not have you afraid of me again."

Brenna rose and straddled him, feeling suddenly shy. But Rourke's big hands cupped her hips, caressing. "Let me inside ye, lass." His voice sounded hoarse with need. "I wish to be inside ye."

And suddenly it was all too simple. She rose onto her knees until she felt him between her legs, then guided him to her entrance. Slowly, so slowly, she lowered herself on his hard length, taking him fully, wonderfully, inside.

She rose again and then back down, feeling the thick stroke in every cell of her body. Perfect.

"Can I help ye?"

"Yes."

Rourke gripped her buttocks and thrust up and into her, sending waves of pleasure spiraling outward. "Is this too much?" His voice was strained and rough.

"No. It's . . . *don't stop*." Over and over he thrust into her as she pressed her hands to his chest. "You don't mind doing it this way?"

The sound that came out of his throat was half laughter, half disbelief, and all male. "Wildcat, there is no wrong way to do this. If 'twould please you, I would make love to you standing on my head."

She grinned and leaned forward until she could kiss him, her breasts pressed tight against his chest. Amazingly, she felt no fear. Only power. Only joy.

She released his mouth and lifted until she straddled him, then arched her back as hot, glorious sensations fired through her, setting her aflame. She rode him harder, faster, driving against his thrusts, forcing him deeper until she thought she would die from the pleasure.

Flying free. Without care. Without fear.

The tension built, winding tighter until finally the spasms broke over her, sending her soaring beyond the bounds of Earth, beyond the reach of men.

Beyond the reach of all but one man.

Rourke pulled her down on top of him and captured her mouth as he drove into her, racing for his own release. He tensed and groaned, thrusting into her once, twice, three times. Then the tension drained out of him on a long, satisfied sigh.

He cradled her against him, stroking her hair. Her cheek found a comfortable spot under his collarbone, and she nestled against him, sated and happy. She'd never known such pleasure. Or such contentment.

"I love you," she breathed against his chest, too softly for him to hear.

But even as she said the words, she knew this fragile peace was destined to be shattered. She was leaving to go back to her own world as soon as they found Hegarty. As soon as she convinced him she wasn't killing anyone, prophecy or not.

And Rourke would go back to sea.

This love she felt for him was doomed, and had been from the start. But she'd lived with loss before and survived. Somehow, she would do it again, though a part of her wondered if *this* wound—the wound to her heart—would ever heal.

Rourke woke the next morning to find sunlight dancing on the papered walls. The hour was late, but he cared not. He had no responsibilities in this place but to see to Brenna's well-being. A satisfied smile curled his lips. He had done that well.

Brenna's warm body was still tucked against him, her silken head resting on his chest. She stirred slightly, her leg twining with his as if she could not get close enough. Desire for her swept through him as it had every time she'd moved during the night.

Sometime before dawn he'd realized what she'd become to him. His life. His breath. The beat of his heart.

It had begun when he'd first seen her lying on his deck in a pool of her own blood, a warrior's blaze in her eyes. And since then, every day, every hour, she'd become more necessary to him until he feared it would not be long before he could not live without her.

He closed his eyes against the damning thought.

She was not of this world. Not of *his* world. She must

go back to her own, for only there would she be safe and content. And only then would he be free to return to his own life.

This morning he would seek Hegarty. The troll would send her back. Rourke would accept nothing less.

But, heaven help him, how was he to breathe without her?

A low rap sounded on the door. Rourke groaned. He should have left before dawn, but he'd slept soundly with her in his arms, then been loathe to let her go. He didn't want to spoil her reputation, but he could hardly hide his presence in her chamber.

As he disentangled himself from her, she rolled over with an unintelligible murmur.

He lifted the sheet over her, then grabbed his nightshirt and pulled it on, letting it fall over his hips before he crossed, barefoot, to the door.

Angus stood on the other side. "The man you warned me about has been spied."

"Cutter," Rourke hissed.

"He makes camp in one of the caves in the hills. Young Broderick saw him watching the castle this morn, then followed him. The lad is certain the cretin did not spy him."

Rourke nodded. "Cutter will not live out the day."

Before he left the chamber, he went back to the bed to gaze down at the beautiful woman lying there. She had given herself into his hands with her body and her trust. *I love you*, she'd whispered just before she'd fallen asleep. Could it be true? The thought both warmed him beyond measure and chilled him to the marrow of his bones.

He leaned over and touched her temple with a feather-light kiss as his heart swelled with tenderness. He was not worthy of her love. If she knew the truth of that day so long ago, she would not give it.

He left her sleeping and made his way to his own

chamber where he dressed and armed himself. Then he went outside to the bailey. To his surprise, he found his mount saddled and waiting for him, along with four other horses. Angus approached him, followed by three of Rourke's kinsmen.

It took him a minute to realize they intended to go with him. He shook his head at Angus. "This is something I must do."

Angus grinned at him, his eyes flashing with determination. "Aye. And we'll be at your back while you do it."

At his back. He'd never had anyone watch his back before.

Angus clasped his shoulder. "Douglases stick together, or have you forgotten? We'll not send you out there alone."

Rourke nodded slowly as the feeling of kinship took on new meaning for him. "Then let us be away." He mounted and set off in a single move, his kinsmen close behind.

They rode into the hills close to the place where the lad had seen Cutter's camp.

"There," Angus said, pulling up beside him. "Between the two rocks on the rise above is a cave. Broderick saw him go in."

Rourke nodded and dismounted. His men followed. While one youth took the reins, Rourke let Angus lead the small party up toward the mouth of the cave.

When they neared, Rourke motioned the other men back, then pulled his gun and sword at once. There was no sense in calling to the man. Cutter would never emerge to such an ambush. A patient man would wait for the fox to leave his den even if the waiting took hours . . . or days.

But Rourke was not a patient man.

The bloody cur had betrayed him. Twice . . . no, three times he'd tried to end Brenna's life. And all because she'd gotten the better of him in an uneven fight.

He would not wait. If luck was with him, his former

bosun was fast asleep and Rourke's approach would go unheeded. If not . . .

He edged toward the narrow opening, silent and tensed for battle. Though he listened, he heard no sound.

Taking a deep breath, he stepped around the corner and into the narrow opening of the cave.

The crack of a firing gun exploded from the rocks.

He felt fire rip through his side a half breath later. Searing pain tore through him as he gripped the wound at his waist. His hand came away slick with blood.

Bloody hell. And why had he thought luck, which had deserted him all his life, would appear this day?

Because she'd said she loved him. Because with her love he had, for a fleeting, foolish moment, thought all things possible.

"Kinross!"

"My lord!"

His kinsmen rushed around him.

His side burned as if the man had used a torch instead of a gun to wound him. Blood soaked his shirt and the top of his pants. He knew with an instinct born of many battles that this wound would be his last.

He would not survive. But neither would Cutter.

Waving off his kinsmen, he lunged into the cave, gun drawn, sword high.

A flash of silver caught the daylight. Rourke parried the thrust barely in time, nearly crumpling from the agony the movement caused. The clash of steel upon steel rang in the narrow confines, echoing with the pounding of the blood in his ears. His eyes, narrowed with pain, could barely make out the form of his bosun.

"You're as good as dead, *Captain*," Cutter sneered. "'Tis no more than you deserve." He fought hard. Too hard.

Rourke struggled to meet every thrust, every blow. "Why, Joshua? Why did you turn over my ship?"

"They paid me well, *Captain*. I'd not have needed the money had you made me first mate after McNeil died. 'Twas my *right* to be mate. Baker is half the sailor I am."

"Aye. There are few your equal upon the sea. But you've never been loyal to me, Joshua. Mr. Baker was."

Cutter turned and thrust, catching Rourke in the thigh.

Rourke stumbled, barely righting himself in time to parry a blow to his head.

Cutter laughed. "I would have been most loyal to you had you shared your earnings with me."

"'Twas you, wasn't it, who took the gold last spring?"

"Aye. You would not share it, so I did it for you. What need you with so much? You already had the ship. And any lass who caught your eye. You horde your gold like a miser."

Rourke clenched his teeth against the twin fires burning his side and his leg. "I shared more than half of every take. I was more than fair, more than generous. But that wasn't enough, was it?"

"You should have made me your partner. I was the best sailor you had. The best! You should have made me your mate. Split your earnings in half with me. And me alone!"

"Why?" Rourke gasped. His strength was draining fast. He wasn't sure how much longer he could hold out, but he must. He could not let Cutter win. *Brenna.*

"Because it was my *right*. I should have been born to wealth. I should have been captain of my own ship. Not you. You had it all—too much for one man. Too much!"

Marshaling the last of his strength, Rourke swung in, catching Cutter's arm, drawing blood, but doing little real damage.

His sword was growing too heavy. *Nay. Hold on.*

"But you haven't got it all now, have you, *Captain*? You've nothing. I've taken it all. Your ship. Your crew. And now your life. When I'm through with you, I'll take care of the bitch, Brenna Cameron. I saw you carry her into your castle. I know she still lives. But she'll not live long, I vow it."

Nay. He could . . . *not* . . . let Cutter win. Brenna. He had to save Brenna.

With a final effort, he swung at Cutter's head. But his strength had all but given out. An upward thrust from Cutter tore Rourke's blade from his hand. It was over.

Nay, it is not.

He felt the heaviness of the gun still clenched in his left fist.

"Brenna Cameron will die, mark my words," his bosun snarled.

Rourke raised the gun with a trembling arm. "You are wrong, Joshua. She will not die. But you will."

He aimed for the sailor's face and pulled the trigger, sending the man straight to the hereafter.

His strength gone, he sank to his knees in a haze of pain, knowing he, too, was headed straight for the fiery pits of hell.

THIRTEEN

"My lady! My lady! Ye must awaken!"

Brenna felt a hand on her shoulder, shaking her out of sleep. Pushing herself onto her elbow, she squinted at the intruder. "What's the matter?"

The young servant wrung her hands. "'Tis the viscount! He's been shot."

"The viscount?"

"Kinross."

God, she needed caffeine. Her brain clicked with a horrified snap.

Rourke.

Her eyes flew open and she sat up abruptly. "How? Where?"

"I dinna know. The old laird said to fetch you."

"Oh, no." Brenna jumped out of bed, realizing too late she was stark naked. She grabbed for her shift and pulled it on, as the servant handed her the corset from last night.

Brenna shook her head. "No time." She grabbed the

deep green silk and pulled it on. As the servant tried to button her, Brenna pulled on the soft kid slippers that went with it.

"That's good enough." Brenna started for the door.

"But, my lady. I've only begun the buttons."

"You got the top one. The dress will stay on." She wrenched open the door and raced down the stairs and into the bailey to find a horse saddled and waiting, two riders mounted beside it, one of them Rourke's uncle.

"He is asking for you, Marie. We will take you to him."

Asking for her. *Not good. So not good.*

One of the men helped her mount, and the three took off.

They hadn't gone far when they came upon a group of Douglas kinsmen gathered about something in the road.

"*Rourke.*"

"He tried to return," the man beside her said. "But he couldna make it."

Brenna pulled up and slid off the horse, then raced to Rourke's side and knelt beside him in the mud. He was conscious, his pale gaze fixed on her, his eyes shimmering with pain. His entire right side, from the waist down, was soaked in blood.

He reached for her.

Brenna took his hand, struggling not to cry. "What happened?"

His hand, always so strong, so sure, shook with the weakness of a child's. "Cutter. He's dead."

"He shot you."

Rourke swallowed. Grimaced. "Aye. From the shadows of the cave. I killed him."

"You fought him *after* he shot you?"

He squeezed her hand. "He would ha' come for ye, Wildcat. The man had lost all reason. Ye had become Lucifer to him. The devil to be vanquished."

"You could have died."

"Ah, lass. I *am* dying. There is naught to be done. The wound is too great."

She shook her head, her own hands beginning to shake. Dear God, she couldn't lose him. Not like this.

"You're not going to die. You can't, Rourke. We need to get you a doctor."

She looked around her at the grief-stricken faces. Why didn't someone *do* something? A wildness tore through her, encased in a steely calm.

She pointed at Angus. "Get a doctor." The man looked at her like a loyal dog wanting to please, but with no idea how to do it. "A physician. A surgeon. *Someone.*"

He shook his head, clearly not understanding.

"Then give me your shirt."

"My . . . ?"

"Now."

Angus whipped his shirt over his head and handed it to her.

"Help me lift him. We need to stop the flow of blood or he's going to bleed to death."

Rourke squeezed her hand. "'Tis done, Wildcat."

"No, it's not! I'm not going to let you die."

If only Hegarty were here. He could . . .

The sapphire. He'd used its magic to heal her leg.

She reached up and closed her fingers around the familiar coolness of the silver. The chain was too short for her to take off and there was no clasp.

She ripped open his shirt and laid her head on his chest to get the stone to touch him.

"*Heal him.*" Tears stung her eyes, blurring her vision. The soft fur of his chest tickled her nose. The metallic scent of his life's blood filled her nostrils even as the gentle rise and fall of his chest reassured her he was not yet dead.

"You can't die, Rourke. I *need* you. I love you, dammit."

She felt his hand in her hair, felt the soft rumble in his chest as he spoke.

"Find Hegarty. The Wellerby cottage in Monymusk. Make him send you back."

A sob caught in her throat as fear wrapped around her heart. She needed Hegarty *now*. Not later.

She kissed Rourke's bare chest and pushed herself to her feet.

"Hegarty!" She shouted to the winds as tears slid down her cheeks. "He needs you, Hegarty! He's dying."

"Wildcat."

"Hegarty. *Please.*"

Brenna felt Rourke's hand tugging at her skirt. She sank onto the ground beside him.

"He canna hear you." His face was drawn taut, his mouth pinched with pain, but his eyes were warm and sure. He took hold of her hand and brought it to his lips. "You are strong, lass. And bonnie. So bonnie. Dinna be afraid."

Her chin began to tremble as she gazed at his beloved face. "I can't lose you."

"You would ha' left me behind when ye returned to your home."

"It's not the same thing. You're supposed to be at the helm of some ship somewhere. Not . . ."

Behind her, one of the men shouted, "A rider!"

Brenna heard the faint clopping of horses' hooves before she could blink the tears from her eyes enough to see.

She stood as a horse and rider trotted down the road toward them. The rider's legs swung freely, several inches above the stirrups, his hair a riotous shock of red.

"*Hegarty.*" Never was she so glad to see anyone in her life. She closed her eyes and sent a prayer of thanks heavenward.

The little man dismounted and scurried to Rourke's

side. His keen gaze traveled over him from head to toe as he knelt as his side.

"'Tis bad, Pup."

Rourke's brows lifted briefly in resignation. "Aye. Too much even for you, my friend."

Hegarty shrugged. "For me, mayhap." He turned his gaze on Brenna, looking pointedly at her throat. "But not for the stone."

Rourke shook his head. "Nay, Brenna. Dinna give it to him." His voice was growing weaker. "He willna give it back. Ye'll ne'er go home."

Hegarty held out his hand to her, his gaze somber. "'Tis the only way to save him."

Brenna reached for the pendant, her fingers closing over the beloved, familiar smoothness of the silver.

"If I give it to you, you must give it back."

"Nay." Hegarty's expression turned hard. "Its return is the price you'll pay for saving the lad."

Nay. The word echoed through her head as an icy numbness spread through her limbs. *You'll never go home.*

But she must.

She couldn't stay here, she couldn't live in this place where people shot at her and aimed knives at her heart. This place with no hot showers, no hospitals, no Starbucks. She had people counting on her to return.

Her father . . . what if he hadn't known where Janie had taken her? What if all this time he'd been looking for her, mourning her loss? What if he was waiting for her to find him?

Rourke grabbed her skirt. "Dinna give it to him, Wildcat."

But it was Rourke's only chance at survival. Her life or his?

As she watched, Rourke's body went limp, his eyes wide open.

No. She grabbed his arm and shook him. "No!"

"Brenna," Hegarty coaxed, his palm open before her.

She turned her shocked gaze on Hegarty. "He's dead."

Hegarty grunted. "Then ye'd best hurry, lass."

The words pierced her grief and her focus snapped to his weathered face. Hegarty could still save him.

She grabbed the necklace. "The chain won't fit over my head. You'll have to cut it."

"Grasp it with both hands and will it gone from your neck."

"Will it . . . ? You mean *wish* it?" She grabbed the sapphire in one hand and the chain in the other. *Go to Hegarty.*

And suddenly it was in her palm, the chain unbroken. *Magic.* The hair rose on her arms. All these years, she'd worn magic without ever knowing. She shoved it at Hegarty.

He laid the silver pendant on Rourke's chest, then placed his hand over the worst of the wounds and began to chant, the same strange melody she remembered hearing that first night aboard Rourke's ship.

She stroked Rourke's hair, waiting, afraid to breathe, afraid to hope. Tears ran steadily down her cheeks as the song went on and on. Others gathered around, drawn out of the castle, drawn to the spectacle. The air grew thick around them. Thick as a fog, yet clear, almost shimmery.

The sapphire began to glow.

Magic. Her heart pounded in her chest as the power of unnatural forces filled the air. He was so pale. So still. So . . . dead.

"You can't die," she whispered, stroking Rourke's hair. "You have to come back to me, Rourke. I need you."

As Hegarty's song continued, Brenna reached for Rourke's hand and raised it to her mouth. "Don't leave me."

Pressing the back of his hand to her cheek with one hand, she felt for a pulse at his wrist with her other, but could feel nothing. Despair settled over her, crushing her beneath its heavy fist. It wasn't working. Not even Hegarty could perform such a miracle.

Hot tears turned to wrenching sobs as she clasped Rourke's beloved hand between both of hers.

She felt something.

A tightening, almost a spasm, in his hand. His eyes swept closed.

Her heart suddenly thudding, Brenna searched desperately for his pulse.

And found it. Her eyes widened at the faint, thready rhythm that tripped beneath her fingertips. Joy swept through her.

"He lives," she whispered, and laughed, a small, choked laugh.

A cheer went up along with whispers of witchcraft and magic, but Hegarty continued his chanting, ignoring them all.

Minute by minute, Rourke's pulse grew stronger beneath her fingers until it fairly thrummed in his veins. Brenna squeezed his hand in hers and pulled it up to her lips as she gave thanks over and over.

Hegarty quit chanting abruptly. He plucked the necklace off Rourke's chest and placed it over his head as if it had always been large enough to fit him.

"He will survive, though he has need of deep rest."

Brenna's gaze followed the sapphire as it disappeared into the little man's shirt and felt her first shaft of fear at what she'd done.

"You can't leave me here, Hegarty. You've got to send me home."

To her surprise, he leaned forward and cupped her chin in his weathered hand, his eyes kind. "There are all kinds of homes, lassie. The trick is finding the one where you belong."

"But . . ."

He released her and went to his horse, and one of

Rourke's cousins helped him mount. With a brief wave, Hegarty rode off into the shimmering mist and was gone.

Just like that, he'd given her back Rourke's life and taken her own.

An icy shock tried to steal her breath, but she shoved it away. She couldn't deal with that now. Not yet. Rourke was her first priority.

His pulse remained strong, his breathing even and calm. She lifted his torn shirt and stared at the small scar in his side, now puckered and healthy. A chill shivered down her spine. Beside him, in the dirt, lay the small metal ball that had shattered his body and nearly stolen his life. The bloody gash in his pants revealed nothing but a scar.

Brenna was beginning to shake. She looked around her at the slack-jawed faces until her gaze met Rourke's uncle's. "We have to get him back to the castle."

The older man nodded slowly, then came to kneel before his nephew. "Does he live? Does he truly live?"

Brenna reached for his hand and pressed his fingers into Rourke's pulse.

The man looked at her, eyes wide and glistening. "'Tis a miracle."

"Yes. Hegarty's good at those." *But at what price?*

Four men carried Rourke back to the castle using a long length of plaid as a makeshift stretcher. Brenna walked beside them, the ground rocky and harsh beneath her soft kid slippers.

Tendrils of panic slid over her skin. Everything she'd ever known was out of her reach now. Her home, all her possessions, her friends. *Everything.*

An icy coldness invaded her body, shock echoing through her head.

Rourke was alive. *Concentrate on that.* He'd been dead and now he wasn't. That was all that mattered.

But, oh my God, she'd lost everything else.

She barely noticed where they were going, paying little

attention as they crossed the courtyard and climbed the stairs to his bedroom. The men laid him on the bed and one of the serving maids started toward him as if to remove his bloodied clothing, but Brenna blocked her path.

"Leave him." She met Rourke's uncle's gaze. "I'm staying with him until he wakes up. He's going to need a lot of rest. Then he'll feel fine."

"You seem certain."

"I am." She had firsthand knowledge of Hegarty's healing process. *Magic.* Now the magic was gone. The magic that would have sent her home.

She pressed her fist against the sudden piercing ache in her gut. She couldn't live here.

The older man nodded and turned for the door. "I will send someone to bring you meals and whatever else you require."

This can't be happening.

She started to thank Rourke's uncle and realized he'd already left. She was alone.

Her fingers interlaced, squeezing until her knuckles turned white. Rourke would help her. Once he woke up, he'd find Hegarty and make him send her back.

There had to be a way out of this. She had to find a way home.

Her body began to quake. She couldn't draw air into her lungs. *Everything lost.* Her apartment, her car. Her job.

My life.

Gone.

The quaking turned into hard shivers and she sank onto the bed beside Rourke and curled up into a tight ball.

Oh God, oh God, oh God.

"What have I done?"

She was stuck in the past.

Brenna paced Rourke's bedroom. A fire crackled in the

hearth, the low flames shadow dancing on the walls of the dark room. It was the middle of the night, but she couldn't sleep. Her mind leaped from one thought to the next as her emotions pinged-ponged back and forth like a grasshopper trapped in a shoe box.

Sometime during the night she'd begun to doubt Hegarty would ever be persuaded to send her home. He'd brought her here for a reason, to kill the Earl of Slains. And she wasn't going to do it. Which meant she probably wasn't ever going to leave. She'd better figure out a way to live here. But not *here*. Not Picktillum. She remembered too well what the black cloud that followed her had done to Rabbie's village. She wouldn't bring that destruction here. These people had been too kind to her to deserve that fate. Besides, this was Rourke's home. His family.

She picked up an apple left from dinner, needing something to occupy her hands as she crossed to the window alcove and back to the hearth in continual, endless pacing.

No, she had to go somewhere else. Somewhere far away. America was out of the question. In 1687 there wasn't much in the way of civilization there yet.

Maybe London. Or even Edinburgh. Somewhere the Earl of Slains wasn't likely to find her. She could go with Rourke when he left, and travel with him to another port. Somewhere safe. Then she'd find herself work in a kitchen.

Staying with him wasn't a possibility. Her fist pressed into her stomach against the knot of misery growing harder by the hour. Of all the times she'd felt lost and alone in her life, this was the worst. Always before she'd believed her dad was out there somewhere, looking for her. That someday he'd find her and take her home. Now she knew she was all alone. The only person on this entire planet who knew where she came from, who knew her at all, was Rourke. But he wanted to go back to sea, and she couldn't possibly go with him. She'd learned firsthand what it was like being a lone woman aboard a ship full of pirates.

She had to make a life for herself.

Her fingers sank into the apple. She could do this. Ever since high school she'd worked in a restaurant doing one job or another. They might not have electric stoves or microwave ovens, but cooking was cooking. She could learn to make things the old-fashioned way.

But even as she told herself she'd be okay, the shadows seemed to laugh at her. She knew *nothing* of this ancient, male-dominated world.

So? She'd learn. She'd fought too long and too hard for her independence to throw it away just because of a little time displacement. A long time ago, she swore she'd never be dependent on anyone again. Somehow she'd manage, even here.

The apple fell apart in her hands and she tossed the mess into the bowl and wiped her sticky hands on her skirt. Despite her pep talk with herself, fear spiked the air around her. This was a dangerous world, especially for a woman alone. If she was going to survive, she needed to learn to wield a sword and shoot a gun.

She had to figure out a way to earn money. And buy things. And darn socks. She wasn't sure what that meant, but people in the olden days always seemed to be darning socks.

A cold chill seeped into her bones. No more cute novelty socks with cats or Christmas trees. No more malls to sell them. No more grocery stores with food lining every shelf. There would be shortages here: She might not always have enough to eat.

Never again would she plop down on a comfy sofa in a well-heated room to eat ice cream and watch TV. Never again would she stand under a hot shower and shave her legs. Never again would she drive the Camry she'd saved to buy.

How long would her beloved car sit in the airport parking lot, waiting for her, before someone finally towed it away?

Oddly, it was the thought of her Camry that started the tears rolling. She sank onto the chair before the hearth as great sobs tore through her.

No more cell phones or Girl Scout cookies or rock music. Forever out of her reach were her makeup and Nikes and bras. She couldn't even reach for a Kleenex. Wiping her eyes on her sleeve, she cried even harder.

I want to go home.

Her fingers sought comfort from the pendant that had always hung at her neck. But her fingernails scratched her throat, her fingers clawing at nothing. Even her necklace was gone. Her only link to the family she'd lost.

Wrenching sobs tore through her for what seemed like hours, finally easing to hiccoughs, the tears subsiding to leave her eyes swollen and sore, her head throbbing.

Exhaustion pulled at her mind and she rose stiffly, unbuttoned the top button of her gown, and let the garment drop to pool around her feet. She stepped out of it and crawled into bed beside Rourke.

Rolling onto her stomach, she took his hand and pulled it close to her face. Enveloped in his warm, comforting scent, she finally fell asleep.

The next morning, as the rain pounded on the castle's many roofs, Brenna sat on the edge of the bed, watching Rourke. He hadn't appeared to have moved during the night, neither did he move while she took a quick, cold sponge bath and dressed in a pretty pink day dress with the help of a servant.

She stroked his forehead, letting her fingers linger on the reassuring warmth of his skin. Even in this deepest of sleeps he didn't seem at peace. His expression wasn't exactly tense, but neither was it calm, as if whatever demons hounded him when he was awake remained even now.

A hard rap sounded on the bedroom door and she rose to answer, hoping it was another servant. Preferably one of the cooks this time. She'd confined herself to the room until Rourke woke up, but she was growing increasingly restless with nothing but her own morbid thoughts. So she'd turned to interviewing the servants. She'd thoroughly interrogated the girl who'd brought her breakfast, demanding to know where every one of the ingredients had come from and how the porridge had been prepared. The poor girl had stuttered and stammered that she was just a serving girl, not a cook.

Brenna had asked her to send up one of the kitchen servants instead. So far, she'd talked to two, learning as much as she could from each.

She had so much to learn, and since computers and libraries weren't options, she was going about it the only way she could—asking questions.

But when she pulled open the door, instead of another kitchen servant, she found two teenage boys struggling to hold a chest between them.

"We've a delivery for the viscount, my lady," one of them said, grunting with effort.

Brenna stepped back, pulling the door wide for them. She eyed the chest with confusion and no small amount of wariness. Who knew they were at Picktillum?

"Do you know who sent this?"

As the boys set the chest against the wall, one of the pair nodded. "From the Wellerby cottage, the man said."

Wellerby . . . ? *Hegarty.*

The lad withdrew an envelope from his coat and

handed it to her. "This came with it. Feels heavy enough for a key."

As soon as the boys left, Brenna's gaze moved to the chest. It looked like a classic pirate chest with its curved top and iron straps over aged wood. A pirate chest for the pirate. Go figure.

The envelope began to get heavy in her hands, weighed down by her curiosity.

The chest wasn't hers. She had no right to open Rourke's stuff. Then again, he couldn't very well do it himself at the moment and there could be something important inside.

Making her decision, she tore open the envelope and tipped it upside down to find a small iron key and nothing else. Not even a note. Kneeling before the chest, she unlocked it to find a true pirate's treasure. *Gold coins.* Tons of them.

On top of the gold lay half a dozen small rag bundles.

She stared at the wealth in wonder. So Hegarty had had Rourke's gold after all. Rourke probably had enough here to buy himself another ship. If any small hope had lingered that he might not go back to sea, with this it was gone. Going back as a simple sailor might have given him a moment's pause. But as captain of his own ship? No. It was what he was made for.

Brenna lifted one of the little rag bundles and felt something hard inside. She carefully unwrapped it to find one of Rourke's carved birds. A small falcon that she didn't remember seeing hanging from the rafters in his cabin.

She unwrapped a second and smiled. In her palm sat a squat little puffin. All he needed was some paint to make him come alive. She settled more comfortably before the chest and lifted out three more bundles until she had a small menagerie of birds sitting on the floor in front of her.

One bundle remained. With curious fingers, she peeled back the yellowed rag . . . and stared. Goose bumps rose on her skin.

A bird. It was just a bird.

She swallowed, hard.

A bird with a head that was merely an extension of its body. A bird with smooth, straight wings lying perpendicular to the torso with funny little knobs sticking out, one on each side.

A bird with no feet and a tail that did not lie flat as a bird's would, but rose straight up like a fin.

She stared at the thing in her hand with reeling disbelief. "Rourke, you son of a bitch," she whispered. "Who are you? What game have you been playing?"

There was no getting around it. The crudely shaped carving was not a bird at all.

She held in her hand an airplane.

FOURTEEN

Rourke blinked against the bright sunlight and yawned.

"Are you okay?"

He jerked his head toward the familiar feminine voice. *Brenna.* She was sitting on the side of his bed, dressed in a pretty gown the same blue as the sky, her sleek, red brown hair hanging loose and lovely around her shoulders.

Her beauty made him ache.

"Aye. I've gone to heaven, have I not, my angel?"

He'd thought to earn a smile, but as he gazed into her eyes, he found not the warmth he'd come to know so well, but the cold eyes of a stranger.

Rourke pushed himself up with effort until he sat on the bed. "What happened, Wildcat?" As he reached for her, she rose and stepped back as if avoiding his touch.

"How much do you remember?" Her voice was tight. Controlled. Too controlled.

His brows drew down as he fought through the murk

of his memories. All he could see in his mind's eye was Brenna's blood. Nay, not Brenna's. One of the earl's soldier's. He'd followed. Rescued her. Brought her to Picktillum.

His gaze took in the familiar surroundings and he knew they were at Picktillum still. Here, in this castle, he'd made love with her. The memory enthralled him, the thought of her riding him, head thrown back in ecstasy. She'd enchanted him with her abandon and set him aflame as he'd never been before.

A knock on the door had ended their time together.

"Cutter."

Brenna nodded. "He shot you."

Shot. He remembered. His hand moved to his side where he'd been wounded. The traitor had blown a hole in his side. But he felt no pain. The wound was gone.

"I should be dead."

"You were for a minute or two. Hegarty came."

"Hegarty." He breathed the word and lifted his shirt until he could see his side, where the wound should be. There, just above his hip bone, was a small, well-healed scar. The hair rose on his arms as it had when he'd first seen the scar on Brenna's leg. Hegarty and his unnatural ways. That damned sapphire . . .

His gaze flew to Brenna's neck. It was bare of the chain that had always been there. Anger sliced through him. "You gave it to him."

His tone was harsh and she answered in kind. "You would have died."

"Where is he now?"

"Gone." Her mouth compressed into an unyielding line and she turned away. "We have to talk."

"Aye." Brenna could no longer go home.

He felt a swift stab of relief even as the knowledge settled like a rock in his stomach. The lass was his responsibility now. He couldn't leave her at Picktillum, for the earl would only come looking for her, destroying everything and everyone in his path. As he had twenty years ago.

No, Rourke would have to take her away. Far away.

If only he still had the *Lady Marie*. If only he had his gold. But he would manage somehow. He would secure them passage on a ship to the West Indies, then barter for what they needed until he could find a way to earn coin enough for them to live.

The rock in his stomach slowly crumbled and dissolved, a measure of relief taking its place as he worked through the problem. Brenna wasn't going back. He would keep her by his side as together they made a life for themselves far away from the darkness that hounded them here.

He gazed at her rigid back. "Wildcat. You needn't worry, lass. I'll take you with me. I'll take care of you. Together we'll ride back to Aberdeen—"

She whirled and thrust her hand toward him. "We need to talk about *this*." In the center of her palm was one of his old carvings. A chill stole over him. *That* carving. He thought he'd destroyed it years ago.

"Where did ye get that?" he demanded.

"Hegarty. He sent your gold. The carving was in the chest."

His gold. Returned at last. Now they would have money aplenty. They would buy the Goodhope Plantation . . .

But the small carving rose like a stone wall between him and his plans. The demand in Brenna's eyes sent dread curling dark fingers around his throat, cutting off his air.

"I'll explain later, Wildcat. I am still recovering, you ken?"

Her eyebrows soared. She snorted softly. "I *ken* you're

recovered enough to make excuses. I want an explanation. *Now.*" Her voice was sharp, lacking any sweetness. She was a warrior once more.

And he had not the strength to fight her.

It was about damned time Rourke was awake. For more than a day she'd waited to confront him about what she'd found.

Brenna sat at the foot of his bed, tapping her foot and watching him coldly. Since yesterday morning, she'd alternated between being furious and feeling utterly betrayed.

How could he not have told me?

Rourke moved back against the headboard, looking as weary as an old man despite the healthy glow to his skin and the clear vibrancy of his guilt-ridden eyes. He stretched his legs, brushing her hip with his bare toes.

She scooted back, avoiding him. She'd thought she knew him, thought she understood what made him tick. Now she knew she'd never understood him at all.

He nodded toward the carving. "What do ye think it is?"

She shot him a scowl. "I *know* what it is. It's an airplane. You're from the future, too, aren't you?" She searched his eyes, feeling betrayed all over again. "Why didn't you tell me?"

His mouth twisted ruefully and he looked tired, exhausted, but she had little sympathy for him. He'd lied to her. Perhaps only by omission, but it was a *huge* omission.

He closed his eyes as if to escape her glare. "I am not from your world."

His words sunk in as she cupped the small plane in her palm. "Then how did you . . . ?"

Slowly, he opened his eyes and met her stare, his expression taught and tense, like a man about to face an operation without anesthetic. Tilting his head back, he looked up at the ceiling as if gathering his thoughts. Or his courage.

Finally, he met her gaze with those pale, intense eyes. His tension bled into her. She was suddenly afraid she didn't want to know what he had to say.

"Brenna. You are not from that world where you grew up. You're from this one. Ye were born here twenty-five years ago."

She heard the words, but their meaning eluded her. *Born. Here?* "You're wrong."

"I told you about the prophecy, aye? You were little more than a bairn when the Cruden Seer named you as the one who would be the Earl of Slains's downfall. Barely five summers, ye were."

Denial flashed hot and then cold. She pushed off the bed and strode into the window alcove, needing to escape. "I wasn't born here." She turned back to him. "You're wrong, Rourke."

"Nay." He closed his eyes, his expression taut. "'Tis time you knew . . . everything."

A pounding started in her ears. She didn't want to hear this. She didn't want to listen to this nonsense. Did he think she was a complete moron? She strode back to the bed. "I don't know who you think I am, but I was not born in the seventeenth century. I know that much."

"Do you?"

The pounding in her ears intensified. "Of course."

"You remember being four or five in that place?"

Did she? She remembered coming to America. Before that, only a few flashes of memory. The man during the storm. A woman singing her to sleep. Riding a horse. She remembered now, there had been horses everywhere.

Doubts began to slip in. She'd never found any evidence of her family in Scotland. No record of her birth. No record of anyone looking for her. When she'd gone in search of her family, the only one who had recognized her name had been the old Earl of Slains. *You burned this castle three hundred years ago, Brenna Cameron. You'll not do it again!*

An icy chill slid down her spine. It couldn't be true.

Rourke opened his eyes and caught her gaze. "Listen, Wildcat. Then decide, eh?"

Brenna felt as if the ground was shifting beneath her feet and she sank onto the bed beside him. "I don't want to hear this," she whispered.

"Aye, lass. I ken that. But hear it ye must. The time is past for you to know. The Earl of Slains was outraged that a bairn, a lass no less, was to be his destruction. He ordered you killed."

"Say *her*. He ordered *her* killed. It wasn't me."

Rourke ignored her. "Your mother was round with babe and too close to her time to travel. Your father was afraid to leave her side. So they sent you to Picktillum with your aunt."

Chills danced along her arms and scalp. "It wasn't me. I don't remember any of this."

"Don't you? You followed me around that entire summer. You used to watch me carve my wee birds."

"*It wasn't me.*" But she stared at him. She had remembered a carver.

"The earl . . . learned where you were. My parents tried to protect you." Anguish flickered in his eyes. "He killed them and set fire to the house."

Her stomach clenched until she thought she'd be sick. "And you *saw* this?"

"Nay. I didna see it done, but I found their bodies as I fled through the castle, just before the fire. My father . . ." He clenched his jaw and turned his head toward the window as if escaping the picture in his mind's eye. "My father had been beheaded."

Bile rose in her throat. The pounding in her ears moved

to her temples. "Oh, Rourke." She reached for him, laying her hand on his arm. "Not because of me." It wasn't. She wasn't the one. But his words sparked old memories that began to swirl in her head, vague and shadowed. Memories of crying and smoke. And terror.

Her hand went to her forehead as she squeezed her eyes closed against the images.

"Hegarty saved us. I dinna ken where he came from or how he knew we were in trouble, but we were trapped and there he was. He saved you and your aunt. And me. I was ten."

She remembered. A blond-headed boy with a sharp tongue and no patience with her.

Rourke's hands rested limply on the bed beside him. His head tipped back to lean against the wall, eyes closed. "We were trapped in one of the cellars. Smoke was starting to seep in, but the earl's soldiers were outside. There was no escape. Nor any way in, but suddenly Hegarty was there with us. He put his sapphire around your neck and tried to send the both of us and your aunt to safety. It almost worked."

He opened his eyes and lifted his head to meet her gaze. "I saw the world where you grew up, Wildcat. For a minute, maybe two. Bare-limbed women playing with small children in the grass while a strange, birdlike creature flew noisily through the air and swift coaches without horses chased one another along a hard-packed road.

"I didna know where we were, only that it was a wondrous place. And then of a sudden I was back in the smoke-filled cellar of my home. We all were. The magic hadna been strong enough for the three of us. Hegarty yanked me aside and sent the two of you by yourselves. You never returned."

Brenna stared at him, not wanting to believe his words, but deep down she knew he spoke the truth this time. It fit too well with her scattered memories.

She was from the past. "I didn't know."

"Before he sent us the first time, Hegarty told your aunt to leave Scottish soil so that he couldna be forced to bring you home until you were grown and able to defend yourself. He told her to bring ye back to Scotland on your twenty-fifth birthday so that he could call you home."

Suddenly so many things began to make sense. Janie's demand that Brenna wear long dresses, even though the other girls wore shorts and jeans. Her insistence on the most old-fashioned of manners. How many times had she said, "A lady does this," or "A lady never does that." And the doctors. She'd been afraid of them even when she lay dying.

Brenna had loved Janie, but she'd hated her, too, fighting her over the unreasonable demands that made Brenna a laughingstock. Her stomach clenched with remorse as she remembered how, in the third grade, she'd taken a pair of scissors and destroyed the dresses Janie had painstakingly sewn for her by hand. She'd reduced Janie to tears that night and forced her to promise to buy her a pair of jeans and a couple of T-shirts.

Now, far too late, Brenna understood. Janie had had an impossible task. If Brenna thought living in the past was hard, how much more difficult must it have been for Janie to live in the future? And more difficult still to raise a headstrong girl to be a lady of the seventeenth century, keeping her safe until the time was right to return her to her family.

"*My family.*" Her heart lurched. "Are they still alive?"

Rourke met her gaze. "I canna say. I told you true when I said I went to sea and never returned."

Brenna jumped to her feet. Thoughts tumbled through her head as chills coursed through her body. Her family was *here*. They hadn't abandoned her all those years ago. She'd been as lost to them as they were to her.

All this time she'd been trying to get back to the twenty-first century, when her home was here.

And Rourke had known all along.

She whirled on him. "Why didn't you tell me?"

"Ye are not safe here."

"That doesn't answer my question." Anger sparked and flamed deep inside her. Anger that because of the Earl of Slains she'd been ripped from her home in the first place. Frustration that Janie never told her, left her thinking she'd been abandoned. And fury at the man in front of her for not being honest with her when he knew. He *knew*.

"What *right* did you have to keep this from me? To decide I was going back. I've spent my whole life wondering why they never came for me, why they never tried to find me. How could you keep something like this from me?"

"'Tis too dangerous for you here." His words were slurred as if he'd been drinking, and she realized he was falling asleep again. He started to list sideways and she helped him lie down. He was asleep almost before his head hit the pillow.

She stared down at him, hurt and confused. He would have sent her back without ever knowing her life was supposed to have been here. He had no right to make this decision for her. No right. He always thought he knew what was best for her. He'd tied her in the cave to keep her safe. Had tried to send her back to the future for the same reason. Maybe he thought he was acting in her best interest, but it had to stop. She was a grown woman. An intelligent woman fully capable of making her own decisions in *either* world.

And she knew the first thing she had to do. She had to find out what had happened to her family.

Her parents might still be alive. The man she'd remembered holding her in the storm might still be here. A wary excitement trembled within her. Twenty years she'd been gone, and this place wasn't exactly conducive to long life. Especially with the Earl of Slains around.

But they might still be alive.

And she'd bet money Rourke's uncle would know.

She smoothed the blanket over Rourke's hips, then left him as she went to discover the truth about her family. As she hurried down the passage to the stairs, her heart pounded with futile rage at the fates. Fates that had torn her from everything she'd known, not once, but twice.

She found Rourke's uncle in a neatly furnished anteroom off the dining room where they'd eaten that first night. The walls were wood-paneled and hung with tartans and swords as was the dining room. A large desk dominated the room. It was a man's room. A war room.

Uncle James was alone, sitting at the desk, a mound of books in front of him when she rapped at the doorframe. He looked up and saw her, then stood.

"Rourke?"

"He's good. He woke up and sat up for a few minutes, but he's asleep again."

Relief softened the lines around the older man's mouth.

"I need to speak with you," Brenna said.

He smiled and motioned her in.

Brenna turned and closed the door, then crossed to where he stood, clasping her hands tight in front of her. "What do you know about the Camerons?" Now that the question was out, her heart spasmed with fear that the news would be bad. Surely she hadn't come all this way only to find out she was too late?

"The Camerons, eh?" He offered her one of the chairs, but she shook her head. She was too wound up to sit.

Her fingers twisted around one another, agitation winding her tight as a drum. "What do you know about the Earl of Slains and the prophecy, sir?"

"I ken all there is to know, I wager."

"Are Brenna Cameron's parents still alive?"

The question startled him. His eyes widened, then narrowed with suspicion. "And why would you be asking, lass?"

Her eyes blurred with tears. "Please. I need to know."

James watched her for long minutes as if trying to make sense of her. Slowly his expression cleared and when he spoke, his voice was warm.

"Last I heard, aye. Alex Cameron was hale. But Ena . . ." He shook his head sadly. "She died in childbirth a long time ago."

Brenna blinked hard, clearing her vision. She knew that. In the deep recesses of her memory, she remembered. It's why she'd never waited for her mother to find her. She'd always known her mother was gone.

But not her father. "Where is he now?"

James gave her a small, gentle smile. "I imagine he's home, Brenna. Deveron House. He'll be muckle glad to have you home, lass."

Home. Brenna covered her mouth against the tide of emotion that welled up and overflowed. He was alive. Her father was alive. Waiting for her.

Tears slid down her cheeks and she began to cry, great gulping sobs. All the loneliness for so many years, all the times she'd wondered why he never came for her. Now she knew.

She felt the press of a handkerchief into her hand and blinked to find James standing beside her, his expression soft and kind.

"Och, lass, 'tis a wondrous thing, your return. He knew you'd be back. I do not ken how, but he knew when you were grown you'd return." Inexplicably, he began to laugh. "I remember you well. You were a wee bit of a thing with a heart like a lion even then. You'd taken a liking to my nephew and near drove him to distraction. You followed him everywhere." He looked at her quizzically. "Where have you been, lassie?"

Brenna wiped her tears on the handkerchief. "It's a long story." The understatement of the year. "I have to get to my father."

"'Tis several days' ride. I'm sure Rourke will take you once he recovers."

Brenna shook her head, knowing what she had to do. "I'm not waiting for him. He's not coming with me." The thought of leaving him broke her heart, but it wouldn't be any easier if she waited. For either of them. Rourke wanted to return to sea. By leaving now, she'd be freeing him of any lingering responsibility he might feel for her.

Besides, if she waited for him to wake up, he'd only start making decisions for her again. He'd probably insist she stay here, safe, while he sent someone for her father or went to get him himself. No, she wasn't playing that game anymore. This was her life, her father, her family. And while it would break her heart to leave him, it was better this way. No good-byes. No having to listen to his false promises to come back for a visit. No chance of giving away just how desperately she didn't want him to go.

Brenna gripped her elbows against the pain of leaving him and looked at his uncle. "Can I borrow a horse? And maybe a guide?" If only she could call for a rental car and pull up MapQuest.

"Yes. Of course." James frowned. "Brenna, I'll not keep you here against your will, but I do not think you should leave while the lad sleeps."

"I want to leave right away. I've been waiting to see my father for far too long already."

"But Rourke . . ."

"He's going back to sea." The man's expression turned pained and she reached out to him. "I'm sorry. I shouldn't have been the one to tell you that."

"You cannot know what he intends."

"He told me he wants to go back to sea. But either way, it doesn't matter. If you know who I am, you know the Earl of Slains is still looking for me. Rourke's lost too much because of me already. He's a good man. An honorable man. And I'm afraid he'll stick by me out of some misplaced sense of duty when all he wants to do is leave. I don't want that. It's too dangerous." She met the older man's eyes, willing him to understand. "If he dies because of me, it'll kill me."

And she knew it was true. She *wanted* him to go back to sea. Far from the Earl of Slains and his soldiers.

"So you're taking the decision out of his hands."

"Yes. When he wakes up, tell him . . . tell him I'll never forget him. But I can take it from here. We each need to get back to our own lives."

James pressed his lips together unhappily, then nodded. "I will ready provisions and an escort. How soon do you wish to travel?"

"An hour? I need to change back into the clothes I came in."

"Nay, lass, the gown is yours. I will have your maid prepare others as well. I'll not have you arriving at Deveron House looking like one of the servants." He smiled sadly. "Your father will be most pleased to have you returned to him."

Her father. In a couple of days she'd be with him again at last. The thought was as fragile and extraordinary as a snowflake, even as the thought of never seeing the pirate again felt like a solid chunk of ice in her heart.

She thanked Rourke's uncle, and returned to Rourke, who remained exactly as she'd left him, sound asleep.

Standing over him, looking down at his beloved face, she could barely breathe. How was she ever going to live without him?

But it was time she took control of her life again. She'd

spent her childhood tossed about like a leaf in a storm and long ago sworn she'd never depend on anyone but herself.

She'd relied on Rourke because she'd had to.

But no more. She'd learned from the lessons of her past, learned to take care of herself. Her world may have changed, but not that. Never that. She was through being the leaf.

The time had come to be the storm.

Rourke woke, unsure of the day or time, but feeling alert and strong as he hadn't the last time he'd opened his eyes. The sun was bright. He could tell that much as he sat up and untangled his legs from the blanket.

His gaze searched for Brenna, but the chamber was empty save for himself. With a sinking feeling, he remembered their conversation when he'd last woken. He'd told her nearly everything. And she'd not been pleased.

He needed to explain. She had to understand why he'd kept the truth from her. Why he'd tried to send her back. The prophecy would destroy her, even now, for the Earl of Slains would not give up until she was dead.

He dressed quickly, then strode toward the door. The wildcat was not an unreasonable woman. She'd understand once he had a chance to explain. Then she'd sail with him away from Scotland.

Far from the reach of the Earl of Slains's sword.

Rourke stormed into the Laird's Hall as the midday meal was being served. The scent of roast lamb mingled with that of fresh-baked bread, making his stomach clench with hunger. But his thoughts were not on food.

His uncle saw him and smiled. "You have awakened at last."

Rourke's gaze scoured the long table. "Where is she?"

He'd found her bedchamber empty. The lass had few enough possessions, to be sure, but naught remained. Nothing. It was as if she'd never been here. Even the soap from the washstand was missing.

James rose from the table and motioned him into his private chambers, then closed the door behind them. "Brenna left this morn for Deveron House with an escort of four men."

Rourke stilled. "Ye know who she is."

"When she came to me to ask after Alex Cameron with tears in her eyes, I kent the truth, aye?"

"Why did you let her go?"

James squeezed the bridge of his nose. "I suggested she wait for you, lad, but she was ill-disposed to do so." He opened his eyes and pinned him with a gaze as pale as his own. "She seemed to think you are heading back to sea."

"I am." The words rang hollow to his own ears. "I was. God's blood, I dinna know what I'm doing." He turned, agitated. "She's displeased with me. I failed to tell her she might have family still alive."

His uncle was silent for several moments. "Why is that?"

"She's not safe here. I wished to send her back to where she's been living. Back where the Earl of Slains couldna reach her." At first, he'd only sought to distance himself from that damned prophecy, but over the course of the days since Hegarty brought her back, that had changed. Brenna had changed him. "I sought to protect her, Uncle."

Because she'd stolen his heart.

His uncle nodded, his eyes warm. "As she seeks to protect you."

Rourke stilled. "What do ye mean?"

"She knows the earl will continue to hunt her. She doesna want you killed when he finds her."

"Brenna said that?"

"She said as much, though 'tis not the message she asked me to convey to you."

"What message?"

"She'll naught forget you, but you each have lives of your own to live."

"Bloody hell." His chest began to ache. He rubbed it as he paced. "She should have waited for me."

"She was anxious to see her father."

Rourke's gaze snapped to his uncle's. "He still lives?"

"Aye."

"What of her mother?"

"Her mother died in childbirth years ago. Before the fire. Indeed, word had reached Picktillum that very morn. Brenna, the wee lassie, took it poorly. I remember watching her fly from this room after your father broke the news to her."

The morn of the fire. He hadn't known. And suddenly the events of that morning made a horrible kind of sense.

"Alex Cameron has never given up hope of his daughter's return, Nephew."

Rourke eyed him with confusion. "He knows, then? That she was sent . . . away?" Had Hegarty gone to Deveron House to talk to her father? He'd never said.

"Aye. He knows. He expected her to return when she was grown, but he's been expecting her for nigh on ten years. Alex has feared her lost to him."

Rourke frowned. He'd never given any thought to Brenna's father—a man who'd lost his wife and daughter within days of one another. His daughter had finally come home. Yet Rourke had conspired to keep her away.

Fool. Aye, she would be safer in her own world, but her world was not without dangers of its own. Her experience at fifteen told him that much. She had family awaiting her return, prepared to protect her with the same fierceness that his had shown when he went to draw out Cutter. Yet he would have denied her that. He would have sent her back to her isolation.

I've spent my whole life wondering why they never came for me, why they never tried to find me.

He poured himself a dram of whiskey and tossed it back, feeling the burn all the way to his empty stomach.

"I'm going after her."

"You are only just recovered, lad."

"If ye know who she is, then ye know well the danger that follows her. I'll not leave her to the mercy of the earl and his men."

"She has an escort of four."

"Aye. Before dawn she'll have an escort of five."

"Seven. You'll not ride alone."

Rourke smiled and nodded. It was a good feeling to have kin at his back.

As he rode out of the castle a short while later, two of his kinsmen at his side, he wondered what had happened to that desperate need that had plagued him since he dove off the ship. The need to escape to the coast and sign aboard the first passage to the Caribbean.

Everything had changed. The sea held no interest for him. The Goodhope Plantation no refuge.

Brenna was not there. She'd taken the light with her when she left him. A light that had only begun to shine within his heart for the first time in twenty years.

When had the bane of his existence become the light of his very life? But she had. With every breath he took, he longed to touch her silken hair and catch a flash of her smile.

He loved her.

And he would do everything in his power to keep her safe. Once he saw her into the keeping of her family, he'd turn to the cause of the problem that had plagued their lives for too long. The Earl of Slains. Brenna's life would be in danger until the earl was dead.

The time was past for running. And that was what he'd been doing. Running. From the prophecy. From himself.

For as long as he lived, he would hate himself for what he'd done that day his parents died.

But he would run no more.

The time had come to fight.

FIFTEEN

Brenna and her escort started out the next morning after a restless sleep on the hard ground. Mist hung heavy, parting then reforming as the small party rode through. She wondered how her guide could possibly know where they were going when she could barely see ten yards ahead.

As they had yesterday, the four men rode two in front of her, two behind, keeping her safely tucked in the middle. The men were friendly and kind, but she missed Rourke badly.

Apprehension rode with her, turning her into a vibrating mass of nerves. Yes, she was excited at the prospect of meeting her family. But she was scared, too. Terrified that she'd come this far, waited all these years, for a reunion that would badly disappoint.

Dread swept over her, swift and unwelcome. She'd longed for her father for so long, and now that she'd found him again, she was seriously worried it was too late. She was too old, too used to being responsible for herself to become the responsibility of someone else. But this wasn't the twenty-first century. Women didn't easily live alone in this time.

She'd struggled too long to earn her independence to give it up now.

What if her father wouldn't allow her that choice? What if he was a chauvinistic tyrant who demanded she remain under his roof and his thumb? The thought made her stomach churn. All she had was a single clear memory and she wasn't even sure the man she remembered was her father.

The horse snorted beneath her as they trudged, single file, across mist-shrouded moors.

How was it possible she belonged in this place and not the other? If not for the Earl of Slains, she'd have grown up here. This would be the only world she'd ever known. Instead, for twenty years, she'd lived more than three hundred years in the future and never realized she was in the wrong time.

Her head ached from the confusing thoughts.

Her heart ached for her missing companion.

Had Rourke woken up yet? Was he angry with her for leaving, or relieved? Knowing her pirate, probably some of both. He liked to be in control, the one making the orders, so he wasn't likely to be happy she'd made the decision to leave without asking him.

But then he'd realize he was free. She was being taken to her family and was no longer his responsibility. And he had his gold.

"Good luck, Pirate," she murmured to herself. Her eyes blurred with the hot ache of longing for something that could never be. And with wanting someone who would be forever beyond her reach. And with the fear that she didn't know how to do this on her own.

Anxiety slowly tied her in knots as they rode over the

heathered moors toward what was at once her past and her future. The horses moved at a slow and steady pace as they avoided the main road. Angus feared the Earl of Slains could have other troops scouring the countryside in search of her by now.

"Riders," Angus warned suddenly.

The men pulled up and circled their horses around her, two drawing guns, two drawing swords.

Heart thudding, Brenna yanked up her skirt and dug out the knife Rourke had given her, feeling a strange sense of warmth as her hand closed around the worn handle. As if Rourke, even now, tried to protect her. As she straightened, her gaze went from her small blade to the huge swords of her companions. She felt a little ridiculous. If she were going to survive in this place, she was going to have to learn to wield a bigger weapon.

The dull thud of distant hoofbeats carried to her through the morning mist. Definitely more than one rider, but fewer than the last time she'd heard the fearful pounding as she'd waited in that cave near Monymusk.

Brenna gripped her knife tight as she waited for a glimpse of the riders. Her heart pounded in her ears, her stomach clenching with dread. She didn't want these men to die. Too many had lost too much already because of her.

At last she caught a glimpse of three riders and recognized the strong, agile carriage of the man in front.

"Rourke," she breathed.

"Rourke, is that you?" Angus called.

"Aye!"

Brenna's heart soared at the sight of him, and then crashed like the small wooden bird they'd tried to fly. She was so relieved he wasn't a bluecoat and dizzy with joy that she hadn't yet lost him forever, but at the same time, she wasn't sure she could deal with his ranting at her for leaving without telling him. How was she supposed to take command of her own life if he wouldn't leave her alone to do it? She knew better than to think she could send him away. The man didn't do anything he didn't want to do.

As the three joined the group, Rourke's gaze met hers, his eyes as pale and intense as ever, but lacking any visible emotion. Whatever he was thinking or feeling, neither his eyes nor his expression gave anything away. He turned to talk to the other men, but her eyes refused to move, instead drinking in the sight of the man who even now held her heart hostage. His color was back, his movements strong and assured. No one would ever guess he'd died just three days before.

The men decided that one of her companions and both of Rourke's would return to Picktillum while Rourke continued on with them to Deveron House. As they started off again, Rourke moved beside her. The others gave them space, riding both farther ahead and farther behind than before.

Brenna didn't want privacy, but heaven knew she couldn't escape him. She was doing well just to keep the horse moving in the right direction. Evasive maneuvers were way beyond her current skill level.

"Wildcat."

She could feel his gaze on her.

His voice wasn't hard with accusation as she'd expected. Maybe he wasn't going to read her the riot act for leaving him. His simple presence soothed and strengthened her as if already he were shouldering her doubts and fears.

This wasn't good. She would never learn to stand alone if he kept holding her up.

"Wildcat, I—"

"Rourke, don't." She held up her hand, not looking at him.

She wasn't sure she could say what she needed to say

if she fell into his gaze. "I didn't want you to come. I need to learn to live in this world, to make my own decisions and fight my own battles. Your being here makes that too hard, especially since you're always so sure you know what's right."

She hazarded a look at his face and found him staring straight ahead, his jaw tight. "I need you to back off, Pirate. Give me some space. Let me figure out who I am. I'm returning to my family. I'm sure you'll be welcome there, but you can't make decisions for me anymore."

His head swung toward her, his eyes piercing. "I'll not let ye come to harm."

"If I'm clearly in trouble, then I'd appreciate the help. But I won't allow you to hold me back and lock me up just because things may get a little dangerous. I have to live in this world. Not hide from it."

Rourke stared at her for a long moment, then inclined his head and met her gaze. "I had no right to try to send you away without telling you that 'twas here you belonged. I'm sorry for it. But I'm not sorry for trying to keep ye safe, Wildcat."

Brenna rolled her eyes. "Which is exactly why I left. You have to back off, Rourke. You *have* to. Or you're going to suffocate me, and I'll end up hating you as much as you'd hate someone who tried to steal *your* choices. And I don't want that to happen."

They rode in silence for several minutes before Rourke finally spoke. "Aye. I'll back up. But I'll never stop trying to keep you safe."

Brenna sighed. She'd asked him to *back off*, not *back up*. But the term probably didn't mean anything to him. As he pulled up and allowed the small party to re-form as before, with him taking one of the back positions, she wondered if he'd understood anything she'd said. He was a man. Worse, a seventeenth-century male. They weren't known for being the most liberal when it came to women's rights. She had a bad feeling she was going to be fighting this battle with every male who crossed her path for years to come.

The specter of a dismal, frustrating future rose before her. Her father marrying her off to a man she hated. A husband who considered her little more than a possession. A society that turned its back on her for her rebellious ways.

At least Rourke seemed to like her despite her stubbornness and her twenty-first-century mind-set. If only she could stay with him.

Longing arced through her. She needed him. She needed his strength and his understanding, especially now as she headed into the unknown.

But she needed her own strength even more.

Blood surged through Rourke's body, his veins pulsing with life, his heart pounding with strength. He knew not if it was the brush with death that made him feel so alive, or the magic that still lingered in his veins. Or simply his nearness to Brenna herself.

She rode just ahead of him, safely between the men as she had all day, the evening sun setting fire to her hair, making the strands sparkle as if dressed with tiny red and gold gems. In the simple green gown, the color of the moors, she was dressed to blend into the landscape, attracting as little attention as possible. But the color only accentuated her beauty until he ached with the need to touch her and hold her tight in his arms again.

Back up, she'd said. He grunted. If she thought he would leave her to the mercy of the earl, she was sorely mistaken.

Despite her strength of mind and will, she was soft. Over the years, he'd met his share of women capable of taking care of themselves. Brenna wasn't one of them.

Aye, she'd taken on his crew, but if he'd not intervened, she'd have lost. She wasn't battle hardened. She'd never fought to the death. Never killed.

Aye, Brenna was strong, but hers was a strength layered with vulnerability. He wasn't certain she could see it, but he could.

If she wished to believe she didn't need him, so be it. He'd walk behind her, protecting her back until she was safe. Then he would go after the Earl of Slains himself.

As they rode, he felt her tension as if it were his own and wished he could ease it. Unfortunately, he feared his presence only added to it. She didn't want him here. But it didn't matter, because he wasn't leaving her.

With night approaching, he began to look for a room with a bed, for he had coin aplenty. When they came upon a small brick house with a sign in front indicating a room available, Rourke negotiated a fair price. Angus and the others would encircle the house, keeping watch through the night while he kept watch over Brenna.

Though he braced himself for her displeasure, she said naught when he ushered her into the small room and closed the door behind them. Instead, she went to stand at the window, not moving even when the matron brought a tray with their supper.

"Come, Wildcat. Eat."

"I'm not hungry."

She had said the same both times they'd stopped during the day to eat the victuals packed from Picktillum's kitchens. To his knowledge the lass had not had a bite since his arrival.

"Ye must eat, Brenna."

"I can't," she said miserably, "I'll throw up."

"The earl willna get you, Wildcat. I'll not allow it."

"It's not the earl I'm worried about." She turned to face him, her knuckles white as she held her elbows. "It's my family."

Sympathy and understanding flowed warmly through him. "Aye. I felt much the same as we drew near Picktillum. 'Tis not easy to go home."

She shook her head, silent, as withdrawn as he'd ever seen her.

"'Twill be all right, lass. Your homecoming will bring much joy." Joy he'd have denied them all if he'd talked Hegarty into sending her back.

"Maybe." She sounded far from sure.

He couldn't blame her. He himself knew nothing of her family nor anything of what had happened over the past twenty years. Only what James had said, that her father still lived and mourned her bitterly.

He walked slowly to where she stood and put his hands on her shoulders, expecting her to pull away. She didn't. He felt a tremor go through her as if on a great sigh. To his surprise, she slipped her hands around his waist, tucking her head beneath his chin, flooding him with sweet warmth.

"I don't need you," she murmured.

"Aye." A smile twitched at his lips, for her arms were locked about his waist as if she were a drowning sailor and he her only hope. He stroked her hair, pushing the sleek strands out of her face, as his heart swelled with love. She did need him. She might not wish to, but she did. And they both knew it.

"What is it?" Brenna eyed the meat on the plate with wary curiosity.

"Boiled mutton." Rourke sat across the tiny table from her, digging into the bland-looking food as if he were starving. "'Tis a wee bit dry, but ye must eat, Wildcat. 'Twill do you no good to be weak and daft-headed when tomorrow comes."

He was right, of course. Despite the knots in her stomach, she cut off a small bite and put it in her mouth. The meat was tough and as dry as cardboard, but her stomach told her to keep eating. Despite the knots, it was empty. And hungry.

She tried to ignore her companion as she ate. His presence was too overwhelming. Her need for him too much. All she wanted to do was stay in his arms. But she had to keep some distance between them. For a lot of reasons, not the least of which was her own survival. She wasn't sure she could live through yet another heartbreak.

Everyone she'd ever loved had left her or sent her away. Her father, her aunt Janie, her first and best foster family, the Changs. None of them had done it on purpose, but the result had been the same. Crushing grief. Debilitating loss.

She refused to go through that again when Rourke left to go back to sea. But the more time she spent with him, the more she needed him. And the harder it was going to be to avoid heartbreak.

When she'd eaten all she could, she pushed her plate to Rourke.

"Ye canna eat more?"

"No. It's all yours." Her gaze moved to the tiny bed in the corner. One bed, considerably smaller that a twin-size bed at home. "Where are you going to sleep?"

"On the floor."

"In here?"

"Aye. I'll not leave you alone."

Great. Though she was glad to have him watching over her in case the earl's men found them, sleeping in the same room with the man was not a good idea. She had to keep her distance. Worse, she had to make him keep his.

He finally finished eating and rose to lay the plates out in the hallway.

"Will ye be sleeping now, lass?"

Brenna sighed, meeting his pale gaze. "I'm not sure I

can, Rourke. I'm too wound up. Why don't you take the bed, and I'll sleep here if I get tired enough."

He didn't answer. Instead, he went to stand behind her to grip her shoulders, his magical fingers pressing and rubbing all the tight spots between her shoulder blades and along the sides of her neck.

"If I'd known you gave massages, I'd have asked for one days ago."

"Ye like it, eh?" His voice held a smile.

"If feels heavenly."

She felt him move and knew he'd knelt on the floor behind her low stool. But his thumbs never stopped their careful strokes, easing the tension in her shoulders.

His fingers trailed along the side of her neck, pulling her hair aside. And suddenly she felt his lips on that sensitive flesh, following the same path his thumbs had worked moments before, sending tendrils of pleasure floating along the surface of her skin.

A moan escaped her throat before she could stop it. Oh, this wasn't a good idea. How was she ever going to build up defenses against the man if she let him touch her like this? Touch her until she was melting in his arms.

"Rourke. We can't do this."

But his tongue replaced his lips and sent fire shimmering through her blood. His hands went around her, his palms sliding up her rib cage to cup her breasts. Her head lolled to the side, then fell back against his shoulder as she released a low moan.

She was losing control faster than she could call it back, and couldn't remember why she cared. Rourke's hands were gentle as those clever fingers turned their magic to her breasts, kneading and caressing through the fabric of her gown.

He nipped at her earlobe. "I want ye, Wildcat." His voice was low and strained as he whispered against her sensitive flesh. "Let me ease your body in other ways."

Bad idea. Bad idea. The words kept going through her head even as she turned and wrapped her arms around his neck, demanding his kiss. Passion flared.

Her senses swam in his taste, his scent, the feel of his hands roaming her body with barely controlled urgency. As one they rose, pulling off clothing with shaking hands until they stood facing one another, the firelight flickering over their naked skin.

She stared at Rourke, at the play of light over the ridges of muscle.

He covered her bare breasts lightly, reverently. "So bonnie. Yer the most beautiful woman I've ever seen, Wildcat." As one hand stayed on her breast, the other tracked lower, dipping between her legs. A single finger delved into her wet heat.

Brenna groaned, melting from that erotic touch. She wanted more. Her fingers closed around his erection, eliciting a hard groan from his throat.

"I need you, Pirate."

He kissed her hard, then swept her into his arms and strode the few feet to the bed. But instead of laying her on the mattress, he set her on the floor, lay down on his back, and tugged her onto him.

Without hesitation, she straddled his hips and took him deep inside, riding him until they both lay sated and spent.

Rourke's hand stroked her back. The flesh where she lay on top of him was damp with sweat. But there was no room on the bed on either side for her to roll off of him. There would be no sharing this bed even if they wanted to, unless they stayed where they were, one on top of the other.

Finally, she got up and pulled on her shift to act as a nightgown. Rourke spread a blanket on the floor and lay down, naked as she settled on the bed.

"Sleep, Wildcat. Sleep well."

"You too, Pirate."

But as she curled up on the bed alone, she knew her dreams would be haunted by the emptiness stretching in front of her.

The next morning, Brenna was strung so tight she was afraid she was going to snap. With every mile, as they drew nearer to Deveron House and the family she'd lost, her tension tightened another turn. If only she could figure out a way to get Rourke to give her another of those body-melting massages as she rode.

She glanced at him and he met her gaze, his head dipping in a silent nod as if he sensed how nervous she was and reminded her she could do this. And he'd be right beside her when she did.

That simple nod, and the warmth in his eyes, calmed her, settling her nerves. *Why?* Why did she need him so much? She feared he was a weakness she couldn't afford.

The miles passed at once slowly and all too quickly.

"We are nearly upon it," Angus announced a few hours later.

Brenna's heart cramped with apprehension. They were almost there. *Home.* Her father. Her family.

What would they think of her? They weren't likely to be pleased. Her manners were good for the society in which she'd been raised, but she remembered Aunt Janie harping at her constantly as a young girl about things that none of her friends were required to do or say. Things she was now certain she should have learned. If only she could remember what they were.

As they turned off the main road onto a treelined drive, a strange excitement leaped within her. *I know this place.* The memories weren't clear, only the knowledge that she'd been there before.

Through the trees Brenna caught a glimpse of a house.

A *mansion*. Her stomach knotted. She wanted to tell them to stop. Not yet. She wasn't ready.

What would they say? If only she could snatch up her cell phone and call first. Warn them she was coming.

As they approached a turn, she knew suddenly it would be the last before the house came into view. Brenna held her breath, waiting for the first sight of home since she'd left so suddenly when she was five.

She barely noticed as the men in front of her pulled up as they rounded the corner, so anxious was she to see her home. She pushed between them only to freeze as her gaze caught sight of what had stopped them. Ice congealed in her veins. Her head began to pound as emotions tore through her. Horror. Anger. Fury at the fates for letting her come so close before snatching it all away.

Before her stood not the home of her childhood that she'd dreamed of and longed for all her life, but a singed, eyeless stone shell.

Deveron House had burned.

SIXTEEN

"It happened recently," Angus said. "The smell of smoke is still strong."

Brenna's head pounded. Her chest felt as if it would explode. She wanted to scream. *It's not fair.* She'd waited so long. So long.

What if her father had died?

She urged her mare forward, pushing between the two riders in front of her.

"Wildcat," Rourke called, but she was driven by a need and a fear that overshadowed everything else.

She'd barely gone ten yards when her horse balked. Clearly, her mount did not share her desire to race toward the scene of this latest disaster.

Rourke pulled up beside her. "She fears the smell of smoke."

Anguish tore through Brenna as she dismounted. "I have to know if he died." She started up the dirt road on foot, half running, half walking, heart thundering in her ears.

"Wildcat, wait!" His footsteps pounded behind her.

The memory of Rourke's tying her in the cave made her hackles rise and she swung toward him, feet braced, ready for a fight.

"Don't you dare try to stop me. This is *my* home. I have every right to find out what happened."

He met her gaze, his jaw clenched. Finally, he nodded. "I'll tend ye."

She turned and continued toward the burned-out structure, her gaze taking in the charred grasses surrounding the mansion. Two trees that had stood nearby had been reduced to burnt timbers. It must have been a heck of a blaze.

Please let him have gotten out.

Deveron House was a huge, gray stone building, large and symmetrical with dozens of hollow windows laid out in neat, black-tinged rows. Chimneys popped out of the crumbling roof at regular intervals, while the front door hung askew, charred and broken.

As they reached the stone stairs leading to the door, Rourke grabbed her arm.

Brenna jerked him loose. "Don't try to stop me."

"Think with yer head, Wildcat, not your anger. The floors will be unstable and the last of the roof looks ready to drop at the slightest provocation. Go around instead. There may be another way to see inside without endangering yourself."

Reason hadn't completely deserted her. He was right, dammit.

She brushed past him as she ran down the steps, then with angry strides crossed the charred grass to the back of the mansion. Behind the house, a low wall encircled an intricate garden, amazingly untouched by the fire. To one side of the garden a building stood, equally untouched, that looked to be stables. To the other side, a low-roofed wing jutted out from the back of the house that didn't appear to be as badly burned.

Rourke was eyeing the wing. "Wait here, Wildcat. I wish to see what's there. If 'tis safe, we can go in together, aye?"

She just stared at him as he strode away. He didn't even hear himself. *Stay here. Wait here. Be a good little girl.*

All she wanted to do was lop off someone's head, preferably whoever set this fire. If it *had* been set. She supposed the house could have burned by accident. But it seemed somehow fitting that the black cloud of disaster that was following her around had gotten ahead of her this time.

She watched Rourke a moment longer, then turned and headed for the gray stone building she'd decided was a stable. As she rounded the corner, she saw one of the doors was ajar. Good. She wouldn't have any trouble getting inside.

"Wildcat!"

Brenna growled under her breath. Her keeper had discovered she hadn't waited where he'd told her to. Well, he could just go to hell. She slipped inside the stable doors, the light dim, her eyes all but blind until they adjusted.

She heard a sound barely a second before a large, strong hand grabbed her arm. "Who are ye?" a harsh voice demanded.

Behind her, the door swung wide and the unmistakable sound of a sword being drawn filled the quiet stables. Rourke, coming to her rescue, no doubt.

I don't need rescuing, dammit! All the frustration, all the anger boiling inside her found a target, and she spun and slammed her knee into her assailant's groin with bone-jarring accuracy.

The man, who looked rather young now that her eyes were adjusting, let out a strangled yell as he released her and doubled over.

Hah. Bull's-eye. Skirts and all.

"Drop your sword."

Brenna jumped back out of the reach of the man she'd just attacked as a second man stepped out of one of the stalls—a big man with a bigger gun pointed right at Rourke's heart.

Please God, not again. There was no Hegarty to save him this time.

Rourke shoved his sword into his belt and raised his hands slowly. "We mean no harm." His gaze flicked to the groaning man and then to her. "*I* mean ye no harm."

"Thanks a lot," she muttered. Her gaze returned to the man she'd injured. He *was* young, she realized as he raised his head to glare at her. He was lean and looked to be rather tall, though it was hard to tell about his height when he was bent double.

The wicked-looking knife at his waist caught her attention and she backed closer to Rourke. Her gaze swiveled to the man holding the gun. This one looked more like a linebacker for the Baltimore Ravens—broad face, mile-wide shoulders. Neither of the men were dressed like dandies, nor were they in rags. Just pants and shirts similar to the ones Rourke wore. On the linebacker's head was a round, floppy hat with a sprig of some kind of wildflower pinned to it.

"Who are ye?" the big man demanded, his gun still pointed at Rourke's middle.

"Rourke Douglas. Viscount Kinross."

The man's eyes widened. Slowly he dropped the muzzle of his gun.

"Are ye kin to Alexander?" Rourke asked.

The man nodded slowly. "Aye. I am his nephew." He nodded toward the victim of Brenna's attack. "Malcolm is his son."

Rourke reached for Brenna and cupped her shoulder. "Ye may be wishing to apologize, Wildcat. Ye may have just ended your own family line."

Brenna looked at him with confusion. "I *what*?"

"Ye've just unmanned your brother."

Her pulse leaped as her wide-eyed gaze went from Rourke to the man and back again. "My . . . ?"

Rourke lifted his brows ruefully. "Brother."

"Oops."

"My . . . sister . . . is dead," Malcolm grunted. He tried to straighten, then groaned and doubled over once more.

She looked at the downed man with shocked dismay. *Brother? I have a brother?*

"Brenna?" The elder of the two Camerons took a step toward her, his gun hanging at his side. "Is it truly you, lass?"

Her scalp tingled as she met his searching gaze. "I'm Brenna Cameron."

Suddenly a grin broke over his face. "Aye, and I should ha' known." He laughed, a deep hearty sound, and glanced at Rourke. "He calls ye Wildcat. An apt name, for you were always a wild wee thing."

He took another step toward her. "You dinna remember me, lass, but I was a great favorite of yours once. Your cousin, Hamilton, I am. I'm ten years your senior and you tagged along after me like a duckling to her mam. I used to carry you on my shoulders when you got big enough to hold on. We were a pair, we were. I missed you heartily when you left."

A wisp of a memory teased her mind. "I remember." She was starting to shake. "Hamilton. I called you Ham and Eggs."

The man chuckled. "Aye, you did, then you fell on the ground laughing at your own jest. Every time." His eyes sobered, a sorrow entering them. "Where have you been, Brenna?"

The enormity of the answer nearly overwhelmed her. *I've been three hundred years in the future, driving a machine sixty miles an hour while listening to music played by a band that wasn't there on my way home to watch people on the other side of the world from a small box in my cool living room during the heat of the summer. I returned home by flying over the Atlantic Ocean inside the belly of a great steel bird.*

"I've been lost," she told him. "I didn't know how to get home."

"But you're here now. You've come home at last."

Brenna nodded, needing to ask the question she most dreaded. "I'm looking for my father. Is he still alive?"

Malcolm growled.

Hamilton's face lost all sign of humor. "I canna say, lass. He was taken two days past by the earl's soldiers."

The earl's soldiers.

This couldn't be happening. Two days. Twenty years she'd waited to see him again, and she'd missed him by *two days*?

"Why? Why did the earl take him?"

"He wanted you. His soldiers threatened to set fire to the house, then slaughter all who escaped unless he gave you up. But you werena here."

She curled her arm around her middle, reeling from the words. "How many died?" Because of her. She hadn't realized she'd swayed until Rourke grabbed her arm, righting her.

"Thankfully, none. Alex convinced them you were not here and agreed to go with them in your stead. They still torched the house, but not until all had escaped unharmed."

Brenna heard the words as if from a distance, through a thick, blanketing mist of bloodred fury.

She jerked free of Rourke's supporting hold. "*That goddamn son of a bitch.*"

Hamilton's eyes widened.

"She is no lady," Malcolm gasped behind her.

"They're taking my father back to Stour. God knows what they'll do to him. I'm going after him." She whirled and pushed past Rourke and out of the stable into the muted sunshine.

"Brenna!" Hamilton yelled.

"Wildcat!"

Rourke and Hamilton caught up with her before she made it to the back corner of the house.

"Brenna, wait," Hamilton said. "You dinna understand."

Brenna slowed only fractionally. "The Earl of Slains wants me dead," she spat. "He's wanted me dead for twenty years, ever since some idiot seer told him I'd cause his destruction. He burned Rourke's castle and killed his parents when they tried to protect me. Now he's torched my family's home and taken my father until you give me up to him. This isn't going to end until one of us is dead." She shot him a hard look. "How am I doing so far?"

"Aye, well, mayhap you do understand. But you canna simply go after him."

She picked up her skirts and strode angrily toward the front of the house. "Watch me."

Rourke grabbed her arm and stopped her. "Brenna, wait."

She glared at him, then flicked her gaze to his crotch. "You're risking your posterity."

To his credit, he blanched only a little. "A battle such as this must be waged with care. I dinna deny your right to wage it, but—"

"Since when?"

He sighed. "I wouldna have ye rush in and get yourself killed."

She was shaking, the hatred choking her. But he was

right. As much as she wanted to go in, knee swinging, she couldn't take on an entire castle single-handedly.

Her gaze went to her brother as he hobbled toward them, leading two horses. In the muted sunshine, his hair shone as auburn as her own. A brother.

Glimmers of memory curled through her mind. Little Malcolm leaning on the other side of their mother as she told them a bedtime story. His hand tucked into hers as they snuck out to the stables to watch the horses being saddled. His warm body tucked against hers in bed at night.

Brenna shook her thoughts out of the past and turned her gaze from Rourke to Hamilton and back again. "I agree we need a plan. But the Earl of Slains is *mine*."

Malcolm scoffed as he joined them. "Yer naught but a lass. What can you do?"

She glanced meaningfully at his crotch. "If I'd wanted to kill you, you'd be dead, little brother."

Malcolm scowled at her and stepped toward her as if he might strike her.

Rourke moved between them. "Wildcat, he's your kin. You'll show him the proper respect."

Brenna clenched her jaw on the choking frustration. Malcolm was right. What *could* she do? If she could *will* the Earl of Slains dead, he'd be frying by now. But this wasn't a battle of wills or brains. This battle required brute force and skillful wielding of a powerful weapon. And she sorely lacked both.

Then again, she might just know something that even the Earl of Slains didn't know. Something that could give her the ultimate advantage.

"Maybe I can't take on the earl. But I can help rescue my father."

"Nay," Malcolm spat. "You will remain with the women where you belong."

"We will discuss this with the council," Hamilton said.

But the younger man was not appeased. "I am acting chieftain of this clan in my father's stead. *I* make the decisions."

Hamilton clapped him on the shoulder. "Still, we must consult the council, aye, for of a certainty this affects us all."

"We should turn her over to the earl and be done with it." The look Malcolm shot her was laced with hatred.

Something inside her shriveled. What had she done?

"Malcolm." She wasn't certain what she would say to him. She only knew she had to say something.

But her brother only turned away. Twenty years she'd longed for this reunion, and she had already ruined the chance to reconnect with the first family member she came across.

"Fintrie Castle used to be the seat of the Camerons of Deveron," Hamilton told them.

Rourke glanced at Brenna, who'd ridden silently beside him since leaving Deveron House, and then at Malcolm. The air was thick with sibling strife. But these two had no shared memories of better times to fall back on and Rourke worried at what the acting chieftain might do.

Malcolm had not physically hurt her. Rourke would never allow that. But her brother could make her life miserable in other ways. And Brenna, poor lass, was in sore need of a warm family welcome. Even if she had brought Malcolm's ire upon herself.

In the distance, a town rose from the coastal plains. A small castle sat in the middle of the village as if naught but another house, looking as out of place as an eaglet in a sparrow's nest.

"Deveron House was started near to a hundred years

ago and took seventeen years to complete," Hamilton continued. "The old laird who commissioned it ne'er saw his creation unfold, but the chieftain has lived there ever since. His younger brother took on at Fintrie and his line remains there still. We'll all be living there now," he added soberly.

Rourke wondered how long it would take Brenna to win over her kin, for he couldn't leave until he felt certain she was safe. But once he was sure, he'd ride for Castle Stour.

After running from the prophecy for twenty years, he was suddenly itching for the fight to come. He was more than ready to face the man who even now threatened the woman he loved, the man who'd had his parents killed. The man who had wreaked havoc on the northeast coast with his greed and callous attitude toward those weaker than him, and caused so much destruction out of fear of a simple prophecy and a wee lass.

Either the earl or Brenna would die, of a certainty. He meant to make sure Brenna survived. It was the one good thing he could make of his wasted life.

"How much older am I than you?" Brenna asked Malcolm.

The young man merely grunted, but did not reply.

"Two years," Hamilton said instead. "Do you remember him?"

"I'm starting to. A few things. He followed me around a lot."

"Och, aye. He was always trying to keep up with you, but you were a wee terror, into mischief more oft than not. Malcolm became the terror when you left. Ye'd have been a pair, if the fates had not intervened."

"Are there others?" Brenna asked Hamilton, her eyes brimming with curiosity. "Do I have any other brothers or sisters?"

"Nay, there's just the two of you. Your mam had three before you and one more after Malcolm, but none of the lot lived to see their first year."

Brenna's brow creased. "The last one killed her."

"Aye. And didna live long herself."

The discussion came to a halt as they rode into the village. It was smaller than Monymusk, but well tended, with houses marching in neat rows along the cobbled streets. The hooves of their horses clattered along the cobbles as they rode toward the thick, turreted walls of Fintrie Castle.

Rourke moved his mount beside Hamilton's. "'Twould be best not to reveal her identity. The earl will be waiting for word that she's been seen."

Hamilton met his gaze, his eyes wise as he nodded. "I was thinking the same."

"She's the Lady Marie, then."

When they reached the thick, studded oak castle doors, they found several armed men waiting for them. Hamilton dismounted and Rourke followed suit, then lifted Brenna down. Malcolm still could not fully stand. Rourke winced in sympathy, wondering what additional pain the ride must have inflicted.

They followed Hamilton into a courtyard very different from the one at Picktillum. Whereas Picktillum had a virtual village within its walls, the village here was just outside. Within the walls was a full garden brimming with roses and other flowering plants his mother would have known the names of.

As they followed the wide path to the steps which led to the keep's door, Rourke grasped Brenna's shoulder, silently lending his support.

She glanced up at him, her green eyes worried, her mouth taut. But as their gazes met, her expression softened and she reached up and took his hand, squeezing it, thanking him silently.

Hamilton and Malcolm led the way into the entry hall where they were met by two women, one round with age, the other round with babe.

"Hamilton, who are . . . ?" The older woman stared at Brenna, her cheeks going pale. "Saints have mercy, 'tis our Ena, back from the grave."

"Nay, Mum," Hamilton said, grabbing the woman's arm to steady her.

Her gaze swung to her son, then back to Brenna as understanding dawned and with it a smile of such hope that Rourke was once again filled with self-hatred for having tried to send the lass back to her own world.

"Brenna," the woman breathed. "Is it you, lass?"

Brenna stood uneasily by his side, raking her teeth over her bottom lip as her gaze went to Hamilton.

Hamilton just shrugged as if to say he should have known there would be no fooling his mother.

She'd not be Lady Marie after all.

Brenna nodded slowly. "It's me."

The woman lifted her hands and shook them, rushing forward to enfold Brenna in a huge hug. When she pulled back, she slapped her palms to her cheeks. "The image of your mother, you are, lassie. The very image." She smiled sadly. "But ye dinna remember. Do ye remember me?"

Brenna shook her head. "No. I'm sorry."

The woman grabbed her hands. "Never you mind. You were such a wee slip of a thing when last you were here. I'm yer aunt. Yer father's sister, Gaira. Praise the heavens, Alex will be beside himself when he hears."

Gaira blanched at the sound of her own words. A silence descended over the group and Rourke knew they all had the same thought. Alex Cameron would indeed be beside himself . . . if he still lived.

"Och, come, lassie," Gaira said, pulling Brenna along at her side as the younger woman joined them. She approached Brenna shyly.

"Brenna? 'Tis me. Larena. Do you remember?"

Brenna gave a helpless shake of her head.

"I am your cousin. We are of an age, you and I. We used to be very close."

"Lari's a year older," Hamilton said behind her. "But 'twas you who was the leader, always gettin' the pair o' ye into one scrape or another."

"That seems to be a recurring theme," Brenna muttered.

Larena grinned. "Do ye not remember the time we tried to saddle and ride one of the hunting hounds?"

Rourke felt his mouth twitch as he tried to imagine the two wee lassies trying to ride the hound. She'd been a wildcat from the start, which might have served her well growing up as she had. Such abandonment might have broken a softer lass. Nothing broke his wildcat.

As others gathered around her, Rourke felt himself slowly pushed to the side, along with the other men. Hamilton clapped him on the back. "Come share a wee dram with me, laddie."

But Rourke's gaze remained firmly on Brenna as the women began to usher her toward the upper stair.

"She'll be fine, Kinross. They'll not harm her."

But as she allowed them to lead her away, Brenna's gaze sought and captured his. Panic shimmered in the green depths of her eyes, telling him she needed him still.

"'Tis time we made plans," Hamilton said when supper was over.

Brenna was seated in the middle of the long table between Hamilton and Rourke. She watched the heads of a number of the men bob in agreement as the women of the clan rose and left their seats. Her aunt came up behind her and slipped her arm through Brenna's, pulling her to her feet. "Come, lass. We've given you time to settle, eh? Now 'tis time for you to tell us a story or two about where you've been."

Brenna braced herself, refusing to be pulled away. She didn't want to be rude, but they sure as heck weren't ready to hear about the twenty-first century. Besides, she fully intended to be part of the battle planning.

With care, she extricated her arm. "I'm sorry, Aunt Gaira, but no. I'm staying here."

Several of the men exchanged disapproving glances. Hamilton watched her calmly.

"This is a man's discussion," Malcolm said from the head of the table.

Brenna met his gaze, biting her tongue from saying what she really wanted to. *Well, I guess that leaves you out.*

"Is it?" She forced herself to remain calm as she stood, staring him down. "I thought you were planning to discuss how to rescue *my* father who was taken in place of *me* because of a prophecy that states that *I* will cause the Earl of Slains's destruction. Forgive me for believing this conversation concerns me."

One of the elders spoke up. "You're just a lass, Brenna. You must leave the warmongering to the men. Now run along with the women."

All the anger and injustice of the past days, past years, bubbled up until she could barely speak through the bitter taste in her mouth. *Screw being calm.*

She leaned her hands on the table, looking directly at the old coot who she knew was some kind of cousin of her father's. Neil, she'd heard him called. But before she could start with her tirade, Rourke rose beside her and put a hand on her shoulder.

Brenna knocked his hand away. She couldn't take it from him, too. "Don't you dare—"

"I agree with ye." In his pale eyes she saw warmth and understanding. And something far more precious—respect. "Ye should be part of this."

He turned to the others. "The prophecy and everything to do with it affects her, aye? But the reasons for her to remain are far beyond mere involvement. The lass is a hellcat. A fierce and courageous fighter. And she kens more about Castle Stour than any man here, I trow. She's been inside."

Exclamations of surprise erupted around the table.

Brenna jerked her gaze to Rourke's, then remembered telling him, shortly after diving off the ship, that she'd toured Stour.

Hamilton nodded. "She should remain."

Malcolm scowled, but Brenna ignored him as Rourke held her chair out for her and she retook her seat. She met Hamilton's gaze with gratitude and earned a quick wink. Some of the men were still grumbling under their breath.

Rourke's hand slid over her knee and she took the support he offered, twining her fingers through his. She met his warm gaze and felt him climb right down into her soul. He'd become not only her protector, but her champion. She knew better than to think he didn't bear watching. He was still all too likely to try to keep her out of harm's way. But he'd supported her just now against a roomful of men and for that she could kiss him.

With a last scowl her way, Malcolm launched into the discussion. "Missives have been sent to eight of our allies. 'Twill likely be days before we receive any replies. If we can amass a great enough force, we shall attack Stour and demand the release of my father."

One of the elders, a man with little hair and fewer teeth, rose unsteadily. "The king, I say. Ye must go to the king."

"Ye auld fool," Neil replied. "The king is beholden to Slains for much of his support. He'll not side with us on anything concerning Slains and Stour."

"Ye cannot know . . ."

Brenna rose. "Why don't we—"

Neil cut her off as he motioned toward Rourke. "The Douglases have always allied themselves with us. We've got Lord Kinross himself here."

Brenna crossed her arms. God, this was going to try her patience. "Why don't we—"

"And the Camerons of Locheil," the elder broke in.

"They'll—" Neil began.

Brenna had had enough. She slammed her hands on the table, rattling the china and silver. She was seething and suspected everyone at the table knew it by now.

"Och, aye, uncle," Hamilton said, a twinkle in his eye. "You dinna want to cross this one. She's got Alex's own temper. She'd as likely kick you in the ballocks as look at you, wouldn't she, Malcolm?"

Malcolm just grunted.

"The lass is no lady," Neil complained.

"She can be," Rourke said beside her. He gave her a sidelong look. "I think. But she is a warrior first. She took down four of my crew with her bare hands. And I was captaining a muckle rough crew."

Hamilton nodded at her. "Say your piece, Cousin."

Brenna looked from one man to the next, daring anyone to cut her off again. Some looked down or away, but most met her gaze with curiosity, if not approval.

"I assume the reason you are not discussing a rescue attempt is that you know of no way into the castle past the guards, am I correct?"

Old Neil scoffed. "And would ye be taking out the earl's army with your bare hands?"

"That will be all, Neil," Hamilton said sharply. "Brenna is your laird's daughter, and you will provide her, at the very least, the respect due to her as such."

The old man grumbled and picked at a stain on the tablecloth in front of him.

Brenna watched him, wondering briefly how many bridges she was going to burn today. "I think I know a way into the castle." Her gaze swiveled to Hamilton. "A way that possibly even the Earl of Slains doesn't know about."

"How do you come by such knowledge?" Hamilton asked, his eyes excited yet confused.

"It's a long story."

Rourke spoke beside her, his voice low. "Are you certain it now exists?"

She met his gaze. "Certain? No. But historians believe it was part of the original construction. They believe none of the Earls of Slain ever knew of it."

Rourke nodded gravely. "I am willing to make the attempt."

Hamilton nodded. "As am I."

All eyes slowly turned to Malcolm, who sat watching the table stonily.

"What say you, lad?" Hamilton asked him.

Malcolm lifted his head and looked from Hamilton to Brenna. He sat up and leaned forward, addressing her. "Where inside the castle would ye take us?"

"The dungeons, I think."

"And will you lead us inside?"

Hamilton and a couple of others made sounds of disapproval, but Brenna met the challenge in Malcolm's eyes. "Absolutely. You're not going in without me."

Rourke put his hand on her arm. "Wildcat. 'Tis too dangerous."

"Aye," Hamilton chimed in. "You can tell us the way."

But her gaze remained on Malcolm's. He would sacrifice her in a heartbeat. But his lack of concern for her welfare was just the weapon she needed.

"If he's being held in the dungeons, I can possibly get you in and out without you ever being seen. I can't promise, because any number of things could go wrong, but

I'm the best chance you have of getting him out of there alive."

"Brenna, nay," Hamilton said. "Your father would ne'er forgive us."

"My brother is chief of this clan until our father returns. If we're going to free him, there's no room for fear. Either for ourselves, or for one another."

Malcolm rose. Now that the pain she'd inflicted on him seemed to have passed, he stood tall and straight. At twenty-three, he still had a lankiness about him, but she saw the promise of power in his build. And the pride of generations of Cameron leaders in his stance.

"My sister has the way of it." He acknowledged her as kin for the first time. "If she has knowledge that we need, we'd be fools to ignore her."

"How do we know she can be trusted?" Neil asked. "She may have turned spy for the earl."

Rourke opened his mouth to defend her, but Malcolm got there first.

"If you'd heard the filth coming from her mouth when she learned of our father's capture, you'd not being asking, Neil. She's risking her life more than any among us by leading us into Stour. If the earl catches her, he'll not be releasing her alive." Malcolm's gaze swung to her and held. "And she knows it well." In his eyes, she saw something dawn and grow. A grudging respect.

Brenna inclined her head in acknowledgment. The two of them had a long way to go to develop any kind of familial relationship, but this was a start. And he was giving her exactly what she wanted—a chance to find her father. And a chance to end this curse upon her family once and for all.

SEVENTEEN

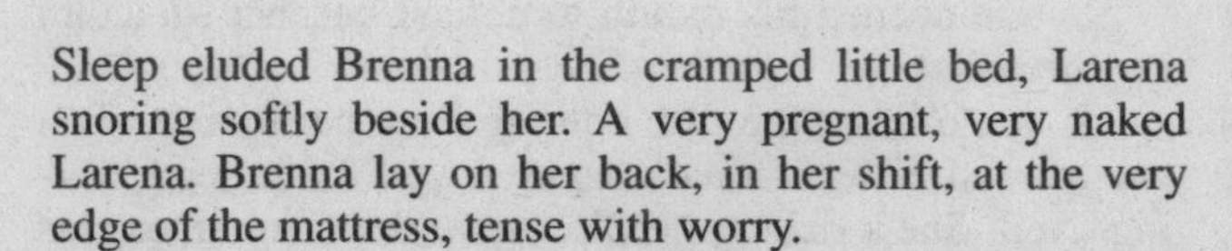

Sleep eluded Brenna in the cramped little bed, Larena snoring softly beside her. A very pregnant, very naked Larena. Brenna lay on her back, in her shift, at the very edge of the mattress, tense with worry.

At daybreak they were heading for Stour. Rourke, Malcolm, Hamilton, and her. Others would follow later, but they didn't want to attract attention by moving too large a force at once. Four travelers would attract little attention. When they got close, they'd lay low until the middle of the night, then go in.

Hopefully. The tour guide had speculated that the third earl hadn't known of the existence of the cave and the entrance. What if he was wrong? The thought made her stomach churn. What if this didn't work? What if they couldn't get in?

But she knew. If she couldn't get her father out the back way, she'd find a way to trade herself for him. He wasn't going to die for her. No one else was going to die for her.

Her old life and all its responsibilities were gone, lost to her. And she'd been missing so long from this life she no longer had a place in it. She was completely expendable. Either she or the earl must die. And if it had to be her, so be it.

This would be her gift to those who'd suffered so much because of this prophecy and, indirectly, because of her. Her biggest fear was that Rourke would get in the way and try to save her. His death had nearly destroyed her once. She couldn't bear the thought of it happening again.

The nearly total silence of the night pressed in on her. Larena was a quiet sleeper and the usual night sounds were missing here. The hum of the air conditioner. The sound of traffic on the street. The distant whine of a siren.

The only sounds that reached her ears were the footsteps of the guards walking the castle walls—or battlements, as Larena called them.

A wave of longing washed over her for the simplicity of that other time. She never would have thought the twenty-first century simple compared to the seventeenth, but for her it had been. Her only concerns had been to keep the restaurant running smoothly and to pay her bills on time.

For a single, harsh moment, she desperately wished Hegarty would appear and offer to take her back there. To that time and place where she'd spend her days off at the mall or the gym and her evenings in front of the television.

Simple. Boring.

Lonely.

She didn't want to die.

It wasn't the thought of death itself that terrified her, but the dying. And what would happen before. She had no illusions the Earl of Slains would merely lop off her head and be done with it. No, he'd use her first. He'd make her suffer. And after twenty years of searching for her, he'd probably make a spectacle of her death.

Shaking, she sat up and buried her fingers in her hair, trying to escape the terrifying scene playing out in her head. Men holding her down, fumbling with their pants.

Her heart thudded. It might not end that way. It might not. The prophecy said she'd win. Or at least take him down with her.

And if the fates were on her side? If she had the chance, would she really be able to slide her little knife through a man's heart?

Oh yeah. She'd never laid eyes on the Earl of Slains, *this* Earl of Slains, yet she hated him with every cell, every molecule, of her body. This man she could definitely kill. If she got the chance. If he didn't kill her first.

Without realizing what she was doing, she climbed out of bed, her breaths quick and shallow.

She needed Rourke. With an urgency bordering on desperation, she needed to feel his arms around her.

Brenna headed for the door.

The soft rap at his door pulled Rourke from a dreamless sleep. He strode, naked, to answer the knock. The moment he opened the door, Brenna slipped inside.

"Wildcat?" Even as he reached for her, she dove into his arms and wrapped herself around him, her body trembling. "What's the matter, lass?"

"Make love to me, Rourke."

And suddenly he understood. She was suffering from battle nerves, the fear and anticipation of death. But she wasn't going to die. He wouldn't allow it.

His hand slid down her back, over the cotton shift and

back up again. "You dinna have to go with us, lass. Tell me where the path is and stay here where yer safe."

"I'm not safe here. I'm not safe anywhere. Besides, you'll never find the way without me."

He felt her fingers slide across his cheeks.

"Kiss me, Rourke. Make love to me."

"Aye." He couldn't deny her, nor did he wish to. He took her into his arms and they came together in a wild recklessness that spoke of need and wanting as much as the fear of looming death.

He pulled the shift over her head, letting it drop to the floor as he swept her into his arms and deposited her in the middle of the bed. The moment she hit the mattress, she pulled his face down to hers as if she couldn't bear to be parted from his kisses for even a moment and kissed him with a wildness that nearly drove him over the edge.

As her soft flesh pressed against his entire length, he tore his lips from hers and buried his face in her neck, drinking in the soft fragrance that was part sea nymph, part rose soap, and all Brenna.

She reached for him, her fingers closing around his engorged root. "I want you."

"Aye, lass. Easy."

Her short nails raked gently over his sensitive skin as she pulled on him, driving him insane with wanting, but rough mating was not her way. She was looking for oblivion. Instead, he wanted to give her a memory to last a lifetime.

"Brenna . . ." With effort, he pulled her an arm's length away and peered into her face, faintly illuminated by the full moon's light. Aye, he saw in her eyes the acceptance of death and the desperation to live until the very last moment.

He took her hands in his, then lifted them gently above her head. "Do ye trust me?"

"I want you inside me."

"Aye, I ken that. But 'twas not what I asked. Do you trust me, Wildcat?"

"Yes, but . . ."

"Keep your hands above your head, lass." He released her wrists, but she remained still as he'd told her to. "Aye, that's it. I'm going to steal the nerves from ye, Wildcat. Then I'm going to please you."

"Rourke, it's the middle of the night."

"Do ye have somewhere ye need to be, then?"

She laughed. The sound, little more than a soft burst of air, was enough.

He smiled and moved his hands to her shoulders, kneading them gently, then lifted each arm and eased the tension out of her muscles.

"Roll onto your stomach, lass."

When she did, he continued the sensual exploration of her back, pulling the tightness out of her muscles as he slowly worked his way down her spine with his thumbs, then retraced the journey with his mouth, eliciting tiny moans from her.

Her skin was like satin, her scent beyond intoxicating. Any tension he released from her body went directly into his. Aye, but he wanted her.

Shifting, he straddled her legs, sitting back on his haunches as he slid his hands over the soft flesh of her rump, her groan of pleasure echoed his own. His body hardened. His breath became labored.

His hands slid still lower, easing the tightness in each trim, muscled thigh. Curving his hands around her legs, he slid his hands upward until his thumbs grazed the damp heat of her.

"Rourke."

He slid his fingers inside her. She was ready and weeping for him.

"Rise on your knees, Wildcat." He helped her pull her

knees up, lifting her rump to align with his root. "I'm going to take ye from here, Brenna."

"Yes."

He grabbed her hips between his hands and pressed himself against her, finding the heart of her. With a single, slow thrust, he buried himself deep within her sheath. Pleasure and tenderness thundered through his body.

Brenna cried out and pressed herself back, tighter against him, driving him deeper.

Over and over again, he pushed himself into her, his body tightening, rising.

"Rourke."

"Aye?" he gasped.

"I want to see you. I want to face you."

Gritting his teeth, he buried himself deep within her and held her tight against him, then slowly pulled out of her. The loss of her heat was torture. But when he expected her to move so that he could lie down, she rolled onto her back and spread her thighs, welcoming him.

"Ye need me beneath you, Wildcat."

"Maybe." She reached for him and pulled him down on top of her. "But I want to feel you over me, Rourke." Her hands caressed his face. "I love you, Pirate. What's more, I trust you."

Her words went straight to his heart like the stab of a well-honed blade. *You shouldn't trust me.* He sank back inside her because his body needed her too much to consider doing otherwise, and shoved his dark thoughts away.

Brenna met his thrust, pushing her hips against his as if she would devour him even as he buried himself within her. She pulled his head down and he kissed her, sinking into the sensations of his body, reveling in the passion that burst between them.

Ah, saints, she was magnificent. Each thrust drew a small moan from her throat, each moan building in intensity until she was nearly shouting her pleasure. Together they reminded him of a pair of wild horses racing for a cliff. Closer and closer they rode until finally, in an explosion of light, they leaped over, falling. Falling.

He rolled to his side, taking her with him in the circle of his arms. "Ye did it, Wildcat. My being on top dinna scare you."

"No." The word brimmed with smiles and she curved her body around his. "Nothing about you scares me."

As he stroked her hair, cradling her head against his heart, a wave of such tenderness as he'd never felt in his life broke over him, tethered by a guilt as deep as the ocean. He'd always intended to take his secret to the grave, but now he wondered if it was fair to her. She thought she loved him. But once she knew the truth, her heart would harden against him. And as badly as he'd wanted to avoid that, it might make his death easier on her, if it came to that.

"You make me weak," she murmured against his chest.

He stroked her back. "There is naught weak about ye, lass. Ye ken that."

"I need you, Rourke. I don't want to need you."

"Needing another doesna mean you're weak."

For several moments she was silent, as if taking in his words. Or lost in her own thoughts. "It does, though," she said finally. "Because if you don't need anyone, it doesn't break you when they leave."

His fingers played with her hair. "Or when they betray you, aye? We all betrayed you, Wildcat. Your mum and your aunt by dying. Your da by sending you away and not coming for ye when you were lost in that other time. And me." The admission felt like broken glass in his throat. "I betrayed you, too."

Her hand, tucked under her chin, moved to stroke his chest. "I understand why you tried to send me home without telling me I was from here. You only wanted to keep me safe from the Earl of Slains. You didn't betray me."

"Aye, lass, I did. And not just then. Another time." He shuddered, then shuddered again. Part of him wanted to push her away, to not be touching her as she stiffened in his arms. But a greater part couldn't bear to lose her until that very moment. He pulled her tighter, as if in holding her he could keep himself from breaking apart with the weight of the guilt. With the bitter, crushing weight of his self-hatred.

"I betrayed you worst of all, Brenna. Worst of all."

She stilled, but didn't pull away. "What do you mean?"

Another shudder tore through his body. "It's about the fire, Wildcat. The one that destroyed my home. It was my fault. My fault my parents died. My fault you had to be sent away. It was all my fault."

"Rourke . . ."

Guilt twisted in his gut. His throat closed against the words. But he had to tell her. He owed her the truth. All of it.

"'Twas I who sent the earl's soldiers to Picktillum that day. 'Twas I who told them you were there."

He felt her stiffen beneath his touch. "You gave me away?"

"Aye. I wanted them to take you." He was glad for the dark, glad he couldn't see the hatred and disgust that would appear in her eyes.

"Why?"

Her soft confusion raked at his heart.

"I was angry with you. You'd broken the swan I'd carved for my mother's birthday. I didn't know . . . until James told me, I didn't know you'd just learned of your own mother's death. The messenger had arrived just that morning with the news. You were bereft and came seeking me as you did every day. But instead you found the gift."

The day unfolded before him as if he were once more there, in that room.

"I'd spent hours finding the right basket, lining it with my mum's favorite wildflowers and heather to set the swan upon. I'd left it on my desk, waiting for the best moment to surprise her. But when that moment came and I returned to my room for it, I found you instead. You'd dumped the basket and flowers onto the floor and were holding the swan in your hands. I was outraged and ordered you to leave my chamber."

He blinked, seeing her as she'd been all those years ago. Cherub-faced and bonnie, her baby's cheeks wet, her lashes spiked with tears. Fury flashing in those green eyes.

"You threw the swan at my head. The bird crashed against the wall instead, and broke. I wanted to hit ye so bad the tears started leaking down my face. I didna want anyone to see, so I fled and saddled my mare and left Picktillum alone. I was almost to Monymusk when I came upon a pair of the earl's soldiers. They asked if I kent ye. If I knew where you were. I told them. I badly wanted them to take you away.

"I returned home a short time later to the sounds of shouts and screams." Sweat broke out on his body as he remembered the sight of his father's head. His mother lying in a pool of her own blood. The fire.

"My fault." He released her to roll off the bed, unable to stand the feel of her against his rancid flesh.

But as he sat up, Brenna grabbed his arm to keep him from leaving. "It wasn't your fault." Her words rang with harsh conviction.

"Wildcat, you don't understand. It was her birthday. I killed her on her birthday."

"You didn't kill her." She rose to her knees and wrapped her arms around his neck, holding him so tightly he thought she was trying to choke him.

But, no. It was the guilt choking him. He pulled her onto his lap and buried his damp face against her neck, desperate for her touch, her words, even as he knew she should hate him. God's blood, but he hated himself.

"You didn't kill her, Rourke. Think about it. The soldiers were already in Monymusk. They must have known I was at Picktillum."

"The earl had soldiers scouring the countryside for you. 'Twas only one of many places they were looking."

"You don't know that. They'd probably followed the messenger who'd brought the news of my mother. You only confirmed what they already knew."

"It doesna excuse what I did."

"What you did was selfish and mean-spirited," she said softly. "But it wasn't evil and it wasn't without justification. I'd ruined your precious gift. Broken it. You wanted to hit me and you didn't. That was huge for a kid your age. You found a more mature way to handle it . . . for a ten-year-old. You tried to send me away. You had no way of knowing they meant to kill me. And even if you did, you were *ten*."

A last shudder rolled through him as he realized she forgave him, crumbling the terrible weight of guilt he'd carried with him for so long. Could he ever forgive himself?

He rolled onto the bed, tucking her tight against his side as he saw that terrible day from a different angle for the first time. Through the eyes of a man grown instead of a horrified wee lad.

"I never meant for you to get hurt, Wildcat." Idly, he stroked her arm. "You annoyed the cockles out of me when you followed me around. But when your attention was turned elsewhere, I enjoyed watching you. I admired your spirit. You were, even then, a bonnie wee thing."

Her hand pressed lightly against his heart. "Is this why you've never gone home?"

"I couldna face my kin after what I'd done."

"They never blamed you."

"They didn't know."

"It wouldn't have mattered." She touched his jaw with her finger. "Do you hate me still for breaking your swan?"

"Nay. You were but a wee 'un."

"As were you. Just as you forgive the little girl who used to be me, you have to forgive the little boy who used to be you."

She rose then and covered his mouth with hers. It was all the invitation he needed. He slid his tongue between her lips, drinking from the well he'd feared all but lost to him. The sweet nectar of her forgiveness swept through him, loosening the dam of self-hatred lodged in his chest. So many years of hating himself. So many years of blaming himself.

Could he let it go now?

And then her tongue met his and all he could think of was Brenna. It was she who'd released him. She who'd liberated him, even though she had every right to hate him.

His spirit soared and he gathered her to him, loving her with a force that stole his breath and threatened to crush his heart beneath its weight.

His wildcat.

She rose and straddled him, taking him deep inside her. He loved her with his body until they were both tired and sated, then held her tucked tight against him as she slept. With his last breath, he would protect her. With his last drop of blood he would see her safe. Yet, as much as he wanted to, he couldn't leave her behind when the sun rose. He'd fought for her right to go after her father and he respected her too much to take that away from her.

Deep in his soul, he knew she sought the final battle with the Earl of Slains. But *that* he would deny her. She would lead them into Castle Stour and aid in the rescue of her father. Then, God willing, return safely to her kin.

The final battle was his and his alone. A retribution that had been a long time coming. For all he'd stolen from Brenna and himself, the earl would pay with his life.

EIGHTEEN

Two days later, Brenna stood at the edge of the surf near the small beach where she and Rourke had swum ashore barely a week ago, watching Castle Stour. Over the course of their two-day journey from Fintrie Castle, her fear and anger had slowly melded to form a single hard knot just below her rib cage. She never thought she'd be calm as she faced the prospect of death, but that's exactly what she was. Calm and deadly determined.

Rourke's big hand cupped her shoulder, holding her tucked against his side to keep her steady against the rolling edge of surf that continually ensnared their feet. Moments before, the sun had set, but the light was still bright enough that she could see the cave's entrance clearly.

"It's there in the cliffs, just below the castle walls." Brenna shaded her eyes from the lingering brightness, wishing she had a pair of binoculars. "A skinny upside-down triangle. It's not facing us head-on, so it looks even skinnier from here."

They'd come full circle, right back to where they started. They'd even approached the castle the way they'd left, taking the path between the surf and the sea caves. As a pair of seagulls soared by on the evening breeze, she turned to look up at Rourke, drinking in the sight of his strong profile, wishing things could have been different.

"I think I see it," Rourke murmured. "The rock just below it looks like a nose sticking out."

And it did. "Yep, that's it."

"Do you know the way to reach it, Wildcat?"

Brenna groaned. "No. But I was standing in the mouth and looked down to find a path leading toward the beach. Precarious, but it's there."

"'Twould help if you knew how to find it, Wildcat." His voice was wry.

"Yeah, I know." She hadn't given much thought to the actual finding of the path. Especially in the dark. "It's not going to be easy to locate or someone would have done it by now. But it's the only chance we have."

He squeezed her shoulder. "We'll find it."

As they turned back toward the cave where Hamilton and Malcolm waited, she looked at him sharply. "Don't even think about leaving me behind, Pirate. Getting into the cave isn't going to get you into the castle. The door's hidden. You won't find it without me."

He didn't say anything, his big hand gently gripping her shoulder. But his silence confirmed that he'd at least considered tying her in a cave yet again.

She could hardly get mad about it, though. Not when she was practically spitting distance from the monster's lair and Rourke had done nothing so far to hold her back. And she knew how badly he wanted to keep her safe. Just as badly as she wanted to protect him.

They made their way back to the sea cave where she and Rourke had briefly hidden a week ago when the bluecoats were chasing them. Hamilton and Malcolm had already opened the pack with their supper and were munching on cold pork and hard rolls.

Hamilton handed her a roll as she passed him. "Did ye find the cave?"

"Aye." Rourke grabbed a slab of pork. "But not the path to it. Once it's full dark, we'll have to do some scouting."

As she ate the quick meal, Brenna thought of the battle to come. For twenty years, she'd waited for this night without even knowing. Finding her father. Destroying the Earl of Slains as the prophecy foretold. She had to believe it would happen. She would fight to make *sure* it happened. Never had she been more ready for anything in her life.

Brenna's gaze went to her brother where he joked about how many bluecoats he could hoist on a single sword. Hamilton laughed. Rourke smiled. Men had strange senses of humor.

Over the past days' ride, she'd come to know Malcolm a little better. He was still cool with her as if he blamed her for all that had befallen the Camerons. And she knew that he did. But she also sensed in him an inherent kindness and had seen evidence of an honor that she greatly admired.

As Brenna sat in the damp cave, tearing off chunks of pork with her teeth, she suddenly wanted him to understand. Especially if she didn't survive. And if they did come out alive on the other end. Well, he was family.

When she was finished eating, Brenna washed her hands in the surf, then went to sit by her brother.

"We need to talk."

He glanced at her, his eyes cool. "Aye?"

Brenna motioned deeper into the cave. "Will you come with me?"

She could see by the stubborn bend of his mouth that he wanted to say no. But Rourke came to her aid.

He slapped Hamilton on the back and rose. "While you talk, Hamilton and I have a wee bit of scouting to do, aye?"

As the two men left, Brenna sat on the rock beside Malcolm. "You're angry with me. And it's not just because I attacked you in the stables."

Her brother only grunted, staring straight ahead.

"You blame me for all this, don't you? The fire. Our father being taken."

He finally met her gaze with a scowl. "You are a curse upon this clan and always have been."

Brenna sighed, hearing the anger in his words, feeling the pain of it pierce her heart. "I'm not the curse, Malcolm. The prophecy is the curse."

She turned until only one hip rested on the rock as she faced him. "Have you ever stopped to think what it was like for me? I was five . . . *five* . . . when I was torn from my family and exiled far away. Our aunt raised me until I was ten and then she died, leaving me completely alone with no understanding of where I belonged. No idea how to get home. I was ten years old and completely . . . *completely* . . . alone. I needed you."

Her voice broke and she turned back, sitting once more with her hands in her lap. "I needed all of you, but you didn't come for me. You left me there."

He turned to meet her gaze, his eyes narrowed and thoughtful. "We didna know where you were."

"I know that. *I* didn't know where I was. But I trusted my papa to find me. For years, I woke every morning hoping he'd finally come for me. But he never did."

"Ye were to have returned when you were grown."

Brenna cocked her head with surprise. "Who told you that?"

"A wee little man, Da said. Came soon after ye left to say ye'd be back when you were grown."

"Hegarty. He told Janie to bring me back when I was twenty-five."

"We expected ye sooner. Da said lasses are grown by their thirteenth year. Every day, he prayed this would be the day you came back to him." His voice turned bitter. "You are all he ever thought of."

And suddenly she understood. In her absence she'd become a ghost, haunting those she'd left behind.

Brenna laid her hand on Malcolm's forearm. "I'm sorry."

He sighed, the stiffness seeping from his spine as his gaze softened. "'Twas not fair of me to say that of Da. He paid me all the attention any lad could wish for. But he didna smile. Our grandmother told me he lost his smile the day he sent you away."

"Maybe." Brenna withdrew her hand. "But our mother died soon after that. It wasn't *me* he was mourning. At least not just me."

"I ne'er asked. 'Twas you he talked about. 'When Brenna comes home . . .' We celebrated your thirteenth birthday with great joy expecting you at any time. Your chamber was readied and day after day we waited. But you didn't come. Ye never came."

Tears burned her eyes as she thought of her father's hope turning slowly to dust as the months, then years went by. She knew all too well how painful hope could be. She pressed her fingers to her eyes, aching for the pain they'd all endured.

"At least I'm here now."

"How did you get here if Janie didna bring you?"

"Hegarty came for me. In his way."

"Where were you, Brenna?"

She met his gaze, then shot him a rueful smile. "I'll tell you about it, little brother. When this is over." If they got out of it alive. "Though I doubt you'll believe me."

"That bad, eh?"

Brenna shook her head. "Not bad. In some ways it was a great place to live. At least once I was an adult."

"How did ye get on as a lassie? All alone?"

"People took care of me. Some better than others."

"Did they hurt ye?" His voice had turned hard again, but this time in her defense.

"Not . . . No. Not really. But I learned to defend myself." She grimaced. "As you know."

To her surprise, Malcolm chuckled. "Aye, and well at that." He reached for her, his hand cupping her shoulder. "Ye'll forgive me, aye? I ne'er considered the situation from your place, as you said. It must have been muckle hard being all alone and lost as ye were."

She covered his hand with hers and met his gaze, so like her own. "You can't know what I would have given to have had a brother all those years." Out of nowhere, tears filled her eyes and slipped down her cheeks. "What I would give still."

His mouth pursed. Slowly, his arm slid around her shoulders and he pulled her against him. "Ye have a brother, lass. I'm told I worshiped ye when we were small. I think, mayhap, we could try again."

She wrapped her arms around him and felt him tighten his grip.

"I should take it as a personal favor, though, if ye'd not make a habit of unmanning me, aye?"

Her laughter took her by as much surprise as the tears had moments before. Pressing her face against his shoulder, she felt his body shake with laughter of his own.

Pulling back, she covered her mouth, cringing, even as she continued to laugh. "I'm *so* sorry about that, Malcolm. I was upset and angry, and I didn't know who you were."

"Did ye really take down half the viscount's crew as he says?"

"*Half?*" Joy bubbled up inside her at the admiration dancing in his eyes. "Just four. But, oh my God, they were pirates, Malcolm."

Brenna swiped at the last of the tears and just looked at him. So much to say. And yet nothing that needed saying at all. Expect for one thing.

"I'm glad you're my brother."

He pulled her close and kissed her on the forehead. "And glad I am you're home."

The sun was fully set by the time Rourke returned.

"Did you find the path?" Brenna asked anxiously.

"Aye. 'Tis well hid, but I found it. Take off your boots and hold up your skirts, Wildcat. The tide's risen."

Brenna did as he said, then took Rourke's hand.

Hamilton eased out of the cave first. Malcolm took up the rear. The night was clear, the moon half full. Bright enough to see where they were going, but bright enough, too, for a sharp-eyed bluecoat to catch the flash of movement. Fortunately, they'd prepared for the possibility of a clear night by dressing all in black.

Hamilton had told her Castle Stour hadn't been attacked since the first Earl of Slains's father seized it soon after it was built nearly a hundred years before. There was no reason they'd be expecting an attack tonight. Especially from the cliffs, by a mere four people.

The element of surprise was definitely on their side. Unfortunately, that might be the only thing that was.

By the time they reached the small beach, Brenna's feet and bare legs were soaked, but the rest of her was still reasonably dry. She took a moment to slip her boots back on, then took Rourke's hand again as he led them to the base of the cliffs. There was no actual path on the lower slope and they climbed single file, Rourke in the lead with Brenna right behind him. This time Hamilton brought up the rear.

Brenna cursed her decision to wear a gown instead of pants, but it was too late to do anything about it. Besides, if she needed to attract attention as she had once before, she didn't want to be forced to prove she was a woman. No way was she flashing anyone with her father and brother around.

Slowly they made their way up the cliffs, with Rourke lifting her up one ledge and then the next until finally they were at the base of the precarious little path she'd seen from the cave's mouth only a week ago.

A week.

Plus about three hundred and twenty-two years.

She remembered the twenty-first-century earl's granddaughter, Lintie, scrambling over the iron railing into the cave. Of course, the iron railing wasn't there yet. It wouldn't be added until the need arose to keep tourists and small grandchildren from falling.

They climbed the path easily. Rourke and Hamilton went into the cave first, swords drawn, while Malcolm lifted Brenna onto the mouth's ledge.

For the first time, her feet trod the same path they had in that other time, so far into the future. A week. A simple week of her life to have traveled so far.

Brenna had told them the cave was deep, so they'd risked bringing a small lantern to light the way. Hamilton lit the lamp and handed it to her. In the dim, flickering light, the cave looked strange and unfamiliar. Clearly, the refuge of seabirds in this time, the floor was thick with guano and crumbling sea grasses.

Brenna led the way, being the only one who knew where to go. The closer she got to the door, the stronger her heart pounded. What if it wasn't there? Or what if it was and they opened it onto a gathering of armed guards?

Worse, what if everything went as planned?

She grabbed for the wall as a hard shaft of fear barreled through her. Within minutes . . . *minutes* . . . she could be standing face-to-face with the Earl of Slains, the man who'd wanted her dead for twenty years.

Oh God, she didn't want to die. Not now.

"Wildcat?" Rourke's hand slid over her hair.

"I'm . . . okay. I just . . . needed a moment." She took a deep breath and struggled to get control over the sudden attack of nerves. It was too late to let them get the better of her. Way too late.

Because the earl wasn't the only one waiting for her on the other side of that door. Her father was, too.

She continued forward until she reached the small alcove at the very end of the cave that she knew hid the door. The wall was cool and damp against her fingertips, soft with moss or lichen in places. Lifting the lantern, she studied the rock, but could see no crevice, nothing to give away the door.

"It's here, on this wall. The door opens inward, into a pantry or a small storage chamber that, in turn, empties into what was originally the kitchens, but which I think are dungeons now. There could be guards anywhere."

"Inward makes little sense," Malcolm muttered. "Too easy to breach from outside."

Rourke shook his head. "There's no room for the door to swing on this side. And who would find it if they didn't know?"

"That's probably the reason no one in the castle's ever found it," Brenna said. "There's no handle and nothing to mark it as a door." At least, that was the theory of the twenty-first-century historians.

They were about to find out.

The men stepped back to allow Brenna to get out of the way. Hamilton took the light and held it high as Rourke pressed his hands against the stone and pushed.

Brenna heard a small groaning of the rock, but nothing happened.

"'Tis here," Rourke said excitedly. "And stuck." He

turned sideways, then slammed his shoulder against the wall.

The door gave spectacularly, with the accompanying crash and minor explosions of dozens of things hitting the floor.

"Close it!" Brenna hissed.

Hamilton pushed her toward the cliffs. "Run!"

Damn. She tore out of the cave and jumped off the ledge to hide where Lintie had that day. Malcolm was right behind her.

Her brother shielded her, knife drawn, as the two of them waited. Blood pounded in her ears, thudding harder with every minute Rourke and Hamilton didn't come. Had they been caught?

Finally, Malcolm moved. "Wait here, lass." He jumped onto the ledge and disappeared into the cave.

Brenna grunted. "Wait here, like hell." Hiking her skirt, she lifted her leg and swung herself onto the ledge. As she crept into the dark, she heard no sound. Neither did she see any light illuminating the end as she was certain she would if the door had been discovered.

As she neared the end of the cave, she heard a soft, "Wildcat." Rourke's hand cupped her elbow and he pulled her tight against him. With their lantern now out, she could see nothing, but the solid beat of his heart steadied her own.

"What happened?" she asked.

"I found a fingerhold and pulled the door closed. We heard voices. They dinna ken what caused the mess."

She felt another body close. Malcolm's voice, rich with humor, spoke near her ear. "Hamilton said they heard the word *earthquake*."

Brenna released a laugh on a puff of air. "Good. That's good."

"They could be a while, straightening the mess we made," Rourke said dismally.

"Or not. It's the middle of the night."

"Aye. We thought of that. We'll wait a bit longer."

Finally, Rourke tried again, more carefully this time. Little by little he pushed. Brenna heard a soft thud as the door hit something, but no crashes and shouts accompanied the maneuver this time.

She heard him move inside. A moment later, he returned. "A light," he said.

Hamilton lit the lamp and handed it to him. He held it aloft to reveal the destruction they'd caused in the small pantry. Sure enough, weapons everywhere. Muskets, swords, knives, shields. And barrels which she could only guess held musket balls or gunpowder.

Rourke ordered her to remain outside with Malcolm, but he must have heard the angry noise she made, for he turned and found her face, kissing her hard. He pulled back, holding her cheek in his calloused palm.

"Wildcat . . . *Brenna* . . . I'll not allow anything to happen to you, lass. *I love you.*"

Then he turned and disappeared into the pantry before she could recover from his words. He loved her. *Loved* her. The words sang through her. She stared after him as he and Hamilton doused the light and slipped out of the pantry into the dungeon.

She started after him, but Malcolm grabbed her arm. "Brenna."

"It's *our* father in there. And you're the acting chieftain. So how did *we* wind up out here?"

His grip softened, then disappeared. "Aye. You're right." He pulled the door open a few inches, then a few more until he could look around. Then he took her hand and led her into the dungeons behind him.

A single torch lit the dank, foul-smelling place, where at least a dozen men were chained to the walls, keys hanging above their heads as if to torment them. The prisoners were all lying on the bare stone floor, asleep, or worse. No guards were visible, but Brenna remembered the layout of the place and knew the dungeons took a turn before reaching the stair. The guards were probably bunked around the corner or in a small anteroom.

Malcolm led her to the right, heading in the direction they'd seen Hamilton go. They'd barely gone ten feet when Malcolm released her and dropped to his knees before an old man.

"Da."

Her father.

Brenna stood as if frozen, as if her feet had forgotten how to move. He wasn't what she'd been expecting. He wasn't the young man of her memory any longer. He looked old and beaten, as if life had taken too great a toll. His unwashed gray hair hung to his shoulders and gray stubble covered his face. As he spoke to Malcolm, she saw that he was missing a couple of his bottom teeth.

Then Malcolm said something to him and his head snapped up. Green eyes, brimming with shock and intelligence bore into hers. Then his face broke into a smile that erased the years with a single stroke. She knew that smile, for she'd seen it a hundred times in her memory—him laughing at the storm.

Tears blurred her vision as a fragile, pounding joy burst within her chest.

"Papa." She took a step toward him, then another, and knelt before him. His strong arms pulled her so tight she was certain she would never breathe again. And she didn't care.

She was shaking all the way to her bones as she clung to him. *At last.* She'd found him at last. Tears coursed down her cheeks.

"Brenna." Malcolm was pulling at her. "We must be away."

She pulled back, but her father held her, gripping her arms nearly until they hurt. "Let me look at you, Brenna lass. You've grown bonnie and strong, the very image of your mum."

"And she's got your stubbornness," Malcolm hissed as Hamilton unlocked her father's chains. "Come. Both of you."

Brenna wiped her cheek on her shoulder. "I missed you so much."

As Hamilton and Malcolm helped him to his feet, he lurched drunkenly, pain flashing over his face.

She frowned. "What's wrong?"

"He's been flogged. You'll have to open the door for us."

"Okay." But as she turned, she suddenly realized what was missing. Or who. "Where's Rourke?"

"He'll be right back," Hamilton said. "Get the door, Brenna."

But he wouldn't be right back. A sick feeling sank to her stomach as she peered into the dungeon, seeing the shadow skirting the far wall, heading slowly toward the circular stair she'd descended with the tour only a week ago. She knew exactly what he was up to. The same thing she'd meant to do herself.

He was going to try to kill the Earl of Slains before the earl could kill her.

God, she loved that man. But she would personally throttle him if they got out of there alive. This wasn't his fight. If he failed, his death wouldn't change anything. Hers would at least end the prophecy's curse.

"Brenna . . ."

She swung around to face them, these three men she would give her life for. Malcolm and Hamilton had her father propped between them.

"He's going after the earl," she told them.

"He canna—" Malcolm began.

"He's trying to save me. I can't let him do it. It's not his fight." She couldn't run and leave him to die. Not that he wasn't a fine fighter, but good grief, the castle was overflowing with bluecoats. Besides, she'd saved him before by distracting his opponents. Maybe she could do it again.

Hamilton held out his hand. "Brenna, you can't—"

"Get my father to safety."

"I'll go after Rourke," Malcolm said.

Brenna shook her head. "I can't hold Papa up. He needs your strength, little brother. I'm not going to be any use to him. You have to get him to safety. And I have to do this."

"Brenna, nay," her father said, his voice strained. "I forbid it."

Brenna met his hard, terrified gaze. "Papa, the prophecy demands I do this. It's my destiny. And it will end no other way."

The pain in his eyes tore her apart. "I have waited for ye for too long to lose ye now, lassie mine."

"I know. But if it were you instead of me, you'd face this head-on, right?"

"But you—"

"Am I right?"

Her father sighed, frustrated and angry . . . and resigned. "Aye."

"She has the Cameron fight in her, Da," Malcolm said. "I'll have to tell you how she greeted me after twenty years," he added ruefully.

Brenna leaned forward and kissed her father's prickly cheek. "I love you." She turned to look at Hamilton, then Malcolm. "All of you."

"Ah, lass," her father said, his voice brimming with misery. Then he squeezed her hand and released her, his voice growing strong and demanding. "Come back to me, Brenna. The prophecy says you'll defeat him and ye will, aye?"

Brenna flashed him a watery grin. "He won't know what hit him."

"Go with God," Malcolm said a few minutes later as she saw them through the door into the cave.

She closed the door behind them, then swiped away her tears and steeled herself for what she had to do. The prophecy would end tonight one way or the other.

Brenna crossed the dungeon, keeping to the outside walls as she'd seen Rourke do. But she'd barely made it halfway along that first wall when a voice erupted from across the room, sending her heart into her throat.

"If you're servicing one of us, lass, you're servicing us all."

Her heart sank to her stomach as a tall, blue-coated figure stepped out of the shadows and started toward her.

NINETEEN

"I'm afraid you've made a mistake."

Rourke froze at the sound of Brenna's voice resonating through the dungeons.

She sounded cold. Haughty. "I'm a guest of the earl's. And though I seem to have lost my way, I am quite certain he will not appreciate your thinking otherwise."

Nay, she was to have been safely away by now. Hamilton should have gotten her out of here.

He braced himself against the stone wall of the stair. He'd been so close, already past the first turn, undetected.

"Forgive me," the guard replied, his tone stiff. "I will escort you back to the—"

"That's her!" another man shouted. "That's my mermaid!"

Rourke's last hope of keeping her out of the fray sank like a stone in his belly. He eased back down the turnstile stair as Brenna's words rang over the stones.

"I'm sure I don't know what you're talking about."

"It's her," insisted the second man. "She said the earl sent her to entertain us. You can entertain me now, lassie."

Rourke turned the corner just as the soldier grabbed Brenna around the waist. The wildcat slammed her head back, catching her unwary captor in the nose. As the foolish man reared back, she spun and kneed him hard in the ballocks.

The lass was magnificent. And near certain to get herself killed.

Drawing his sword, Rourke lunged forward and took out two of the guards before they realized what was happening. Only two more stood between him and Brenna's tormentors. He took on the two at once, parrying every blow, getting in an occasional thrust with little success.

Sweat rolled down his temples, his pulse thudded as he fought to reach her. He had to get her out of here.

But as he fought, a sound reached his ears that sunk his heart to his boots. The echo of multiple heavy footsteps descending the stairs. The swish of a dozen swords being drawn.

Brenna yelped and he saw she'd lost her fight and was being held, a blade pressed to her throat.

"Drop your weapon or she dies," her captor yelled.

"Rourke, no!" No fear glittered in her eyes, only fire and determination. She'd intended to face the earl this night, as he had. And it seemed that was precisely what they were going to do.

Bluecoats swarmed into the dungeon. The fight was over. Rourke backed away from his opponents. When neither made a lunge for him, he dropped his sword to the stone floor. Three guards lifted their sword points to his throat. A single move and he'd seal his death.

The captain of the guards circled around him, eyeing him with interest. "Who are you and how did you get in here?"

Rourke clenched his jaw, his only regret that he'd

failed to save Brenna. If only Hamilton had taken her when he left. But his wildcat had a mind of her own.

"I'm Brenna Cameron." The lass's voice rang through the dungeons, clear and loud. "And he's Rourke Douglas, Viscount Kinross. The Earl of Slains is expecting us."

Without warning, the hilt of a sword slammed into the back of his skull and darkness swept him away.

Brenna gasped as Rourke fell. He couldn't be dead. *Please don't let him be dead.*

"Brenna Cameron, eh?" The bluecoat who'd hit Rourke walked toward her, studying her with cold eyes. When he reached her, he grabbed her hair and yanked her head back, bringing sharp stinging tears to her eyes. "How did you get in here?"

She'd never tell. They'd find her father and the others, and she could not let that happen. Especially when she'd known from the moment she entered this castle she would probably die here tonight.

But as his knife pricked her throat, threatening to slice her open, cold terror iced through her veins.

A voice yelled from behind her. "Alex Cameron's gone."

The leader yanked her hair harder. "Tell me how."

"Magic." She bore her hatred into him with her eyes. "I'm a witch, or hadn't you heard?"

The coldness in the man's gaze slowly turned to wariness as his eyes moved from the empty chains where her father had been, back to her. He released her slowly and took a step back, but his expression remained hard.

"If you hurt another of my men, your friend will die." Brenna nodded, rubbing her stinging scalp. Rourke wasn't dead.

The bluecoat motioned toward the stairs with his knife. "Move." To his men he said, "Take Kinross, too."

Brenna climbed the stairs, all too aware of the soldiers

at her back dragging Rourke's limp body between them. There was no escape, not with Rourke out cold. Had she signed their death warrants by trying to fight a war she could never win?

Bluecoats surrounded her as they made their way through the dark and silent hall to another set of stairs. Finally reaching the top, the bluecoat leader rapped on a heavy door. When the door swung open, a large hand shoved her inside.

"Tell the earl we've got Brenna Cameron here to see him."

The servant nodded, lit one of the tapers on a nearby candelabra, then hurried through a far door. To fetch the earl, she presumed. While they waited, one of her guards used the single taper to light the rest of the freestanding candelabra and its twin, standing on the other side of the large, intricately carved wooden table.

The room slowly brightened, revealing a large, richly decorated room covered in wood paneling and lined with more than a dozen framed portraits. The earl's ancestors?

Rourke's captors dragged him into the room behind her, then knelt to bind his hands and feet with a thick rope. Brenna watched him, desperate for a twitch or a sliver of tension that would reassure her he was alive. But she knew he must be, or they wouldn't bother to tie him.

It would be far better for both of them if he remained unconscious until after the earl was through with her. She didn't want him to have to watch her die. Nor did she want him trying to fight to save her, because he'd only wind up getting himself killed in the process.

She couldn't bear to be the cause of his death, too.

As the minutes piled up and the earl didn't come, her pulse began to lose a bit of its urgency. After looking for her for twenty years, she'd have thought he'd be anxious to get his hands on her, but maybe the guy was a sound sleeper. It was, after all, the middle of the night.

Finally, after what seemed like at least an hour, the far door opened and she realized what had taken so long. He'd dressed for the occasion.

Into the room walked a man who looked like he'd stepped out of an old French painting. Dressed in the fashion of Rourke and his uncle, times ten, he wore a deep green brocade jacket trimmed in gold bows. The bows were everywhere—hem, sleeves, shoulders. On his head, he wore a huge velvet hat, also trimmed with bows, and on his feet, square-toed buckled shoes with a good three-inch heel.

Long black ringlets framed his face and hung halfway to his waist, not quite concealing the wisps of gray hair that poked out from beneath.

His eyes, as they focused on her, were clear and cruel even as they flashed with cunning delight.

"Brenna Cameron. At last, we meet. You're every bit as bonnie as your mother."

As he strode toward her, his lips curled in a hard smile, a flash of ivory burst from the room behind him in the form of a naked girl. She couldn't be more than fourteen or fifteen. Scratch marks striped the girl's breasts and blood streaked her pale inner thighs, filling Brenna with fury.

One of the bluecoats stepped into the girl's path, blocking her way. She screeched and tried to dart around him, but he snagged her around the waist and hauled her against him, both his meaty hands sliding over her bruised flesh.

Brenna started forward, unable to stand by and watch this horror, but the guard beside her snared her wrist. As she whirled on him, knee at the ready, she suddenly found the tip of a knife pricking the underside of her chin.

The earl flicked his wrist at the naked girl. "Tie her to my bed."

As the child was hauled, screaming and kicking, back

to the bedroom, Brenna's fists clenched at her sides. "I see you make a habit of warring on girls."

This monster had to die. He *had* to die.

The earl flicked his fingers at her causing her gaoler to push her forward. Close-up, the earl looked older, his fleshy face well lined. His cruel eyes looked her up and down, taking on a lecherous gleam that had her blood turning cold.

"The seer did not tell me you would grow to be a beauty. Before I kill you, I will take you thoroughly. As will all of my men."

A chorus of pleased grunts rumbled through the room.

Panic flared. Death she could handle, it was rape that would destroy her.

Another flick of that weathered hand. "Put her on the table and hold her."

With the knife still at her throat, she couldn't fight, could do nothing but submit as guards seized her arms on either side.

Brenna met the earl's gaze, her own hard and challenging. "Are you so afraid of me that you can't even rape me without the help of your guards?"

The man's jaw clenched and unclenched, sending the wrinkles writhing like snakes through his skin. Slowly his face flushed red.

"Release her."

"But . . . my lord," the bluecoat leader said. He'd seen her fight.

The earl threw the guard a look of disdain. "Do not touch her again unless she tries to escape. This is between her and me and none will interfere."

The blade left her throat as the guards on either side of her melted away. Brenna was left facing her greatest nightmare. Fear lapped at her courage, freezing the air in her lungs. She struggled against it, taking deep, ragged breaths as she desperately tried to calm herself.

This was it. Her only chance.

She fought against the terror, gathering her hatred for the man standing before her. *The Earl of Slains.* The bastard who'd ordered her killed when she was five. The monster who'd had Rourke's parents killed and destroyed the lives of both of their families. The asshole who'd forced her to flee, stealing her home, her family, her entire world.

He might rape her. He'd likely kill her. But she wasn't going down without one hell of a fight.

Brenna braced herself as the earl approached, his eyes glittering a little too brightly. Too late, she realized the hand coming for her was swinging in a fast arc. The backhand across her face sent her flying. She crashed to the floor, head ringing, her face on fire. As she pushed herself to her feet, she touched her face and felt the sticky dampness of blood.

The jerk had cut her with his ring.

She *knew* she should have signed up for those karate classes. Self-defense was all well and good, but she seriously needed a better offense. Her hand reached for the knife strapped to her thigh, then stilled. No matter what the earl said, she couldn't believe his guards would let her stab him. No, she had to get closer before she revealed she was armed. She had to get close enough to do what she did best.

Brenna thought of the pirate she'd downed in the hold of Rourke's ship. Heaven help her. How could she pretend with this man?

What good will it do anyway? part of her cried. He was going to kill her one way or the other. Stopping the rape wouldn't save her. There was no escape.

It didn't matter. She wasn't giving up. And she sure as hell owed the Earl of Slains *something* to remember her by.

Brenna closed her eyes and raked her hair back off her face. "I don't know why I'm fighting you," she breathed, making herself ill from the sexiness she managed to inject into her voice. "I want you. We're two of a kind, you and I. Craving power." She swept her eyes down to his crotch, then back up again. "And I crave yours."

The asshole's eyes near to ly popped out of his head, then slowly filled with lust.

Brenna cupped the undersides of her breasts, lifting them, unsure what else to do to make it look like she wanted him. Beneath her skirts, her knees shook so hard she was starting to get nauseous. If she wasn't careful, she was going ruin the whole sham by vomiting.

"Take me," she cooed. "Let me *feel* your power."

Yeah, she was definitely going to throw up.

The other guards were making low noises deep in their throats. One was cupping his groin. *Great.* While Slains just stood there, his men were going to jump her.

Finally, the earl started toward her on those high heels, his tongue sliding out to lick his thin, disgusting lips.

Brenna kept her hands on her breasts and tossed her head, running on pure instinct now. No plan, no thought beyond the driving need to take him down in any way she could.

"Take me," she whispered huskily. This was not exactly how she'd envisioned ending her life . . . sounding like some back-lot porn star.

Closing the distance between them, he brushed aside her hand and grabbed her breast. "I'll take you, lassie. I'll take you and drive you up, then slit your throat while you scream your release."

The flowery words every girl longed to hear.

"If you must," she breathed. Then she reached up as if to kiss him and instead, drove her knee hard into his groin.

"You wee *bitch*!" His fist shot out, catching her deep in the gut, stealing her breath.

She wanted to kill him so bad she shook with it.

She needed her knife. As the air started to ease back

into her lungs, she grabbed the hem of her skirt and dug out the small blade. If she went for his neck . . .

Her wrist was caught from behind in a vise like grip.

"My lord?" said the bluecoat leader close at her back.

The earl looked up, his eyes watering, his wig askew, a vicious twist to his mouth. "Get me my sword. And hold her!"

Brenna got a fleeting sense of satisfaction at the earl's voice, now a good two octaves higher than a minute ago. He'd remember her, all right. For a day or two.

The knife was yanked from her fist and once more she was strung between two guards while a third brought a wicked-looking sword and handed it to the injured earl.

If there was any good news, it was that she'd apparently avoided the raping. She'd never really expected to come out of this alive, despite the prophecy. Her poor father was going to mourn her bitterly.

And Rourke. What would happen to her pirate once her head was rolling on the ground? Would his follow? Was there any chance the earl might let him go?

Her heart broke for him, crumbling beneath the weight of her love and sorrow. She glanced over her shoulder to where he lay, needing to see him one more time. But as her gaze skimmed his beloved face, she caught a flicker in his cheek, a muscle tensing.

She swung her gaze quickly forward, her pulse suddenly pounding a whole new rhythm. He was awake.

The earl came to stand before her, the candelabra at his back wreathing his head in flame as if he were, indeed, the devil's disciple. Slowly, he lifted his sword over his head . . . over *her* head . . . and she knew he meant to cleave her in two.

Her heart thudded. Was Rourke awake enough to know what was happening? Could he escape while they killed her?

Her answer came flying through the air to bury itself to

the hilt in the Earl of Slain's forehead. For the space of two heartbeats, a stunned silence blanketed the room, then the earl crashed backward into the candelabra and all hell broke loose.

Brenna's gaolers released her, one to rush toward the earl, who was quickly going up in flames, the other to pull his sword and turn on her rescuer.

Rourke.

Metal rang as he battled with two bluecoats. Somehow, while they'd all thought he was unconscious, he'd managed to free himself from the bindings. Where he'd gotten the sword, she didn't know and didn't care.

The other guards were more concerned with dousing the flames that now engulfed the earl, carrying him to a hell she hoped would never release him. The guards tried to cover him with the rug that draped the table, but the rug caught and they had to leap away.

The fire.

Suddenly she remembered the tour guide. *Castle Stour burned in the year 1687. This year. This night.*

"Get out!" Brenna yelled. "The whole castle's going up in flames."

Amazingly, most of the guards—used to following orders—followed hers. They took off for the door without a backward glance at their charbroiling lord. Only the bluecoat leader remained, battling Rourke, but she fully trusted the pirate to win. He didn't need her help this time. And she had something she had to do.

Grabbing up her knife where it had fallen on the floor, she ran for the earl's bedchamber, where the naked girl sobbed, her wrists tied to one of the bedposts.

"The earl's dead," Brenna told her. "I'm getting you out of here." The poor kid hadn't been as lucky as Brenna at fifteen

As the ropes finally parted beneath her blade, Rourke burst into the door.

"Wildcat!"

Brenna grabbed the earl's nightshirt and shoved it at the girl. "Hold it to your nose until we get through the smoke, then you can put it on." She ran to Rourke and threw her arms around him. "He's dead."

"Aye." Rourke pressed a quick, hard kiss to her hair, then pulled her and the girl across the burning room. At the doorway, the girl paused to don the nightshirt while Brenna stared at the flames that were destroying her enemy.

As the three raced down the now empty passage she glanced at Rourke. "I thought *I* was supposed to be the one to kill him." Shouts and screams echoed up from the lower levels of the castle as the occupants fled. Only one room was on fire, but in a castle like this, with the floors made of wood, the entire structure would be gutted by morning and all within knew it.

She and Rourke would have no trouble getting out. There would be no one left to keep them here. And no reason.

Rourke grabbed her hand and held tight. "The prophecy said ye were to be the earl's destruction, aye? Not that ye would be the one to kill him."

Brenna reached back and grabbed the girl's hand in turn, in a strange way feeling as if she had hold of herself at that age. In one hand she held her past, in the other, her future.

"'Twas his obsession with ye that killed him, ye ken?"

Brenna felt the weight of twenty years lift from her shoulders and laughed. "*Now* you tell me."

Malcolm met them halfway down the sea path. His gaze flew to hers. "I was coming to find you."

"He'd dead, Malcolm," Brenna told him.

Her brother nodded silently, but as he turned to lead

the way back down, his teeth flashed in the moonlight in a feral grin. He led them to where Hamilton and her father sat on the rocks on the tiny beach watching the flames slowly consume Castle Stour.

"She did it!" Malcolm crowed. "My own sister killed the Earl of Slains." He grabbed her up and swung her around, laughing.

"Actually, Rourke's the one who killed him."

The moment Malcolm set her down, her father enfolded her in his strong arms and held her so tightly and so long, she was pretty sure he wasn't ever going to let her go.

Finally, he began to sway and she helped him sit back down on the rock. But he pulled her down beside him and kept hold of her hand as if afraid she'd disappear on him again.

Malcolm took the girl aside and gently questioned her about her family and where she belonged.

Hamilton came to Brenna and hugged her hard, his face wreathed in grins. "Ye did it, lass. Ye fulfilled the prophecy, and brilliantly, too." He sat at her feet in the sand. "I wish to know everything, aye? What happened in there?"

Malcolm and the girl joined them and she told the tale, all watching her with rapt attention.

All but Rourke.

He stood alone, the night's breeze toying with his hair as he watched, not the burning castle, but the sea. As if he were already plotting his escape.

Her joy and relief at their unparalleled success dimmed with the sudden and overwhelming dread of his leaving.

She wrapped up her story, then gave her father a quick peck on the cheek and rose. "I'll be right back."

Rourke smiled down at her as she joined him, then turned back to the sea, making no move to touch her. Her heart squeezed painfully. In the passage to the dungeons, he'd said he loved her. Had he meant it? Or had he been intentionally distracting her so he could slip away?

"Will you be leaving soon?" Brenna asked, afraid to hear his answer.

"Aye. I am needed."

Tears burned her eyes and she was suddenly glad for the dark. The jubilation she'd felt only moments before washed out, leaving a bruising pressure in her chest. She had her answer.

How can I live without him?

She would. She had to. And it wasn't like he'd be leaving her alone. She had a family and a home, now. He knew where to find her if he ever wanted to see her.

The pain sharpened. Tears slid down her cheeks.

"Will you be able to round up your old crew, or will you have to find another one?"

He reached for her, sliding his hand beneath her hair. "I'm not going back to sea, Wildcat. I'm returning to Picktillum to take up the reins of responsibility my uncle would pass to me."

The constriction in her chest eased. He'd be close. A couple days' ride. Even if he didn't offer to visit her, there would be nothing stopping her from visiting him.

"That's great," she said sincerely.

"Aye, I'm not certain. I dinna ken what kind of viscount I'll be."

"You'll make a wonderful viscount, Rourke. And you've got your uncle there to guide you. He's a good man." She dashed the tears from her cheeks under the pretense of brushing her hair out of her face, but the move didn't fool him.

"Wildcat." His voice contained a soft ache as he turned her to face him. "Yer crying."

"I'm happy." She tried to laugh, but choked on the sound. The tears only slid faster.

"What's the matter, lass? Are ye hurt? Did that bastard . . . ?"

"No." She didn't want to cry. She didn't want him to know how painfully her heart was breaking, but she couldn't seem to stop the tears.

His thumb brushed across her wet cheek. "Brenna? Tell me what ails ye, lass."

She slid her arms around him and pressed her face to his chest. "I don't want you to go."

His hands didn't go around her, but instead tightened on her shoulders as his body went ramrod straight. Her heart shattered in her chest. He didn't want her.

Humiliated, she released him and tried to push away, but his hands gripped her shoulders tight, holding her in place.

"Wildcat."

She looked up into his face and her breath caught at the look in his eyes.

His eyes, illuminated by moonlight, shone with love. He pulled her hard against him and kissed her, the kiss at once tender and fierce.

A hard clearing of a throat behind her had Rourke lifting his head and growling. "Leave us, Hamilton."

"You'll be asking for her hand, then?"

"Aye."

Brenna gasped, her gaze flying to Rourke's. He glared at Hamilton, then turned to her, cupping her face in his hands, looking suddenly unsure.

"I'm not worthy of ye, Wildcat, but I love you more than life itself. You've given me back my soul and made my empty heart beat again. All I want from life, *all* I want, is you. Marry me, Brenna, and I vow to make you happy."

Tears ran down her cheeks, unchecked, her heart overflowing with joy.

"I love you, Rourke. There's nothing I want more than to be your wife. But . . . you're a viscount." She winced. "I'm not exactly that kind of a lady."

"Then you'll be whatever kind ye choose. And if ever again you have a need to go a-warring, I'll not hold ye back, aye? I'll fight by yer side." His thumb stroked her cheek. "But I'm hoping you'll be more content to teach our bairns to fly paper birds off the parapets."

Rourke grinned, making her laugh as joy tumbled through her, unconstrained. Her two worlds would always, in small ways, be intertwined. But it was here that she'd always belonged. Here she'd found love, both old and new.

Here that she'd finally found home.

EPILOGUE

The great hall of Picktillum Castle glowed with a thousand candles. The wedding feast had lasted half the day and now well into the evening, but the celebration was only starting to wind down.

Sitting at the high table beside her new husband, Brenna grinned, happier than she'd ever been in her life. The feast had been a spectacular success, all the more gratifying since she herself had planned it. The remnants of elaborate desserts still sat on the long tables, the revelers too full to complete the final, delicious course.

She might be a viscountess now, and the lady of the castle, but the kitchens were hers. At least until she had little ones taking up too much of her time. It was too soon to be sure—there were no neat little pregnancy tests in the seventeenth century, but Brenna thought the first wee 'un might be making an appearance a bit before his or her parents' nine-month anniversary. She couldn't wait to tell Rourke.

She turned to look up at him, her chest aching with love. He met her gaze, his pale eyes shining with adoration, a wicked smile curving his mouth as he leaned forward and kissed her long and slowly until her heart spun wildly.

Cheers erupted around them and they pulled apart, laughing.

Rourke rose, pulling her up beside him. Her father met her gaze with laughter in his eyes and she smiled at him, her heart full of love. He looked years younger than he had in the earl's dungeon that night, having healed quickly and regained his strength under the watchful, and very loving, eyes of his two children. In a single short month, they'd become a family again.

"Come, Kinross," Rourke's uncle James said. "There's a wee surprise awaiting you in the lass's bedchamber. We've arranged for you to be traveling for a few days."

Traveling? Brenna looked at Rourke, but his eyes shared her confusion. This wasn't the twenty-first century. It wasn't like they could surprise them with a pair of plane tickets to the Bahamas or something.

Her father grinned. "Aye, and ye'll be leaving this eve, so ye'd best get to your chamber, eh?"

Rourke laughed huskily. "Aye, we'll be seeing her chamber, but we'll no' be traveling this eve, I assure you."

James shooed them away from the dais. "Off wi' ye then."

Rourke met her gaze and shrugged, then pulled her, laughing, through the great hall as hoots and whistles followed them. They barely made it to the top of the stairs before Rourke pulled her into his arms and kissed her hard.

Brenna giggled and slapped at his chest. "The room, Pirate. No ravishing on the stairs."

With a grin, he grabbed her hand and rushed her to the door of her chambers. They stumbled into the room and fell into one another's arms. As his tongue swept into her mouth, someone cleared his throat behind her.

Rourke leaped back, reaching for his weapon, then froze. "Hegarty!"

Brenna whirled to face the little man, who was standing at the foot of her bed in a wholly anachronistic T-shirt. Hard Rock Cafe Edinburgh, it read.

She took a step toward him, a strange sensation traveling down her spine. "*You've been there.*"

"Och, aye." His eyes sparkled with mischief. "'Tis a bonnie place, to be sure."

"Wildcat." Rourke's hand cupped her shoulder, his sudden tension leaching into her.

She looked up to find his smile gone, a bleakness in his eyes. "What's the matter, Rourke?"

Rourke's pale gaze bore into hers. "If ye wish him to take ye back, I'll understand. 'Tis a wondrous place ye left."

Brenna's heart clenched at the fear she saw in his eyes. Fear that she would leave him.

She pulled his hand from her shoulder and kissed it, never looking away from his eyes. "Yes, there were wonderful things about that time, but I was lonely there. It was never where I belonged. And the only place I ever want to be from now on is at your side."

"Aye, I just thought . . ." He pulled her hard against him. "Christ, I couldna lose ye now."

Hegarty grinned, dancing from one foot to the other. "Ye were always meant for one another. Even the prophecy said so."

Rourke released her slowly. "The prophecy said only that Brenna Cameron would destroy the Earl of Slains."

"Och, aye. More or less."

"More or less," Rourke murmured. She felt the tension go through him. "Tell me *exactly* what it said, Heg."

Hegarty stilled. "When asked when he would die, the

seer told Slains that Alex Cameron's young daughter, Brenna, would be his destruction with the aid of her pirate paramour."

Brenna's gaze flew to Rourke's, her eyes wide. "Pirate paramour?" A giggle got away from her.

Rourke's puzzled gaze stayed fixed on Hegarty. "But . . . she couldna have meant me. I'd never have left Scotland, never become a . . . sailor . . . if the earl hadn't come after Brenna, destroying my family."

Hegarty nodded. "Aye. 'Twas meant to be, Pup. All of it. And you were involved from the beginning, though 'twas a few years before I realized the pirate must be you."

Rourke stood there for long seconds as if letting the words sink in. Then he pulled her close as a shudder tore through him, and she sensed he'd released the last lingering bit of guilt over his parents' deaths.

Slowly he straightened, pulling away from her even as he looped his arm around her shoulders. "And what mischief are ye about this eve, ye wee blighter?"

Hegarty chuckled. "Well, now, I been thinking of a fittin' gift to give ye on yer nuptials, Pup." He looked at Brenna. "Did yer da not tell ye?"

She gaped at him. "They know you're here?"

"Och, aye." He cackled at the looks on their faces. "Three days, they said. And only if I go with ye. Canna have anyone gettin' lost this time."

Brenna felt her eyes grow wide and her chest tighten with excitement. "The future?"

"Aye." He nodded to Rourke. "I couldna send ye before, Pup, but I'll make up for it now. And I be thinkin' your lassie wouldna mind a visit back."

Rourke had gone still as stone. She looked up to see both trepidation and excitement sparkling in his eyes.

"But . . . I thought the stone couldna send three."

Hegarty waved a hand in the air. "Och, it couldna.

Then. Old Inghinn has a way with the magic, aye?" His eyes glittered good-naturedly even as he motioned them with impatience. "Come. Yer room's awaitin' ye in the finest establishment in Aberdeen along wi' a few other things ye'll be needin'."

Brenna began to laugh, her happiness too great to contain. "How . . . ?"

"A wee bit o' gold in the right hands will get ye what ye desire in any century, lassie. Now come on."

He grabbed each of their arms even as they clung to one another. Brenna looked up at Rourke's pale, but excited face and grinned.

"Pirate, this is going to blow you away."

He bent and kissed her hair. "Wildcat, ye canna ken how much I love you."

But she could. She felt it deep inside, twisting and braiding with the love she felt for him, creating a ribbon of such steel that nothing would ever tear them apart. She pressed against him and laughed as the sapphire around Hegarty's neck began to glow.

FOUR DAYS LATER

Hegarty dropped the sapphire into Old Inghinn's aged hand.

"And how was yer trip?" she asked.

Hegarty grinned. Brenna had returned with so many *necessities*, the stone had nearly not been able to carry it all and the three of them, too. And the lad . . . well, the pup's eyes hadna stilled for three days. When he managed to tear his loving gaze from his bride, that is.

"I thank ye, Inghinn. 'Twas a fittin' wedding gift for the two o' them."

"Aye, and ye must keep yer end of the agreement, Hegarty. Ye've a soft heart and a foolish head, my friend."

"Only for the bairns."

"Aye. But the children grow up, do they not? And that soft heart of yours stays with them, I'm thinking."

Hegarty eased toward the door of the Wellerby cottage. He was feeling the itch to be away as he did whenever the witch got on her scolding.

"Ye must fetch me the rest of the stones, Hegarty. 'Tis past time, as well ye ken. They were ne'er yours to take."

Hegarty shrugged, shifting from foot to foot. "I canna reach 'em, ye ken that. Only the sapphire comes to my call."

"They'll all answer to the amethyst. And that one remains in this place, this time. You'll get it back for me."

"The laddie needed it, aye?"

"Mayhap he did. But that was a score of years ago, and he's a laddie no more. Ye must get it back."

"But . . ."

"Fetch the amethyst, Hegarty. And once ye have it, ye must call back the others. 'Tis certain, the Jewels of Kindonan were never meant for this world."